The Paris Herald

A NOVEL

JAMES OLIVER GOLDSBOROUGH

PROSPECTA PRESS

WESTPORT – 2014

Copyright © James Oliver Goldsborough 2014

Prospecta Press
P.O. Box 3131
Westport, CT 06880
www.prospectapress.com

Hardcover ISBN 978-1-935212-32-4
Ebook ISBN 978-1-935212-31-7

Book and cover design by Barbara Aronica-Buck
Cover photo by Henri Cartier-Bresson, courtesy Magnum Photos

To James Chace and Buddy Weiss,
two good teachers.

"Names, names, names."

– James Gordon Bennett, Jr.

AUTHOR'S NOTE

Any American traveling in Paris in the late nineteenth or early twentieth century came across the *Paris Herald* at one time or another. It was available in the same kiosks on the Champs Elysées and quais along the Seine as the latest article in *l'Aurore* by Zola or the newest installment by Proust in his never-ending search for lost time. The *Paris Herald*, founded in 1887, belonged to Paris as much as did Zola or Proust.

Between the world wars, that same traveler would have found the *Herald* not only in Paris but anywhere he went in France. Each evening at 10:30 trucks lined up along the rue du Louvre to receive stacks of newspapers fresh off the press and bound for the rail stations. Hemingway, Fitzgerald, Cole Porter, Gertrude Stein, Josephine Baker, any American who could afford to live or travel in France at the time could be sure his newspaper would be at the Paris stations in time for the eleven o'clock trains to Normandy, Brittany, the Côte d'Azur.

In the 1920s – that brief, giddy interlude between catastrophes – Americans began to find the *Herald* outside France as well. Those same trucks from the rue de Louvre now carried newspapers each night to the Gars de l'Est, du Nord, and St. Lazare for journeys northward. Across Europe, the *Paris Herald* was the one way, the only way, to stay in touch with things American. In 1928 it became the first newspaper to be distributed by air, with daily planes to London. It was as much America's gift to Europe as the Statue of Liberty was France's gift to America.

James Gordon Bennett, Jr., founder of the *Paris Herald* in 1887 and son of the founder of the *New York Herald*, died in Paris in 1918, but there was never any question of scrapping his newspaper. In 1924, with the merger of the *New York Herald* and *New York Tribune*, the *Paris Herald* became the *Paris Herald Tribune* and moved from the cramped rue du Louvre to the rue de Berri, off the spacious Champs Elysées. In all those years, the only break in publication came in the early 1940s. But Hitler was soon gone from Paris and the *Herald Tribune* back to the rue de Berri.

From Bennett, ownership passed to the Reids of New York and then to Jock Whitney, also of New York. As the American presence in Europe grew in the 1950s, the *Paris Herald Tribune* could be found everywhere in Europe, including in Communist East Europe, though behind the Iron Curtain you had to know someone to get it.

Naturally, it attracted imitators. The *Wall Street Journal* planned and canceled a European edition in the early sixties. The *New York Times* launched a Paris edition in 1961, but lacking the *Herald*'s name and history was never successful. In 1966, when union strikers forced the *New York Herald Tribune* to close its doors, the *Washington Post* bought into the Paris paper. The following year, the *Times* closed its Paris edition and bought a minority interest in the joint Whitney-*Post* Paris paper, hating every minute of it and vowing revenge. The new paper became the *International Herald Tribune*.

The *Paris Herald* has seen a lot, and now must suffer the indignity of seeing its hallowed name forever erased by the *New York Times*. Some of this story has been told, nowhere better than in Charles L. Robertson's history of the newspaper. But having lived through the critical years, 1965–1970, when the newspaper and the regime of Charles de Gaulle were both fighting for their lives, I've always thought those intertwined stories, and the people responsible for them, deserved to be told. This is an historical novel with a few names changed just to be nice.

I

He walked off the train and out of the Gare d'Austerlitz and looked over Paris for the second time. The first time, six months before at the Gare du Nord, it looked brighter. There was nothing bright about the Gare d'Austerlitz, old and dark, tucked into a gloomy corner of the city, barges lined up on the Seine with their loads of coal and gravel, ugly buildings on the far side, probably warehouses. The first time had been for just a few hours, changing stations on his way from Berlin to Barcelona. He had no idea how long it would be this time. Wayne said there might be a job at the *Herald* and how long he stayed would depend on that. First he had to find Wayne.

Paris had never attracted him. He'd gone to Berlin for a year and then to Barcelona to start an export business with an old college pal. Six months in Barcelona had been more fun than profitable and when his friend returned to the States, Archer knew he was next. Then came the letter from Wayne. He'd have to write his parents for money to get home anyway and could just as well write from Paris as Barcelona. Now the task was to find a phone, call the *Herald*, ask for Wayne Murray and get the lay of the land. Wayne would give him a place to stay, set up an interview, and Archer would find out how much longer his little European adventure would last.

He bought a token for the telephone, dialed the *Herald*, and was passed to the editor's office where a woman's voice informed him that Wayne Murray was on a month's vacation, probably somewhere in Greece. It was a moment before he thought to explain his situation.

His name was Rupert Archer. He had worked with Wayne in the States and come to Paris because Wayne said there might be a job. After a pause, the woman, who spoke with a New England accent, said he could come by the newspaper at two o'clock when Mr. Stein would be back. Cross the Seine to Bastille and catch the Metro to George V. "Make sure you take the train direction Neuilly," she said. "When you leave the train walk down the Champs Elysées to the rue de Berri and turn left. We're at twenty-one."

He saved a franc by walking, stopping for a sandwich along the way. Why not see more of Paris than its tunnels since he might not be around long. At Concorde he looked up at the Arch of Triumph, great granite block towering over the wide avenue. He walked under the chestnut trees for shade and was so fixed on seeing everything that he almost missed the rue de Berri, insignificant side street two-thirds up the hill. From the corner he spied the word HERALD jutting out over the sidewalk in vertical letters across from another smaller sign: HOTEL CALIFORNIA. Slice of America in Paris.

Inside, someone waiting by a rickety elevator directed him to the second floor, first door on the left. He climbed the stairs, pushed through an old door and entered an empty office, actually three small offices stretching toward the street and the Hotel California. The only eyes to greet him were those of a large bronze owl maybe five feet high, perched on a filing cabinet in the second office and staring at him with suspicion. He examined the surroundings: old wooden desks, old wooden chairs, old wooden coat racks, old wooden station clock ticking away, metal files, typewriters, owl. No names anywhere. He opened a newspaper. It was 1:40. He sat down to read and to wait.

If there was a job, did he want it? Could he do it? Not that Mr. Stein would offer it since he was totally unqualified, but what if he did? He'd worked on three newspapers in the States but done nothing in Europe but write a bad play about the Berlin Wall and sell a few Spanish rugs and pots to Sears. It hardly qualified him for a job on the *Paris Herald*, elite newspaper for Americans abroad.

He'd been woolgathering, exchanging stares with the owl, hadn't read a word and not heard her come in. He stood and looked into the face of a slim young blonde, dowdy, mussed, even sloppy, no makeup, a girl more attractive than she cared to show. "You're early, but I understand. I'm Connie Marshall. Please sit down."

She took her place, looked up, started to say something and stopped, smiled at him, and set to her work. He read the newspaper. He'd gotten out of touch: Things not going well in Vietnam. Trouble at home. When he looked again it was 2:15.

He was restless. "Do you mind if I ask about the owl?"

"Minerva, goddess of wisdom, transferred wisdom to the owl, her favorite bird," she said, mechanically, continuing to type.

"I see."

She looked up, saw he wasn't satisfied. "James Gordon Bennett, Jr., brought the owl with him from New York in 1887. Owls were his fetish . . . that owl has a history."

Definite New England accent, he decided. Good worker. No schmoozer. She leveled her sensible gaze on him. "I don't understand what's keeping Mr. Stein. He's not one for long lunches."

On cue, a mostly bald, natty, square-jawed gent in horn-rims came in and stood a moment staring at Archer.

"This young man is Rupert Archer," said Connie Marshall, "a friend of Wayne Murray's. He's come in to see you about a job."

"Sonny Stein," said the man, holding out his hand. "Come on back."

That was easy enough, thought Archer, walking past the owl toward the rear office, simple, plate glass windows on two sides, one of them looking across a low roof to other *Herald* offices, the other across the street to second-floor rooms in the Hotel California. Stein sat down. Archer handed him his résumé, sat down and waited.

He hadn't known what to expect at the *Herald* but certainly not this. The building was dilapidated, the elevator a rickety cage, the furniture ancient and encrusted. Though it had not been a conscious thought as he sat waiting, he supposed Mr. Sonny Stein would be a suave and elegant product of the best Ivy League schools, Lippmannesque, no doubt chosen from the cream of the Eastern newspaper establishment for what had to be the plummiest newspaper job in the world. He half expected the conversation to start off in French and that his inability to speak it, let alone his ignorance of copyediting and the elite New York newspaper world from which Sonny Stein sprang, would immediately disqualify him from any hope of employment.

"So you're a Californian, eh? Like Wayne Murray."

"Wayne's from Arizona. We worked together in Phoenix. He was on the copy desk. I was a reporter."

"How's your French?"

Archer shrugged. "Imperfect."

Stein smiled for the first time. "I came here three years ago and still can't pronounce the name of the street where I live. I carry a card to show the cabbies."

Archer wondered if he might have a chance.

"I see you've worked in San Francisco, Honolulu, and Phoenix – never for very long. What's up, Rupert – wanderlust?"

"Laid off in San Francisco at the merger. Honolulu – can't really explain it. Kind of claustrophobia sets in out there. People call themselves mainland rejects. Lot of them are. A year was enough."

"Phoenix?"

Archer had been fired in Phoenix but wasn't going to mention that. "Phoenix . . . right. I was there when Kennedy was killed. Kind of lost it, I think."

Stein looked back at the résumé, single-page, single-spaced, slightly crumpled from living in a suitcase. The last eighteen months were not included. Waiting, Archer felt embarrassed. His career couldn't possibly be impressive to a guy from the *New York Herald Tribune* who could pick up the phone to New York and have the pick of the litter. On the other hand, Wayne Murray from Gila Bend was hardly a member of the journalistic elite. Stein had a quiet, easy, almost shy way about him, probably a good man to work for, a pro not a maniac. Still, the way he kept his eyes on the résumé was telling him this was not a match made in heaven. Stein could see he had no copy desk experience. Archer had never even written a headline.

"You ever worked on a news desk, Rupert?"

"I've always been a reporter."

"Reporters we don't need. We do need a copy desk man – badly. We're getting two feet of copy a day on Vietnam alone, keeps two guys busy."

Stein fell quiet awhile, reflecting. Archer heard the outer door open and a man's voice. Finally Stein laid it down, leaned back in the swivel chair, and put his feet up on the desk. Behind him, across the street in the hotel, Archer saw a woman holding back the tulle sheers and staring at him. His eyes went to Caesar. Thumb up or down?

"You know, ordinarily I'd tell you the usual: We'll file your résumé and let you know. But I'm going to level with you. We need somebody now. The guy you'd be replacing was a linotypist from Pittsburgh – a *linotypist!* That's how desperate I was. Why not, I thought: a guy who sets type ought to be able to edit it. Disaster. Everything had to be redone. Let him go two weeks ago. Now I've got two guys on vacation – European law, have to give them their six weeks. Wayne's somewhere in Greece and Joe Marder, the news editor, is back in Canada. What I'm saying is that I'm ready to put you out there tonight. You've got four years daily newspaper experience even if it's not editing. You must have picked something up. The guys will help you. Don't tell them I said this, but it's not that hard. Telling a story by cutting and pasting. And with Joe gone for a while – I have to tell you, Joe is a bear – it'll be easier. You up for it?"

Caesar's thumb was up.

Am I up for it? The equivalent of twenty bucks in my pocket, no place to stay, not enough money to get back to the States, and he wonders if I'm up for it.

"Show me the way to the newsroom, Mr. Stein."

"Call me Sonny." He called into the next office. "Al – you there?" Archer turned to see a man come in from the owl's office, probably in his late thirties, more horn-rims, receding brown hair slicked back, open angular face, slightly skullish, no smile lines, intense. Stein handed him the résumé. "This is Rupert Archer. He'll start his three weeks tonight. Four to midnight. Hour for lunch. Hundred a week, bumped to $110 if he survives Joe Marder. Many don't."

The man, whom Stein, oddly, had not introduced, led him to the next office. "Al Lodge, managing editor." He held out his hand. "Sit down." Connie Marshall walked through to Stein's office, closing the door behind her.

Lodge looked up as a woman came in. "Helen Lodge, features editor," he said.

Archer introduced himself and looked into the face of an attractive late-thirtyish woman, long auburn hair piled in loops on her head, cigarette in hand. "Also Al's wife," she said. "He doesn't like to admit it."

"Rupert is starting tonight," said Lodge.

"Good luck," she said. "Be happy Joe's gone. Let's hope we still have a newspaper when he's back. Al, my page will be a little late tonight. I want to get Tom's review of *Man of La Mancha* in." She left.

"What did she mean about there still being a newspaper when Joe's back?"

Lodge lit a cigarette. "You've heard about the New York newspaper strike?"

"Uh . . ."

"*New York Herald Tribune* owns us. If it closes – that's the rumor – we've got a problem. But that's not your concern. You've been to Paris before?"

"I don't know Paris."

"Probably don't know the *Herald* either," he said, swiveling around to look up at the owl on the cabinet behind him. "James Gordon

Bennett, Jr., brought that bird with him from New York in 1887. Loved owls, lived here thirty years right around the corner on the Champs Elysées. Buried in Passy Cemetery." He continued staring at the bird. "This newspaper is the second oldest in Paris – survived two world wars, survived Hitler, survived the *New York Times* opening a Paris edition, so far has survived de Gaulle and may even survive the New York newspaper strike."

He turned back to Archer, trying a smile, which didn't work well on the tight skin of his face. "Some of the guys on the desk – you'll meet them tonight – have been here through a lot of it. Some of them – like you, like me, like Sonny – didn't know a thing about Paris when they got here. Others are as permanent as the owl, never go back to the States, *can't* go back, if you get what I mean. When you come here you don't know if it's for three weeks or forever."

That's how it started. When Joe Marder returned it was instantly clear what a break it was that he'd been away. Unlike Lodge and Stein, who had some tolerance for human error, Marder was a perfectionist insulted to have a neophyte on his desk. The job consisted of constructing a flowing news story from a half dozen thick wire agency reports, some of them, like those from Vietnam, filed daily in a dozen versions from a dozen reporters in several languages. Two people in particular helped him: Frank Draper, whose voice was so loud you thought he was deaf, which he wasn't; and Dennis Klein, a small man with a knifelike face and a friendly manner. By the time Marder returned, Archer had some idea what he was doing.

"We'll probably keep you around for a while," Marder told him one night. "Shows how hard up we are. Don't like reporters on my desk. Make lousy editors."

It was a strange cast of characters and after a month Archer still only knew about half of them. At the Berri Bar, the next-door café where the staff congregated nightly between editions, he usually drank with Klein, who'd come to Europe to write a book about the

Nazi occupation of Paris and couldn't stand the thought of going to Germany to finish it. Draper was a loud, intimidating man who'd fought with the Lincoln Brigade in Spain. Byron Hallsberg, the red-bearded, chain-smoking, Viking-like sports editor who'd gone to Hungary during the '56 uprising, seemed slightly crazy, rosy lips smiling through the bushy red beard as he expounded nightly on the decline of Western civilization. Dick LePoint, who wore a permanent bandage on his left hand, apparently from a war wound, came down each night with his girlfriend, Suzy de Granville, an elegant blonde half his age who worked in the *Herald's* library. According to Klein, they'd been mutually attracted by their French names.

Wayne still wasn't back, but another ex-Phoenix hand, Steve Fleming, was there, owing his job, like Archer, to a letter from Wayne. Fleming came down at 10:30 to flirt over pinball games with Gretchen Kilic, a short, bountiful girl with dancers' legs and miniskirts who worked in the library with Suzy. Molly Fleming, Steve's pretty and monumentally naïve wife whom Archer remembered from Phoenix, often came by to pick up Steve when he was off at 10:30. For some reason Molly seemed to like Gretchen, who, according to Klein, who said it with some envy, was fucking her husband.

All these people, even the ones with exotic names, were Americans. Suzy de Granville was from Altoona, Draper from New York, Hallsberg from Indiana, Gretchen Kilic from Chicago, LePoint from Virginia. The only non-American among the editors was Marder, who was from Toronto. The only Brits were the proofreaders, who worked downstairs next to the composing room. The compositors and pressmen were all French, members of the CGT, the Communist labor union. They too congregated in the Berri Bar between editions. The various groups were joined each night by a crush of distributors and vendors arriving in every imaginable kind of vehicle in a cacophony of honking and shouting in the street, to pick up first editions as they came off the presses.

The ground floor office, which handled ads and subscriptions during the day, was taken over by sorters after 10:30, mostly young women who according to Klein worked at night selling more intimate wares down around les Halles, on the rue St.-Denis. "St. Denis," he said, "my patron saint, the patron saint of all Jews. Ha-ha."

One vendor came on foot. He was Eddie Jones, a tall, stooped American Negro who Klein said had been in Paris since the war. He wore a yellow sweater bearing the logo PARIS HERALD across his chest. Eddie came in nightly with an empty canvas bag over his shoulder that the girls filled with newspapers before sending him off into the night. He sat off by himself at one of the little formica tables in the dining area. He was, Klein said, unapproachable.

"Has his cognacs, fills up his bag, and starts down the street – summer, winter, rain or shine. He takes fifty papers, hawks them in all the joints where expats go – Crazy Horse, Lido, Calavados, Harry's, Lipp, Deux Magots, Dome, Select, whatever. You're there between eleven and one you get your *Herald* from Eddie. Been doing it for twenty years. Doesn't talk much."

"Paper sells for fifteen cents," Archer said. "That's seven dollars and fifty cents if he sells them all."

"Oh, he sells them all. Comes back at twelve-thirty for the second edition and goes out with fifty more."

"Walking?"

"He gets rides. I hear he's got some kind of deal with the cabbies. I've been in Harry's when he comes in and seen his bag emptied. Guys are so happy to get the baseball scores they don't ask for change. Eddie does all right."

Archer discovered he liked Paris. Not knowing the language or people he hadn't been sure, hadn't been attracted to France like he was to Germany and Spain, but he liked the *Herald*, liked the work and got along well enough. He found a little apartment on rue St.-Dominique close enough to walk to work and set about learning

French. It was a break, he saw, not only that Joe Marder was gone when he arrived but that Wayne was gone. Staying with Wayne would have been awkward.

"If you hadn't written I'd be back in the States by now," Archer told him when he was back from his six weeks in Greece. "Doing what, I have no idea. Eighteen months away from newspapers probably made me unemployable."

Wayne Murray was a once-solid man running to chubby; hearty, friendly in a forced way for he was basically a shy guy. He'd been miserable in Phoenix, wrote the *Herald* in a desperate attempt to escape and was surprised when by return post Sonny Stein offered him a job.

"Maybe it made you more employable. More sophisticated."

"Not in Phoenix."

"Who's going back to Phoenix?"

"Hard to understand," Archer said as they nursed their demibeers, "how a newspaper like this could hire someone like me. For two weeks I didn't have a clue."

"Lucky Joe was gone."

"So why can't Sonny pick up the phone and hire ten guys from New York?"

"At a hundred bucks a week? Guys with families? He tried it for a while, and you know what happened? They all went across town to the *Times*, which pays one fifty. I'm going over for a tryout myself next week."

"You're kidding."

"Why not? I hate to tell you but one of the reasons you got this job is that this newspaper has no future. Jock Whitney is fed up with the New York unions. No way he'll give in again and lose more money than he already is – twenty million dollars a year is what I hear. If the *Herald Tribune* folds why would he hang on to the *Paris Herald* which loses another three million? And here the unions are communist. Even if Jock wanted to hang on, how do we survive in Paris without New York? When New York closes, we close, that's how I see it. And the *New York Times*, which has been in Paris for six years compared to the *Herald's* eighty, will own Europe."

"Maybe you're wrong."

"And maybe not. Anyway, that's why I'm going over for a tryout. If they need people, I'll jump. I need the money."

"Look at you, just back from the Greek islands. How hard up can you be? I'm living on a hundred dollars a week – made more in the States but never lived as well. And what if the *Herald* survives and the *Times* folds? It's not doing so well either, I hear."

Wayne eyed him warily. "One of the problems . . . if you must know" – he broke off to swallow some beer – "is that I have a family."

"*What?*"

"A boyfriend is what I mean."

"Ah."

"Jojo is his name. Not everyone is as cold a fish as you are, Rupert."

2

Ben Swart held the cold black metal phone against his ear and listened. He'd feared it, they'd all feared it, but knowing Jock Whitney he'd expected something to be worked out. Jock was a doer, a fixer, a *macher* in everything he did – business, horses, yachts, politics, women. The fight with the New York labor unions wasn't something he hadn't faced before. But it hadn't worked out this time, he was saying, the words coming in short bursts through the cable under the icy Atlantic. He hadn't faced this kind of adversary before, like Jap kamikazes, he said, people who want to die. "Suicidal, nihilists, anarchists . . . " and then came a big crack in the line and Ben didn't catch the next word.

"What was that, Jock?"

" . . . never seen anything like . . ."

"You're not coming through."

"*Communists*, I said, goddamn communists set on wrecking everything."

Ben waited for him to get his breath and go on. Jock Whitney was a man who measured his words and if he was calling the New York unions communist, then Swart, who knew something about communist unions, wasn't going to disagree. The merger with the *World* and the *Journal* would have cost a thousand union jobs but would have saved a thousand others. Now the unions were out two thousand.

"Their goal was to destroy the *Herald Tribune*, pure and simple,"

Jock said. "They hate anything that smacks of liberal Republicanism. They stomach Hearst's right-wing crap and the left-wing *Times*, but print a newspaper that appeals to normal, middle-of-the-road Americans and they bring you down. I should have known. I saw the Reds at work when I was over there. Heighten the contradictions they call it. That's why the German Reds supported Hitler. Conflagration leads to revolution. Insanity. You still there, Ben?

"I'm still here, Jock."

"Anyway, Ben . . ." His voice faded again. "That's not why . . ."

"Lost you again . . ."

"Listen, Ben, why don't you just stop talking for a while. We'll do this like telegrams. When I'm through talking, I'll say stop. Then you can start stop."

"Got it, stop."

"We're dead here, Ben, that's what I called to say. We're dead here but we're going to try to hold on in Paris." Again came the cracking, but this time Swart stayed silent, waiting for Whitney to continue. "Try, I said – nothing guaranteed. It'll be hard for you for a while. You'll get nothing from New York – no columnists, features, sports, stock tables, no more Washington bureau." (crack, crack) "Do what you can with the wire services, freelancers, anything. Just hang on while I look for a partner for you. I've got some ideas. Keep your head up, stop."

It took a minute for Swart to digest all that.

"Ben, I said *stop*. Are you still there, stop?"

"We'll manage, Jock. Somehow we'll manage, stop."

Nestling the phone against his ear, Swart leaned back, feet atop the nineteenth-century oak desk that had been in the publisher's office at the *Paris Herald* back to Bennett's time on the rue du Louvre. He loved listening to Jock talk in that snooty accent cultivated from years of boarding schools, yacht races, and diplomatic cocktail parties. Through the door he saw the back of Martine Treuherz's pretty neck as she typed something. He could tell she was listening, but since Jock was doing all the talking what would she hear? Down the way he could just see into Theo le Tac's office, and the little Frenchman would already know what Jock was saying through his secret contacts.

"Oh, and Ben – one more thing. Walter thinks we should start thinking of pulling out of Paris."

Swart was semi-tuned-out and focused on Martine's neck and it was a moment before the words hit his cortex. Walter Thayer was Jock's director of operations, chief negotiator, hatchet man, tough man to buck, but Jock had done it in sending Ben to run things in Paris over Walter's objections.

"Say that again."

"You heard me. Walter's as sick of the unions as I am. He wants you to start looking around – Zurich, Munich, maybe Geneva, cities with good transportation and no communist unions. Send le Tac. Talk to the ministries. See what they offer."

"*Leave Paris?* Did I hear you right?"

"Call it contingency planning. Don't jump to conclusions."

"Bennett is turning in his grave as we speak."

"Times change."

"You'd let the *Times* drive us from Paris?"

"Not the *Times*, goddamn it . . . *the Reds*! Anyway, even if we don't go, it gives us leverage."

Depressing, he thought, hanging up, standing up and looking from his fifth-floor window across to the Hotel California. Down on the street he spied a chic couple climbing out of a taxi and heading into the hotel bar. It was nearly five o'clock and Swart realized he could use a drink.

"Martine," he called. "Come in and shut the door behind you."

He wanted to tell her without le Tac overhearing – just in case he didn't know everything already. Of course le Tac, an old Vichyite, hated the communists as much as Jock did, but le Tac was French and so better to let him wait. Martine was French, too, for that matter, but Martine was different.

"The *Herald Tribune* is folding."

She showed nothing. It was what came next that interested her.

"In Paris we stay in business." He waited a moment and added: "For now."

The face remained impassive. She could sit through endless meetings with the comité de l'entreprise, which represented all departments at the newspaper, and give nothing away. With Martine, no one ever suspected anything. He decided against telling her anything about Walter Thayer's latest brainchild. Was he serious – pull out of Paris after surviving eighty years and two world wars? Maybe not . . . gives us leverage, Jock said. Munich, Zurich, maybe Geneva.

"Pour me a scotch with a little seltzer, would you?"

She poured the drink and sat down across from him. He sat on the desk and looked down at his girl Friday. She had on the white angora sweater that shed a little and the skirt in green plaid with the big safety pin. He was so dumb the first time he thought you had to unpin it.

"I better go down and announce it before they hear it from the unions."

"Go before six – before they head to dinner."

The scotch felt good. He'd had an early lunch to be back in his office for Jock's call and had eaten nothing since. The scotch, the safety pin, and his coming task helped lift his spirits. "I come over tonight?"

"I'm going to the theater tonight."

"Oh." He tried to hide his disappointment. "What's on?"

"Molière – *L'Avare*."

"Got a heavy date?"

"Not that heavy. Come over later if you like."

They kept the damndest hours, the French. He finished his drink in a gulp and got up, frustrated. She looked wonderful in that angora but he didn't want to hang about until whatever time five acts of Molière ended. Damn her! She knew Norma was out of town.

He checked the clock. "Gotta go. You coming? Tell le Tac, will you? No, come to think of it I'll tell him myself." When the time came le Tac would be in charge of finding a new site. Send him to Munich, Jock said. As an old Vichyite he'll be right at home.

Three floors down Joe Marder looked with exasperation at the headline that had just crossed the copy desk:

U.S. SEES SOLUTION IN STRATEGIC HAMLET

"Jesus, Archer," he cried, throwing the file back across the desk. "Whadaya doing, reviewing Shakespeare? Write a headline that someone can understand. What's with you lately?"

Byron Hallsberg's fluffy red beard tickled Sonny Stein's bald head as he leaned over the editor. "Goddamn it, Hallsberg – stop!"

"Got the latest *Sporting News* for you. Cubs picked last."

"So what else is new?"

For reasons no one, including himself, fully understood, Sonny Stein, from New York, was a Chicago Cubs fan. He was picking up the *Sporting News* to have a look when the siege started: Helen Lodge came through the door from the features department, bearing down on him; Frank Draper, in his ridiculous stentorian voice, shouted something at Dan McGillicuddy, slotman on the news desk, who was calling to Stein; Marder was chewing out Archer on the copy desk; behind Helen, Steve Fleming, the political reporter, was approaching with news about de Gaulle's press conference; on the next desk financial editor Johnny Restelli was arguing about column space with Al Lodge, voices rising because Restelli was sick of Vietnam crowding out the business news.

Thinking things couldn't get worse, Stein looked up to see Martine Treuherz in the doorway mouthing words he had no trouble reading: Ben's coming.

Swart rarely came to the newsroom. Since the day they'd arrived together from New York three years before, he'd come down no more than a half dozen times. He knew everyone on the staff, made a point of it, but the thing Stein most liked about Swart was that he was an editor's publisher, which is to say he left Stein alone to edit the newspaper. Swart didn't even step onto the second floor on his way upstairs, always taking the elevator. His presence now could mean only one thing.

Martine held the door and there he was, natty in tweed and a two-tone, blue-white shirt and tie that fit the collar perfectly because it was Brooks Brothers silk. Stein and Swart were the same age but the publisher looked ten years younger. Blond hair versus baldness and rosiness versus pastiness was part of it and so was Stein's chain-smoking. Following Swart, Theo le Tac slithered in and then came Martine. One by one people looked up, laid down their pencils, watched, and waited. This was it, they knew. Suzy and Gretchen came out of the library, copy boys crept in from the telex room, assistant editors from features and finance drifted over, even Maurice, the old-school French messenger who proudly did not understand a word of English, looked up from his racing form.

Next to enter, much to Stein's surprise, was Eric Hawkins, editor emeritus, the little Englishman hired by James Gordon Bennett, Jr., May 7, 1915, the night the *Lusitania* went down. Hawkins became managing editor after World War I, holding that position until Jock Whitney bought the *Herald* in 1958. Hawkins still had a little second-floor office by the elevator but hadn't entered the newsroom since the day he was replaced. His real office was across the street in the bar of the Hotel California, where daily he nursed his drinks, memories, and resentments.

Swart crossed the room and whispered: "New York's folding; we're not."

Expressionless, Stein looked up into the publisher's rosy face. Ben wore a faint smile. Sonny did not. He'd expected that after his little Paris sojourn he would return to New York as editor of the *Herald Tribune*, the newspaper that had given him everything. It looked like he might be in Paris longer than expected.

The madhouse hushed, only the clackety-clack of telex machines interrupting the silence. Stein sat on a corner of the desk, nearly on a level with Swart. Across the room old Eddie Jones trooped in wearing his yellow *Herald* sweater and sat down next to Eric. Eric and Eddie, the two old exiles, thought Stein. How did they find out, he wondered? If they knew, then the unions knew. Even as he held that thought, Stein heard the library door to the basement squeak, and there stood the enormous shape of Tonton Pinard, head of the union local, the communist CGT, come up from the pressroom to listen, though Tonton pretended to speak no English.

Swart, lanky frame leaning on the desk, looked out over the room. "I've just come from talking to Jock Whitney," he began. "First the bad news: the *New York Herald Tribune* ceased to exist as of today, ending a tradition, as I'm sure you all know, going back to James Gordon Bennett, Sr., in 1835. It's a black day in New York, and I have no hesitation at all" – Swart, too, had noticed Tonton Pinard and inclined his head slightly in his direction – "in saying that the *Trib*, as well as the *World* and the *Journal*, were killed by the New York unions. For the newspapers it was murder; for the unions, suicide." He glanced at Stein. "We'll have the story in tomorrow's newspaper.

"Now the good news. Jock is neither selling nor closing the *Paris Herald*."

They erupted in cheers. Swart glanced at Martine, who gave him a little nod and left for her date. Date with whom, he still wondered. Damn it! Why had he turned her down? She might have left before the fifth act. He should have asked.

"We will go on," he said as the room quieted. "Maybe not quite the same as before for we've lost our parent, but we will go on. Jock is looking for another newspaper to partner with us," in Munich or Zurich or Geneva he might have added but didn't. "For a while we'll be on our own, but the important thing is that we still have our job to do. We've still got the *Times* across town, no doubt thinking they've run us out of New York and now will run us out of Paris.

They'll be salivating at the news."

"How do we know Jock isn't talking to the *Times* right now?" asked Dan McGillicuddy, good copyeditor but great blob of a man who needed to lose a hundred pounds.

"Jock sell to the *Times*?" said Swart, "interesting idea." A slight smile crossed his face as his eyes swept around the room, seeking eye contact, building tension, getting the timing right. "I've worked for Jock Whitney for fifteen years." Pause. "Sell to the *New York Times*?" Longer pause. Then, vigorously: "He'd sooner burn in Hell!"

Again the cheer, this time not quite so loud, for there were doubters.

"Anyone but the *Times*," muttered Joe Marder.

Across the room, Byron Hallsberg, legs up on his cigarette-scarred sports desk, sifted bony fingers through his red beard and called out: "Don't want to be a party-pooper, Ben, but who's going to get me the sports scores on time?"

"I've thought about that, Byron. I'll be talking to the Associated Press about sports scores and late financial tables. The *Times* already beats us on stock prices because of their transoceanic teletype setting system. We can't let it get any worse. The AP will have to push up their deadlines. It'll cost, but we'll do it."

"Does Jock have any idea how long it will take to find a new partner?" asked Wayne Murray.

"He has some ideas, that's all I know," said Swart.

"Aren't we losing money, Ben?" said Hallsberg. "Isn't that what you tell us each time we ask for a raise? So who's going to buy into a money-loser?"

Swart considered the question. He liked Hallsberg. Crazy as a loon, but utterly fearless. "Because we're losing money doesn't mean we'll go on losing money."

"So who's he have in mind?" asked Dick LePoint.

Swart decided to probe. "I don't know, Dick. Any guesses?"

"*Wall Street Journal*?"

"Jock wouldn't turn this into a financial rag, would he?" said Hallsberg.

"I don't know what he's going to do," said Swart. "The *Journal's* been trying hard to get into Europe. It's not news they tried to buy us awhile back. Jock wouldn't sell. Doesn't like the Bancrofts."

"Those stock tables sell newspapers," said LePoint, news editor and the only man on the *Herald* to wear an ascot.

"Yeah, but to whom?" said Hallsberg.

"Who cares?" said LePoint.

"I care," said McGillicuddy. "Stock tables aren't news. We do news. Let the *Journal* do stocks."

"What if there are no takers?" asked Martha Gates, the best headline writer.

Swart missed the question. "What was that, Martha?"

"What if no one wants to buy into this money-losing proposition?"

"Ah, yes," said Swart. "What if there are no takers?" He thought about it for a minute. "Well, then, I'd have to say that James Gordon Bennett, Jr., lying across town in Passy Cemetery, will roll over in his crypt, knowing that the *Paris Herald* was beaten by the hated *New York Times.*"

Swart found himself staring at Eric Hawkins and Eddie Jones at the far end of the room, the editor emeritus and the newsboy. Eddie wouldn't care who bought into the *Herald*, but Eric would. Swart reminded himself to drop in for a drink with Eric at the California. "Whadaya think, Eric?" he called to him. "How about the Brits? Think they'd like a piece of the action?"

Surprised, Eric sprang up like he'd been called on in a classroom. "Don't see how that would solve your problem, Ben," he said, hint of a smile on his face. "I believe Byron was talking about baseball scores, not cricket."

It got a laugh, relieving the tension.

"How about you, Eddie?" called Swart. "You want to wear a

sweater with Paris edition of the *Cleveland Plain Dealer* on it?"

Jones's reading glasses balanced on the end of his broad brown nose as he stared, silent and expressionless, at Swart. No one expected him to answer.

"Just joking," said Swart. "I have no idea who Jock's talking to. I'd guess it has to be East Coast to keep the time difference to a minimum."

"That means Baltimore, Boston, or Philadelphia," said LePoint.

"And New York if you include the *Journal*," said Swart.

"Sounds like the *Journal* to me," said Hallsberg. "Hey Draper – wait till the boys in the Lincoln Brigade find out you're working for Wall Street."

Draper, who'd joined the Lincoln Brigade to fight against Franco and was known as the man who never laughed, suddenly laughed.

"Who's going to find out?" said McGillicuddy. "Frank's the last one alive."

"What about the *Washington Post*?" called Suzy de Granville from the library.

Immediately all eyes shot toward Suzy, though Dick LePoint's eyes got there first. More than one copyeditor had tried to make it with Suzy but after LePoint moved in things were settled. Most of them sensed that a leggy blonde like Suzy deserved a guy in an ascot, even if she was from Altoona. LePoint was twice her age but she seemed to like that, might even have set her sights for Sonny himself had not Connie Marshall been around. Beautiful, elegant, and aloof, Suzy had come to Paris in search of the noble roots implied by the *de* in front of her name. Suzy shared the library with Gretchen Kilic, petite but muscular dancer whose main distinction was that she never, whatever the weather, wore anything on her legs, claiming the elements were good for them.

For some reason no one had thought of the *Washington Post*. The *Post* was run by a wealthy, ambitious widow whose sole motive in life, rumor had it, was to make the *Post* better than the *New York Times*. That meant not only transforming it from a local to a national newspaper but competing with the *Times* internationally as well. The *Times* operated thirty-five foreign bureaus at an average cost of $1 million per bureau. Saigon alone cost $10 million a year. Was Katharine Graham ready to spend that much?

"Why not?" said Suzy as the room waited for her. "*Washington's* on the East Coast – sort of."

3

Maryanne and Claire, two young women from Toronto, won a week in Paris from Air Canada. One of Klein's literary pals called from Toronto to ask if he'd show them around town. Klein was taking them to the Tour d'Argent for dinner. He asked Archer to make a fourth.

"On a hundred dollars a week I'm supposed to entertain at the Tour d'Argent – or are *you* paying?"

"*They* are paying, you fool. They're inviting us. It's part of what they won."

Archer was working that night, a Wednesday, but switched with Martha Gates, another copyeditor.

He had no expectations other than it would be the first three-star meal of his life. Two Metro trains took him from La Tour-Maubourg to the Hotel de Ville. He walked across the Seine to the Ile de la Cité and across the passerelle to Klein's place on the Ile St.-Louis. He had a nice little one-bedroom flat not far from where Baudelaire had lived, one he clearly didn't pay for on his salary. Klein's family, from Great Neck, was in New York real estate.

Archer had not been with an American girl since Phoenix. The Berlin girls were accommodating, but Spain, under Franco and the church, was another story. In Paris he'd met no one, gotten no closer to a woman his age than Suzy and Gretchen in the library, neither of whom needed another bee buzzing around. He couldn't remember his last date with a girl who spoke English.

He remembered the apartment, which looked out on the rue des Deux Ponts, from a little party Klein gave for him after word came that he'd survived Joe Marder. They'd toasted him with pastis and then all dashed down the island in a rainstorm for a beery bistro dinner at the Brasserie de l'Ile. In six months in Paris he'd become an expert on bistro food – lapin chasseur, petit salé, ragout, coq au vin, blanquette, sole meunière – mostly thanks to the Berri Bar. The Tour d'Argent was a big step up.

The girls were side by side on the couch, drinking kir. Klein had a fire going against the bitter January weather. Maryanne was speaking French. Klein's French was not good but he was indomitable and Maryanne seemed to understand him.

Archer smiled at Claire. "I hope you speak English."

She smiled back. "If you like."

The girls were sharing a room at the Hotel Madison on the boulevard St.-Germain. Claire was in advertising at Air Canada, had never been to Paris, and told him of her shock winning the company lottery. She was a winsome girl with short, thick auburn hair and bright hazel eyes. She wore a blue silk blouse, beige skirt, and light makeup, maybe none. Gold bangles dangled on slim wrists. She talked slowly, smiled a lot, said, yes, she was bilingual for she'd grown up in Montreal. He looked immediately, as men do with pretty girls, for rings, and saw that neither wore one. But they would take them off to come to Paris, wouldn't they? Just before eight they bundled up and came down to cross to the Left Bank. The Tour d'Argent was the tall building on the corner, just across the Seine. They rode the elevator up to the restaurant, on the top floor.

"Beautiful view from here," said Klein after they'd ordered their ducks. "You can see all the top tourist attractions – Notre Dame, the Seine, my apartment. Proust had a table here, you know. Might have been this very one."

The sommelier handed him the wine list. "If monsieur wants the full list, I will gladly bring it. Most visitors prefer the short list."

Klein hesitated, glanced at Maryanne, and slid the list to her. She pushed it back. "Really, Dennis, I have no idea."

"If monsieur wishes," said the sommelier, "I would be happy to recommend something."

He opened the list, and Archer watched Klein follow his finger down the page, wondering how far down he'd let it go. Klein could have no idea what kind of budget the girls were on. There would be $100 bottles on that list, tempting when you're not paying. Klein looked up at the sommelier. "Something suitable, please, agreeable, not pretentious. We're on a budget."

"Well done, Dennis," Archer said when the sommelier was gone. He looked at Claire. "You know how much he wanted to order from the top of that list."

"We have spending money," said Maryanne. "The hotel's paid for and the airline tickets were free. We can afford a little pretension."

The sommelier was soon back, showing Klein the label and pouring a taste into his glass, which Archer found odd since he knew the girls were paying. Man's job. Klein sniffed, tasted, smacked his lips and the wine was poured.

"You're so fortunate," said Maryanne. "Distinguished journalists living in Paris."

"I don't know how much longer we'll be distinguished journalists if Jock Whitney doesn't settle with the New York unions," said Klein.

"Any jobs in Toronto?" Archer asked.

It was an excellent Burgundy. The way they were going there was a good chance the bottle would be empty while they were still on the soup. He thought of asking the sommelier to put the wine on a separate check, but how much money did he have in his wallet? Klein, of course, would have more.

"Didn't you say you were leaving for Germany anyway?" Maryanne asked.

"I've done all I can do in Paris," Klein said. "Have to go to the source."

"What's the problem with Germany?" asked Claire.

By this time Archer knew he was smitten. They'd paired up some-how, Dennis with Maryanne, he with Claire, not by chance, not really by choice, just mysteriously been pulled that way. He knew he was vulnerable, that in eighteen months he hadn't come close to anything resembling romance. It was so much easier to be with someone he could talk to without being stuck for a word half the time. Knowing nothing of Claire Lambert except that she was from Montreal, had gone to school at McGill, lived in Toronto and worked for Air Canada, he already was plotting to keep her in Paris.

"I'm a Jew," said Klein. "The thought of stepping onto the soil where . . ." He stopped. "It's stupid, I know. The Nazis are gone. I knew the time would come. From my first day in Paris I knew I'd have to go to Bonn and Munich to finish – and probably Berlin. The Nazis took almost everything with them. The stuff here is the just French side of things. Even most of the stuff on Vichy was hauled back to Germany."

After dinner they walked to the Latin Quarter where Lee Konitz was playing at Chat qui Pêche. They ordered cognacs to keep off the cold and it was after midnight when they emerged onto the boulevard St.-Germain, heading toward the Hotel Madison. The sidewalks were empty and they walked four abreast until Claire stopped to look in a shop window and Klein and Maryanne pulled ahead. Claire took his arm and pulled close as they walked in step. She'd taken a red knit cap from her pocket to pull down over her ears. It had not yet snowed in Paris but was bitterly cold – colder than Toronto, she said.

"We have three days," he said. "When can I see you again?"

She didn't answer. They were almost alone on a Left Bank boule-vard that would be flooded with people on a summer night but on a cold January midnight was nearly abandoned. A few cars raced along toward the river.

"I don't know," she said after a moment.

He sensed from the start that she liked him, a sensation that grew over dinner and later at Chat qui Pêche where she'd pulled close to him and he'd put his arm around her so they could hear each other over the wailing sounds of a saxophone trapped by the cold stones of a sixteenth-century cellar. He'd kissed her cheek and she responded with a squeeze of his hand. He'd looked up to see Maryanne staring, seeking Claire's eyes, settling on Archer, something in the look that didn't fit.

"We leave Sunday, you know. Saturday's our last day."

"Save it for me."

Again she fell silent. She had her arm through his and he felt her pulling him toward her as they walked. "I'll talk to Maryanne."

She was bubbling with excitement when they met the next day. "Cézanne's still lifes – something mystical, like he was painting fruit for the gods."

It was just as cold as twelve hours before except that black night had turned into ominous midday gray. The wind off the Seine whipped down the boulevard and nipped at their faces. She pulled the loden tight, wrapped her scarf, adjusted her knit cap, and tucked in close as they walked. People were bustling along, moving fast, heading for indoors. At Chez Lipp they pushed through an outer door into the vestibule and through a second door into the dining room. People waited by the door, loosening coats, shifting feet, letting warm air engulf cold bodies. Waiters bustled about in long aprons with platters of oysters and choucroute, glasses of Sancerre and Beaujolais and beer foaming over the rims of tall schooners.

He'd been there before, once with Byron Hallsberg, bon vivant sports editor who'd introduced him to M. Cazes, the owner who stands sentry at the door. Lipp is a place you go to be seen as well as to eat. "You come here for a while," Hallsberg said, "and you recognize everyone – le tout Paris." He'd pointed across the room where François Mitterrand was about to drop a raw oyster down his gullet. Mitterrand had come within a few points of defeating de Gaulle the year before.

M. Cazes remembered him and asked about Hallsberg. They were shown to a table under the long mirror of the main wall. The room was buzzing, people nestling close on banquettes and leaning across paper tablecloths to better hear each other. Sliced baguette arrived in a little metal tray. Claire talked about museums. They'd been to the Louvre, the Orangerie, and the Flemish collection at the Petit Palais. Archer ordered for two: lentil soup, a dozen oysters, céleri rémoulade and a bottle of Sancerre.

"Your French is quite good," she said.

"Café French, they call it."

He would never forget that lunch. It was the first time he'd really felt at home, like he belonged in Paris, like he was just as important as anyone else in that restaurant and in that city; that the other men were secretly envying him, and the women were wondering who she was. Drinking a half bottle of wine was not something he normally did before work, especially with the Vietnam file waiting, but every table had a bottle of wine or glasses of Alsatian beer, the famous Lipp one-liter *sérieux*, and if the others could manage it so could he. The cracking of oysters, sloshing of beer, calls from one table to another, loud laughter and joking as people fortified themselves against the cold would live in his mind forever. As would the bright eyes of Claire Lambert.

He had little recollection of their conversation. She may have asked him how he came to be in Paris. Or perhaps that was the night before. He didn't have much to say about his personal life for what had he ever done? He'd already begun to think that his greatest achievement was being in Paris and working for the *Herald*, begun to understand what a stroke of luck it had been. Klein said it was all an illusion; that he'd been brought onto a sinking ship because no able-bodied seamen could be found, but if that were the case at least he'd be able to say that he'd lived in Paris, worked in Paris, and fallen in love in Paris. He had this amazing thought: From a life of no pre-vious distinction suddenly he was somebody, working at the *Herald*,

commanding a table at Chez Lipp, entertaining a beautiful girl, surrounded by le tout Paris. He belonged. The gods were smiling.

They created their own hermetic world during their four days
together, worlds without pasts, sufficient unto themselves. He knew
it would last. He did not know *how* he knew, did not know precisely
how young love sustains itself when soon to be parted by a great
ocean, but they would find a way. They would write; one of them,
probably her, would come to join the other. After all, he would be
inviting her to live in Paris. How could she, a bilingual Canadian girl
brought up in Montreal, turn down an offer to live in Paris? Air
Canada had an office in Paris. He'd seen it somewhere, on the rue
Castiglione, or maybe it was the rue de Rivoli. On the Right Bank
somewhere.

They held hands across the table. They drank wine and picked
oysters from the platter of ice and lemon wedges, sliding the slimy
creatures down their throats and chasing them with bread and wine.
She wore a red turtleneck that set off her auburn hair – my Christmas
sweater, she called it. He wanted to ask about her Christmas but did
not. She laid her hand on his and he wondered if it was true that
they'd just met. They'd not known each other twenty-four hours and
yet her eyes told him she returned his feelings. These things happen
in Paris. He'd heard about that. Couples meet by accident, fall in love,
old lives are shed, as in molting, new lives taken on.

You're amazed and doubtful and even afraid because it's such a
huge risk but you have to give it a chance, especially in Paris. Anything less would be to live forever in doubt and regret. I felt something
that day, that night, that week, you would say, felt something I'd never
felt before and yet went away before knowing if it was my one true
chance. We know there's someone out there for us, someone with
whom we will be happy as with no other. We go through life looking
for that person, rejecting perfectly fine, decent people because as
much as we admire them we know they're not our destiny.

And so to meet that person, not only meet her but know it is her and then walk away after seventy-two hours would be an enormous crime against ourselves. We know that, and so when the thing happens we're willing to risk everything for it. We willingly embrace, as D. H. Lawrence put it somewhere, the "new cycle of pain and doom."

"Black, black, black, a bottomless pit, the abyss. I can't think up there tonight, Klein. I'm making mistakes. I am rattled all the way down to the bottom."

"Maryanne told me."

It was Sunday and they'd come down to the Berri Bar for dinner at six o'clock, though outside it felt like deep in the night, which is how Archer felt inside. He ordered a cognac to try to compose himself after two hours of drowning under a foot of Vietnam copy with a hungover, under-slept, short-circuited brain. Klein was eating lapin chasseur but Archer had no appetite. He slathered hot mustard on a piece of baguette to last him until 10:30.

"*When* did you know?" he asked Klein.

"Not before last night. Believe me, I would have told you. She told me Claire was up all Friday night crying. She didn't know what to do."

"Just twenty-four hours ago I was going to marry that girl."

"These things happen."

"Not to you."

"So I got lucky."

"You don't mean . . . ?"

"Look, I don't want to make it worse for you."

"The hell you don't. Black, black, black."

"Quit saying that, will you. You're ruining my rabbit."

"For Christ sakes Klein – you're a Jew. Those girls were Catholic."

"You think being a Jew is a disadvantage?"

"I can't talk about it. You were in bed with her while I was being destroyed."

"I don't confuse things."

"What does that mean?"

Klein laid down his fork and sipped his Beaujolais. He examined the menu on the wall blackboard, choice of tarte tatin or crème caramel for the prix fixe dinner. Klein felt sorry for Archer.

"It means that different situations require different solutions."

"What the hell does that mean?"

"It means, you fool, that those girls came to Paris to have a good time. They won a goddamn prize and came over here for four days of escape and freedom and relaxation and yes – sex. You got all moony when Claire just wanted to get laid. Just like Maryanne. Think about it: They come to Paris for four days and then go back to their little lives. They work in offices, take buses to work, hang out in Laundromats, for God's sake. They come to Paris and they want something to remember. So ask yourself this: What can a man give a girl that she'll never forget?"

"Claire didn't come here to get laid."

"*How do you know that?* Did you even try – did you take her back to your place to see what she wanted?"

"My God, you're cynical."

"Cynical – for wanting to please a woman? Archer, I hate to tell you this but you are screwed up."

"Black, black, black."

"You're making my point."

"I have to get rid of Vietnam tonight. I can't think."

"They're gone, Rupert. It's over. She's back with her husband by now."

He hadn't slept at all. Trapped in the cycle of pain and doom and the awful thing was he had known it would happen. He'd tried to pretend he didn't but Nemesis had whispered in his ear.

The waiter came for the plate of little rabbit bones. Klein explained in his Great Neck French that he would take the tarte and coffee. He finished his Beaujolais and dabbed at his lips.

Archer loathed him. "You have no feelings."

"Look, you're a pro, Archer. Get a grip."

"I'm a pro with a knife through his heart."

"She loves you. I already told you that."

"You think that makes it better? She also loves her husband."

"What can I say? This is Paris."

4

Steve Fleming was cool, as cool a customer as had ever come to the *Paris Herald* or maybe ever come to Paris, which is not a cool place. Oh, in eighty years there might have been someone else at the newspaper who was equally calm and smooth and self-assured, who walked with the same muscular beach swagger, but no one thought of them as cool. Cool was something special that came out of the 1950s and came out of L.A. and was jazz at Hermosa Beach and waiting for the right wave at Malibu Pier and tooling around the Strip at midnight in your Impala convertible looking for action.

Cool was not just that you were composed under pressure, but that you were always composed, flustered by nothing, not by Paris rudeness, not even by the riffraff that lives in the Metro and pinches wallets, purses, and girls' bottoms. Cool is a way of talking, slow and casual; and walking, the shoulders rolling but not too much, which would be uncool. No one at the *Herald* could remember anyone quite like Steve Fleming, but that's what happens when you hire sight-unseen from the West Coast. Steve had the build to go with it, too, and the blue eyes and blond hair over his forehead, and a smile that might even have melted the heart of Mme. Defarge as she sat knitting and waiting for his pretty head to fall into the basket beside Dr. Guillotine's new invention.

Molly was thinking about Steve as she sat at her dresser in the sixth-floor walkup combing her hair, hair just as golden as her husband's and much longer. Her eyes were half on her hair and half out the window running over the Paris rooftops. When you're in L.A. you never much notice rooftops, but high in a Paris building overlooking a gallimaufry of orange and black tiles and slates and little chimney pots sticking up at all heights and angles from dozens of buildings as far as the eye can see, you get interested. They had no television in the apartment and Molly was not a reader.

The first months were wonderful. They'd go out every night after work, eating at midnight in the Marais or Les Halles and staying up with friends until three or four in the cafés of St.-Germain and Montparnasse, drinking and rolling joints, coming home for sex as the sun came up. She transformed herself from a morning to a night person, from living in Santa Monica sunshine to Paris nights. The language didn't bother her because she spent all her time with other Americans. Steve knew French well enough because he'd studied it and was a quick learner, but Molly knew very little. The thing they'd missed most when they arrived was the beach but then Byron Hallsberg found this little lake called l'Etang de Hollande out by Rambouillet, and he and his Irish wife, Doris, would drive them out on weekends with their children and they'd meet others from the *Herald*.

It was like a vacation those first summer months and even when winter came it was fine for a while. Then it got cold, colder than anything she'd ever known, and without swimming at l'Etang and sitting up all night with friends in cafés Paris seemed dark and gloomy. Days were short and nights long and sometimes she didn't feel like taking two Metro trains to get to the *Herald* and found herself going to bed before he was home and getting up while he was still asleep so she could take advantage of whatever daylight or sunshine there might be. They lived on different schedules and Molly began to feel marooned, isolated with no company but the mirror and the rooftops.

By the end of the second year, she was thinking of going home. She was twenty-two when she married Steve and how could she have imagined she'd wind up in Paris? He was working for a little Santa

Monica newspaper and expecting every day to be hired by the *L.A. Times*, but instead was offered a job in Phoenix. Molly loved Phoenix, though Steve did not. The Phoenix newspaper had a nifty little club out near Shadow Mountain where she lay in the sun all day and they had a nice place in Scottsdale with its own swimming pool and she grew to love that hot, dry weather that everyone else hated. And then Wayne Murray, desperate to get out of Phoenix, was hired in Paris and wrote Steve that he should come over, too, and Steve knew French and so they came.

She wondered what she'd be doing at home. She'd have her own friends again, not just Steve's, and probably have a job like before, cocktail waitress at a place called The Point on the ocean at the foot of Topanga. She'd liked the hours, four to eleven with mornings free for the beach. She hadn't said anything yet to Steve about going home but thought he might be ready for it. They would find some nice little West L.A. stucco near Pico and hit the beach every morning. And maybe – she was twenty-five years old – it was time to start thinking of children.

They should have sat down and discussed these things. She kept telling herself to do it but she wasn't much of a talker or Steve much of a listener. He just smiled and never interrupted and was cool about things, but didn't really pay attention. Steve was the *Herald*'s political reporter, spending more time in French circles, not able to meet up after work at Lipp or Deux Magots as they used to do. And there was this new girl, Gretchen, who worked with Suzy in the library and seemed always to be around Steve.

She was ready for a showdown when she got a surprise: She was pregnant. Neither wanted children, not yet, not in a top-floor walkup in Paris. Steve began looking for a doctor, but as time passed and they talked it over they grew more used to the idea of having a baby. She talked to Doris Hallsberg, who had three children and still lived in Paris, in the Sixteenth Arrondissement. Many on the *Herald* had moved to suburbs like Meudon or Maisons-Laffitte but that meant putting down roots and neither Molly nor Steve wanted that. But they could find another Paris place, on a lower floor or with an elevator, have the baby, and in a year or two go home.

The came the second surprise: miscarriage. Dr. Tom Boswick, the handsome obstetrician at the American Hospital in Neuilly said nothing was wrong with her, that it was an accident of nature and she would have many more babies. Molly liked Dr. Tom and liked the hospital, almost felt like she was back home again, like when she had her appendix out at St. John's in Santa Monica. She had an instant crush on Dr. Tom, tall, white-haired Bostoner who the pretty English nurse named Tessa said was married to a Frenchwoman. Dr. Tom was the first American she knew married to a Frenchwoman.

When Steve came to bring her home Molly feigned a relapse. There was something about the hospital that appealed to her, something she needed, something about how everyone had a purpose and a role to play and pulled together to get the worst jobs done even when they had their own problems. She knew something was going on between Tessa and Dr. Tom. Tessa, from Devon, was dark and curvy, brisk and smiling in her tight white uniform and probably half Dr. Tom's age. They were having an affair, she could see that, but she wondered if it made either of them happy.

Two days later, Dr. Tom said she would have to move into a ward and she decided to go home. She didn't call Steve this time, just packed up her things and called a cab, which dropped her off on boulevard St.-Germain in front of their building. It was a sunny, crisp morning, the kind of winter day in L.A. when you needed a wetsuit. It felt good to be back on her feet, though she felt weak. Steve would still be asleep so instead of heading around back to start the climb upstairs, she went into the corner café, put down her little suitcase, sat down by the window and ordered a café crème and croissant.

She stretched out her legs in the sunlight and when the croissant came found herself tearing through it and ordering another. It felt strange to be empty again after so many months and she needed to fill up. She thought about the baby, a boy, Dr. Tom said, though she hadn't wanted to see it. Now she'd get Steve to write that letter to the *Times*. She needed to get him back on her own turf, back where they were equals again. She couldn't get Dr. Tom and Tessa out of her mind, thinking how natural it was for them to be drawn together on their little English-speaking island in France. There was another such island at the *Herald*: Steve was on it. She was not.

She thought of him six floors up under their quilt, sleeping late. "Wait awhile," Dr. Tom had said about making love again. Steve was probably very frustrated. Her head felt light and she wondered if she could climb the five flights. She'd leave the suitcase and Steve could bring it up later. The coffee and sunshine warmed her and with her belly full from two croissants she was feeling randy. It was five days since the miscarriage, and sex would feel good. She'd make him be gentle and then it would be time for him to go and she would fall back into dreamless sleep until going out to the corridor to use the toilet and there wouldn't be a sound in the house.

The toilet was a problem. The top floors of Paris buildings, the fifth étage, are for the family maids. From each of the family apartments, one or two to a floor, a rear door off the kitchen connects to the back stairway. Through these doors the maids – once young Bretonnes but more recently Portuguese or Spanish girls – climb the stairs each night to the top, where their rooms are bunched together. The toilet is a common one, outside in the corridor. It is Turkish style, that is, with no toilet bowl or seat, only a slab of porcelain on the floor with two raised places, like giants' footprints, over a hole. The Flemings' proprietor had purchased six rooms from owners who no longer kept live-in maids and made them into one apartment. It was a fine apartment, quiet and with a good view of the rooftops. The drawback was no toilet or elevator. But for tenants young and healthy enough not to care about the climb or the squat, the apartment was a steal.

Molly paid her bill, left her suitcase with the patronne, and went around back. Her legs were shaky and she took the stairs slowly. There are no landings on the back stairways, for healthy young maids and the young men who visit them don't need to rest. At the top of each flight, outside each kitchen door, Molly paused, and twice she sat down on the top step. The stairwells are very steep and narrow, with no space wasted. Molly had her purse slung over her shoulder and took her time. She counted the kitchen doors as she mounted. She'd never had trouble with the stairs before, but for a moment wondered if she'd make it. As she started up the last flight, she knew she was bleeding.

Reaching the top, she leaned back against the wall to rest. She stayed like that for a moment, remembering six days before when she'd felt the baby coming and gone rushing downstairs to find a taxi, alone, for she couldn't reach Steve. The thought depressed her. She turned toward the toilet and was aware it was occupied. She heard a paper scratchy sound and then the chain and the flush. None of the maids would be home at 11 A.M. They were allowed to use the apartment toilets downstairs during the day. It had to be Steve.

She stood and waited, ready to surprise him. Their apartment was at the front and she was still at the rear, near the stairs. After a moment, the door swung open and instead of Steve, a girl emerged, small, barefoot, athletic-looking with dark, tousled hair, dressed only in a man's T-shirt. She had remarkable calves. Molly expected her to turn toward the maids' rooms but she did not. She darted quickly, on little dancing feet, in the other direction, pushing open the door to their apartment and closing it quickly behind her.

"C-h-e-r-i-f," he said slowly.

Some of them were taking coffee in a café on the boulevard Raspail after French class, and the Arab boy who'd been reluctant to come had just spelled out his name.

"Like sheriff," the German boy said in English, and Cherif smiled though he didn't understand.

"It's the same word," said the Egyptian girl.

Molly enjoyed these meetings more than the classes because making mistakes in French over coffee didn't matter. They met for the camaraderie of it; rarely the same people because the faces at the Alliance française changed every week.

She'd seen him in class a few times, always shy, rarely saying anything though he seemed to speak French better than the others, never joining them after class. On this particular day, Molly had gone up to him boldly after class, put her arm through his, and said, "venez avec nous pour le café." She felt the recoil in his arm but then he relaxed and even smiled. "Oui," he said after a hesitation, "pourquoi pas?"

He was an Algerian sent to France following the peace treaty to study and learn to love the French again. He was small and retiring with quick, darting black eyes that were vulnerable and appealing to Molly. He was very young and on his guard as Algerians must be in France. He was a very handsome boy.

Their class was a mixed group of foreigners, some necktied businessmen who rushed away afterward and girls who disappeared to tend babies or do the shopping for their mistresses. But there was a rotating group that didn't have chores and headed across the street to the Relais Raspail. It was upon Molly's return to class after her miscarriage that she asked Cherif join them. It seemed like a nice thing to do.

The next time, Cherif came up to her afterward and asked if she would take coffee with him at a Turkish place he knew, on the rue du Dragon. "I will tell you about Algeria," he said in French, "and you will tell me about America."

She'd said nothing to Steve about the morning she returned from the hospital. She'd stayed alone in the corridor awhile, gone into the toilet to staunch the bleeding and then made her way back down to the café. She had nowhere else to go. She waited until they came down and then she trudged back up those five flights and collapsed onto a bed whose disorder and odor left no doubt about what had taken place. She was in no state to be fastidious. She fell immediately into a deep sleep of escape and was not awakened until evening when Steve came home.

"Sorry about the bed," he'd said with his winsome smile. "I didn't expect you."

She smiled back at him. "I know you didn't."

She continued to take coffee after class, sometimes with the others, sometimes with Cherif, either at the Raspail or on the rue du Dragon. It was several weeks before he invited her to supper. He knew she was married for she wore her ring, but she never mentioned her husband and he never asked. She accepted because they spoke French together and being with him was like having her own tutor. It turned out to be a night when Steve was off early, but she stuck to her guns, saying she was having supper with classmates and couldn't meet him. She knew he would find company elsewhere.

They met at the Procope, which was decent enough if you didn't mind the occasional cockroach. The food was cheap and nobody minded who was seen with whom. Cherif was *basané*, as the French say, swarthy, easily spotted as an Algerian, and there are places in Paris where a pretty blonde in a miniskirt on the arm of an Algerian are not welcome. Procope, with its long Left Bank student tradition, was not one of them.

After dinner (Molly insisted on splitting the bill), they walked up to Deux Magots, finding a table inside where they could watch people passing without being observed. They ordered coffee, and Cherif lit a Gauloise.

She was aware she was being courted, though in a strange Arab way, a mixture of deference and desire. Later, she would realize it had been in her mind all along, though at the time she was not aware of thinking ahead. One thing just led to another.

Back on the sidewalk, Cherif held out his hand to say good-bye.

Molly lived up the boulevard St.-Germain, and he had the Metro to catch at Odéon, in the opposite direction. He lived at the Cité universitaire in the southern part of the city.

"Would you mind walking me home? You can catch the Metro at Bac."

It must have been the way she said it, for he hesitated. Was it something more than just a request to walk her home? The boulevard St.-Germain was very safe. He was a guest in France; he had to be careful. Molly saw doubt flicker in his eyes and so took his arm and led him in her direction.

Outside her building they stopped. The café was closed. They held each other's gaze a moment. "Viens avec moi," she said, taking his hand and leading him toward the back. She saw he did not know what to expect.

"Cinquième étage," she said, pointing upward.

She saw his puzzlement that Americans would live in maid's quarters, but when they reached the top and entered the apartment, he understood. Molly was used to surprised looks when people visited the first time, but nothing quite like what she saw on Cherif's face. What did it mean for him to be here? Where was her husband?

She, too, should have felt apprehension. Or nervousness, doubt, fear, anything but what she felt, which was desire – raw, naked, lusty desire. She'd never done anything like this before. She'd been a good wife. She'd worn a jacket all evening and her hair up but now took off the jacket to reveal a low-cut sweater bulging with breasts still swollen for the baby. She let her hair fall down to her waist. If he hadn't understood before, now he did. She moved closer, sliding both hands under his open shirt and running her fingers over his hairless chest. She had long, manicured nails and felt him grow aroused when she dug in a little bit. She saw desire in his large, dark eyes and felt the pressure in his pants against her. They were the same height and she felt it exactly where it should be.

For Cherif the circumstances were beyond imagination. He'd

heard something about American women but not entirely believed it. And he'd never been close enough to a French woman even to think about it, never been this close to any woman but his mother and grandmother. He stood motionless as she unbuttoned his shirt. He was down to his cotton briefs and in a state of high arousal. Molly led him into the bedroom where they kissed, an open, hungry cavernous kiss. She dropped her skirt, slipped from her sweater and bra and grasped his penis. Her heat radiated through him. They fell on the bed and she instantly guided him inside her, the first time he had ever been in such a place. He came with such a massive jolt that he felt her entire body buckle.

He stayed inside her. She bucked like a goat as he came again. He pulled out and she felt him melt in her arms. The same as with Steve, she thought, all that swaggering masculinity suddenly limp like a wilted flower. What power she had! She seemed a maniac to him, a different person from the pretty, polite girl who sat across from him at coffee speaking French. She didn't talk. She moaned and scratched, and he wondered about her husband. Did he do this to her, too? Or was it because he did not do it?

At some point Molly felt an ebb. She lay her head on his chest and something told her she should be worrying. Instead her hand went to his penis and she massaged it into an erection and as she prepared to mount him she heard steps on the stairs.

Cherif was not aware of any sound at all. He was feeling the new sensations brought to him by this amazing girl. He found himself thinking of the white sands by his home, of the blue waters off the coast of Oran. In the distance he heard the sound of a whistle, the clank of the tramway, the cry of a child. He was a teenager and the French wives were there on the beach in their bikinis and the boys, hiding in the wadi, could only look and dream and lust. He wanted a cigarette, but first wanted to do it one more time. He was gorged, greedy, addicted. He felt her above him, inserting him into her, and he opened his eyes and saw her mounted on him, her large breasts bouncing under the long cascade of blond hair that came down and tickled his face.

Molly stayed like that even as the key entered the lock and Cherif tried to sit up. She kept him like that inside her, beneath her, stuck, pinned, under her control, intent on squeezing one more orgasm out of him. It was a good position, probably not that much different from how Steve and Gretchen had done it.

5

Eric Hawkins hoisted all five feet two of his pink body onto the corner stool at the bar of the Hotel California and waited for Marcel to bring his gin and bitters. The hotel owner, Lucien Montsouris, had set out after the war to decorate the bar in authentic Californian, the problem being that Lucien had never set foot in California. The garden terrace, with its white iron tables, yellow umbrellas, and potted palms, was occasionally sunny enough to pass for California, but for Hawkins, who'd never been to the States despite working forty-five years for a U.S. newspaper, the bar had nothing of what he imagined California to be. For him, its high ceilings, deep red Morocco leather chairs ,and ornate glass lamps along the walls were more Second Empire than anything else.

Not to complain. Since leaving the *Herald*, the California was his primary home, where he spent far more waking hours than in the cubicle they called an office across the street and nearly as many as in his flat off avenue Wagram. From his barstool he could look outside and see everything, from the magazine *l'Express* on one side of the *Herald* to the Berri Bar on the other. Above all he could see the *Herald*, making sure they kept to schedule – his schedule. Under Eric Hawkins, the *Herald* had never missed an edition – except for the second war, of course, something he couldn't do anything about. It hadn't been a problem in the first war because the Germans never got to Paris.

He'd not spent the entire forty-five years at 21 rue de Berri, but between December 8, 1930, when they moved from the rue du Louvre, and June 13, 1940, and the arrival of the Nazis, it was home. And between his return August 28, 1944, and September 10, 1960, when he was retired, it was home again. He knew those dates better than his birthday, which he tended to forget. He'd lived at the *Herald* so long he once talked to Lucien about taking a room at the California. Lucien just smiled and gave him another gin and bitters. He'd slept there a few nights as the Germans closed in. Later he joined a few million others on the roads south, slipped into Spain, crossed into Portugal, and sailed for England, a place he hadn't been since arriving in Paris twenty-five years before. Despite what his passport said and his somewhat shaky command of the language, Eric Hawkins was a Parisian.

There were maybe a dozen other people in the bar, a smattering of journalists from *l'Express* and some German tourists at the tables, but Eric sat alone at the bar. It was a long bar but had only four barstools because Lucien, being French, didn't believe in them. In French bars you stand up at the bar or sit at tables. Since Lucien didn't want to attract the kind of people who stand up, he'd put in four large, swiveling barstools to occupy the space and force people to the tables where tips for unsalaried waiters like Marcel were better. Eric Hawkins was a special case. Eric had sat on that same barstool every night since his return to Paris in '44.

Hawkins looked up from his *France-Soir* to see a young man come through the door and stand a moment surveying the large room. He remembered him from the newsroom the night Swart came down. Eric knew personally only the people he'd hired himself – Marder, Draper, Hallsberg, Mac the fat man, Martha Gates, the Brit proofreaders, a few others who were still around like Eddie Jones and Maurice the messenger and the copyboys, who weren't boys at all. He'd turned down Art Buchwald when he came scrounging for a job in '49, but that had worked out anyway. For him, the new *Herald* crowd was just a lot of strange faces he saw around the building. Sometimes they nodded, usually not. It was amazing to him. He'd been captain of that ship for forty years (with a few years out for the Nazis), and now most of them looked right past him. Damn maddening how they'd lost all sense of history – with a few exceptions, like Hallsberg and Al Lodge. Bennett would have known what to do with the rest.

"Mr. Hawkins. My name is Rupert Archer. I'm the new boy over there."

"Eric will do, laddie."

"I've heard enough about you."

"Well, I hope you're talking to the right people." He was sizing him up, wondering if he would have hired him. "Where you from, Rupert?"

"California."

"You don't say. Well, you've come to the right place. First time at the California?"

"First time I've been off at 10:30. New boy gets the worst hours." He hoisted himself onto the next barstool. "You know why I came here tonight? I came for a Canadian Club. Since about nine o'clock I've been thinking how good a Canadian and soda would taste. I like it with a twist of lemon."

"There's your bottle, right up there," Eric said, pointing. "Why Canadian?"

Archer hadn't made the connection but suddenly did, feeling the pain. But it wasn't her at all. He'd always liked Canadian whiskey.

Eric turned to the tables. "Marcel, s'il te plait."

"J'arrive, M. Eric, j'arrive."

Suddenly the old gamin's face came alive. "Listen – you hear that? The music has started."

Archer heard nothing.

"That's the presses, Rupert. You not only hear them, you *feel* them underground – low kind of rumble, like the troll under the bridge beating his drum." He checked his watch. "In ten minutes Eddie Jones will push through that door with my *Herald*. You can set your watch by it – every night. Until then, you've got this to read." He pushed across the *France-Soir* he'd been reading. "How's your French?"

"Improving."

"You can read that headline, I imagine."

DE GAULLE CONTRE LBJ

It consumed most of the top half of the front page: "*That* I can read."

Marcel fixed Eric another gin and bitters and got down the Canadian Club, pouring a stiff shot, dropping in ice, and passing Archer the seltzer bottle.

"How do you say *twist* in French, Eric?"

"Tweest. Un tweest de citron pour mon ami, Marcel, s'il te plait."

At 10:40, Eddie Jones came in and handed Eric his newspaper.

"What are you hearing over there, Eddie?"

The old newsboy looked at him over his half moons, glanced at Archer, and then back to Eric. "Tonton's been down to *l'Humanité*. He's worried about this New York thing. Don't know what transpired."

"Eddie, do you know Rupert Archer?"

Archer put out his hand and Jones touched it lightly. "Gotta go."

He turned and then turned back to them. "Funny rumor, Mr. Eric. Something about the *Herald* moving to Zurich. You know anything about that?"

"Where'd you hear that?"

"One of the pressmen."

Archer watched Hawkins's eyes move up and down the tall green neon HERALD sign across the street. "Tactics," he said, "never happen."

"I'm sure as hell not going to Zurich."

They watched him shuffle away.

"Amazing man. Knows everything, says nothing. Hired him in forty-five, stayed on after the war, disappeared for a while. Never went home. Good man."

"*Zurich . . . ?*"

Eric shook his head. "Now tell me. What brings you to Paris?"

"I'd been wandering around Europe."

"Where'd you work in the States?"

"San Francisco, Honolulu, Phoenix."

"Never been to the States myself."

"Well, I'd never been to Europe."

"Why'd you leave?"

"Just after Kennedy's murder."

"That drove you to Europe?"

He was savoring the drink and his mind drifted. She'd told him to write her in care of Air Canada Toronto and he'd written two letters with no response. Little things would bring her to mind, which would short-circuit him for a while. He needed a way to shock her from his system. "That and the fact I was fired in Phoenix."

Watching him in the mirror, Hawkins swung sideways to look closer. "So you know how it feels. How long had you worked there?"

"One year."

"One year, ha! How'd you like to be fired after forty years?"

"After forty years you just call it retirement."

Eric didn't like that and turned away. "You tell Sonny you'd been fired?"

"No."

"No disgrace, you know. Why'd they fire you?"

"It's a long story. The short version is that I was the labor reporter in a right-to-work state. The publisher didn't like what I wrote."

Eric turned back to him. "You know, Rupert, you've just made an old man feel better. Allow me to buy you a drink."

Marcel pulled *France-Soir* across the bar to read. He tapped the front page. "Le vieux cherche la bagarre," he said as someone hailed him from a table.

"Bagarre?" said Archer.

"He said the old man is looking for a fight. De Gaulle hates the Vietnam War, which is why he's throwing American troops out of France. Thinks Johnson is crazy – doesn't want to cooperate with someone he doesn't trust. Say, how come you're not in Vietnam? You're not a shirker, are you?"

The whiskey relaxed him, made him remember how much he missed it. "Drafted. I already served. I don't know what I'd do if I was five years younger." He held up his glass. "Maybe go up to the place where this stuff is made." He stared at the glass. "No, come to think of it. I couldn't do that."

"It's a new world, Rupert. No one shirked in the two wars, no one would have dared. This war's different, like the French in Algeria. That's why de Gaulle pulled out. It's why the British got out of India. Colonialism's had its day. You Yanks just haven't gotten the word."

"I don't think I'd want to die for Vietnam."

The little man stared into his drink. "You know, Rupert, I once asked Mr. Bennett if he thought Henry Stanley was ready to die for Livingstone. Bennett sent Stanley off to find Dr. Livingstone, you know. Imagine what it was like in the Congo in those days – savagery, disease, heart of darkness. I'll never forget Mr. Bennett's answer. Twirling his mustaches, he looks down at me and says, 'Hawkins, if you believe in what you're doing you never worry about dying.' There was a man, James Gordon Bennett, Jr. They loved him, the French did, like one of their own. They've loved a few of you, you know – Ben Franklin, Pershing, Lindbergh, Kennedy. They loved Bennett as much as any Yank. Maybe more. Knew he was one of them. Wasn't going home. Not like that today."

In the mirror they watched some people shuffle in from the hotel lobby and noisily seat themselves at a table, Americans, fat, friendly, noisy, insecure, doing Europe on the strong dollar, homey in the

California looking out on the *Herald*, nice rooms at $15 a day, American newspaper at breakfast. They were being bubbly to Marcel, who kept a fish eye on them, though he depended on their tips. Marcel was *un homme sérieux*, and one thing *un homme sérieux* does not do is get friendly with strangers. You are friendly with your friends – if that. Marcel spoke no English but knew the English words for every drink he'd ever been asked to make.

Eric caught Archer's glance in the mirror and nodded his head back toward the Americans. "That's what you're sending over today. Rich tourists. Mind you, we can't complain. They keep us in business. But Bennett, he came to stay. I came to stay. What about you, Rupert . . . you come to stay?"

Archer looked back at him in the mirror. "In Zurich?"

Hawkins ignored it. "Say, how would you like to meet Bennett?" He pulled closer and Archer smelled the sweet mixture of cologne, sweat, and bitters, noticing the white stubble sprouting in pink crevices of the old editor's cheeks. "I think of him, you know." He wore a gnomish smile on his lips. "Sometimes I talk to him."

Archer eyed him in the mirror. Dotty? He pulled back from the smell. "How do you do that?"

"I visit him."

It took a minute to catch the meaning. Ben Swart had mentioned the crypt in Passy Cemetery. "You go to the crypt?"

"Exactly so – been there many times, usually after hours when it's private and we can talk. You work on the *Herald* you should visit the crypt. Like to go?"

Archer hesitated. "Sure . . . of course."

"Let's do it." He grabbed the tabs. "Allow me to sign, Rupert. I get a price, you know."

"Wait – you mean . . . ?"

He signed, sprang to his feet, and grabbed his coat.

Archer stood up just as the door opened and in rushed Molly Fleming, breathless, looking around, approaching them when she saw no sign of Steve. Her long blond hair serpentined over one shoulder, tumbling almost to the bottom of the short leather coat that descended to a level just below her rump and showed no signs of anything under it, though there was probably a skirt down there somewhere.

Molly turned as Steve came in. "Some horrible little Frenchmen just goosed me – stuck his hand right up on the Metro and pinched."

"Got you on the Metro, did 'e," said Hawkins, dropping his *h*'s for the first time. "Must 'ave 'urt." He chuckled as they pushed outside.

A taxi was just dropping people off and Hawkins had them in the door and on their way before Archer could protest. Soon they were whipping down avenue Kléber and pulling up outside high walls just off Trocadero. He produced a key and opened the gate onto a vast black space.

"You've got your own key?"

On little light feet, Hawkins was already down the path, pulling a penlight from his pocket to jet a small beam through the darkness. "Stay close," he whispered. "Don't want to lose you. Don't step on anyone." He chuckled again.

Veering off the path, nipping his way through a maze of tombstones, monuments, and mausoleums, suddenly he stopped. "There," he whispered, pointing his light on a sculpted head, "Manet – you know your impressionists?"

Why was he whispering? He stopped again, shining the light on a black marble crypt. "Debussy," he whispered. "Horrible death . . . almost there. Bennett wanted to be in the back. Modest for a great man. Can you believe that the only time his name appeared in the *Herald* was for his obituary, May 14, 1918. Same thing for the crypt."

"What do you mean?"

He stopped. "Just this . . ."

The beam flashed onto the bust of a bird, bursting from the dreary night like Poe's raven, perched on a pedestal above the entrance to the thanatorium.

"An owl . . . ?"

"An owl it is, Rupert. It was his fetish, you know. Had owls every-where – claimed it was the hoot of an owl that told him to start up the *Paris Herald*. Saw it one night at midnight. Like Napoleon's star, a sign. Made it his signature. Look around, Rupert, you won't find Bennett's name anywhere in this crypt. Just the owl." He took Archer by the arm. "Come along."

Inside, the beam moved up the wall to a large stained glass window depicting a sleek yacht knifing her way through blue water. "The *Lysistrata* – his yacht – named for a Greek lady both beautiful and fast."

Nowhere was anything written. How many people had come by this tomb, paused by the bird, and wondered who its mysterious inhabitant could be?

"He was different from the others, Rupert . . . knew right from wrong, he did – oh, maybe not in the little things. He was something of a rogue. Hated the Kaiser . . . blamed him for the war, for those thirty million dead . . . right, you know."

His light fixed on the yacht, he was in full flight.

"The *Lusitania* – my God, it was my first night on the *Herald* if you can imagine it, up all night sorting out dispatches of survivors and missing. Horrible, it was. I was the grim reaper, sorting names, this one dead, this one alive. We ran dozens of little black boxes, like caskets, on the front page with just the words: 'In Memoriam of the Men, Women and Children Lost on the *Lusitania*' . . . stayed up all night putting out new editions with the latest list of casualties . . . posted it in the window on the avenue de l'Opéra for the crowds out-side. My God we hated the Kaiser that night."

The old gnome was gone, transported from the *Lysistrata* to the *Lusitania*, reliving the night a half century before when he'd been thrown onto the news desk to do something never done before – a newspaper's minute-by-minute accounting of the deaths of twelve hundred people. How do you forget something like that?

"Bennett wrote the unsigned editorial himself that night," he said. "'What a pity Mr. Roosevelt is not president,' he wrote. 'He would know what to do.'"

6

Ben Swart stepped into the rickety elevator, clanked the outside metal door, slid shut the inside wooden gate, and pressed number four, which took him to the fifth floor. The elevator was a relic. One day it jerked to a stop between floors, trapping him. He pushed every button but red SECOURS, which would have been too embarrassing, and stomped a few times before deciding that stomping was not a good idea. Nothing worked until, like an angry ape in its cage, he began rattling the gate, apparently rattling it closed. The thing started up with a spine-shattering jolt and he continued on his way down.

Stepping off on the fifth floor, he carefully closed the gate and door and sent the elevator back down, which he sometimes forgot to do. He headed into his office, wondering what Martine was wearing. Whatever it was it would be more than she'd had on a few hours earlier. Even when Norma was in the States and he slept over with her he always left early, enjoying the walk from her little place off the avenue Mozart to his house in Villa Montmorency. Better not to arrive together at the *Herald*. She should arrive first. She was, after all, his secretary – in addition to the other thing.

Spring had come and she was dressed in a tight sleeveless yellow jumper. It was new and he liked it.

"The Elysée Palace called," she said, not looking up. Sometimes when he left her too early she came in cranky. He'd never taken her to his house, which with the neighbors and friends of his children was risky. "They'd like you and Mr. Stein to come down at four today – if that is convenient of course. I am to call them back."

"The Elysée Palace?" he said, surprised. "Who, de Gaulle himself?"

"No, *not* the president." She *was* cranky. Perhaps tomorrow he'd take her to breakfast. "You have an appointment with M. Henri de Saint-Gaudens, chief of staff."

"Sonny and me?"

"Sonny and you."

"Why Sonny?"

She didn't bother to answer.

"Why me?"

"How should I know?"

"You didn't ask?"

Finally she looked up and he could see the color in her face. God how he loved her when she was like that. "Of course I asked."

She was making him squeeze it out of her. "He must have said *something*."

"Something about the future of the *Herald*."

"Ah. I don't suppose you were speaking English to him."

"Why would two French people be speaking in English?"

"Do you know if he speaks English?" How could women be comfortable in clothes that tight, he wondered.

"It would be extraordinary," she said, slowly, "for a Frenchman in his position not to speak several foreign languages."

"Yes, yes, I know how superior you all are, but sometimes they *won't* speak English. De Gaulle, they say, speaks English. The man lived in England for three years – how could he not speak English? He simply refuses. Apparently he wouldn't even speak English to Churchill. You'd better come with us today."

"Of course I won't come with you," she said. "When M. de Saint-Gaudens sees that you both are – how should I put it – linguistically inadequate, I'm sure he will accommodate you."

"Have you told Sonny?"

"He isn't in yet. I left the message with Connie."

Swart felt a little nervous. "So what's this all about? Why is the Elysée suddenly interested in the future of the *Herald*? I didn't even know de Gaulle read the *Herald*. Of course even if he did he wouldn't admit it. Apparently he won't even serve whiskey at receptions anymore – either kind. He hates us equally."

She smiled. "Perhaps, but I hear the champagne is very good."

Now she was being snotty. "Say – whose side are you on?"

"Must I choose?"

She was making him angry – deliberately. "Tell Connie to have Sonny come up when he's in."

"Yes, sir!"

Al and Helen Lodge walked in after lunch at the Val d'Isère, the rue de Berri's best restaurant. "Sonny back yet?" Helen asked.

"He's upstairs with Ben Swart," Connie said. "They've been summoned to the Elysée Palace this afternoon."

"*Whaaat?*" said Helen.

Helen and Connie had a decent enough relationship, more or less the same relationship as Al had with Sonny, which is to say they would never have been friends if they weren't colleagues though they might have been friendlier as colleagues if Al and Sonny had been closer. Helen was friendly with Rachel Stein, Sonny's wife, and Connie knew it, which was part of the problem.

Sonny saw the surprise on the Lodges' faces when he walked in.

"Don't ask because all I know is that the Elysée wants to see us at four. I didn't even know de Gaulle read the *Herald*."

"Tea with the General," said Helen, "how quaint. Take notes, Sonny, and we'll run it on the back page."

"Ha-ha."

"Sonny," she said, "before you disappear, here's my thought. With Steve Fleming gone, we need a Paris features writer. What about Archer?"

"Hey, we've just made him into a decent editor."

"We've got Wayne back," said Al.

"Oh, the *Times* didn't offer him enough?"

"Something like that," said Helen. "Anyway, I need someone. He says he speaks French so why not try it?"

"What, he learned French in six months?"

"Some do, you know. Anyway, here's how we find out. This new book everyone's talking about – *le Défi Américain*, by our neighbor at *l'Express*, Servan-Schreiber. We'll have Archer do a book review for the back page."

"The one about America taking over Europe?"

"That's it."

"It's in English?"

"Not yet. They're translating it as *The American Challenge*. Jean-Jacques called me about it."

"Are you sure you want to give it to Archer?"

"I'm sure."

"OK by me." He turned toward his office and motioned for Connie to follow. "Say, by the way. That thing with Fleming was weird. He never even came in to say good-bye."

"He called," said Al. "Said L.A. wanted him right away. Apologized – said they were on their way."

"It had something to do with her miscarriage," said Connie.

"Probably did," said Helen.

At 3:30 that afternoon Swart and Stein set out on foot for the Elysée Palace, down the rue de Berri, right on the rue d'Artois, angling over to Faubourg St.-Honoré. It was a short pleasant spring walk, acacias budding, shops lively, a walk they'd made many times though never together and never heading for the Elysée. When Swart went that way he was usually going to see Charlie McCloud, a crony of Jock Whitney's who since being named ambassador had become his own friend, though Norma's absences were making socializing difficult. With his own money, McCloud had renovated a beautiful old mansion next to the Elysée purchased a few years before by the State Department. Just beyond the new residence was the British Embassy, where Swart had also been a guest.

When Sonny Stein went that way it was because he'd taken the evening off and was walking Connie home to her place in the Marais. In truth it was *their* place since he'd moved out of the house on the rue Vaugirard that he shared with Rachel. Sonny had never been to the Elysée. He'd been a few times to ambassador's residence and once to a garden party at the British Embassy. What struck him was that the front gardens of the Elysée, the U.S. residence, and the British Embassy all connected with each other, separated only by a few hedges. Someone could just pop over for a cup of sugar. He liked walking with Ben. In New York they used to walk together around Bryant Park after lunch at Manny's deli on Forty-Fourth Street. This was their first walk together in Paris.

A blue-uniformed member of the Garde républicain stopped them at the entrance and took them into a little office where passports and French identity cards were checked against a list of visitors. A call was made and they were led across the courtyard, up the broad marble stairs on which de Gaulle greeted foreign dignitaries, through the main entrance, past gilded furniture and ancient tapestries, and upstairs to the first floor. Apart from the uniformed huissier who guided them, they saw no one else. They entered an anteroom, took seats on an antique sofa under a tapestry showing a fleet of longboats and a helmeted warrior with sword ready to debark.

"William the Conqueror," said Swart, "about to make England French."

In front of them the wide Elysée lawns and gardens stretched toward the trees of the Parc Champs Elysées.

A well-tailored French woman emerged from an inner office and M. de Saint-Gaudens was at the door to receive them. "Thank you for coming on such short notice," he said in impeccable English, leading them into a spacious inner salon. "I know how busy you are and won't intrude on you for long." He motioned toward a corner alcove where a tea service was set out.

Henri de Saint-Gaudens looked his name and looked his position. He was tall, pinstriped with silver hair, an aquiline nose, and thin, pale lips in a face that would no doubt wear that same ironic smile whatever the circumstances. It was the face of a French diplomat – an aristocratic French diplomat – long, elegant, world-weary behind hooded eyes. His English was of England, not America. He made pleasant small talk while pouring tea from the Limoges service and inviting them to help themselves from the plate of madeleines.

"I read the *Herald* every day, gentlemen, do you know that?"

Ben smiled, but Sonny couldn't resist nodding toward the gilded double doors leading deeper into the palace. "And . . . ?"

"Ah, you wonder if the General . . ." he chuckled and sipped his tea. "All the Paris newspapers are on his desk each morning, Mr. Stein. Naturally, I cannot say which ones he reads and which he does not. But all are there." He gazed outside at the gardens. "Paris in the springtime. I can't think of anywhere I'd rather be. Can you?"

"Certainly not New York," said Stein.

"You are both from New York?"

"We both worked there," said Swart. "I'm from Rhode Island."

"Ah, Rhode Island, of course. Then you know of the Battle of Newport, where the French under Admiral d'Estaing destroyed five British frigates during your revolution. I believe it was 1778, was it not?"

"August eighth, 1778," said Swart. "And a fierce storm then drove the French fleet into Boston harbor for repairs. I was in the navy. We studied that battle. Do you know Rhode Island?"

"Lamentably, no. I've spent a good deal of time in the States over the years, Washington mainly, but with a bit of traveling, regrettably never to Newport. Washington in springtime is very nice. Summer not so nice."

"Neither is New York," said Swart. "Perhaps sometime when we're both in the States you will come up to Newport. We have lovely summers. Do you sail?"

"My paternal family is from Saint-Gaudens, of course, landlocked in the Pyrenees, but on my mother's side they are sailors. La Rochelle – do you know it? You have a New Rochelle in New York, I believe. On my mother's mother's side, the family is from Orléans. Surely you know Orléans."

They nodded. M. de Saint-Gaudens dipped a madeleine into his tea and bit into it.

"What we see here, gentlemen, are some of the – how should I say it – the common points between our two countries, the history we share. We both know it; we don't have to go over it – Admiral d'Estaing, Lafayette, Pershing, Normandy, Newport, New Rochelle, New Orleans. It is a long list."

"Very long," said Swart, "very impressive."

"A friend of mine at the Quai d'Orsay – I am a diplomat, you may know, seconded to the presidency. In any case, my friend likes to refer to Franco-American ties as de la sauce Lafayette."

The Americans smiled.

"It may be de la sauce Lafayette, but it is a rich, wholesome sauce, sauce that is good for everyone. Good for the world, you might say. For two hundred years we've always stood together. Despite our differences, despite Algeria, despite Vietnam, the basis of our friendship is – de la sauce Lafayette, wouldn't you agree?"

"Absolutely," said Stein, a touch giddy with the magnificence of it all but with no clue where Saint-Gaudens was going.

"Oh," said de Saint-Gaudens, "how could I have failed to mention Bennett? Few have done more to make la sauce Lafayette rich and savory than James Gordon Bennett, Jr. Wouldn't you agree?"

For the first time Swart understood the purpose of the visit and wondered how Saint-Gaudens could possibly have heard and why he would be interested. Theo le Tac's trips to Zurich, Munich, and

Geneva were the *Herald*'s most guarded secret. On the second floor only Sonny (and probably Connie) knew, and on the fifth floor only Martine and le Tac. In the basement, where Tonton Pinard ruled, no one could possibly know.

"They tell me the *Herald* is the second oldest daily newspaper in Paris, just behind *Le Figaro*. In two years you will celebrate your eightieth anniversary in Paris – eighty years – do you know that's longer than Louis XIV ruled? Imagine that." He looked from one to the other, the delicate smile never leaving his lips. "We would like to help you celebrate your anniversary. What better way could there be to cement our friendship?"

"I can't think of any," said Swart, wondering why the seventy-fifth might not have been even better. "What a generous offer."

"So you accept?"

Lying in bed that night, he told Martine he'd felt intimidated and had Suzy look up Henri de Saint-Gaudens in the library: noble family, distinguished diplomatic career as first secretary in Washington and Bonn, ambassadorships in Italy and the Netherlands, poised to be named ambassador to the court of Saint-James when called by de Gaulle to the Elysée. In 1940 he'd been among the first of the diplomatic corps to join the General in London and later was dropped behind German lines in France.

"Impossible," Swart said, running his hand over her silky body, "not to be impressed. A man like that, you know it in your gut, is afraid of nothing – not the Gestapo, not torture, nothing. A man who knows how to die."

"I'm sure you held your own," she reassured him.

"I can see why he's chief of staff – tough, elegant, well-honed steel."

"But how did he know about le Tac?" she said. "It must be through the unions."

"The CGT is not present in the cities Theo visited."

"No, but there are communists in the unions in those cities. They keep in touch with each other, you know. " She ran her hand through his fine blond hair. "Did he explain why the Elysée wants to help?"

"Not exactly."

"Did he explain *how* the Elysée wants to help?"

"He was vague about it. He knew the *Herald Tribune* had folded and that we were on our own. He knew Whitney was talking to people about buying in. He knew we had someone going around Europe looking at other sites."

"So he knew everything."

"He knows more than I do. And then came the strange part – how much the government can do to help us, not to think that because we have certain problems – taxes, unions, distribution, et cetera – that solutions can't be found. French law is more flexible, he said, leaves more room for the human element."

"The French way."

Surprised, he came up to an elbow. "*Exactly*. How did you know he said that?"

"I'm French."

He chuckled. "Speaking of the French way, I told him how one of our managers once tried to fire a union maintenance worker for putting French toilet paper in the johns, the scratchy stuff we can't stand – you know, the stuff you use."

She pinched him. "Don't be rude."

"We kept telling old Pierrot to put in American toilet paper and he kept refusing. 'If it's good enough for us it's good enough for you,' he said."

She rolled over to him. "Good for old Pierrot."

"Old Pierrot had twenty years seniority, I told Saint-Gaudens. It would have cost us a half million francs to fire him. *That's* the French way. It was the only time he laughed all afternoon – threw back his head, showed his teeth and belly-laughed."

"Why does de Gaulle care if the *Herald* stays in Paris?"

"The *Herald* makes Paris seem like the center of Europe."

She snuggled closer. "We like being the center of attention."

7

When Eddie Jones was younger, still in his fifties, he could leave the *Herald* at 10:40 and be at Harry's Bar by midnight having hit every American hangout in Paris along the way. He was on a tight schedule because he had to be back by 12:30 to pick up the second edition and start out again. It wasn't that the second edition was much different from the first – not much happens in the world in two hours and it was still too early to get in the baseball scores – but editors know how to fiddle with stories and headlines to make it seem like a new paper.

Eddie had his route, adjusting if one place seemed slow or another especially lively. He did a lot of walking, but for the big crosstown moves he hailed a cab, especially as he grew older. He stayed on the lookout for cabbies he knew and they looked out for him. Just as if you catch the 6:40 local to work every morning and the 5:40 home again you get to know the people, it's the same at night. There aren't that many cabs late at night and cabbies and riders get to know each other.

Leaving the *Herald*, Eddie worked the Champs Elysées and then caught a cab to Montparnasse. After hitting the Dôme, Sélect, Coupole, and Rotonde, he needed another ride to St.-Germain, which he used to walk but lately had been riding. From St.-Germain he caught another cab to Pigalle and another to Harry's, where he did his best business. If he was low on newspapers, he told them he'd be back in a half hour with the second edition. He did his second run in the opposite direction, starting with Harry's.

The midnight cabbies liked Eddie and didn't charge him for he kept his pockets full of goodies he got through friends from the embassy PX. Eddie also made a special barbeque sauce for the annual Christmas party he gave in his rooms near Ternes, his one social event of the year. The French liked his sauce and so he bottled it and doled it out during the year. Most of the cabbies live in the workers' suburbs where it's easier to have a barbeque than in the posher districts. Eddie liked the barter system, which benefited everyone and saved him money.

He finished up at La Calavados, across from the Hotel George V, where Joe Turner played piano. Like most of the American Negroes in Paris, Turner had come back after the war. He played until two and Eddie would be there for the final set, sitting at the corner of the bar, eating whatever the cook left for him, having a nightcap with Joe before they closed up. Joe was from Baltimore, though told people he was from New York. When people asked him to sing "Kansas City" he'd smile and say he wasn't Kansas City Joe Turner, he was stride piano–playing Joe Turner, but he'd still do "Kansas City" for them and even throw in the vocal. He preferred playing Fats Waller. Joe was proud that Oscar Peterson once called him "the greatest stride pianist."

Lately Eddie was falling behind. It wasn't that he walked slower or was having trouble catching cabs and it wasn't that he was talking to people, for he'd never done much of that, not white people at any rate, except for Eric. The problem was he was lingering too long, accepting drinks he didn't used to accept. He knew he should cut down his route. He'd saved enough money to retire, though knew he never would. He couldn't imagine life without his route. What would he do?

"Right on time," said Eric as Eddie crossed the room at the California. "You watch yourself tonight. It's a hot one."

"Move over, sonny, do you mind? I'm going to let Mr. Eric buy me one tonight."

Instead of moving over, Archer stood up. Eddie dropped his newspaper bag and swung onto a barstool. Marcel, serving the tables, came back to the bar when he saw Eddie sit down. Eddie never sat down at the California.

"Un cognac, s'il te plait," Eddie said.

"You feeling all right, old friend?" said Eric.

"Movin' slow, Mr. Eric, movin' slow."

Eric knew better than to suggest he slow down. Like the mail, newspapers have to be delivered on time. When Eric was still in charge he'd hired a half dozen pretty girls, dressed them in tight yellow *Herald* sweaters, called them the "golden girls," and sent them out on the streets. They took some business from Eddie, but Eric convinced him they were more for publicity than sales. The best publicity came when Jean-Luc Godard put a *Herald* sweater on sexy Jean Seberg for the movie *A bout de souffle* and even shot a scene at the *Herald*. The girls didn't last because Eric didn't pay them and soon Paris belonged to Eddie Jones again.

Marcel brought the cognac and Eddie shot in some seltzer. He finished it, set the snifter down, and looked at Archer. His face was a pale shade of brown, freckled and crisscrossed with lines and furrows like cracked earth. He was a man of medium height, large-boned with a big head and receding hairline that made it look even bigger. He had large hands with slender but strong-looking fingers and well-tended nails. A thin mustache filled in the large expanse between mouth and nose, a broad nose with half glasses perched on its tip and lashed around his neck with a thin leather cord. Peering over the half moons of his glasses, he studied Archer's face.

"I've seen you, around, young man. A year or two – am I right?"

"You're right."

"Archer's the Paris reporter," said Eric. "Took Fleming's place."

"Ah," said Eddie, his milky eyes fastened on Archer. "I remember Fleming. Pretty little wife."

"Back in L.A.," said Archer.

"I heard something about that."

"Eddie hears something about everything," said Eric. "Should have been a reporter – knows how to listen."

Eddie flicked his finger against the snifter, and Marcel came back to fill it. Eddie was chuckling. "Knows how to listen but Mr. Eric didn't think Eddie could write. Might have done a Paris column . . . like Buchwald."

"Chubby little fellow in big glasses drifts one day. I didn't hire him, went on vacation and they hired him anyway. A star is born. Wrote a column: 'Paris After Dark.'"

"Or I could have done a sports column . . . like Sparrow."

"Ahhh, the Sparrow," said Hawkins. "Always wore a homburg. What a reporter! Stayed on after the Nazis came – sat in the little office by the elevator I use now. Came in every day to an empty building, typed his stories, shoved them in the desk and went home again. Dropped dead in June of forty-one. A year of the Nazis was all he could take. I found the stories when I came back in forty-four. Stood there crying. The Sparrow couldn't stop writing – even without a newspaper."

"I've seen you in some of the jazz spots," Eddie said.

"I do a jazz column. Hitting some spots tonight."

They watched him go, disappearing among the cars, trucks, and people overflowing street and sidewalk outside the *Herald*. Across the street, behind the plate glass window, they saw women in bandanas bent over long tables bundling newspapers that soon would be delivered across Europe. Horns sounded from blocked motorists who should have known better than to be on the rue de Berri at 10:30.

"How old is Eddie?" asked Archer.

"How old is Eddie Jones?" repeated Hawkins. "How old would you say he is?"

"I'd say in his seventies."

Let's say he's seventy-five, which would make him fifty-three when the war ended – that sound right to you?"

"The army, right?"

"Sergeant Eddie Jones of the Five Hundred and Eighty-Second Dump Truck Company. Ask him about it."

"Dump Truck Company?"

"They didn't like giving them guns."

"He doesn't talk much."

"Depends who he's talking to."

"How could he be a fifty-three-year-old sergeant?"

"Well, you know, I asked him that once. I asked him that the day he came into my office in forty-six looking for a job. Sat him right down under the owl and when he told me his age I asked him how that could be. 'Well, sir,' he says, 'I saw early on that white folks can't tell a black boy's age. They asked for my birth certificate when I went to join up in New York and I said I was from North Carolina and down there sometimes things get lost. So these sergeants look at each other and damned if they'll turn away a healthy black boy. How old are you, son, one of them asks and I said I was surely into my thirties. They signed me up. Worked out for everyone.'"

"Maybe I could do a story on Eddie," Archer said.

Eric swung around to face him. "You don't think others have tried? The problem is that Eddie Jones doesn't exist. In the States he's listed as missing in action. He didn't desert. I wouldn't have hired a deserter. The war was over. He went a little AWOL so he wouldn't have to go back to the States and pay his way back to France. Washed dishes in Pigalle; lived with a French woman. If the MPs had found him they'd have taken him back, but they didn't. If the French had picked him up there would have been trouble, but why would they pick him up? Eddie's never caused anyone any trouble. Plenty of West Africans in Paris. All Negroes look the same to the French. He doesn't exist here either."

Eddie made a few sales outside the Lido, crossed the Champs and headed up Pierre Charron to the American Legion. Across from the Legion was a bar where the fight crowd used to hang out. Eric had told him about it. All the top fighters came over in the thirties – Kid McCoy, the Dixie Kid, Sam McVey, Joe Jeanette, Sam Langford – came to fight the French boxers. Boxers weren't the only ones: Josephine Baker and Sidney Bechet came. After the war musicians like Bud Powell and Dexter Gordon and Kenny Clarke came and then writers like Richard Wright and James Baldwin.

"Where you been, Eddie," a marine at one of the tables shouted at him. "You army guys are always late."

"Hey, I heard that, buddy," shouted a guy at the bar. "Gimme a paper, Eddie."

Always busy at the Legion. Some came for the sour mash bourbon you couldn't get anywhere else, and they had a television that showed the latest sports tapes. Mostly though the clientele was guys getting away from France for a while, getting back into their language and themselves. Not that anyone talked much at the Legion. They came to nurse their drinks, hear the music, watch the games. If someone said something, someone else might answer but he'd do it without caring much. Then the other guy would say something and the first guy would chuckle and return to his drink. That's how it was.

Eddie dropped his bag and ordered a Jack Daniels, neat.

The thing had been bothering him for weeks, not really a pain but a kind of tiring ache that had grown worse. Summer or winter he could make his rounds in whatever pain and in twenty years he'd had all kinds. Fatigue was another matter. With pain some part of the body tells you to take it easy, slow down if it's the feet or shift the bag if it's the shoulder or get some painkillers if it's the back or the head. With fatigue there's no relief, not even sleep. The body's telling you to stop. Maybe he'd just do Harry's and Montparnasse and finish up with Joe at Calavados. He'd see how he felt after that.

Archer was at Bud's, in Montparnasse, listening to a young Frenchmen at the upright who was nothing special. He wouldn't have stayed but Lucy brought him a cognac and so he couldn't leave right away. Lucy had been good to him, told him the story of Bud Powell that he'd made into his first two jazz columns. She tended bar under rows of bottles and photos of Powell. The young Frenchman was playing on Bud's piano and was probably intimidated by it, like sitting at Shakespeare's desk.

"You going to give Jacques a mention, Rupert?"

"I'll mention him. I'm doing a piece on Martial Solal down at Club Saint-Germain, but Jacques is worth a mention. Who knows in a few years?"

"I'm trying to hang on. Kenny comes in sometimes. So does Dexter. Just old friends being nice to a lady."

He'd sat down for two nights with Lucy Freeman, who'd taken over from Buttercup, who came over with Powell in '59. Lucy told him all about Bud, the greatest jazz pianist. It took him two columns because she had a lot to tell. She'd put the columns in glass cases outside. The problem was that Bud's was on a side street that didn't get much street traffic. Lucy couldn't afford top talent. It was 11:30 and there weren't fifteen customers. She'd probably give the pianist fifty francs for the night. Ten bucks.

The photos showed the handful of good times in Bud Powell's short life: one with Thelonius Monk outside Minton's in New York after Bud made the first recording of Monk's "Round Midnight"; another with Monk in a studio recording "In Walked Bud," Monk's homage to his friend; another with Bud and brother Ritchie, also a jazz pianist, as young boys. The only Paris photo was at a session at the Blue Note, around the corner from the *Herald*: Bud at the piano with fellow exiles Kenny Clarke and Dexter Gordon.

Archer's second column told the rest of the story: Powell's schizophrenia, a year at New York's Creedmoor mental institution for electroshock and his lifelong dependence on antipsychotic drugs. There was alcoholism, a beating by New York police, memory loss, tuberculosis, Ritchie's death in a car accident with Clifford Brown, and finally the flight to Paris. Buttercup opened the club, Bud did some gigs and concerts and, by then a wreck, returned to New York to die.

Archer sipped the cognac and was ready to go when Eddie Jones walked in, dropped his bag at the bar beside him, and collapsed. Archer caught him, Lucy screamed, and Jacques, in the middle of "I Remember Clifford," hit a great crash of notes and jumped up. Eddie clung to Archer as he dragged him to a table. He started to slide off the chair. His glasses dangled from the cord around his neck.

"Get him to the hospital," Lucy cried. "Rupert, get a cab. We'll bring him out."

Archer had the cab waiting when Lucy, Jacques, and two customers brought Eddie out, leaning heavily on them, one of them lugging the newspaper bag. They helped him into the taxi. "Neuilly," said Lucy, "hôpital américain."

"*Mais non!*" cried the cabbie, waving his hands. "*Pas Neuilly!*"

"L'homme est malade," said Jacques. "*Partez, partez!*"

The cabbie refused to go. Jacques opened the front door, handed him something and closed it again.

"He said he'd never get a fare back from Neuilly. I gave him fifty francs. Bonne chance." Archer reminded himself to mention Jacques in his column.

At the hospital Archer ran inside and emerged with attendants and a rolling stretcher. Eddie mumbled something as they strapped him down. Of course! Archer grabbed for the car and pulled out his newspaper bag.

"Your friend will be examined," said the nurse after Eddie was gone. "Fill out these forms with everything you know about him – name, age, address, next of kin, everything."

"I don't know much beyond his name: Eddie Jones. We're colleagues, but I don't know him personally."

"You were with him tonight, were you not?"

"He collapsed in a bar where I happened to be."

"He had been drinking?"

"No, madam. He had been walking."

An attendant came out and said something to the nurse in French.

She looked at Archer. "His pockets are full of many strange things, my colleague says, but no identification papers."

Archer shook his head.

The nurse stared at him for a while. "Write down here," she commanded, tapping the forms in front of her, "what you know of him. If you are colleagues write down the name, address, and telephone of your place of work – also the name of someone who knows M. Jones personally. We must have some identification." She pointed toward a waiting area, empty, a few worn armchairs, desolate. "When you are finished you can wait in there."

Sometime near dawn he was shaken awake by the duty doctor, a young, prematurely balding Frenchman in rimless glasses who seemed entirely too rested and composed for someone dealing with important things at such an hour. He held the form that Archer had sketchily filled out. He spoke English.

"Have you notified Mr. Jones's family?"

"I don't believe he has family."

"No family in France? And in America?"

"I'm not sure. I can let you know later today. Is he all right?"

"Your friend has had a stroke. We are doing tests. How long was it between his first symptoms and his arrival at the hospital?"

"Maybe a half hour."

"You know that time is crucial in these matters."

"Yes." His gaze was so steady that Archer had to look away.

"It will be awhile before we have a prognosis. You should go home and when you come next please bring all his identification papers."

"I'm not sure he has any."

"Of course he has. You've written here that he's been in France for twenty years."

"It's what I have been told."

"Twenty years, " he said. "Believe me, sir, if he has lived in France for twenty years, he has papers – carte de séjour, carte d'identité, carte de travail. You must bring them. If he is not of French nationality, he will also have his passport, n'est-ce pas? It is impossible to live in France for twenty years without papers."

8

Martine was still sleeping when Swart left the hotel room, closing the door gently. He'd showered, shaved, dressed, combed his fine blond hair, and slipped into the corridor without waking her a second time. Taking the elevator down, he ordered breakfast and looked out over the room where the string trio had entertained the night before. With its ornate salon and huge brass cage of exotic birds, the Barclay was his favorite New York hotel. He poured more coffee and opened the *New York Times*, a paper he would not normally be reading but with the *Herald Tribune* gone what was the alternative – the *Daily News*? The usual headlines: Vietnam War, arms race, Cultural Revolution, civil war in Indonesia, Nixon ready to run again, same old gray lady. He put down the paper and watched the birds. The E train from Lexington would get him to Times Square in five minutes, but why not walk? He didn't have to be in Walter Thayer's office until 10 to prepare for the meeting with the *Times* at 10:30.

His thoughts went to Martine, that exquisite young body lying naked upstairs under the silky Barclay sheets with the high thread count. Bringing her was a risk, but she deserved it. He didn't see how Norma could find out, but what if she did? Whatever happened, *that* was beyond repair. He had no idea what the meeting with the *Times* would produce, but if it was good news Martine would help him celebrate and if bad, which was more likely, commiserate. Regardless of what happened they'd have the weekend. For the evening he'd ordered tickets to *Hello, Dolly!* and made a reservation at Sardi's for 10:30. She planned to spend the day shopping on Fifth Avenue. She'd wanted to meet for lunch at Rockefeller Center, but he'd be lunching with Jock and Walter.

The call from Walter was a shock. He and Jock were meeting with Punch Sulzberger, Sam Hecht, and Sydney Gruson to discuss a possible partnership between the *Times* and the *Herald*. Since Punch wanted Gruson, publisher of the *Paris Times*, at the meeting, Ben should be there as well. He was stunned: Jock Whitney talking to the *Times*? Bennetts selling out to Sulzbergers, Republicans giving way to Democrats? Did Jock think he could maintain any influence in an arrangement with the *Times*, which devours everything it touches? He recalled his words in the *Herald* newsroom that night – how Jock would rather burn in hell than sell to the *Times*. Had he misjudged him?

He signed the bill and stepped out onto Forty-Eighth Street, walking briskly in the sharp fall day, autumn in New York. He waited at Park, made the lights at both Madison and Fifth, glanced down at the morning skaters as he weaved through Rockefeller Center, and spied the restaurant where Martine would be lunching – alone, poor thing, his pretty Parisian girlfriend by herself for a day in New York. Shopping would make up for it. Crossing Sixth Avenue he thought, my God, it's come to this: face-to-face with Sydney Gruson who will be taking my job. What treachery! How could I ever tell them in Paris? Let Walter do it. He's good at things like that.

Arriving outside the somnolent *Herald Tribune* building he stood a moment remembering how it once had been at 230 West Forty-First Street: lobby filled with people frantically dashing about – reporters, photographers, messengers, copyboys, like Penn Station at rush hour. The *Trib* not only had the best reporters but all the big stars – Clementine Paddleford, Walter Lippmann, Walter Kerr, Red Smith, Marguerite Higgins. The old, gray *Times* around the corner could only dream of such verve.

He stepped into a lobby he scarcely recognized – quiet, nearly empty, stars all gone to other newspapers or worlds, everyone but Walter Thayer, still holding down the fort at Whitney Communications, though without the *Trib* it wasn't much of a fort and they didn't have much to communicate. They still had the *Paris Herald*, but for how much longer – days, weeks, months? Elevators still running, but he didn't recognize the operators. Time was when he knew them all.

"Ben, good to see you – thanks for coming."

Walter Thayer, white mane combed back over his extraordinarily high forehead, crossed the room to shake hands and lead him to the leather chairs by the windows overlooking Midtown. Nothing in the office changed.

"Jock's running a little late. I suppose this is all a surprise to you."

"You could say that."

They dropped down into the soft leather. "Short notice, I know. Don't worry, nothing is settled. Jock will tell you himself. You can imagine what it would be for him to sell an interest in the *Herald* to Punch Sulzberger."

"That's what we're talking about – just an interest?"

Walter Thayer could never quite hide the condescension in his blue-lipped smile. For some reason Swart never understood, Thayer had opposed sending him to Paris. Swart owed his job to Jock himself, who went more on instinct. Thayer was a straightlaced, humorless, by-the-books executive who'd learned from his jail-warden father how to stay one step ahead of those out to get you.

"It's a negotiation, Ben. Remember Napoleon's adage: 'Start fighting and see what happens.' That's what we're doing – listening to everyone. The *Wall Street Journal* wants to buy the *Herald* lock, stock, and barrel, which Jock won't do. We're talking to Lord Thompson at the *Times*. My instinct tells me it's going nowhere with the Brits, but it's good leverage. We've got to do something about Paris – you know the figures better than anyone. I've read le Tac's reports and I'm not impressed. Zurich's the best of the lot, but I wonder if we shouldn't start looking at Frankfurt."

"Don't forget we have the Elysée behind us."

"Our trump card. You think Punch knows?"

"Why would the Elysée leak to Syd Gruson? I don't see it. They want us to stay – why let the opposition in on it?"

"To make sure the opposition stays if we go."

"Frankly, Walter, what puzzles me is how we can be thinking of moving when we're thinking of selling?"

Swart watched as this tough old dog, a top Wall Street lawyer before politics brought him together with Whitney, pondered the question. "It's the way I do business, Ben, lots of balls in the air, confuse the opposition. On a case you're always probing, looking for a new angle for your side and weakness on the other. No different in business. Put yourself in the mind of Punch. He's sitting there around the corner with Sam and Syd going over everything that could come up this morning. My job is to make sure there are things they don't know about. You know what I mean – of course you do. It's what you do when you're negotiating with the labor unions. What's that fellow's name – the one with the belly who heads the printers?"

"Tonton Pinard."

"Funny name."

"Nothing funny about Tonton."

"I suppose not. How is it the communists run your shop?"

"I asked Eric Hawkins about that once. They held union votes after the war: communist, Christian, and socialist unions. Because they'd been active in the resistance and strong in Paris, the communists won at all the newspapers. That's why de Gaulle backed a new newspaper, Le Monde, owned by journalists and noncommunist. Irony today is that Le Monde opposes him, thinks he's violating the constitution, his own constitution; thinks absolute power has gone to his head."

He wanted to get to the point. "Why am I here, Walter?"

"Of course, Ben." He was looking out the window toward the Empire State Building. "You're here because Sydney Gruson will be here. So why will Syd be here?" He turned back to Swart. "Well, reading Punch's mind I would say it's because Punch expects to walk out of this meeting with a deal to take over the *Paris Herald* and that with you and Syd here we can begin drawing up plans for an orderly transition."

Before Swart could react the door opened. Thayer looked up. "Jock – good morning."

They both stood for Whitney, tall, regal New York blueblood whose exploits in business, politics, diplomacy, movies, horses, yachts, and women were known to anyone who knew anything about society. On both sides, Jock could trace his lineage to the Mayflower and on both sides his fortune to banking, railroads, tobacco, mining, and oil. He was a very rich and busy man. Newspapers were his hobby.

Very different men, Whitney and Thayer had been at the center of New York Republican politics for two decades. In '52 they'd persuaded Dwight Eisenhower to leave Columbia University and run for president and were instrumental in Ike's defeat of Bob Taft at the convention. Nixon was their man in '60 but after his loss to Kennedy and defeat in California in '62, they'd backed New York's own Nelson Rockefeller – only to see the GOP taken over by Barry Goldwater. With Goldwater and his radicals massacred by Lyndon Johnson in '64, they were working to swing the GOP back to Rockefeller in '68. Their problem for the '68 election, unlike previous ones, was that they wouldn't have a newspaper to back their agenda – or at least not one in America.

"No more transatlantic calls until we get a new cable," said Whitney, and they all laughed. After some small talk they got down to business.

"This meeting is Punch's idea," said Whitney. "Punch called Walter, and Walter invited him over. Why not? We'll listen. Depending on how bad they're hurting we might hear something interesting. If he wants to buy in, we're interested. We don't have any other fish on the line at the moment. Punch doesn't know that – at least I don't think he knows. With the *Trib* closed, the *Herald* is in a delicate position. But as long as Punch thinks we have a chance of finding another partner and staying in business he'll be interested. He knows by now that the Paris edition of the *Times* was a big mistake."

A tap at the door, and the receptionist peeked in. "They're on their way up."

"Is survival in Paris worth selling a piece to the *New York Times*? – *that's* the question we face," said Whitney.

"I don't think those are the only options, Jock," said Thayer. "If they are, we've misplayed our hand."

The three of them – different ages, different incomes, different pedigrees, two from New York, one from Rhode Island; two from Yale, one from Princeton, stood up and moved toward the board room. They were different, but also similar: three smart, successful, self-confident, worldly Republicans, all handsome, trim, healthy, and over six feet tall, the best America had to offer.

"We mustn't be boxed in," said Thayer. "We're hardly out of options."

"Speaking of options," said Swart. "Has anyone talked to Kay Graham?"

Whitney spun to face him. "Kay? With that dinky little operation she runs? Why would she would be interested – or for that matter why would we be interested in her?"

"Just rumors," said Swart. "With her husband dead, her father's money, the *Post's* new deal with the *L.A. Times*, their new wire service. The scuttlebutt is she wants to take on the *Times*, prove a woman can do it."

"*Punch!*"

Whitney called out to Sulzberger as the door opened across the room. "Welcome. Sam, Syd – come in and make yourselves at home – or should I say chez vous."

They shook hands under the twin portraits of James Gordon Bennett and Horace Greeley, founders of the *Herald* and the *Tribune*, portraits that the men from the *Times*, who had never been in the *Herald Tribune* building, eyed politely. Whitney led them across to the window with its fine view up to Times Square, across to the Empire State Building and over to Midtown, unlike anything they had in the dark and cramped *Times* building. Swart noticed that the visitors were all shorter – shorter but also (with the exception of Thayer) nattier. Whitney dressed as a multimillionaire sportsman who didn't care. As for Swart's wardrobe, it needed an overhaul.

They paired off naturally – Punch and Jock by the window talking New York real estate, Sam and Walter strolling to the end of the room to discuss labor unions, and Syd Gruson cornering Swart to tell him about the pigeon dish on the menu at Lasserre. Swart had run into Gruson at various Paris functions, where they were as cordial as any two people out to destroy each other can be. A side buffet offered coffee, tea, and biscuits.

"I was the one who called," said Sulzberger when they were comfortable, a benign smile on his heavy face, "so I suppose it's right that I start off by telling you what's on our mind. We're both losing money in Paris, which suggests to me that Europe is not big enough for both of us. You're losing less money than we are, but without the *Herald Tribune* your losses are surely mounting."

Sulzberger had a square-jawed, ruddy face, thinning gray hair, and horn-rimmed glasses. He was the most agreeable of the guests, the noblesse oblige that comes from being heir to a rich, powerful newspaper empire.

"I don't see how you do it without a home newspaper," said Gruson.

"We manage," said Swart.

"But for how long?"

"We're looking for a partner," said Thayer. "We're in no hurry. We can sustain losses because we intend to come out of this a stronger newspaper, looking to the future, better adapted to a wealthier, united, more self-confident Europe."

"Have you found a partner?" asked Hecht, bluntly.

Whitney looked to Thayer, who responded: "We have many suitors, Sam," he said, his face a mask. "We're having trouble deciding among them."

Many people had sold Sam Hecht short as he rose from city editor to managing editor to vice president of the Times Corporation. He'd lost out for executive editor, not because Punch thought the other guy was better, but because Syd Gruson, ten years younger and smarter, was being groomed for the job. Gruson would take over, the smart money said, after a few years getting the Paris Edition in the black.

"But what will you gain, Walter?" asked Gruson. "Whomever you choose, *we'll* still be there. We've already hired a half dozen of your best Paris people. Ask Ben. They're calling us every day. The *Times* grows stronger as you grow weaker and even if you find a partner the best you can hope for as long as we're there is more losses."

"Who would buy into such an operation?" said Hecht. "I'm not saying I know everything, but what I hear is that when these suitors take a good look at the dowry – suddenly the bride's not so attractive anymore."

"You're wrong," said Thayer, "to think that we lack options. That said, we're ready to listen to your offer. Isn't that why we're here?"

"Fifty-fifty," said Hecht. "We use your building until we find a better one."

Whitney immediately shook his head. "Fifty-fifty, no. We keep control."

"The *Times* does not participate in ventures it doesn't control," said Hecht.

"*You* caused the problem," said Thayer, studied lawyerly petulance coming into his voice. "Had you not come to Paris six years ago, we'd be turning a profit today and you wouldn't have had six years of heavy losses. Not only that, but we'd surely have moved out of Paris. The unions are as bad there as they are here."

"We may have caused the problem, but now it's your problem," said Gruson. "We're not going anywhere. *We* haven't lost our newspaper in New York."

"Syd," said Sulzberger, gently laying a hand on his worsted sleeve, "let's not forget that it's our problem, too. That's why we're here today."

"Sorry, Punch," he said, "but I don't see how we get around the fundamental problem: Jock won't give up control. We have to have control."

They're good, thought Swart. Punch is the neighbor who helps you put out the fire and Syd and Ben are there with the papers to sign.

"Our position," said Whitney slowly, "is that we are prepared to offer you a minority interest in the *Paris Herald*, which is clearly the superior newspaper, the one with more readers, more pages, more ads, more income, more tradition, more potential. You benefit by taking a position in a, shall we say, historic enterprise, and pulling the plug on a venture that hasn't turned out very well."

Swart watched Sulzberger as Whitney spoke. Gruson wanted to reply, but again Sulzberger's hand went to his arm. The publisher of the *Times* took a deep breath, looked down at the table, back up again, and smiled. "I don't see how we can square this particular circle, at least not at the moment. Perhaps we should leave things as they are for today. The fundamental issue remains: One too many newspapers in Paris. We'll let the pain increase a little and see if that brings us back to the operating table."

Martine was ravishing in a low-cut black mini with fringe at the bodice and the gold collier he'd bought her at Cartier's. They celebrated Jock's decision over cocktails with the cockatoos and set out for the play. Afterward it was on to Sardi's and then back to the Barclay, a perfect day, start to finish. Jock Whitney had done what anyone who knew him would have expected, and Swart would not have to apologize to the newsroom. He still had a newspaper, still had a job, and was on a three-day trip with a gorgeous young Parisian who turned heads wherever she went.

As he rolled to his side of the bed, he wondered if he wasn't falling in love. Norma was not returning to Paris. The children were better off in Newport, she said. Paris was too turbulent. About Martine, she'd said nothing, but she knew. Somehow she knew. He hadn't argued because he wasn't sure he'd still be in Paris himself.

Now he knew: Gruson would not be taking his job. Jock was committed to keeping the *Herald* alive, even if it meant moving from Paris. The next decision was up to him. Seeing Martine in New York had changed everything. She was perfect. If they moved from Paris, would she go with him? He needed to make up his mind. As she was constantly reminding him, she had her own friends.

9

Byron Hallsberg opened the deck chair and slowly eased his long white body into it. It was his time of day – cocktail hour – and he badly needed one. He reached for his gin and tonic and took a long swig. It was cheap French gin – Saint Peter's from Bordeaux – but the tonic was Schweppes so it would do. He'd mixed it nearly half and half with ice and he could feel the alcohol shoot into his hungry bloodstream. Bordeaux, he reflected, is to gin what Liverpool is to wine, but he'd run out of Gordon's on the weekend and didn't feel like driving to Fauchon's for more.

"Dad," came the call from inside, "you wanna play checkers?"

"Nah," he called back, sifting bony fingers through the red beard that rested on his chest. She knew that 7:30 was his time of day, especially on a day like this. He'd seen death before. In '56 he'd gone to Budapest and seen Soviet tanks run people down and was lucky not to be one of them. They'd put him in jail but the embassy got him out. And he'd been to funerals before, plenty of them, but the one today had shaken him: something about not getting out in time.

"How about some chess?" came the voice.

Little squirt, he thought. She'll never play chess when I want. He took another swig and was smiling to himself. Her problem is that she hates losing – bad as me. Thinks a good dad should let his daughter win. Let her learn the hard way. If I have another drink I might play her. "Maybe later," he called.

"You're no good later," came the voice.

He let out a loud guffaw. Thank God for kids. Life goes on for them even after a fucking depressing funeral. Doris didn't want to take her, but Tilly wanted to go. She was not a girl with illusions. The boys wouldn't have liked it but the boys were with friends for the weekend.

"Who's playing tonight, Dad?" came the relentless voice.

Hallsberg was looking around, checking out the territory. Behind him loomed six stories of stone apartment building – his building. In front of him, beyond the tall iron fence with the Bismarck spikes on top, stretched the property of one Axel Kirchener, trees and lawn leading to the ugly gabled mansion in the distance. Kirchener, industrialist, was rich enough to own several acres of land in Paris's very exclusive Sixteenth Arrondissement. Turning back, Byron could see his daughter on her bed reading Nancy Drew and glancing at him when she thought he wasn't looking. She was in a mood for pestering and he had an idea why. Hot August night like this at home and she'd be at the club swimming or playing tennis. In Paris, kids had nothing to do but hang around and pester. He'd wanted to move to the suburbs after Tommy, their second, was born, across the river to someplace like Meudon or St.-Cloud, but Doris declined. While we're in Paris, we're in Paris, she said. When we go home we'll live in the suburbs.

"How would I know," he called. "You never know until game time." He took another swig, lit up a Gitane, slouched down, and laid his red head back against the dark twill of the deck chair. Dusky blue sky at twilight. The big lawn beyond the iron spikes looked so inviting. Take a football and throw a few passes – didn't need the boys because Tilly is always game. She's better than they are anyway. "I wouldn't mind living in that old place over there," he said.

"What?" came the voice from inside.

"Just talking to myself."

"You're not supposed to do that."

"Who says?"

"Mom says."

The Kircheners had two acres. Easily. On his side he had ten by five paces. It was his domain, where he had his drinks in summer and where he went to smoke, summer or winter. It wasn't big enough to throw a ball in but was big enough for a deck chair, a hammock stretched from fence to building, a folding table for eating, and a hibachi for cooking hamburgers on the weekend. The apartment was a great find. Where else could he have a hammock and barbeque in Paris – and with Eddie Jones's homemade barbeque sauce, rest his soul. Lying in his chair and looking west (if it weren't for the iron fence), he might have been in the countryside.

"We do something tonight, Dad? I'm bored."

She'd crept up, and he wrapped his long arm around her hard, round little fanny and pulled her to him. "It's Saturday, Til. Game's on at nine."

"Who cares?"

"What's eating you – not the funeral, I hope."

"I'm just bored." She slipped into the hammock and starting swinging.

"The game will pick you up. Maybe it's the Cubs."

"It never is," she said, keeping one sneaker on the gravel to push off. "Anyway, they stink. And nobody can understand anything but you."

True enough, he thought. De Gaulle's fault. When he kicked out the U.S. forces he also kicked out the Armed Forces Network. Used to be able to get the Saturday games as clear as back on Lake Michigan. Now the nearest antennas were in Germany and Spain. He'd gotten only static until he bought the Telefunken shortwave with all the bands. He had to flip bands awhile to get the right one, but he always found something.

"Byron, have you started the fire?" came the voice from inside.

"Aye aye, sir," he called, jumping up, lighting a match with his cigarette and putting it to the hibachi, which was ready to go.

He sat back down again, his eyes on Tilly, gently rocking herself in the hammock. Pretty girl, he told himself each time he studied his daughter's face, equally composed of Doris's round Irish bones and his own sharp Viking angles. She had his red hair and her green eyes, too much for any man. She was strong and hard as nails and when that girlish sinew started to flesh out and soften, his pretty girl would be something.

His mind went to the funeral. He doubted Eddie Jones had ever set foot in the American Church on the Quai d'Orsay, but so what? Lots of people. Surprising. Eddie had been in Paris for twenty years, but a hundred people is a good turnout for anyone. It helped that Sonny ran the little obit with the photo of Eddie in his *Herald* sweater. Eddie was just a paperboy but he was *our* paperboy.

He sipped his gin, watched his daughter, watched the coals getting redder and wondered how many people would come to his own funeral. Wouldn't be any ambassador there for sure. Goddamn if Charlie McCloud didn't show up with his wife in a black lampshade hat and even make the drive to the cemetery with the rest of them. Probably thought: AMBASSADOR AT NEWSBOY'S FUNERAL would make a good headline. He finished his drink.

"*Matilda!*" Doris shouted, standing in the double doors with a tray piled with food. "Don't swing like that. What if the rope broke? Byron, say something to your daughter."

"You ever think that if the rope broke you'd end up impaled on those spikes – like a shish kebab."

"*Daaaad!*" she cried.

"Come down and put the hamburgers on. The fire's hot."

Doris went back in and returned with mustard, ketchup, napkins, and cutlery. She wore white shorts and a plaid blouse, and her just-washed dark hair with little tinges of grey was loose to her shoulders. She opened a plastic liter of red wine, filled her glass, and sat down. "I'm done. It's been a day. The rest is up to you two."

Tilly took the spatula and carefully placed three large patties at the center of the hibachi. It was a small one, just wide enough for five large patties, which is what they needed when everyone was home. They had a larger metal barbeque that they used with guests, but for the family they preferred the hibachi, which caused fewer problems with the neighbors upstairs, who weren't used to people on the ground floor with barbeques.

"Watch the hamburgers, Til, we don't want them black."

French hamburgers, they'd learned from early adventures, are made from steak, which the butcher grinds up in front of you. Since the French eat their hamburger raw in the form of steak tartare, there's no fat, which means no sizzling when you cook it, which means if you don't pay attention you end up with shriveled little black balls that even ketchup, mustard, and onions cannot completely save.

It was after nine when they finished and cleared the table, except for the wine. Tilly went in to collapse on her bed while Byron lit another Gitane and switched on the radio. Through heavy crackling he discovered that it was Baltimore and Boston. He turned it off. "It gets better closer to ten, the night air transmits better," he said to Doris, knowing she didn't care. He filled the wine glasses again and sat down.

"Quite a day," she said. "More depressing than your run-of-the-mill funeral."

"Are any funerals run-of-the-mill?"

"After a certain age I guess some are."

"Are we getting close to that certain age?"

"My God, Byron, we're still in our forties."

"What got me was Eddie being buried here. You die here, you're buried here. I don't want to be buried here."

"You want to talk about that?" she said.

"You know what I mean."

Doris was ready to move home. They'd met in Budapest, where she'd gone, as had so many, with hopes of building Hungarian democracy. Afterward, they kept in touch. She came to Paris a few times and then they married. Every other summer they went back to visit his parents in South Bend, swim in the club pool and drive to Lake Michigan for the beach. The way to a Dubliner's heart is through sunshine, he'd discovered – making sure he never took her back for a South Bend winter. When she talked about home she meant South Bend, not Dublin. With Tilly ready to start junior high school and the boys right behind, she wanted to go home. With life at the *Herald* uncertain, she thought this was the time.

"It wasn't the church," he said. "It was that fucking cemetery."

"It was getting lost."

"I'm supposed to know there's a separate cemetery in Puteaux for Americans?"

"Couldn't you have gotten directions?"

"I *know* where the Puteaux cemetery is. I just didn't know there were two of them? *Why* are there two of them? We were allies, weren't we?"

"Where do you want to be buried, hon?"

"We're at that point, eh?"

"It's a fair question."

"I promise you that when the time comes we will not be in Paris."

"Where will we be?"

"Somewhere in the States – wherever there's work. Maybe Chicago. Maybe L.A. Fleming's doing fine on the *Times*."

"Molly's happy to be home."

"She did a number on Steve."

"Hey, who did the number on whom?"

"Good grammar, bad thought."

Soon it was dark. Turning, he saw that Tilly had fallen asleep reading. It was a clear night, warm, bright moon. Through the iron fence they saw lights from the Kirchener mansion. The wine was good cheap French rouge. They weren't picky. Mellow. When Doris went to bed he'd turn on the game, which by then would be coming in clearly. She was staring at the tall ash tree that grew out of a clump of bush and bramble just beyond the fence. One long branch reached over the fence into their little plot.

"I mentioned the tree to old lady Kirchener the other day," he said. "She was poking around out here and I was ready to lay into her about that damned thing."

"That would have been effective, I'm sure."

"But I didn't. Instead I decided to be charming."

"When were you ever charming to the French?"

He ignored that. "She didn't know who the hell I was. Just some red-bearded prole from beyond the walls. I coaxed her closer in my very best French and said how I loved her house and her yard and it was so nice for us to have a view like that from here instead of staring at another building or into the street."

"You said all that?"

"I did. And when I got her almost smiling I told her that there was this one branch on the tree here that hung over into our yard and it was a fine branch on a fine tree but that it was really a bother for us for it stayed in the exact line of the sun into our yard in summer and that if it weren't for that branch my wife and children would have sun all afternoon instead of being in the shade. I said that she had probably never even noticed that branch or that tree for that matter, and I asked if she could have it sawed off."

"What did she say?"

"Nothing at first, just stared as if I'd crawled from the sea. Then she came closer. She looked at the branch and after awhile pronounced it a very beautiful branch on a very beautiful tree and to saw it off would be atrocious."

"*Atrocious?*"

"*Atroce* was the word she used."

"So she won't do a thing. Typical. Without the tree we'd have sun all afternoon."

"Not the tree, luv – the branch. Just the branch."

"One frustration after another."

"Oh – there are others?"

"Like trash from upstairs. It's lovely to be sitting here trying to get a little speck of sunlight through the branch while the biddies up there are emptying their dustpans."

"They still do that?"

"They do it on purpose. Look around the yard – cigarette butts, peach pits, hairpins. The other day I found a tampon."

He laughed. "New or used?"

"You don't toss them out new, luv. I've talked to everyone in the building – explained how maybe no one used this yard before but now our children play out here and it would be better if they stopped tossing down their trash. They know. They just don't care. People on the ground floor are the lower classes – like the concierge. They should be used to trash."

"It's the barbeque," he said. "Revenge for the barbeque."

"We cook out once a week. Saturdays."

"How do they even know? I thought the upper classes are all off in their country houses on the weekend."

"That's the top floors. It's the middle floors can't afford country houses yet."

When she went in he turned the game back on. He didn't care about the American League but between innings the army announcers gave scores from other games and he could keep up on how much the Cubs were losing by. He poured himself more wine and examined the tree, outlined against the sky, running his eyes over it branch by branch until arriving at the large branch that arched over their yard. European ash, it was, with spiky little leaves and useless buds that never bloomed and fell into his yard.

He stood on his chair, grabbed some leafy twigs, and pulled down. He could reach the main part of the branch, pulling it down over the spikes. The base of the branch was high enough to get good leverage. When he let it go it shot up like a catapult, leaves slapping through his beard, twigs scratching him. The branch had drawn first blood. It quivered in defiant anger. He saw it could not be snapped from the ground.

He sat down to sip his wine and think about it. His hands were red and black. Leaves and twigs littered the gravel of his yard. As he stared at the tree he realized he was angry. The useless branch was causing trouble in his family. A branch hanging from one property into another was surely the responsibility of the tree owner, but the lady had brushed him off. What was he supposed to do, go to the commissariat, hire a lawyer?

That thought was followed by another: Who, other than his own little family, would know if the branch was gone? Mme. Kirchener would never notice.

Anger vanquished by reason becomes resolve. He went through the quiet apartment into the corridor off the kitchen where the garbage cans were kept. Careful to make no noise that would stir Mme. Lucas, the concierge, he took the ladder off its hook and slipped back through the apartment into the yard. He leaned the ladder against the fence and mounted until he was at the height of the spikes and then slightly over them. He could not reach the place where the branch joined the tree, but from this height he had an advantage. Pushing away smaller branches and leaves he wrapped his arms around the main part of the branch. Good leverage but not enough to snap it. He would have to jump.

He climbed down and took a good swig of pinard to fortify him. He climbed back up and grabbed the branch, which immediately swung him into the spikes, one of its points grinding across his shirt and into his ribs. He let go and felt inside his shirt, feeling a large welt. In a duel he would have been nicked twice before he got off a single thrust.

The trick, he saw, was to grasp the branch as high up as possible but far enough from the fence to be able to launch himself into the air and avoid the spikes as he fell. He couldn't afford to get it wrong.

Waiting, like a first-time parachutist, he gathered resolve. The

Cubs, said the announcer, had just won, momentarily were out of last place. It was the omen he needed. He cast his 175 pounds into the void, becoming momentarily suspended as the branch resisted and prepared to spring upward and drop him on the spikes. But he had weight and gravity and leverage and the tree knew it. With a mighty crack, it sighed and gave up. He was prostrate on the ground with the branch on top, pinning him underneath a great mass of leaves and twigs.

Pushing it off, he stood to examine his maimed body, looking up to see if anyone in the building was looking. Nothing. Everyone in front rooms watching the telly. No sign of Doris, asleep with Boules Quies in her ears to blot out the radio. He inspected the fallen foe spread across yard, enormous, far bigger on the ground than on the tree. It consumed half the yard. He'd never get it back over the fence and if he did Mme. Kirchener would see it immediately. God knows what French crime he was guilty of.

He returned the ladder to the corridor, grabbing some garbage bags and his saw from the kitchen on the way back. He would cut the main branch into pieces and saw off the small branches to keep them from ripping the bags. But where to put the bags? Movement somewhere, inside, upstairs? He stood listening, resuming his chore, annoyed at not having thought the thing through. But the branch was down. Doris would come out outside to read tomorrow and when the sun came over the building it would be shining down on her. She'd look up and they would open the Champagne.

He sawed until he had blisters and then sawed some more, throwing small pieces over the fence where they disappeared into the bramble. He was covered in sawdust – clothes, skin, beard. All around lay pieces of branch and twig, and through the sawdust he saw blood from multiple scratches and welts across his arms. Straightening up was painful. He started filling the bags.

Finished, he sat down, lit a Gitane, and stared at the half-dozen bulging black bags that filled his little yard. He felt good. The world was right again. Midnight and the Sixteenth Arrondissement was asleep. He closed his eyes to consider the next step and when he opened them he saw Doris at the window, curtain held back, ghostly in her white nightie. How long had she been watching? After a moment she opened the window, closed to keep out the radio. Still she stared, saying nothing. He supposed it was suppressed shock, like coming across a grave robber and deciding it best to just keep on going.

"And what," she said, finally, "do you intend to do with the corpus delicti?"

"That," he said, "was the one flaw in my plan."

"I'll put something on," she said. "We'll scatter the bags about the neighborhood. People will think the tree trimmers were around."

"But they weren't around," he said, loving her Irish energy.

"Byron, isn't it time we went home?

I O

It was mid-afternoon, quiet time at the Berri Bar. Archer stood by the pinball machine, ordered a demi beer and began going over his notes from the Foreign Ministry. Looking up, he glanced in the mirror and there, behind the dining room partition, was Dennis Klein talking to a young woman whose face he could only partly see in the mirror. My God, It was her! His heart thumped.

She'd finally written to apologize for not writing. Let's keep writing, she said. The letter was affectionate and encouraging. She missed Paris and missed him and he got the impression she was unhappy with her work and her marriage and Toronto and that their brief encounter in Paris was not the end of things. He immediately wrote back. He never heard from her again.

How could she come to Paris and never say a word? He watched her shoulders, the perfect neck, the way her head moved when she laughed, which she was doing now with Klein. He paid for his beer and walked toward them, heart still thumping. Dennis waved and when he was closer he saw it was not Claire.

"Rupert, this is Sophie, from l'*Express*. Sophie, meet Rupert, our Paris reporter."

"Practicing my English," she said, "which is not good. How do you do, Rupert?"

He was stunned at the likeness, stunned and relieved. It was over. He sat down. "Sounds good to me – better than my French."

"That's what Dennis said, but his French is good."

"If you like New York accents. So how did you two meet?"

She laughed again, an insouciant girlish laugh. It was remarkable how she resembled Claire – younger, but the same shape face, same hair, about the same build. Blue eyes, though. Claire's were hazel. He had to stop thinking like that.

"Dennis came over and introduced himself."

"Typical rude American," said Archer.

"Oh, I don't mind. We're neighbors, you know. We share this café."

"Sophie is a stagiaire at *l'Express.*"

"I work with Marc de Thorigny, the political columnist. He is my – how would you say? – my patron."

"Thorigny," said Archer, recalling. "He has a weekly column."

"He's coming to meet me here. He's late."

"I have to get upstairs," said Klein, leaving some francs on the table. "Nice to meet you, Sophie. I'm leaving you in good hands."

"Good-bye, Dennis." She turned to Archer as he left. "What a nice man."

"He is a nice man. You mind if I stay awhile? Could we speak French?"

"Of course. Oh, here comes Marc. Would you like to meet him?"

"Yes," he said, lying. "But could we meet again? Coffee some day – or perhaps lunch?" He would not let a girl like this escape.

"Of course," she said, writing her name and number on the paper tablecloth and tearing off a corner. "What is your family name?"

"Archer – Rupert Archer. And yours?"

"There," she said, handing him the paper. I've written it out. Sophie de la Tour."

Archer stood and looked into the long, sallow face of a man who did not smile as Sophie made the introductions. He saw immediately that though this man was her mentor, there was more to it.

"You're American," he said in French. It was not a question.

"Yes. I work at the *Herald.*"

"Rupert is the *Herald's* Paris reporter," she said.

"Ah, yes. You were at the Foreign Ministry?"

"I was."

"Things are not going so well for you in Vietnam."

"No."

"You have been there?"

"No. And you?"

"Oh, yes. I covered the French retreat. I will go back shortly to cover yours."

It was as good a way as any of dismissing him. "I must go. Nice to meet you. Good-bye, Sophie." He checked the scrap of paper as he left the café. She'd given him her home phone.

They had lunch a few times and one weekend toward the end of July, shortly before the French were to leave town for the month of August, he invited her to l'Etang d'Hollande, the little lake with the little beach on the road to Rambouillet discovered by Byron Hallsberg. Doris and Byron were driving out one last time before leaving for Los Angeles. Like Steve Fleming, Byron had been hired by the *Times*.

It's a forty-minute drive to Rambouillet if traffic is light, though a bit longer in the ancient VW beetle Archer had purchased for getting around Paris. He'd met Sophie's parents by this time, an elderly, formal French couple living in an apartment on the rue Vaneau, who unlike Sophie's mentor at *l'Express* seemed unconcerned that their daughter was seeing an American. As a teenager, Sophie had spent time in England as an au pair and also lived in Spain and Germany. She had a wide circle of Parisian friends, but seemed to like the fact that he wasn't French. Klein pretended to be annoyed that Archer was dating the girl he'd met first, but with Fleming's departure Klein was concentrating on Gretchen Kilic, whose bare legs obsessed him.

It was Saturday and a nice crowd had gathered at the lake, Parisians trying to get pale skins ready for Brittany and Normandy –

or, for the upper floors, the Côte d'Azur. Many from the *Herald* had already arrived, marking their space with blankets, tents, and umbrellas. The Hallsbergs came with children; Dick LePoint and Suzy de Granville with a wine cooler; Klein, khaki shorts and T-shirt covering most of his white, hairy frame, had brought Gretchen, whose hard dancer's body was injected into a black one-piece bathing suit. Red-haired Hallsberg, beer in hand, huddled back in his tent like a bear in its cave. LePoint, elegant in silk shirt, beige slacks, and sun hat, sipped white wine under his umbrella while Suzy, languidly gorgeous in a yellow one-piece bathing suit, stretched out in the sun with white plastic orbs over her eyes. She removed them long enough to watch Sophie slip out of a little wraparound skirt and tank top to reveal a red polka dot bikini. Archer had not expected anything so daring from this very correct young woman.

"Now what could a pretty girl like you see in a schmo like Archer," Hallsberg called from his lair.

She was a sight. Archer had not yet seen her in any state of undress, and her polite reserve led him to believe it wouldn't be anytime soon. In Paris she tended toward sweaters and knee-length skirts.

"Can you swim in that?" he asked.

"I'm a good swimmer," she said. "How about you?"

They swam out past the pier and under the rope toward the middle of the lake. It was the largest of les Etangs d'Hollande, the series of small lakes that Louis XIV created from the rivers of Yvelines to serve the Palace of Versailles, a favorite lake of kings and princes. They had it to themselves, most people deterred by the rope and fear of cramps and water snakes. There was a lifeguard on the beach but if he noticed them beyond the rope, gave no sign of it. He was there for the children.

That was the day Sophie became pregnant. They'd driven back to Paris in late afternoon, stopped at shops along the rue St.-Dominique, brought their packages upstairs to Archer's apartment, and had a picnic supper to the music of Jacques Brel and Georges Brassens on the phonograph. She got a little high on wine and chattered away in French. He knew she wanted to move into her own apartment but he'd not yet detected the streak of independence, even rebellion, that made her want to be free of her parents. Her two sisters, much older than she, had married and moved out years before.

He saw she was not quite what he'd thought; that the initial shyness he'd found so appealing came not from temperament but from the subtle inhibitions of speaking a foreign language. In French, she had firm views on everything from politics to Frenchmen, and after they finished a bottle of rouge they ended up in bed, where she was as eager to be as he. Afterward they lit up Gauloises with the wonderful black tobacco, gabbled away in French, made love again.

"I'm not a virgin, you could tell, couldn't you? You were surprised?" She snuggled up to him. "Of course, Rupert," she said, laughing, "you could not possibly comment on such a thing. You are un monsieur . . . ein Herr . . . un caballero . . . a gentleman." She was funny and irresistible. "Do you want to know how many times?"

"Ahhh . . ."

"Yes, of course you do. Four times."

"Four different men?"

"Ah, non, monsieur. I am only twenty-one. Just one man."

"Marc du Thorigny."

She sat bolt upright, as though on a spring, her young breasts, still straight and hard, thrusting into his face. "How did you know that?"

"Just a guess."

She lay back down again. "I shouldn't have, you know. But I wanted to – with him, not with some pale French boy in a dirty pullover and a mégot in his mouth. Marc wanted me badly and so I gave in. He has four children, you know."

"Hmmm."

"He wants to go on, but I said no. That day at the Berri Bar, that's when I told him. Things are difficult between us now."

"I can imagine."

"He took precautions, though – if you know what I mean." She thought about it for a moment. "You didn't take any, did you?"

He had not. How could he have planned for such a day?

She was gone the whole month of August, sending him two post-cards from Saint-Malo. He was surprised how much he missed her and knew it wasn't just the sex. It was late September when she told him her periods had stopped. They were meeting for lunch at the Val d'Isère, down the street from the *Herald* and *l'Express*.

"Let's get married," he said.

He'd already thought about it. He was twenty-eight and wanted a family. It looked like he would be in Europe for some time. Despite the cultural gap, they enjoyed each other's company and were intrigued by each other. It was not the mad passion he'd felt for Claire, but that kind of folie à deux brings only the worst kind of pain. With Sophie it was pure pleasure. He was sure he would have proposed even if she weren't pregnant.

She reached across the table for his hand. "Pourquoi pas?"

The de la Tours were not quite the conventional family he'd thought. Originally from Brittany, land of Celtic voyagers and emi-grants, the family wasn't surprised anymore when someone took a foreigner to bed or to the altar. Bernard and Florence, Sophie's par-ents, accepted the news with equanimity. In the months he'd known Sophie, her parents had been unfailingly friendly and welcoming to him, inviting him to family dinner on Sundays and introducing him to cousins visiting Paris.

Bernard had retired as a sous directeur at Renault autoworks and now spent his days walking the quais and visiting old bookstores. He was a bibliophile, an erudite and humorous man who liked to corner Archer to test his literary and historical knowledge. For Bernard it was one thing for his daughter to marry an American, quite another to marry an uncultured American. Sophie had two older sisters, one married to an Italian industrialist in Milan, another to a Paris bureaucrat. No one in the family had any problem with Sophie marrying an American.

But Archer had not yet met everyone in the family.

As for Marc de Thorigny, Sophie, at her request, was assigned to another mentor at *l'Express*, but he continued to pester her.

"Look," Archer said one day, "you gave him a taste of what it was to be twenty-one again. You have addicted him and he's having trouble kicking the habit. In the old days I suppose I'd have to fight a duel."

"Ahh," she said, laughing. "How I would love that. Men dying for me – a woman's dream. Why don't you do it?"

"It's not for me to challenge him – *I won!*"

She frowned. "*That's* how you see it – like I was a prize at the fair?"

"If you want to be rid of him, tell his wife, tell his children. Do they know?"

She didn't laugh. "That's terrible, you know."

Over dinner at the Berri Bar he asked Klein to be his best man, which was only right. Klein was still waiting to give his notice at the *Herald*, to get on with what he'd been putting off so long, moving to Germany to complete his research on the Nazi occupation of Paris.

"Why not ask Wayne Murray, your pal from Phoenix?"

"Wayne's still sore at me. It's an old story."

"Look, if you want me, I'd be honored. Where's the wedding?"

"Sainte-Clotilde."

"Ah, Sainte-Clotilde, very nice. Designed by a German architect, you know. A favorite church for the German occupiers – Catholic ones, that is. Are you sure you want a Jew as your best man in the very Catholic Sainte-Clotilde? The priest may not like that."

"The priest isn't the bridegroom. And there is the fact that there would be no wedding without you."

"True, isn't it? And there is the fact that I might be the bride-groom without you."

"You would never marry a French Catholic."

"To say nothing of whether she would marry me."

"How are things with Gretchen?"

"I prefer not to answer."

"Don't tell me you still haven't . . ."

"I think Gretchen may be anti-Semitic."

"What, the girl won't fuck and that makes her an anti-Semite?"

"God, you are crude. How can that delicious French pastry possibly want to marry a barbarian like you?"

They were married on a crisp October day in the Basilica de Sainte-Clotilde, Gothic masterpiece designed in the mid-nineteenth century by German Franz-Christian Gau and declared a basilica by Pope Leo XIII. The several hundred people at the church were mostly friends and family of the bride gathered from across France, all of them, with a single exception, friendly and even affectionate toward Archer.

The exception was a cousin, Vincent Bertrand, whom Sophie embraced and kissed on the lips despite the young man's shabby clothes, unshaven face, and scraggly appearance. When Sophie introduced them, Vincent barely looked at him, hardly touched his extended hand, and went quickly away. Archer stared at his bride, seeking an answer.

"We spent summers together as children in Saint-Malo," she said, "every summer since we were babies. You have to excuse him. He has an artist's personality. Vincent is a gifted painter." She hesitated. "He has always been in love with me."

"But you are cousins."

"Vincent is adopted."

Following a short honeymoon in Spain, Sophie gave notice at *l'Express* and set about to find an apartment big enough for three. She found a place in a modern high-rise on the Place St.-Ferdinand, and they settled in for the winter of Sophie's first pregnancy.

It had all happened so fast for her. In a matter of months she'd gone from being a girl barely out of school and living with her parents to a young woman with husband, bourgeois apartment, and baby on the way. She didn't give a second thought to leaving *l'Express*, knowing that under French law she could return when ready. The apartment was close enough for Archer to walk to work and for Sophie to visit old friends at *l'Express*. She never mentioned Marc de Thorigny.

By March Sophie's stomach was round and smooth as a beach ball. One evening when Archer came home early he found her entertaining cousin Vincent.

"He's done a painting for us," she said happily, pointing to a large canvas on the floor against the couch. "We're discussing where to hang it."

Vincent was a surrealist. Saggy, pale, big-breasted women floated in the air with nymphs and cherubs peering from sea and sky and various fierce-looking animals and overgrown insects staring out of the jungle. There was a lagoon and a moon. Archer found it dark and ominous and hideous.

"What do you think, Rupert – here over the couch or maybe over there by the dining room table?"

"I don't know. What do you think?"

"I like it better over the dining room table, don't you, Vincent?

She'd made a kind of chicken stew for dinner and Archer opened a bottle of Beaujolais Villages. Afterward Vincent lit up a Gauloise. Sophie had given up smoking and Archer mainly smoked during sex. "I've decided the baby is going to be a girl and we were discussing names. We like Marie-Claire. Like the magazine. What do you think?"

"*No!*"

She was in a gay mood, taking a little wine and obviously happy to have Vincent visiting. They'd been out walking in the Bois. It had been a benign cousinly day and Archer's sharp negative jolted her. "You object to the Marie or the Claire?"

"The Claire."

"Well we can't just call her Marie; it's too common. What would you suggest?"

"I suggest a name that works well in both languages, something like, let me think, something like – what about Charlotte?"

"Vul-gaire," said Vincent, drawing out the word.

"No, Rupert, that won't do. What else?"

"What about Isabel? Isabel Archer is a famous name in litera-ture."

She frowned. "No. Isabel is not good in French. But I like Agnès."

Archer's turn to frown. "In America Agnes is the name of maids and old maid aunts. Like Gertrude . . . or Amelia."

"Gertrude . . . no," she said. "Too German. But Amelia, Amélie – Amélie Archer, yes, I like it. Amélie Anne. That's what we will call her."

"Amelia Anne Archer," said Archer. "I don't like it. Too soft, too many a's. A name needs a bit of a bite."

"Like Rupert," said Vincent.

"Amelia – Amy – I could live with that," Archer said. "But not Amy Anne."

"A girl has to have a saint's name. I have one – Sophie Anne Marie de la Tour."

"In America we use family names as middle names. We could use my grandparents' name, Shields. Amelia Shields Archer. Initials ASA. I like that."

"Amelia Anne Shields Archer," said Sophie.

He laughed. "Done. Let's just hope it's a girl so we don't have to go through this again for a boy."

In the kitchen, she whispered: "We have to pay him for the paint-ing."

"It's awful."

"It is original, which is what every artist seeks. You must give him something."

"Five hundred francs?"

"Oh, no, that is an insult. At least a thousand francs. You can write a check."

"I'll give him a thousand francs as long as you don't hang the painting."

"I will hang the painting."

"It will scare the baby."

"Perhaps by then I'll be tired of it. I'll have him do another."

11

The transatlantic connection was good for once. Swart hung up, smiled to himself and swiveled around, looking across at the Hotel California. A couple stood at a window, holding back the sheers and staring at him. They waved and he waved back. Americans, he thought, thrilled to be staring into the *Paris Herald*.

"It went well?" asked Martine, at his door as soon as he'd hung up.

"Very well," he said, "as I'm sure you heard. Call Connie, will you? Tell her to get Sonny up here."

"Already done."

It was after four o'clock, the newsroom was just getting started, and Stein was upstairs within minutes. "The deal is done," Swart said when the door was shut. He didn't mind Martine hearing, but he'd tell le Tac in his own time. "The *Washington Post* is now part owner of the *Paris Herald*."

Stein ran his hand over his bald head, a habit formed by bald men in good hair days and continued out of nostalgia. He got right to the point. "Who has control?"

"Jock keeps control. The *Post* bought a minority interest, forty-five percent – in the *Herald* only, not Whitney Communications."

"Any personnel changes? Didn't Ben Bradlee start with *Newsweek* in Paris?"

"Don't know yet."

"This'll kill them at the *Times*."

Swart checked his watch. "They announce it at noon today in Washington. Everyone will be there: Jock, Walter, Kay, Fritz Beebe, Bradlee. It'll be six o'clock here. Syd Gruson will be on the phone within seconds."

"They're finished over there."

"He expected my job. They thought it would be weeks until we folded. They never dreamt Kay Graham would be interested."

"So who put it together?'

"Walter called Fritz, who had him down for lunch. Walter says that in his first meeting with Kay she could hardly sit still she was so exited. She hates the *Times*. Thinks the *Post* can be a better newspaper. She knows this will bring Punch crawling to us sooner or later, crawling to *her*, begging to get in on the deal – on her terms."

"How long can the *Times* can hold out?"

"Kay has deep pockets – they know that."

"You're sure she's not sending anyone over?"

"She'll have to restrain Bradlee. Walter said something about maybe someone at the assistant ME level, someone familiar with the *Post*'s writers and correspondents."

"I already have an assistant managing editor, Joe Marder, a damn good one."

"And the managing editor?"

"I don't think Lodge wants to leave. He loves the *Herald*."

So Ben Swart, who made a point of staying off the second floor, was downstairs for the second time in a year with the feeling that the third time wasn't far off, depending on how the *Times* reacted. Walter's call couldn't have gone better, and he would take Martine to Vattier's afterward to celebrate. Martine's family was from Alsace, and she liked nothing better than choucroute and a good Mosel – or maybe champagne on this night. They'd walk around les Halles to work up an appetite. They'd done a lot of walking in New York. He was ready to hail cabs but she wanted to walk.

He had another piece of good news for her: Norma was filing for divorce. She didn't mention Martine, didn't say she'd met anyone, just said their lives had taken different directions. She was good about it, a proud New Englander, knew he wouldn't contest it. She wanted the children to go to school in Newport. He agreed of course. It meant no more sneaking around in Paris. Martine could move in with him.

"It's just been announced that the *Washington Post* has purchased a minority interest in the *Herald*," he began, looking around at anxious faces wondering how much longer they'd be in Paris. "Big deal for us . . . means we survive. Sonny will go into details but one thing it means is that on big stories, like the war, we'll no longer be at a disadvantage. The *Times* has its people in Vietnam, and the *Post*, as I understand it, has just as many."

"So what's the bad news?" called Frank Draper. "How many new guys and how many of us have to leave?"

"They did not take us over, Frank," said Swart. "They bought in. I stay. Sonny stays. You stay. With attrition, as I understand it – when Klein leaves for Germany or to fill the spot left by Hallsberg – for that they might send someone over."

"They're going to love this across town," said Wayne Murray.

"We don't know what it means for the *Times*," said Swart. "The *Times* has long anticipated that it, not the *Post*, would be our partner, and that it would be the senior partner. You know what that would have meant. With the *Post* coming in they are likely to be, shall we say, extremely pissed. Some of the people who left us to go across town will regret the move. It goes without saying that they will not be welcomed back."

"Let's not forget," said Martha Blaine, "*why* people went across town."

"Money," said Swart, "yes, I know that. On that subject I can promise nothing. There is a prestige to be working on the *Paris Herald*."

"Oh, balls, Ben," said McGillicuddy. "*You* can live in the Villa

Montmorency. Paris isn't so sexy when you live in the suburbs. Sure, we'd rather work here than at the *Times*, but you can't feed your children prestige. We are obscenely underpaid."

"*Hear, hear!*" called Draper. "Pass that on to Kay Graham. She wants to compete with the *Times* – tell her to compete in salaries as well."

"She knows. She's seen the books. Obviously I can't speak for her. By the way – she'll be coming over here soon to meet you all, along with Fritz Beebe and Ben Bradlee. What I *will* do is point out that because of company losses over the past few years, losses that had a lot to do with losses in New York, salaries here haven't kept up with the *Times*. How she intends to address that is up to her."

"What's your best guess about the *Times*, Ben?" asked Helen Lodge.

Various thoughts flashed through his mind as he considered her question. He still had a vivid picture of the meeting in New York with Sydney Gruson, white teeth flashing, insisting to Jock that the *Times* had to have control. They'd been through too much at the *Trib*, forced by the unions to close the paper people thought had the greatest newspaper talent in the country, maybe ever.

"The *Times*," he said slowly, "has dug itself into a deep hole in Paris. Jock would have sold them a minority interest, but they got greedy. The *Times* is the second American newspaper in Europe and its one big hope was that Jock would throw in the towel. But he didn't. *When* they close is up to them, but when you meet your friends from the *Times* at Harry's Bar, tell them this: the sooner they close up the better for everyone."

"I'll drop you off and pick you up at nine," he told Martine when they were back upstairs. "The later the better at les Halles."

"*Les Halles?*"

"I'm taking you to dinner tonight, my dear, to celebrate."

She stared. "Ben, I already have a dinner date."

"With whom . . . anyway, cancel it."

Her face colored. "At seven o'clock you're asking me to cancel a dinner date?"

"This is important to me."

Her stare was icy. "Why didn't you say something?"

"How could I know the deal would be done today? Anyway, I have other news."

"What?"

"That's why we're going to dinner."

"Ben, you can't do this. I have to tell you – I have my own friends."

He felt a surge of anger, jealousy, fear, all of them. She was trying to ruin a very good day. "I've heard that before. Tell me – what exactly does it mean?"

Martine Treuherz was Alsatian, which meant as much Frank as Gaul, as German as French. Her hair was pale yellow, flaxen, her eyes blue and her face rosy from genes and a lifetime of skiing and skating. She was not stocky and muscular like many skiers, but built more like a figure skater, sleek and athletic. She was smart, classy, and had a figure she liked to show off. Men had never been a scarcity.

"It means you're assuming too much, that's what it means."

"After New York I didn't think I had to assume anything."

"Don't ever assume."

"Are you coming with me or not?"

Her eyes flashed. "You're such a bastard."

"Asking my girlfriend to dinner – that makes me a bastard?"

"So I am your girlfriend?"

"What did you think you were?"

"I try not to think about it."

"Maybe that's what I want to talk about."

She slumped in her chair, staring at the telephone. "All right," she said, more in anger than agreement. "I'll cancel."

Everything went wrong that night. The affair had always been difficult to manage. Ben Swart was a well-known figure in Paris and to be seen around town with his secretary was never a good idea. In the past they would never have gone to a place like Vattier's, hardly a hushed lobster palace where you sit discreetly with your mistress in some dark velvet corner. Vattier's is a big bustling Alsatian bistro where people go to make noise and toss down glasses of Kronenbourg with their choucroute and laugh and talk to their neighbors and above all to be seen.

His second mistake that night was trying to undress her. She was stunning in tight pants and white sweater and as she puttered around her apartment putting on finishing touches – he could tell she was still angry – he was overcome with lust. There was something about angry women that made him want to fuck them. It was the same with his wife. When they quarreled she wanted nothing to do with him and that's when he wanted her most. He knew it had something to do with rape, that taking her when she didn't want it was when he wanted it most. He'd never really quarreled with Martine before so it was a new experience. She'd never said no to him before, but when he put his arms around her, she pushed him away.

"I don't feel like sex with you," she said. "Let's just go to dinner."

Hired by his predecessor, Harold Breckenridge, Martine Treuherz was always too good to be true. Breckenridge hired her away from Barclay's Bank on avenue George V by the simple means of doubling her salary. She'd gone to business school in London, was trilingual, gifted with numbers, and absolutely reliable. She was also, Breckenridge said, a great help in dealing with the comité de l'entreprise and Theo le Tac. She was terrific with dictation, would work weekends when needed, though once a month went home to Alsace to visit her parents, to whom she was very close.

"She's a very sweet girl in all respects," Harold said, "and Mary and I love her as a daughter. I'm sure it will be the same with you."

Not exactly. He hadn't been in town a month, was still living in

an hotel, when he'd driven her home after work one night. Knowing
he was on his own, she asked him in for a drink. He stayed all night
and in two years it never stopped. Eventually Norma found out. He
promised to end it, but was unable. Martine had another lover, a nice-
looking boy from Barclay's named Jean-Claude whom Swart had seen
hanging around. She dropped him. Though Swart suspected Jean-
Claude was one of what she now described as "her own friends," he
was sure she wasn't sleeping with him.

"I never," she told him once, "sleep with more than one man in
the same month."

Swart had slept with her at least once a month for two years.

A cold February wind swept through the open pavilion as they
arrived at les Halles. They could see their breath as they walked under
the massive iron structure among carts and trams racing about with
fresh products from lines of trucks outside. Voices shouted in incom-
prehensible argot, a scream rang out as something loud and heavy
crashed to the ground somewhere, dirty water sloshed in gutters
behind the stalls, beefy men in blood-stained aprons over undershirts
tossed sides of beef around as if they were loaves of bread. Overhead,
lights shined from ironwork as intricate as the Eiffel Tower and a giant
cupola of leaded glass held by swooping iron beams rose above everything, creating the sense of being inside a cold and drafty cathedral.

Smells changed every few meters as they passed from meat to fish
to produce to live animals screeching their displeasure. Carts and trams
honked and dark-suited inspectors with clipboards strutted about like
cocks. From their stalls, hawkers leaned forward to shout their wares,
for while les Halles is primarily a place of wholesaling, for centuries it
has attracted le tout Paris out for a night of slumming and looking to
take home a jambon de Bayonne or wheel of Cantal for the next soiree.
Or maybe looking for something else: one street down from les Halles
is the rue St.-Denis, where the girls are on display – not by accident,
for meat markets tend to complement each other.

It was after ten when they were led to their table at Vattier's, across the street from the pavilion. Martine had hardly spoken a word.

He ordered a '64 Veuve Cliquot brut, Yellow Label, and choucroute for two. A half baguette was cut into the metal basket, and they slathered on mustard for they'd not eaten since lunch. Swart proposed a toast, "to us" and they clinked and Martine tried on a faint smile for the first time that evening, though she'd hardly spoken two words. Soon the choucroute arrived on a heaping, steaming platter, and the waiter dished it out, first sauerkraut, then carefully distributing nuggets of ham, sausage, kielbasa, and potatoes.

They ate and drank, and he watched the anger drain slowly from her face, replaced by something he couldn't quite identify.

"Such a perfect night it could have been," she said after awhile. "Choucroute, champagne, I have to say you know my favorite dishes."

"I know you're a good daughter of Alsace."

"And I am, you know, Ben. I am a very good daughter. Do you know what Treuherz means in German?"

"I don't know German."

"True heart. I have a true heart, Ben."

She said it with emotion and it pained him. "I know you do."

"You mustn't pressure me like that."

Was she softening?

"Sometimes you have to be flexible," he said. "I know you have your friends, but when certain occasions come up – well, you just have to be flexible."

It was the wrong thing to say.

"*Me?*" Her blue eyes narrowed. "I have to be flexible. Not you."

"I don't know if you realize it, but this was a really big day – not just for the *Herald*, not just for me – but for both of us. If things had gone differently I'd be on my way back to New York. As for you – you'd be out of a job."

She dabbed at her mouth with a napkin and stared at him icily. "I assume you'd have given me a recommendation."

"Not if you're going to sulk all night."

The anger was back. "Do you know what you just said?"

"What did I just say?"

"That you'd be on your way and I'd be out of a job. And that would be that, as you say in English."

"Oh, look, forget it. It didn't happen. We won. The *Herald* lives!"

"You said you had something else to tell me."

"I do – but only if you stop sulking."

"Can't you stop being so . . . so . . . *condescendant*. I am not sulking. I am quite angry with you, that's all. You made certain assumptions that . . . well, never mind. What do you have to tell me?"

"Norma has filed for divorce. She's not coming back. I'm supposed to pack up her stuff and ship it home. Just like that."

Her expression never changed. She sat there in her maddening twenty-something seductiveness and just stared at him, making it hard.

"Just like that . . . that's life for you, isn't it, Ben . . . lots of just-like-thats."

"What does that mean?"

"I'm sorry for you, Ben."

"*Sorry* for me . . . why?"

"You have a fine wife and fine children."

"I happen to be in love with you."

Still that stare. Her tongue moved over her lips, moistening the gloss, exciting him, though her tone gave him misgivings. All the time her eyes said nothing. "I think it's the first time you ever told me that."

"I thought I told you that in New York."

"I think I'd remember . . . do you have a cigarette?"

"Before we finish eating?"

"If it's all right with you, of course."

He offered her a Gitane, lighting it. "Strange to see you smoking."

"With you I usually don't."

"Just with les copains, eh?"

"You might say that – and not Gitanes."

The icicles had begun to stab deeply. "I want you to move in with me."

"Before or after you pack up for Norma? And don't forget the children's things."

"Why are you doing this?"

"I was mad at you. But now I can see why you insisted that I come tonight."

"So the sulk is over?"

"It was never a sulk. What I have to say is not said with petulance. I would say the same thing even if we were going back to my place tonight for sex, which we are not. I would say to you Ben that you have been an education for me – from the first night I invited you in for a drink and we slept together. Our affair has been good for both of us – despite all the sneaking around – and I regret absolutely nothing. Our three days in New York were – well, I suppose that's what a honeymoon is like. Unforgettable."

He felt a stab of panic. "You talk as though it's over."

"I don't say that."

"Then what are you saying?"

Their gazes locked until he had to look away. It was the smoke. "Ben, you are my father's age. You are, in fact, a little older than my father. If my parents knew of this . . ."

The arrow struck deep. He was stunned, shocked into crushed silence. Never had she even hinted at such a thing. It took a moment for the full meaning to sink in. "Isn't it a little late to be – "

"I can't move in with you," she interrupted. "You want to go around town to all your fancy dinners and receptions with me on your arm as – as what? As your girlfriend . . . your petite amie . . . if I move in with you I'd be more than that, wouldn't I? I'd be your concubine. No. I won't do it."

"I love you, Martine."

She shook her head, slowly, exhaling smoke. Behind the smoke he saw tears.

"You have nothing to say to that?"

"Sex."

"What?"

"You like to fuck me."

She said it too loud. Heads turned. He stared in disbelief.

Her falling tears left marks on the paper tablecloth. "You don't love me, Ben. You're just afraid of going home to that big house alone."

12

Suzy stepped from the bathroom with her white terrycloth bathrobe wrapped loosely around her and towel over her wet blond hair. She didn't know how long she'd been in there; the hot bath felt good and it was the only really warm room in the apartment. Dick was on the bed wrapping his hand. After years of practice he was used to it but preferred having Suzy do it. The cold parquet floor hit her bare feet as she made for the carpet, actually just a rug but in furnished Paris apartments you're lucky to get anything. They had a two-room ground floor place on avenue Emile Deschanel near the Champs de Mars. It wasn't much of a place – cramped, cold, next to a creaking elevator and with a single curtained window onto a dark courtyard. But it was the snazzy Seventh Arrondissement, close enough to walk to work and better yet, close enough to walk to the rue Cler, which was less a street than an open-air market where Suzy did her shopping.

Suzy and Dick had been together long enough to look for a bigger place but never felt permanent enough. Draper, McGillicuddy, Wayne Murray, Helen and Al, Martha Gates, Tom Blaine, a few others, those were the permanent ones. And of course Eric Hawkins who'd been in Paris forever. Byron Hallsberg with his three children had been permanent, but now he was gone. They agreed that if the new deal with the *Post* brought salary increases they'd get serious about looking for something better, though it would have to be close to the rue Cler.

Dick didn't look up as she came out from the bathroom. The way he wrapped his hand took eighteen inches of gauze. He cut it carefully to the right length, gripped it between left thumb and index finger, and started wrapping, making sure the gauze stayed tight and allowed the thumb free movement from the rest of the hand. Done, he taped both ends. He'd been doing it since he was wounded and it took six minutes. He never talked about it, never told the war stories you might expect. Fortunately, it was his left hand. Suzy could wrap it in half the time.

She took the towel off her head and let her long, damp hair fall down over the bathrobe. She parted her hair with her hands and held it out in two long tresses ready for drying and braiding. She'd have a French braid tonight, perfect to impress everyone at the reception. Dick had just started the wrapping. She took the gauze from him and held his wounded hand against her robe, which, untied, came open. His fingers brushed the fine blond hair of her pubis.

"Jesus, Suzy."

One of the first things she'd discovered with Dick was that she had to seduce him. He wasn't one of the studs at the newspaper who fluttered about her like butterflies or the Frenchmen in overcoats who followed her along the Champs Elysées whispering, among other things, that they could get her a tryout with Truffaut. She'd been fighting off male lust since she was in pigtails in Altoona. "Just so happens we need a librarian," Sonny had said when she told him she'd worked in the library at Penn. Sonny was attractive in a bald, New York Jewish kind of way, but she hadn't been there long before she saw he wasn't available. It was better with Dick, who put few demands on her, wore an ascot, and had beautiful gray hair. She liked older men.

She finished the hand and slid his suspenders off. The bathrobe slipped to the floor as she began undoing the buttons of his shirt. "I want to share."

"I think we're going to be late," he said a few minutes later as Suzy erupted into a series of sustained moans that penetrated through the wall into the rooms next door.

The rooms next door belonged to Mme. Florence Dumesnil,

concierge at 78 bis avenue Emile Deschanel and a woman who'd heard many sounds in her time but never anything like those made by Suzy. As the moaning started, Mme. Dumesnil got up to turn down her television. The wall between them was particularly thin because it had once all been a single apartment – her apartment. Several years earlier the building co-proprietors voted to split her rooms in two (what possible use could an elderly widow have for thirty-five square meters?) and compensate her by splitting her remaining room in two again, giving her two rooms again but with half the space. With the new space they created a small rental whose income went toward building taxes, so high in the Seventh.

Usually Mme. Dumesnil was in bed and the moans would awaken her. It was rare to hear them at six o'clock in the evening and though French television (the studios were a stone's throw away on rue Cocnacq-Jay) presented the first of their two Saturday movies-of-the-week at six, which Mme. Dumesnil never missed, she didn't mind turning down the sound to listen to Suzy. She was certain that she had never made sounds like that, not on her honeymoon nor any subsequent occasion.

For her marriage at l'Eglise de la Trinité in the Ninth Arrondissement (she only came to the Seventh after François passed away), she'd received from her parents a pair of fine linen sheets, one of which, le drap fendu, came with an embroidered hole in the middle. She kept it wrapped in tissue in her armoire and would take it down from time to time to admire the needlework. It was through that hole that François was allowed to penetrate her, the only contact between their perineum in thirty years of marriage. Sitting on her bed with the television sound turned down, Mme. Dumesnil found the hole and gently massaged it as she listened to Suzy. Never through that hole (and despite having had three children), had anything occurred to elicit the sub-human sounds now penetrating her wall. When she ran into Suzy in the foyer she had to turn away.

Little girl, big girl, young woman, Suzy de Granville had always turned heads. What she loved most about Paris was how it appreciated beauty. As a student she'd seen a statue of Aphrodite caressing her long golden hair, holding it apart in two long tresses before braiding, exactly as Suzy did. The statue was in the museum at Penn, and she decided that it was Aphrodite, goddess of love, beauty and sexuality, who'd given her the idea to come to Paris to search for her origins. They called her Suzy Granville in Altoona, though her real name was Suzanne Marie Vallette de Granville. What did the "de" mean? What Norman king had elevated her family into the aristocracy?

They arrived at the Hotel Lancaster on the rue de Berri a half hour late. A bouncing black Citroën DS bearing government plates screeched up behind them as Dick paid the taxi outside the hotel.

The distinguished gentleman in tuxedo climbing out and ready to rush inside clearly was someone important. He stopped when he saw Suzy.

"Madame, s'il vous plait. After you."

Dick, grasping that entering with a government official would cover their late arrival, held out his hand.

If it had not been awaiting the late arrival of Charles de la Belle-fontaine, sous secretaire d'Etat, chargé de Information, the receiving line already would have disbanded. Henri de Saint-Gaudens, secretary general of the Elysée Palace, also in attendance, could have insisted that any minister in de Gaulle's cabinet (with the exception of the prime minister, M. Pompidou, and the minister of culture, M. Malraux) sacrifice his country weekend to attend the reception for Katharine Graham, but settled on Bellefontaine, whose job, after all, was information. Further, he knew that Bellefontaine had served in Washington and was acquainted with Mrs. Graham.

Jock Whitney was at the head of the receiving line and next to him was Graham, who, with a regal smile and a touch of petulance, called out, "Charles, enfin." Suzy preceded Charles through the line.

Graham knew, or at least was pretty sure, that the beautiful young woman in the strapless white gown and in such high color was not with the minister, though in Paris you could never be sure.

Suzy gave a demure smile as they touched hands. She saw that the new owner, stately with a thick gray bouffant and an aging debutante's face, was curious about her. "I'm the *Herald's* librarian," she offered, noticing that her eyes were slightly higher than those of the very tall Graham.

"I have to say, my dear," she said, smiling back, "you don't look much like a librarian."

Proceeding along the marble hallway and down three steps into the Lancaster's elegant salon, they joined Dennis Klein, Gretchen Kilic, Rupert Archer, and Helen and Al Lodge. Helen wore a green taffeta dress matching her eyes and setting off her deep red hair. In the course of an evening her fingers would run many times through that hair and it always came to rest as it had been, thick, lustrous, brilliant.

"I see everyone's here," said Suzy.

"Connie Marshall isn't here," said Gretchen.

"Sonny came with Rachel?"

"Looks better for the new boss when you bring your wife," said Klein.

"I see Martine's here," said Suzy. "Did she come with Ben?"

"They came separately," said Helen.

"I thought Ben was being divorced."

"He is," said Helen.

Waiters passed with flutes of champagne and platters of amusebouches. Across the room the stentorian voice of Frank Draper rose above all others as he made a point to CGT union head Tonton Pinard. Old Tonton had probably passed the stately Lancaster five thousand times on his way to work without ever stepping inside. Charlie McCloud, the ambassador, stood near a garden window talking to Bellefontaine as Graham and Whitney, having left Saint-Gaudens, toured the room arm in arm, stars of the show.

Some of the men wore tuxedos. They would be going on to dinner at the ambassador's, Suzy knew. She and Dick, the most stunning couple in the room, everyone would surely agree to that, should be going as well, but the cutoff point for tuxes seemed to be Sonny. Al Lodge was in business suit. That must be why Sonny had come with Rachel, she thought: he could hardly take his mistress to the ambassador's party. Al, she saw, was spaced out, eyes fogged behind his horn-rims. Helen was on edge, as though something had happened or was about to.

"What do you know about Bradlee?" Archer asked no one in particular.

"Graham, Fritz Beebe, Ben Bradlee, that's the troika," said LePoint, who'd worked in Washington. "When Phil Graham killed himself, Kay knew next to nothing about newspapers. She ran her little salon, but Phil kept her out of the business. Suddenly she has control of the *Post*, *Newsweek*, the whole operation and knows nothing of any of it. Some on the board tried to push her out. Beebe, the chairman, sided with her. So did Bradlee, then managing editor, now executive editor."

"Virtue rewarded," said Klein.

"I'm going to cruise," said Archer. "Might pick something up. Funny atmosphere around Paris these days."

"The election last year," said Helen. "De Gaulle was insulted that he didn't win on the first round. Why don't you do a piece for me on his moods?"

From sharing an office with her, Archer knew how good an editor she was. He also knew that he owed his reporter's job to her.

"*On his moods . . . ?*"

"His style, if you prefer."

"Psychoanalysis," said Klein.

Suzy stood back from Helen and Al to escape their cloud of cigarette smoke. Odd couple, she thought, Helen a smart and lively New Englander who unlike Al was sassy and liked to laugh. She was Al's first wife though he was her third or fourth husband, something

Helen had never been clear about – something to do with an annul-
ment somewhere along the line. She'd obviously been smashing
enough to have a swarm of men around, and her mistake was to
marry too many of them.

"When we went through the line," Helen said, "Mrs. Graham
asked me how many wives worked at the *Herald*."

"Good thing she didn't ask how many mistresses," said Gretchen.

"Odd question," said Klein.

"Sounds like a woman whose husband kept her from working at
her own newspaper," said Helen.

"The *Post* came to Phil from Kay's father," said LePoint. "Like a
dowry."

Eric Hawkins, who'd arrived too late for the receiving line, came
over. "You just missed Archer," said Helen. "He went off to find out
why de Gaulle is testy."

"De Gaulle is always testy," said Eric. "It is his greatness."

"Why weren't you in the receiving line, Eric?" asked LePoint.

He was drinking something that looked more like gin than
Champagne. "Don't own a tux. These are new times, my boy. Like
Napoleon at Valmy: a new era begins."

"You're the link to Bennett," said Al, breaking his silence and slur-
ring his words. "The last one. You should have been there. That's
Sonny's fault."

"More like Ben's," said Helen.

"By the way, I hear the *Times* is – if you ladies will excuse me –
pissing its pants," said Eric. "Thought Jock would sell to them."

"They're losing a bundle," said LePoint.

"This lady brings deep pockets," said Eric. "Nothing wrong with
losing money while you get established but at some point it has to
stop. You know Bennett never turned a profit until 1917 – thirty years
after he started the *Herald*. Lot of good it did him."

"Meaning?" said Klein.

"He died the next year."

Frank Draper came up with his wife, a French woman named Odile who spoke no English. At sixty-six, Draper was the oldest man on the news desk, though with his loud voice, erect bearing, and slim build only his white hair showed his age. He lived in the suburbs with his wife and two children. He was convinced the merger would lead to his forced retirement, which he intended to fight. He spent as much time as possible at the *Herald*, working more hours than he was paid for. Escaping his family was the general opinion.

"You think they'll say anything tonight about Zurich?" Draper asked.

"I thought it was Frankfurt," said Wayne Murray, who joined them along with Jojo, sleek little man of indeterminate nationality whom they knew from the Berri Bar, where he came nights to await Wayne. Next to Wayne stood Dan McGillicuddy and wife. People were getting in better position to hear the dignitaries, who were gathering at the front of the room. If Draper's main interest in the merger was his job, McGillicuddy's was money.

"This newspaper is going nowhere," said Draper. "The thing these people don't understand is that you don't get into this business for the money. If Jock Whitney wanted to make money he should have stayed with his horses. Newspapers are a calling, not a business. Pay a newspaperman too much and you corrupt him."

"Jesus, Frank," said McGillicuddy, "You are a dinosaur."

One of the tuxedos came up. "Eric I know," he said, "though I doubt he remembers me when I was at *Newsweek*."

"Of course I remember you, Ben, mostly from the bar at the Crillon."

Bradlee was a man of medium height, trim, athletic, with gray hair and a lined leathery face. Unlike most people in the news business, which tends to be proletarian, Bradlee was a Boston Brahmin on both sides, with pedigrees as long as Jock Whitney's, back to the Pilgrims. He had the reputation as a gregarious guy, as outgoing as Katharine Graham was private, as bold as she was shy.

"I think they want you up front, Ben," said Eric.

The dignitaries mounted the marble steps leading up to the hallway. Ben Swart introduced them and turned it over to Whitney, who said a few words and then took Kay Graham's hand, raising it high. There was applause.

Regal in a powder blue Chanel gown and standing out in the sea of tuxedos like a dove in a row of crows, she looked uneasy, unused to the spotlight. "It is an honor for me to join forces with such a great team, such a marvelous Paris institution," she said, smiling and stopping. Those who knew her best thought she was done.

But she was not done. After a brief hesitation while myopic eyes looked down, then out, unfocused, on the faces beneath her, Kay Graham resumed, her voice harder:

"If it is an honor, it is also an opportunity. Together we will not only be the best American newspaper in Europe, we will be the *only* American newspaper in Europe."

If not everyone was paying attention, suddenly they were.

"Jock and I are in total agreement," she said, looking to him.

"There is no room in Paris for two American newspapers."

Those watching Fritz Beebe, chairman of the Washington Post Company, would have seen the twitch in his face, an involuntary convulsion followed by a hand quickly rising to conceal it. Beebe knew, as Kay Graham did not, that such a challenge would only make the *Times* dig in deeper, as troops do when they know the charge is coming.

Glancing around, Beebe saw discomfiture, not only among the French officials but on the face of the ambassador. They would be wondering about their presence at such a declaration of war. Wasn't Sydney Gruson coming to the ambassador's dinner?

"Ladies and gentlemen," she said, voice softer now: "I sincerely hope you're ready for a good fight."

How they loved it! The old newsroom vets, the French employees from the business offices, even Tonton Pinard who pretended to speak no English, clapped as Kay Graham beamed down on them, any trace of nervousness washed away in the ringing applause. They cheered and clinked flutes and spontaneously turned looking for Eric Hawkins, while those around him backed away so he was standing alone. He raised his glass as they raised their flutes.

Yes, Eric thought, this lady has restored spirits sinking for months under rumors of impending doom. She talks like the old man himself.

13

Amelia Anne Shields Archer was born March 8, 1966, the same day de Gaulle formally announced that France was withdrawing its armed forces from NATO's integrated military command and gave the allies one year to remove all men, bases and equipment from French territory. She was a happy baby who didn't much care what the French president was doing to Franco-American relations. She never cried, which was a good thing because it was soon clear that the apartment on Place St.-Ferdinand was too small. One day in August, Archer returned home to find Sophie, her sister Marie-France, and husband Philippe Gauthier at the dinner table awaiting him. A nearly empty bottle of Côte de Rhone waited as well.

"Philippe has found an old farmhouse near Anet, near the chateau that Henri II built for Diane de Poitiers," said Sophie.

"Not really a farmhouse, more like a manor," he said. "An hour from Paris with an acre of land. The buildings are in wretched shape but there's potential."

Archer liked Philippe, a smart, good-humored, soft-spoken man a few years older than Marie-France, who was eight years older than Sophie. The two couples met for dinner from time to time, but the sisters saw each other every week, sometimes at their parents' house but usually on rue de la Pompe, where Marie-France lived in a large apartment with her husband and two school-age children. Sophie had already mentioned Philippe's dabbling in real estate, how he would spot old places, buy cheap and through his own and local labor restore and sell them to double his money. They'd been relatively small jobs. This would be something far grander.

Five of them drove to the country the following Saturday, out through the St.-Cloud tunnel to Bois d'Arcy, right for forty kilometers to Houdan and right again toward Anet on the Eure, though their destination was St.-Ouen, a village on the Vesgre, a stream feeding the Eure a few miles east of Anet. The fifth person in Philippe's Peugeot 404 was not the baby, who stayed with the grandparents, or either of Marie-France's children, who had Saturday school, but Vincent, the family cousin, whom Sophie had invited. Philippe had strapped a large folding table to the top of the car, and folding chairs plus cooler and picnic lunch prepared by Marie-France were in the trunk.

They approached the house down a one-lane country road off the two-lane Houdan-Anet road. The main building, two limestone stories covered with ivy and a partial slate roof, looked across to a small church, the only common building in the village, which was too tiny for commerce. Philippe drove into a grassy allée, through an open gate, and onto a large dirt area. The buildings formed a perfect square, like a fort, one side of the square formed by the two-story main building, with two one-story stone annexes running down each side toward the rear where they joined a row of low buildings for the animals. The rear section opened onto fields in the back, which stretched down to the valley and the Vesgre.

Archer had no trouble imagining a marvelously restored French manor with luscious lawns, guest houses running along the peripheries, sculpted hedges outside and a path through wild raspberries and crocuses down to the stream. But if what faced him was a fort, it was one that had been under heavy siege. Stones had fallen from underneath the beams supporting the roof of the main house and craterous holes in the slate showed into the upper story, where birds came and went. As for the rest of the buildings running around the square, all but one needed major structural work.

"Definitely needs some fixing-up," said Marie-France as they climbed from the car, and everyone laughed.

"You do this kind of work yourself?" Archer asked Philippe.

"Roofs, no. We'd find a local contractor. Pay cash, of course." Sophie and Vincent went off to explore the main building while the others walked to the rear and outside the walls. Vast fields of corn waved to the tree line running along the stream at the bottom of the valley. Philippe picked an ear and pulled back the husk.

"Bright yellow kernels," he said, "dry and hard. Picking season soon."

"This would have been picked a month ago in the States."

"In the States you eat corn," said Marie France. "Have you ever seen corn on a French menu? Here it's for animals, who like it dry and hard."

"We wouldn't buy the fields," said Philippe, "just the house and fifty square meters in back to make a garden. There's a path through the fields to the river."

They came back in as Sophie and Vincent emerged from the main house, Sophie in a little pink tank top and wraparound skirt looking like a schoolgirl. Vincent was scraggly as always in jeans and a sweater and the two of them might have been Sorbonne students walking through the Jardin du Luxembourg on the way to class. Archer helped Philippe and Marie-France set out the table and chairs. It was a lazy, warm summer day with a few high drifting clouds shielding the sun enough for them to have their picnic in the center of the square, away from the shadow of the main house.

"We'll have company," said Philippe. "I've invited the notary to come for lunch."

They climbed to the second story of the main building. The floors still seemed solid enough, though rain through the open roof and birds in the rafters had made a mess of things. Through a hole in the wall, Archer looked out to the yard and saw that Sophie and Vincent were gone again.

"They're asking two hundred thousand francs," said Philippe, "but I'm sure we can get it for one hundred and fifty. My rough estimate is that with another hundred thousand in restoration we can sell it in a few years for half a million, double our money."

They walked through the second story and down a second staircase. "This is why I call it a manor," said Philippe. "A farmhouse would have only one staircase. I don't know all the history, which is why I asked the notary to come by. Apparently it's been in the same family for two centuries and they're only selling because the family has no more farmers. That's the Common Market, you know – get rid of the farmers."

Philippe was a bureaucrat, a functionnaire in the French Ministry of Education, but he was an erudite man, having traveled and published articles in French travel magazines. He'd been to the States, South America, and the Far East and had served in the French Army in Algeria during the war, becoming a passionate anticolonialist. He was good with his hands, a true *bricoleur* who according to Sophie had done most of the work himself on his previous houses. But he couldn't finance an investment of $30,000 alone and, like most French, didn't like borrowing.

At the bottom of the staircase they came to a locked door. On the other end of the building there was no inside connection to the outside annexes, but on this end there was.

"Ah, yes," said Philippe, looking at the door.

"Tell Rupert about Mme. Mignon," said Marie-France. "It is so old France."

They walked outside and turned to face the house. "The notary will explain all the complications at lunch. But you see what you see."

What he saw through two front windows was a neat little one-story cottage attached to the two-story main building and cozily arranged. It gave every impression of being inhabited. Through one window was a bedroom, the bed lying under an ancient quilt, a lamp on the bedside table, a tall armoire at the rear of the room. Through the front window they saw a central table and chairs, two sitting chairs separated by lamp and table, and shelves along the rear wall with old books, bibelots, and framed pictures. The table had a lace tablecloth.

"Someone lives here," said Archer.

"Mme. Mignon," said Marie-France.

"Not exactly," said Philippe. "It's complicated, not true *rente viagère* because that allows you to buy property and only take possession when the owner dies. Here we would take full possession of all the property except the cottage of Mme. Mignon."

"Who is she?"

A car pulled in from the side gate.

"Ah, here's M. Bourdon. He will explain." Philippe left to fetch him.

"I wonder what happened to Sophie and Vincent," said Marie-France, who was setting out provisions – paté, ham, chicken, baguette, carrots, tomatoes, cheese, apples, a country feast. She handed Archer a bottle of Côte du Rhône and a corkscrew. The sun was still hidden behind the high clouds, but Marie-France, with her pale skin so unlike Sophie's, had donned a sun hat. She laid out cutlery and paper cups and opened a large bottle of Evian.

He wondered if Sophie in a few years would look anything like her sister, who, though only thirty, looked years older. Covered from neck to ankles, Marie-France wore no makeup on her pale face and kept her figure carefully hidden. Of all the de la Tour family members, she was the most conventional, most bourgeoise, staying at home, raising children, shopping each day for the midday meal. She'd never held a job nor apparently ever considered one. She lacked Sophie's spontaneity and sparkle but was sociable and well informed and Archer always learned something about France in her company. The sisters were close, but to Archer their relationship seemed more like one of an aunt and niece or mother and daughter than of two sisters.

"Still no sign of les enfants," said Marie-France. "Rupert, go out back and call them. Surely they'll hear you."

Outside the walls, he let his eyes follow the cornfields down the valley to the tree line hiding the stream that meandered to the next village. Rooftops and a single steeple poked up over the trees in the distance. A path ran between cornfields toward the stream.

"SOPHIE!" he called into the silence. "SOPHIE!"

Her name brushed the cornstalks and rode the wind through the trees and across the valley. Anyone down there would hear. There was no other sound and he called again, listening as the words faded into the silence. Nothing answered but the ripple of the breeze. Where had she gone? Why had she gone? Coming here was her idea; joining her sister in buying a maison de campagne and spending a few years fixing it up was her idea. Archer had no desire to be a French squire.

He also had no money to invest, though was sure he could get $5,000 from his mother and another $5,000 from his uncle. They'd be thrilled to make a small investment in the French countryside. If he decided to join Philippe it would not be because he had any taste or talent for home restoration or needed to escape Paris. He did not need to escape Paris. He liked Paris and in any case his job was not one that allowed him much escape. If he joined Philippe it would be for Sophie and Amy, nothing else.

M. Auguste Bourdon had driven over from Rouvres, the nearest town big enough for a notary. Dressed in black except for a nylon shirt trying to be white, he was exquisitely formal, touching on obsequious, but also extremely long-winded. Fortunately, he was also a big eater, giving the others, while he was swallowing, time to get a few words in.

He explained how he'd been chosen expressly by Mme. Mignon to represent her, which for him was a very big honor. It was also for him, he made clear, a very big deal. Larger firms, from Houdan or perhaps even Dreux, could have been brought in, but Mme. Mignon, for family reasons, preferred M. Bourdon. Archer knew from Philippe how a French notary differs from his English and American counterparts, how he is a kind of broker, agent, lawyer, escrow officer and, when needed, banker rolled into one. The house had been on the market for two years, M. Bourdon explained, or since Mme. Mignon left to take up residence in a retirement home in Anet.

"Mme. Mignon is quite happy in Anet," he said. "You need not worry she will reappear to occupy her maisonette. But she insists it remain in her name while she is still alive. I've talked to her, of course, told her how much more the house would be worth on the market if she could see her way to abandoning any claim on it. But she is adamant."

"For you it must be hard," said Marie-France.

"Oh, yes, Madame, very hard," he said, slathering paté on his baguette and visibly pleased that someone could sympathize with his predicament. "We notaries live on commissions, you know. Her attitude will cost her several thousand francs perhaps. As for me . . . well, obviously a more insignificant sum."

"I would imagine it will cost her more than several thousand francs," said Philippe. "Two years on the market is a long time. In France, the land – la terre ferme – nothing is more sacred, not even gold. It sells quickly. Surely Mme. Mignon understands that given the conditions, given the fact that she is maintaining a claim on part of the property – its only presently habitable part – she is asking too much."

M. Bourdon sighed. "Ah yes. And between you and me, I believe she is ready to come down to one hundred and fifty thousand. But no more. Anything less would be an insult."

"I don't see a problem," said Marie-France. "I quite understand why she would feel like that."

Philippe frowned. "You don't see a problem? Mme. Mignon would have every right to move back to her maisonette until the end of her life."

"Oh, no, no, monsieur," said Bourdon, quickly, "she would never do that."

"Then let's make it part of the contract," said Philippe.

"Alas, no," said the notary. "We have been over that. She insists that her frame of mind allow the possibility of her return. That's all it is – an old lady's frame of mind."

"But she *could* return at any time," said Archer.

"Monsieur, if you could see her you would not say that. She is ninety-four years old and in no state to live here again. And alone! Understand that she was born in this house and that her father and grandfather were born here. Mme. Mignon's grandfather, Eustace Plichon, was born during the reign of Louis XVI. Imagine that! Before the Revolution, and this has been a working farm since long before that. Mme. Mignon lived here alone after M. Mignon died and her sons moved to Mantes to work in the Renault plant. But she was younger then and in better health. And something else explains her attachment to her house – in name only of course: It is that all her memories are here. All of them."

"Of course," said Marie-France.

"To be frank," he went on, "it is possible she could have someone bring her by one day to peek into the cottage, perhaps one last time, to renew all those memories. But she is happy in Anet. The home is near the famous chateau and they take the residents to visit quite often. Have you been to the chateau, the former home of Diane de Poitiers?"

"Oh yes, yes," said Marie-France, enthusiastically. "Diane de Poitiers. Extraordinary woman. My parents took us through the chateau, the marvelous chapel."

"Ah yes, the chapel," said M. Bourdon, crunching on a cornichon. "What perfection! Mme. Mignon goes there quite often."

"So she is ambulatory," said Philippe.

"Only short distances," he said quickly. "Those who attend mass are driven to the chapel." The notary's glass was empty and Philippe poured more to allow him to finish his pâté. "I understand they drove them over last week to watch the film they are shooting at the chateau.

There's quite a buzz in town over it. A new James Bond film, I hear."

"I wonder what Diane de Poitiers would think," said Philippe.

"As Henri II's mistress I imagine Diane would rather like James Bond," said Marie-France, and they all laughed.

"Those were the days for mistresses," said Archer. "They got their own chateau."

"I imagine you had to be a very good mistress to get your own chateau," said the notary, reddening as he said it. "By the way, it may interest you to know that the film director Roger Vadim and his wife, Jane Fonda, have a farmhouse just up the road from here. You would be neighbors with a very famous couple. Have you seen *Barbarella*, Vadim's latest? I am something of a cinephile. Not his best but very entertaining."

"*You didn't wait . . .!*" called Sophie, erupting through the rear gate with Vincent.

"Where have you been?" said Marie-France. "Poor Rupert was shouting over the rooftops trying to find you."

They looked like they'd been on a cross-country hike. Vincent, always scraggly, looked more or less the same except for a sweater covered in what looked like corn husks, but Sophie's little wraparound skirt was half backward and her tank top was dotted with burrs and brush.

"We made it through the corn to the next village, Berchères," she said. "Look, we've got a fresh baguette. Is there any food left?"

"It looks like the birds got to your baguette," said Philippe.

"We were starving," said Sophie.

Archer was angry, glaring at his wife who studiously avoided his gaze. Her irresponsibility occasionally annoyed him, but put her together with cousin Vincent and things spilled over. It was like they were twelve-year-olds again, free to run off wherever and return in their own good time. Since Sophie wouldn't look at him he glared at Vincent, but Vincent never looked at him.

"You're out of bread," she said. "It's a good thing we bought the baguette, which was Vincent's idea."

"You'll find the boulangerie in Berchères is excellent," said M. Bourdon. "I'd say it's the best between Houdan and Anet." He smiled. "Of course, it is also the only one."

"You're angry with me, Rupert," she said when they'd returned to Paris that evening. "You haven't said two words to me all day."

Amy was bubbling over when they picked her up, so happy to be reunited with her parents. They fed her, played with her, and finally persuaded her to go to bed. Later they had a light supper and headed for bed themselves.

"I don't think your sister appreciated your disappearance any more than I did."

"Don't be silly. She's used to it."

"I'm not."

"Maybe you should be."

"What's that mean?"

"I need my independence, you know."

"You don't seem to need independence from Vincent."

"Vincent is not my husband; Vincent is my friend."

They'd showered and were getting ready for bed. "Do you realize what you just said? I am your husband but not your friend?"

"Oh, don't be obtuse, Rupert. How can you do this piece on de Gaulle if you don't understand French nuances? The same words have different meanings, you know. If I say, je t'aime, je t'aime bien, je t'aime beaucoup, they all mean different things. You have to understand these things in French. If I tell you je t'aime bien it really means I don't like you at all. If I say you are my husband and not my friend it means I sleep with you and not with him. Get it?"

She could always soften him up. He'd be angry over some outrageous thing but she'd put on a little nightie that barely reached her thighs and made her look like she was sixteen and the anger would wash away in a great wave of lust. She was not only sexy, but clever, surprising him with comments showing she knew more about what he was doing than he thought. When had he mentioned the de Gaulle article? He was keeping quiet about it because he wasn't sure he would do it, wasn't sure he *could* do it.

He'd decided to spend the next day, Sunday, at the newspaper to see if he could get anything down on paper. De Gaulle had become increasingly obstinate and impulsive in his second term, attitudes French commentators ascribed to being forced into a runoff against Mitterrand, a man he detested, the previous year. What everyone seemed to agree was that his politics had become arbitrary to the point of eccentricity. The French press was turning against him his own words about Marshal Pétain, "old age is a shipwreck," words penned years earlier in his memoirs to explain how Pétain, hero of World War I, his former mentor and godfather to his only son, Philippe, could be the same man who signed the peace treaty with Hitler.

Pétain was eighty-four when he took France out of the war against the Nazis and set up the Vichy government. De Gaulle was only seventy-five. But was there a parallel?

The day's quarrel was forgotten and when Archer slipped into bed Sophie rolled right over to him. Later, when he thought about it, he was certain that was the night she became pregnant with Christopher, their second child.

14

"What are *you* doing here?" he asked.

Helen was at her desk when he arrived Sunday morning.

"Getting away from Al."

"Saturday night on the town?"

"I wish."

Her desk was across from his in one of the *Herald*'s front wings. Built in the shape of an H, the building was an oddity to everyone but its architect. From their wing on the second floor, Helen, Archer, and the financial editors looked across an empty roof area to the offices of Connie Marshall, Al Lodge, and Sonny Stein in the opposite wing. It was the same setup for offices in the rear. The idea was to provide open space and sunlight. The reality was that the space was wasted and the sun never came in.

"The new guy?"

"Al's convinced Eppinger was brought over so Sonny could fire him."

"What do you think?"

She took off her reading glasses and looked across at him. "I don't think Eppinger has anything to do with Al. Ben Bradlee said he might send someone over who knew the *Post*'s writers. So he did."

Archer spread out his notes, took two sheets of copy paper, inserted carbon paper between them, and rolled the package into the shiny black Underwood. He glanced across the low roof to the Hotel California, tulle curtains in the rooms carefully drawn. Helen was bent over her work, smoking a Winston. He stared at the paper in the typewriter. Nothing came. He waited. He looked back at Helen and waited some more.

After awhile she looked up. Every weekday they were like this, looking across at each other, noticing when things were flowing and when they weren't. Helen had a steady stream of writers and reporters dropping off copy, phoning, arguing, complaining, pleading. Writers and editors: not a relationship made in heaven. Archer, focused, good on deadlines, could work through all of it. She wasn't used to seeing him blocked.

"You want to talk about it?"

"The French say he's out of touch. The thing is, I don't think he was ever in touch – not the way others are."

"So write that."

"But that's who de Gaulle is, incorruptible, unafraid, totally focused on the right thing. Take Algeria: The French hated him for pulling out, tried to assassinate him three times. He didn't care because he knew colonialism was over. Take Vichy: The whole nation embraced Pétain for making a deal with Hitler. Peace at last! Alone, de Gaulle flies to London. An obscure brigadier general ignored by everyone except the one guy who counts, Churchill, who looks at him and sees himself: someone who never gives up."

"Write it!"

"Nah, that's just repeating the Gaullist line. The point is . . ."

"What's the point?"

"It's this business about old age being a shipwreck. In the past de Gaulle was out of touch but he was always right. He exposed everyone's worst instincts. They hated him for it, but he was right. Eventually they had to accept it."

"Go on."

"He's still out of touch, but now he may be wrong. Opposing

NATO, fighting with Washington, recognizing Communist China, pushing the gold standard, boycotting the Common Market, signing a pact with Moscow, he's turned into a contrarian – not doing something because it's right, but because everyone else does the opposite."

"You've got your story."

"Yes, but what if he's right again? What if again he sees what no one else can? It *looks like* he's lost his touch, but how can we be sure? He's always been a prophet, a prophet with a touch of magic."

"So he hasn't lost it?"

"Maybe it's timing. Timing is everything, they say."

"For example . . . ?"

"China. Two years ago France becomes the first Western nation to recognize Communist China. Protocols are signed. Next month, Chou en Lai is supposed to visit Paris and de Gaulle will visit Beijing next year. But there's this little problem: Mao launches the Cultural Revolution and his Red Guards start killing people, hundreds of thousands of them. France has just cozied up to a government committing genocide against its own people. China is not opening up, it's shutting down."

"You can work it into a great piece."

"There's too much. It's a book – volumes."

"Boil it down. Focus on the timing angle."

He stood up. "I need to let things simmer. You interested in a walk, lunch?"

She shook her head. "You mind if I unload on you?" She lit another Winston, inhaling deeply. She hadn't come in to work as much as to escape. "I trust you, Rupert, more than anyone at this newspaper."

Another drag. A sigh. "I think Al is cracking up."

They were alone together. He felt a shiver. He remembered it from other times, other cities: Sunday mornings . . . the deathly quiet of empty newspaper buildings . . . something wrong . . . the ominous silence of the great beast asleep.

"He's been treated for depression and I think Paris saved him –

saved both of us because the last year in New York was bad. Paris turned out to be the best medicine and he's afraid of losing it. He's stopped taking his medicine."

Another drag. Smoke swirling. No sound inside or out. Paris still quiet.

"Sonny sees it and doesn't like it. Sonny doesn't like aberrations. Al gets through the day on sheer willpower. It's worse when Sonny's here. Sonny can't delegate. Both of them work better alone. Since Sonny's not going anywhere, Al thinks he's the one."

She'd had a rough night, red hair in perfect loops accenting the fatigue of the face. They could have used a cup of coffee, but the Berri Bar didn't open until four.

"Depression is a weird thing, Rupert, like migraines only worse. You're fine until it hits and then you're afraid it won't go. That's the horrible thing – you just don't know. With migraines it can be a day or days. With depression you just don't know. We've been married eight years and it's not like I haven't seen it before, just not in Paris. The worst thing is when they start hating their medications, start thinking it's better to live with their true selves, even depressive selves, than be turned into someone else. It becomes a personal test: I will endure this awful thing until it goes away."

"Anything I can do?"

She shook her head, not interested in commentary. "He's on at four. You're coming back"

"Can I bring you anything?"

"Thanks. When the B. B. opens I'll call down."

He walked down avenue George V, thoughts on Al Lodge. Paris in August: hot and empty. At the Pont des Invalides he turned up the avenue Franklin Roosevelt. He liked how the French honored foreign greats with streets and monuments – Wilson, Roosevelt, Eisenhower, Kennedy, Churchill. No avenue Charles de Gaulle in Washington. Even Roosevelt had his Paris avenue: Roosevelt, who recognized the foul Vichy regime and opposed de Gaulle to the point that Churchill and Eisenhower thought him obsessed.

His thoughts switched to de Gaulle, such a juicy target in America, right up there with Ho and Mao. The columnists called him a dupe of the communists, a change from the Roosevelt days when he was labeled a fascist. The exception was Walter Lippmann, who'd moved to the *Washington Post* when the *Herald Tribune* folded and now ran twice weekly in the *Paris Herald*. Lippmann understood de Gaulle's greatness.

He headed back up the Champs Elysées to Fouquet's, ordering ham and cheese on baguette and a demi beer. The next day he'd take Sophie and Amy to Gare Montparnasse, direction Saint-Malo. He knew he couldn't write the story Helen wanted. He needed more evidence that de Gaulle, like Pétain, was a shipwreck. He didn't believe it.

The beast was just coming awake when he was back, grumbling, rubbing its eyes, not quite ready for the new day. In the newsroom a half dozen people were at their places with coffee and cigarettes, settling in with war – in Vietnam, cold war in Europe, civil war in Indonesia, cultural war in China, the brink of war in the Middle East. He missed the newsroom. It was the first time on any newspaper he'd worked in a separate place, away from the organized confusion of a newsroom. Real writers work better off by themselves – Flaubert in *solitude sombre*, Proust in his cork-lined room on boulevard Haussmann; Balzac around the corner on rue Balzac. He wasn't that kind of a writer. Reporters need the rhythm of a newsroom, the heart and soul of the beast.

Al was alone at the editor's desk. Trouble with Al was you couldn't tell his good days from his bad ones. Skull head, horn-rims, slicked-back hair, pale lips, steely look, cigarette, nothing changed. To Archer he didn't look any worse than Helen, maybe no worse than anyone looked in Paris after a heavy Saturday night.

"Have a look," he said, pushing a small pile of copy toward him.

The top story was from the French News Agency. A group of Chinese from the Paris embassy had tried to rush a Chinese national, described as "nearly unconscious," past police controls at Orly Airport onto a Pakistani Airlines plane leaving for Shanghai via Cairo and Karachi. The Chinese showed their diplomatic passports, said the man was an employee of the embassy in Algiers, was ill, brought to Paris for treatment and they had to get him home to Shanghai. Emergency please, chop-chop. When airport police smelled something fishy, the Chinese formed a flying wedge to rush past controls, shouting "Fascists!" Police relieved them of the man and took him to the hospital Hôtel-Dieu. Instant international incident.

"What do you think?"

"Maybe the guy doesn't like the Cultural Revolution."

"Can you get something?"

"I can try."

He caught a taxi to the Hôtel-Dieu on the Ile de la Cité and found a handful of colleagues waiting behind a police barrier. "Press conference at the Quai d'Orsay at six," someone said. Archer walked to a café on the rue d'Arcole and telephoned Lodge, saying he'd be back before seven with something. It was just after five. Looked like a good story. He drank another demi beer and decided to walk to the foreign ministry.

"The man's name is Chang Shi-jung and he is of Chinese nationality," announced Charles de la Bellefontaine, who'd returned by helicopter from his country home. Obviously this was more than a routine counselor matter. "M. Chang is resting. I'll have nothing more until he awakens."

"Was he drugged, Charles?" was the first question.

"The medical report is that he was sedated, yes."

"Was he being taken aboard against his will?"

"Alas, gentlemen – until he is recovered, you understand . . ."

"Why was he sedated, why was he struggling?"

Bellefontaine looked down at his notes. "The police had reason to believe that he did not wish to board the plane."

That was the lead, and Archer saw one of the two AFP reporters rise and quickly leave the room.

"So he was a defector?"

Bellefontaine grimaced at the word. "I've told you what the police said. The man was sedated and struggling with his companions. That's all we know at this point. We've sent a translator. He will be interviewed as soon as he's awake."

"Will we be allowed to interview him?" asked Archer.

Bellefontaine hesitated. "I'd have to say that I doubt it. The man is an employee of the Chinese embassy in Algiers, a technician, a junior employee. It's up to his superiors, not the French government whether he meets with the press."

"Not if he's a defector," said the AFP man. "If he's a defector it will be up to him, not the Chinese embassy, am I not right?"

"You're jumping to conclusions, Jean. I'll let you know when I have something more. It won't be before tomorrow."

"It looks like the police and foreign ministry are not on the same page."

Bellefontaine stiffened. "The police did their job. We will do ours."

Back at the newspaper, Sonny had taken over. "It smells," said Archer. "It's a good bet the guy wants to defect. Problem is that de Gaulle's China policy is at risk if France grants him asylum. Big debate going on I suspect."

Wednesday morning, sometime before dawn, three limousines arrived at the Hôtel-Dieu and Mr. Chang Shi-jung was rushed to Orly where he departed French territory. The news agencies, staked out at the hospital, alerted their correspondents at Orly, but the limousines drove straight onto the tarmac. At noon, the Foreign Ministry put out a short statement saying that after interviewing Mr. Chang Shi-jung, the French government was satisfied that he wished to return to China.

The French Foreign Ministry on the Quai d'Orsay is an enormous Second Empire building of five visible stories with labyrinthine passageways running over miles of worn beige carpet over creaky floorboards along which are clustered hundreds of offices all containing people with some responsibility for the foreign affairs of France. Sometimes it is a very small responsibility – third secretaries looking after relations with Lesotho or Paraguay and clerks typing up their reports. Sometimes it is a large responsibility, a bureau headed by a ministre-plénipotentiaire who has been ambassador to that country and has aspirations for something higher. Though the government alone is responsible for foreign policy, not everyone along the passageways necessarily agrees with the government. Some are more than willing to add their two cents, though of course, never officially. To whom they are willing to pay their two cents depends on what audience they wish to reach and how much trust they have in the person they are paying.

Along one of those passageways sat a man, neither a third secretary nor a ministre-plénipotentiaire, but someone who read the cables, knew the facts, and knew Rupert Archer. Armand Damrémont was the man's name, and Thursday morning, after reading Archer's story about the disappearance of Chang Shi-jung, he called and invited Archer for a drink at the Café de Commerce on the boulevard St.-Germain.

"Raisons d'état," said Damrémont as they sat over demi beers. "Mr. Chang Shi-jung was sent back to China for reasons of state. He did not wish to return home. He said they would kill him or make him a slave laborer and he asked for asylum in France. He was refused. I will say no more. Draw your own conclusions."

He rose and turned to go. "You can say you learned it from reliable sources. I will say no more. Au revoir, M. Archer."

"One thing, Monsieur. May I ask why you are telling me this?"

The diplomat looked down at him. "I will answer your question with one of my own. Is France not the birthplace of the Declaration of the Rights of Man?"

The story ran Friday, on the front page over four columns:

THE TRUTH BEHIND THE CHANG SHI-JUNG AFFAIR
FRANCE DENIES ASYLUM TO DRUGGED DEFECTOR
by Rupert Archer

It was an exclusive, and when Archer arrived at the newspaper Friday morning Connie came over to say he was wanted in Ben Swart's office. Sonny had already gone up. "They've been summoned to the Quai d'Orsay."

He took the three flights two stairs at a time, greeted Martine Treuherz who told him to go in. He'd not been there before. Swart did not ask him to sit down.

"What do I tell them?" said Sonny.

"Whom are you seeing?"

"M. Cambronne, the undersecretary."

"A bear. Not friendly to us. Tell him the information came from reliable sources."

"You want to tell me who?"

"You want to know?"

Stein considered it. "Any doubt whatsoever?"

"No."

"You think Cambronne will deny it?"

"He'd be lying."

Behind his desk, Swart watched them like at a tennis match, eyes moving back and forth. "You know, Rupert, this could hurt us. We have friends in the government, people working to help us."

He hardly knew Ben Swart at all, but why would he? Even for something like this Swart stayed off the second floor. Seeing him up close, he looked younger than he was, probably fifty, Archer thought. Good-looking man, obviously stayed in shape. Being divorced was the scuttlebutt, something about his secretary. What else is new?

"Can't let that affect the news, Ben," said Stein.

"Of course not. It's just that – well, the timing. It's inconvenient."

"The news is often inconvenient."

"I gather that M. Cambronne has not requested my presence," said Archer.

"He has not," said Swart.

Turning to leave, Archer had a thought. "I said Cambronne would be lying if he denied it. There's another possibility. He could be out of the loop."

"So which is it?" said Stein.

Archer hesitated. "They hate lying, you know. It's so vulgar."

Henri de Saint-Gaudens sat in his office under Delacroix's superb depiction of Apollo slaying Python, on loan from the Louvre. He gazed out over the Elysée gardens, still lush green in the waning days of summer. His eyes came back inside, settling on the photo of his wife, Eleanor, surrounded by children and grandchildren on the lawn by their chateau in Saint-Gaudens, where his family had lived for centuries, and where Henri, like so many of his ancestors, served as mayor. There were previous Augusts in the service of the General when he'd spent the entire month in Saint-Gaudens, surrounded by family and friends, enjoying the air off the Pyrenees that cools the valleys of Haute-Garonne. This was not to be one of them. The General was restless, and when he was restless he stayed in the capital during the week, even in August.

He waited to be buzzed in. Arriving that morning, de Gaulle had smiled. "Eh bien, Saint-Gaudens, here we are, alone again, as in London."

He'd smiled back. "Oui, mon Général."

That was forty minutes ago. Though the capital was empty, the General was keeping to his regular schedule, convoking the council of ministers Wednesday afternoon and not planning to leave the city until late Friday. With the affair of the Chinese defector, the week had been unusually busy for August. The matter had not been discussed by the council of ministers. Instead, the General had summoned the prime minister, foreign minister, and interior minister to the privacy of his office and the five of them (Saint-Gaudens naturally remaining) resolved the matter quickly and without dissent.

Raisons d'état. French foreign policy has not changed since Richelieu, thought Saint-Gaudens. Was that not why newspaper cartoons depicted the General in ermine robes – to compare him with the ancien regime? He thought of de Gaulle's words to the rebel generals who defied him over Algeria: "The war is over, messieurs. France's destiny no longer coincides with that of the French Algerians."

Raisons d'état. Salutes. Au revoir, messieurs.

De Gaulle didn't read newspapers. He had too much contempt for them, contempt that went back to the 1930s and fights between socialists and fascists as France drifted into anarchy and Germany rearmed. At Liberation he'd thrown his weight behind a new newspaper, *Le Monde*, owned by its journalists and free of partisan agendas. Hubert Beuve-Méry, who'd fought the Germans and joined the Resistance, became editor and twenty years later still remained in the job. Now even Beuve-Méry had turned against him. Occasionally the General read one of Beuve's essays to stay up on what the intellectuals were saying, but most of his news came from television, which remained under government control. Often when Saint-Gaudens was called in for the morning briefing he noticed the pile of newspapers he'd left for the General still untouched.

This morning was different. Saint-Gaudens had carefully laid the *Paris Herald*, with its story about the Chinese defector, on top. Unlike the French newspapers, the *Herald* revealed that M. Chang Shi-jung was a defector who had been denied asylum. Saint-Gaudens knew all about the *Herald* story. It was he who called Armand Damrémont at the Quai d'Orsay, who'd served under him in so many posts, and asked him to meet with the reporter. "Are you sure, Henri?" Damrémont had asked. "I am sure, Armand," was the reply and no more was said. Both men knew that Saint-Gaudens never had, never would, never could, take an action against the interests of France.

The buzzer sounded. He gathered up his dossiers and went

toward the gilded double doors at the rear of his office, next to the Delacroix painting. He knocked and went in, seeing immediately that the *Herald* was the only newspaper displaced from the pile. The General looked up as he entered and tapped the newspaper. "You've seen this story, Saint-Gaudens? There has been a leak."

"Oui, mon Général," he said, sitting down.

For his cabinet ministers and most of France, Charles de Gaulle was "Monsieur le Président," but for those who'd served with him from the beginning he would always be simply, "mon Général." The two men had been together so long there was a familiarity between them that de Gaulle had with few others. All those others, without exception, had joined him and the Free French in London. As Churchill would write of the plane that brought de Gaulle, alone, from Bordeaux to London on June 16, 1940: "De Gaulle carried with him, in this small airplane, the honor of France."

Four months later, October 23, 1940, a day he would never forget, Lieutenant Henri de Saint-Gaudens was summoned to St. Stephen's House, where the Free French were installed across from the House of Commons, for his first meeting with de Gaulle. That night he would be dropped into German-occupied France with instructions for the FFI, the internal resistance. De Gaulle stood to greet him as he entered the room. "Good day, lieutenant," he said. They shook hands. "It is an important mission you undertake tonight. If you die you will have died for France. Au revoir, lieutenant."

They joked about it sometimes. De Gaulle had a whimsical sense of humor born of keen observation, an encyclopedic memory, and sharp wit. He rarely displayed it in public. The French people, he said, prefer a leader with a sense of mystery, not a sense of humor. One place he did use it was in his private meetings with Saint-Gaudens.

He ran a hand across his eyes. He was myopic, his eyes watered, and in private he often dried them with his fingers. Soon he would turn seventy-six, a massive man with that extraordinary head and a name perfect for a leader sprung from the fertile soil of eternal France: a unique name, the man of Gaul.

"Inevitable, I suppose," he said, staring at the newspaper.

"I believe so, mon Général."

The slightest hint of a smile appeared on the General's expressive lips. "It serves our purposes, though, doesn't it, Saint-Gaudens? I suppose I don't have to tell you that."

"Non, mon Général."

"I don't suppose you know anything about it."

His eyes went to the brilliant tapestry behind de Gaulle, an unsigned Gobelins execution of the battle of Tours, Charles Martel with slashing sword cutting down the Sarazens. At first he'd thought it an odd choice, for the General received many Muslim leaders. But for de Gaulle, Franks defeating Muslims seeking to invade Europe represented the very basis of his philosophy: each people, each nation, in its time and place, free to carry on its affairs without interference. The Arabs had no more right to Europe than Europeans had to Arab lands. Saint-Gaudens laughed at those who compared de Gaulle to Napoleon. He was the anti-Bonaparte.

"It does not hurt the world to know there are those in France who still believe individual rights take precedence over those of the state," said Saint-Gaudens. "I suppose that's why the leak was to the *Herald*."

"So the world would know, eh?"

"I believe so."

Their eyes spoke more than words. "It is a balance, Saint-Gaudens, is it not?"

"Oui, mon Général."

"A balance that, a priori, must tip toward the state."

"Toward the people."

"Yes, the state is no more than the sum total of its people."

"That is the point."

"Why can't the communists understand that? Mao is crushing his people."

"You're still hoping to visit China?"

He shook his head. "Impossible, but the invitation to Chou en-Lai is already extended." He was looking out the window. Saint-Gaudens wondered what those tired old eyes could see. Colors only? Vague shapes? He didn't like wearing glasses. "This Cultural Revolution, as they call it, changes everything. Will Mao still let Chou come? Perhaps we should have let the defector stay."

"But we couldn't, could we?"

The General sighed. "Alas."

Saint-Gaudens let a moment pass before pointing to the open newspaper. "I'm told those in charge at the *Paris Herald* have been summoned to the foreign ministry."

"Why would Couve do that?"

"I don't believe it was the foreign minister, mon Général."

"Who then?"

"Cambronne."

"Ah, Cambronne, of course."

"Great-great-grandson of Napoleon's general."

"If he is as loyal as his ancestor we have nothing to fear. Wounded at Waterloo."

"Ran off with his Scottish nurse."

The General smiled. "Couve explained to Cambronne what was decided?"

"I do not believe so."

"Ah, and so Cambronne believes the Chinese returned home voluntarily?"

"I believe so."

"And so will ask the Americans for a retraction?"

"I believe so."

"Will ask them to retract the truth?"

"Oui, mon Général."

"Which they, of course, will not do."

"Oui, mon Général."

Saint-Gaudens observed the General softly chuckling. "You're quite sure Couve said nothing?"

"Quite sure, mon Général."

"We will see if Cambronne is as good a soldier as his great-great-grandfather."

Ben Swart and Sonny Stein hailed the cab as it came down the rue de Berri. It was not a long ride to the foreign ministry, just across the Seine at Invalides, but with one-way streets they were leaving a half hour early to be sure. The appointment with M. Cambronne was for 11:30.

"What do you hear from across town?" asked Stein, settling onto the cracked seat of a worn-out old Peugeot 304.

"Syd Gruson apparently spends all day on the phone to New York."

"I doubt they're talking about the Yankees – not this year."

"Le Tac's trying to get information on their advertising. He thinks they're giving space away, padding figures."

"By the way, Ben, Joe Marder's leaving. Did I tell you?"

"First I heard of it."

"I'm moving Mike Eppinger into his spot."

The taxi drove down Faubourg St.-Honoré, heading for the avenue de Marigny. They'd been told to enter the rear of the Quai d'Orsay, closer to the ministers' offices in the huge building. On Marigny they turned south toward the Seine.

"How's he working out?"

"Top notch – could easily step in for Al Lodge."

"Eppinger will be under Lodge, correct?"

Stein was silent, looking into the shops along avenue Marigny. It still amazed him how everything could shutter up for an entire month. In effect, the French fiscal year covered only eleven months. "I'm wondering if Al doesn't need a leave of absence."

"Why?"

"I don't think he's well, Ben. He's rattled."

Swart turned to face him. "*Rattled?*"

"I have trouble working with him."

"Just bear in mind, Sonny – this is France. You can't put people on leave of absence just because you have trouble working with them."

They announced themselves in a small office off the rue de l'Université and waited to be called. Nothing impressive about the back door of the Quai d'Orsay. The front door was pillared, arched and gilded, but the front door was not for them.

Escorted upstairs to a waiting room, they sat in stuffed, worn chairs, nothing like the elegance of the Elysée Palace. After a wait long enough to make the point, they were ushered in to meet Jean-Yves Cambronne, ministre d'état, chargé des affaires étrangères.

Cambronne advanced to shake hands and bid his guests sit down. He returned to his desk, quickly established they did not speak French well enough to proceed and switched to English. A copy of the *Paris Herald* lay open and he held it up.

"Forgive me, gentlemen, if I come right to the point. We are all pressed for time. This story you have printed is nothing less than an insult to France. No other newspaper has written anything comparable. How dare you print such lies? It is an outrage."

It was to Stein to answer the charges, but the minister cut him off before he spoke. "Do you have something against France? Do you really think you can live as guests in our country and print such lies? Had this been printed in a French language publication we already would have brought charges under Article Thirty-Six of the press law. You're familiar with Article Thirty-Six, I presume."

Their looks showed that any familiarity with Article Thirty-Six was not intimate.

"Article Thirty-Six deals with insults to the nation and its representatives," said the deputy foreign minister, not concealing his exasperation.

"We printed the truth," said Stein.

"The *truth*? That France, birthplace of the Declaration of the Rights of Man, would deny asylum to a political refugee? That is not the truth; it is a lie and an insult."

"Mr. Chang Shi-jung sought asylum in France and was denied," said Stein.

"Outrageous! Do you really want us to prosecute you, M. Stein?"

"How can you prosecute us for printing the truth?"

Cambronne picked up the newspaper. "'Reliable sources,' I read here. Who are these reliable sources?"

"You don't really think . . ."

"How can you call them reliable when they lied to you? Whoever leaked this story to your reporter – assuming of course that he did not invent it – is a liar and an enemy of France."

Swart did not like being ignored. He also was curious. What was the source of the deputy foreign minister's outrage? The Gaullist Party, the foreign minister, the Elysée, the General himself? "Perhaps it is you, sir," he ventured, "who is misinformed."

The deputy foreign minister turned to Swart, who for some reason irritated him more than Stein. Cambronne not only had the manner of a bully, with none of the finicky fastidiousness associated with diplomacy and the Quai d'Orsay, he was also physically intimidating, ruddy and solid, with the build of a rugby player.

"It is a pity that we cannot deal with journalists like you as we deal with diplomats who are unfriendly to France – by declaring them persona non grata – though come to think of it, perhaps it's only because it's never been done. You understand of course that your newspaper operates in France by our indulgence."

"We have been in France since 1887," said Swart, reddening and rising to the challenge. "It is both an honor and a privilege to be guests in your nation. But as a newspaper, we have our job to do. Surely you understand that."

"And we have our job to do, too, sir, a job based on French law.

Are you familiar with French libel law? It is quite different from Anglo-Saxon libel law."

"The truth is not libel," said Stein.

"That is where you are wrong, sir. Even if these lies were true, which they are not, under French libel law truth is not always a defense. You cannot slander someone – or by extension, slander the nation – just because something might be true."

"We have not slandered anyone," said Stein.

"Ah, but you have – and for that there must be reparation."

"*Reparation?* said Swart, dumbfounded.

"We would like you to print a clarification."

"What is there to clarify?"

"It must be made clear that France is the champion of the universal rights of man; that we have always offered asylum to the persecuted of other nations. We would never force anyone to return to a country where he could be persecuted for political reasons. We respect the rights of political refugees. It is our vocation."

"I would see no problem publishing a short commentary written by you to make those points," said Stein.

"But it is you who must make the clarification," said Cambronne, vigorously.

"We will not publish a retraction," said Swart.

The deputy foreign minister fell silent, considering his options, turning to look out a window into the courtyard, noticing a pigeon on the ledge across the way. Couve naturally had the view onto the Seine and the city. "We will not close your newspaper," he announced. "We have that right, of course, but it is not our intention – not at this time. You will not, however, be allowed to continue to violate our laws." He stood up. "You have been warned. We will be watching you. Good day, gentlemen."

He rang, and a woman came in to fetch them.

"Oh yes," he said, as they turned to go. "We will write the commentary you suggested. Please leave the information with my secretary as to whom it should be addressed. We will write it in English and I trust you will publish it immediately."

They couldn't wait to get downstairs and into the fresh air.

"My God," said Stein, "what an ass."

"I wonder if he knows Henri de Saint-Gaudens," said Swart.

16

Sonny Stein laid down the receiver and called for Connie. "Shut the door."

"No one here."

"Shut it anyway."

Connie Marshall had become an attractive woman. She'd always had the essentials: a lithe, girlish figure, short blond hair, and the kind of angular face and high *pommettes* admired in Paris, where pug noses and dimples aren't as appreciated as at home. As far as the essentials went – face, coiff, body – some said she reminded them of Jean Seberg, stripped down as she was to play Joan of Arc. When she'd arrived in Paris Connie had that same stripped down look, no makeup, not much done to the hair besides washing it, baggy flannels perfect for the town square in Bennington, Vermont, her hometown, but that didn't do much on the Champs Elysées. They didn't even do much on the Pletzl, the Jewish quarter of Paris where she lived. She was Bennington in Europe.

"That was Walter Lippmann," he said.

"I know."

"He's coming to Paris to see de Gaulle."

"And you're giving a party for him."

"You read my mind."

"I listened in."

He didn't care. She knew everything. She'd showed up one day out of the blue and he'd hired her on the basis of her French, a decent résumé, and the good luck to show up two days after his previous secretary quit. It worked out in more ways than one.

"We're old friends, met at *Herald Trib*. Secular newspaper Jews."

"We'll use the Lancaster. Or if you want something bigger, the George V."

"Oh, no. Helen would hate that."

"Helen?"

"Walter's wife. She's particular. Wouldn't like a hotel."

"So?"

"My house."

"With Rachel?"

He didn't answer right away. It still all seemed so strange to him. Four years ago he was a shirt-sleeved city editor at the *Herald Tribune* living in Roslyn with his wife of twenty years, taking the Long Island Railway to work and for going to Manny's on Forty-Fourth Street for pastrami and pickles. Now he wore three-piece pinstripes, was invited to the Elysée Palace, lunched at Taillevent and Lasserre, and lived with a twenty-seven-year-old blonde from Bennington in a third-floor walkup in the Pletzl. Inside he was the same guy. Rachel still occupied their house on the rue Vaugirard, refusing to return to New York. She knew about Connie and couldn't imagine it would last. That was two years ago.

"Yes, with Rachel."

"So you go back to her for parties."

"Look, Connie, what can I do? I owe this to Walter. He expects it. It'll be a *Herald Tribune* reunion."

"He knows Rachel?"

"Of course he doesn't know Rachel. How in hell would he know Rachel? That's not the point. I can't very well throw a big party in your apartment."

He watched her pale face darken. He still didn't understand her, why she was attracted to him. At first he thought it was because she liked taking care of people, but she wasn't the motherly type. Through the rough times with Rachel, Connie remained blasé to the point of indifference, unable to understand his conflict or empathize with the woman whose marriage she was breaking up. Her attitude was simple: make up your mind, buster – who gives you more? She saw Rachel and her thick legs as an embarrassment to Sonny and to the *Herald* and had no problem taking her place.

"November, right? Who's coming?"

"That's what we have to decide. I think everyone on this floor should be invited."

"Does that include me?"

That surprised him. "You *want* to come?"

"Of course I want to come."

Goys, he thought – so goddamn different. That wasn't news but until he lived with one he had no idea how different they were. She'd been raised a Congregationalist and had an uncle who still preached somewhere in Vermont. Congregationalists are independent, she said, each congregation runs things as it wants. To a Jew, even a secular one, religion is the opposite of independence. Religion unifies.

"Come to a party hosted by my wife? You would put me through that?"

"You bet I'm coming. Sorry, but you're not going to hide the woman you're living with."

"No, but do we have to advertise it?"

He turned to watch Helen Lodge walk into an empty office in the wing across the way. Helen was Rachel's friend. He wondered how much of what Rachel knew came from Helen, one more reason to get the Lodges packing. She looked over and waved.

"OK, so you're coming. Now who else? Walter and Helen like celebrities, which means we'll ask Couve de Murville . . ."

"Who won't come – so invite your friend Mr. Cambronne."

"Who hates Americans – perfect."

"So, maybe he'll change his mind."

"Good point. Lippmann loves de Gaulle."

"And we'll invite your Elysée friend, M. Saint-Gaudens."

"Definitely. And the ambassador and *chargé* – and Cy Sulzberger from the *Times*, all the U.S. bureau chiefs, some French editors. Walter will like that."

"What about Sydney Gruson?" she asked.

"*Gruson?* We want the *Times* at this party? This is supposed to be a *Herald Tribune* reunion."

"Cy Sulzberger is the *Times*."

"That's different. Cy and Walter are columnists, veterans of foreign wars so to speak, old antagonists. They enjoy hating each other."

"You don't like Gruson, do you?"

"It's a *Herald Tribune* party, damn it!"

"Back to Gruson . . ."

"After Kay Graham threw down the gauntlet at the Lancaster – I don't think it's a good idea."

"So no Gruson."

"What about Ben? You going to tell him or shall I call Martine?"

"I'll tell him. He'll hate the cost, but it'll be worth it. Be good for the *Herald*."

"Why don't I call Lippmann at the *Post*, see if there's anyone in particular he wants."

"Good idea. You'll get his secretary, who'll call Helen."

Toward the end of August, Archer returned to St.-Ouen. Alone. Philippe had hired a local handyman to work on the roof, but handymen, too, vacation in August, and the only change in the roof was that a large piece of plastic now covered the main hole. The ground floor was better. They'd put in windows, done some plastering, and had the kitchen working. They'd found an old bathtub with porcelain paws and had a water heater installed. In a rudimentary way, the house was livable. They'd begun laying paving stones from the gate to the kitchen and Archer planned to get a few more down so they'd have a solid path before the fall rains arrived. He stopped in Houdan and bought groceries. He had books and newspapers and planned to stay the weekend.

He'd never been alone before at the house. Usually Sophie or Marie-France invited friends who would arrive just in time for pastis and lunch on Saturday and then the afternoon was shot and Archer kept thinking how much more they'd get done if they were alone. So now he was alone and it felt funny. He worked all day and then washed up. He poured a glass of red wine and took a chair outside to enjoy the summer evening and admire his work. For dinner there was ham, cheese, lettuce, tomatoes, and baguette, everything fresh, the kind of French food he loved. No animal insides. No sauces.

He sipped his wine, sat listening to the silent sounds of the countryside and contemplating his French life. Soon he stood, loaded the car, locked up and left for Paris.

It was nearly eleven when he arrived at La Calavados, slipped his VW between two black Mercedes beside the Hotel George V across the street and took his place on the barstool closest to the door, where Eddie Jones used to sit. He ordered a sandwich and beer and settled in for a night of Joe Turner's stride piano. Turner tended to stay near the piano even on his breaks, accepting drinks, sliding over to a nearby side table if a musician he knew showed up and wanted to try his chops.

When Turner spied him he waved him up. He'd moved to the side table to join a small black man with small hands and a slick mustache. He introduced Errol Garner. Archer ordered three *fines*. Someone came up to get autographs.

"I'm trying to get him to play. Guys come in all week and want to play. The horns all think they can play piano. Most of them can't. Charlie Shavers, there's an exception. And Milt Jackson. So now I get a real piano player and he won't play."

"Haven't touched a piano in a week," said Garner. "Just tooling around. I ended up down at les Halles the other night. Late, all by myself. That's the way I do things. Now I'm thinking of maybe flying to Vienna. Why not? Just like I went to Barcelona last year. Just get on a plane and go. Don't tell anybody. They find out anyway. They even had me on a television show before I got out of there."

Turner eyed Archer. "I'm stuck here until two. You know all the joints, man. Why don't you show Errol around?"

"I could do that."

"You know what I'd like to see," said the little man, "one of those French go-go places, you know, the discothèques you hear about."

"The hot one is called La Boite, on the rue Mazarine, not far from where Memphis Slim plays. You want to hear Slim?"

"Heard Slim the other night."

"OK, we'll go to La Boite. You mind a Volkswagen?"

He laughed. "I fit in everything."

Turner went back to the piano and they heard a series of lightning arpeggios on Honeysuckle Rose. "Hey, Tatum," Garner called as they turned to leave. "Not so fast."

He would go over that night many times. It wasn't just how it ended, but how it began. He'd gone to St.-Ouen for a quiet weekend on the first piece of real estate he'd ever owned. Something drove him away, drove him back to Paris and into the clubs. He didn't like the French countryside. He probably didn't like any countryside. He was a city boy. More than that he was a newspaperman, and there are no newspapers in the country.

The problem was that Sophie loved the country. He hadn't known it when he married her. Soon they'd have their second child in three years and she'd still be only twenty-four. Though they'd moved from the cramped quarters on the Place St.-Ferdinand into a spacious Left Bank flat on the rue du Four, Sophie wasn't happy in Paris. She was happy in places like Saint-Malo and St.-Ouen. She didn't think big cities were right for children.

Archer pointed the VW down avenue George V to the quai,

crossed at the Pont Concorde and headed up the boulevard St.-Germain toward the rue Seine. Garner was bubbly, a talker, a chatterer. He was from Pittsburgh and started talking about the Pittsburgh musicians he'd known over the years – Earl Hines and Roy Eldridge and Art Blakely – "lot of guys came out of Pittsburgh. Eldridge lived in Paris for a while, you know that? Lot of guys, like Joe and Slim, came over here to stay. I never could see it. I like tooling around Europe. But the clubs, the hot clubs, that's the States."

He parked on the rue Seine and they walked to the rue Mazarine. Like Garner, Archer had never been to a French discothèque. Why would he? The music was neither live nor jazz. He'd been to one in Berlin, in Dahlem where the GIs went, a go-go discothèque where girls showed up in short-shorts and knee-high boots and wiggled to the frug and the mule. He was surprised that Garner, who could have gone to the Blue Note to hear Kenny Clarke or Chat qui Pêche to hear Stèphane Grappelli or the St.-Germain to hear Martial Solal would be interested. Did the little man dance?

Outside, a few people queued in front of the booth where a woman was selling tickets. A red padded door with a window opened and shut to admit those who'd paid. Garner hung back while Archer approached. A sign said fifty francs entry fee. The discothèques billed themselves as private to keep out rowdies, but they weren't rowdies and it didn't occur to him to show his press credentials. He asked for two admissions. The woman shook her head. "You, yes, your friend, no," she said.

"What?"

"You OK – not your friend."

"What are you saying?"

"You heard what I said – now pay or get out of line."

A face behind a pane in the padded door watched. The door opened. "A problem?" He was young, burly, and not smiling.

"I'm trying to buy tickets."

"This is a private club. Are you members?"

The man glanced at Garner, insignificant in dark suit and tie.

"Do you know who that is?" said Archer, angrily. "That is Errol Garner."

The man looked again and his eyes showed recognition. So did those of others in line. Anyone who knew anything about jazz anywhere knew the name Errol Garner. No jazz musician played more, recorded more, traveled more or was more popular than the little man in the dark suit, the man with the small hands and the perfect ear, self-taught, the man refused entry into the Pittsburgh musicians' union because he couldn't read music and now refused entry into a Paris discothèque where they apparently didn't want little black men dancing with leggy white *ye-ye* girls.

"Ah, Mr. Errol Garner, you are our guest," he cooed in English. "Come with me."

Garner was already walking away.

They walked in silence to the car. What could he say – apologize for the French being as racist as Americans? Back in the car he headed down the rue de Seine, dark, narrow, one-way street leading to the river. He was angry and embarrassed and sped along until his headlights caught a car parked, abandoned apparently, in the middle of the street. He braked quickly, holding out his arm so Garner didn't fly forward.

Still Garner said nothing. This chirpy man had not said a word since being refused at the club and now was stuck with a strange man on a strange street in a strange situation in a strange country. Archer was ready to back up along the dark street when he spied a space along the curb ten yards ahead. Why hadn't the driver taken it? It was a small, dark Renault 4. If it was open he could release the hand brake and push it to the curb. He walked up to it and opened the door.

He saw immediately it was not a normal car, slammed the door, and turned back toward the bug. It was a police car, and the shouting figures running from the surrounding buildings left no doubt about it.

Archer's press credentials made no difference to these cops, nor did the name Errol Garner. They had to show what happened to people who tried to push Paris police cars off the street. They put Garner in the Renault, a policeman climbed into the Volkswagen with Archer, and they drove to the commissariat on the rue de l'Abbaye.

It was cleared up in minutes. The sergeant in charge, who knew American jazz, promised to pay a personal visit to La Boite. After all, France was the birthplace of the Declaration of the Rights of Man, was it not? As for the car in the street, it was on police business. Naturally his agents would have taken the empty space had it been there when they arrived.

Back in the car on the way to La Calavados, Garner began talking again.

"Some of the cats worry more about that stuff than I do. They say there's less of it over here and maybe there is, but it still exists. It is a state of mind. I just go about my business. If people don't want me around I don't want to be around them either. Plenty of people want me around. That's good enough for me. Maybe I'll play a little for Joe tonight."

Archer put it all in his column. For once, the States didn't look so bad. Racism was international.

17

Sydney Gruson was in a foul mood. Everyone who mattered in le tout Paris had been at the party for Walter Lippmann. Cy Sulzberger came into the office the next morning bubbling over with accounts of the snappy repartee between him and Lippmann. "First-rate party at Sonny's house, Syd. Where were you? Ha-ha."

Why would they have done that, he wondered? Why would they specifically have left me off a guest list like that? Raymond Aron was there, for God's sake, and Jean-Jacques Servan-Schreiber and even André Malraux put in an appearance. It was a terrible slight. Who was responsible – Swart? He'd have no reason. Lippmann wouldn't have done it. He'd almost had Lippmann for the *Times* before Whitney bribed him away, convinced him he should be writing for Republicans instead of preaching to the choir. That left Sonny Stein. Stein would have done the guest list because Stein knew Lippmann from the *Herald Tribune*. There would be a reckoning.

He sank down deeper into the devouring velvet of the Citroën DS. The party wasn't the only thing that ruined his mood. "Call Swart," Sam Hecht had said on the phone. "Feel him out, plant the seed, see if they're ready."

"Why here, Sam? New York's where the deal will be done. Invite Thayer to the Century Club and do it over martinis."

"Punch wants to do it this way, OK."

Why the icy tone? But of course! Punch wanted *him*, Syd Gruson, in on it, which was why Hecht was touchy. "Right, Sam, right. So how far should I go?"

"The message is that Punch is ready to talk if they are. Got it? Punch is ready to talk if they are."

The DS bounded around Place de la Concorde and headed up the wintery Champs Elysées. No strollers in the park today. Why don't these cars sell in the States, he wondered? Best thing the French ever invented – aside from baguettes and foie gras, that is. At Rond Point, the driver turned onto avenue Franklin Roosevelt, pulling up outside Lasserre. Gruson stared at the gold-tipped iron fence around the German embassy next door, like so many spikes on the Kaiser's helmet. Who was there first, he wondered, Lasserre or the Germans?

Ten minutes late, just right, Swart thought as he bounded on long legs down the Champs toward Rond Point. "Ridiculous," he said when Martine offered to call a taxi.

"It's freezing out there," she said.

"Bracing, we say in Newport."

But it was damn-ass cold – cold and dark and gloomy. Europe was so dreary in winter. But he'd bundled up and was moving briskly along and not too late and looking forward to the meeting if not the lunch. The wind swept down the avenue from the Arch of Triumph, blasting dozens of strange, colorful flags that rattled their chains against the lampposts. He'd probably just missed a motorcade for some African potentate to lay a wreath at the Arch. At Rond Point he turned toward Lasserre – three Michelin stars, top of the line. Too bad he didn't like long winey lunches, would rather be eating pastrami and pickles at Manny's on Forty-Fourth Street. "Pigeon André Malraux," Martine said. "Try it." He wondered who'd taken her to Lasserre.

Gruson hailed him as he approached from the cloakroom. Swart hoisted himself onto the next barstool. "I'll take one of those," he told the bartender, pointing at Gruson's martini. They hadn't seen each other since New York.

"Jean knows how to make them – right, Jean?"

"Oui, M. Gruson," said the bartender, enunciating the name slowly, swallowing the *r* as the French do and as Swart could never do. "For you, eight to one. Précisément."

"Précisément, Jean." He turned to Swart. "I come here a lot, have to say it's my favorite. Vefour is nice and I can walk there but it's too old Paris for my taste – reminds me of guillotines. Something brighter about Lasserre – plants, the skylight, serre means greenhouse in English, did you know that?"

Dapper was the word for Syd Gruson, impeccably dressed in fine pinstripe worsted with smart two-tone shirt and silk tie and matching handkerchief, both red polka dots on white. Everything about him gave the impression of being fresh and rosy, like he'd just shaved and bathed in Old Spice. Swart admired the type – small, vigorous, elegant, compact bodies easier to control than big ones, full of energy, reputedly good in bed. Swart had met Gruson's wife, Flora Lewis, a few times around town. They were the best kind of American ambassadors abroad, elegant, cultivated, courteous. They both obviously loved Paris. Too bad they'd be leaving. He wondered if Gruson would have a second martini. One before lunch was all Swart could handle.

But no, their table was ready upstairs. "He never lets me have more than one," said Gruson, leaving a fifty-franc tip for the bartender. "Says it ruins the palette."

They settled in at the table. Swart had no doubt what lunch was about – how could it be anything else? Gruson took his time, leisurely enjoying a Montrachet '64 over hors d'oeuvres of quail eggs: If you're in the office until after midnight, who cares if you don't finish lunch until four? For the pigeon Malraux with foie gras and wild mushrooms in truffle sauce, they switched to a '61 Mouton. They chatted about Paris and New York and newspapers and politics. For Swart, the food touched on nauseating.

Over two courses and two hours, Gruson chattered away about everything but what he'd invited him to talk about. Over the quail eggs they discussed Vietnam and China; over pigeons, Bobby Kennedy and LBJ; over dessert, women. Anything but newspapers. Bon vivant with an iron constitution, Gruson liked talking about women. Swart, who had only his wife and secretary and wasn't doing that well with either, listened with envy. He hadn't seen his wife in six months, and his secretary, with exquisite timing, took the occasion of his divorce to return to her French friends. He was alone in a four-bedroom house in the Villa Montmorency. Even his maid deserted him.

For dessert Gruson insisted on the timbale Elysée Lasserre. Coffee arrived. Gruson sniffed the cigars and chose two Partagas Carlottas. Maybe we're getting to it, Swart thought. You don't invite someone you've been trying to drive out of business for six years to a $500 lunch at Lasserre because you want to talk about girls.

"You know," Gruson said, masticating the smoke, "how much they'd pay in New York for one of these? I'll tell you a story. A guy from the Johnson Administration comes to town – we'll leave him nameless but let's say he's high in the State Department – very high. We're at Maxim's. So afterward I light up a Partagas – or maybe it was a Montecristo, I don't remember. We'd had a couple of bottles and suddenly I'm telling him that one of the really stupid things about not recognizing Castro is that the Russians get all his cigars. Whaaaat, says the guy? No, I said, don't get me wrong. Here's the thing: You can't meet a Russian today who doesn't have a pocket full of Havanas to hand out. What I'm saying is that if we did business with Castro he wouldn't have to have the Russians around. No more Bay of Pigs, no more Russian missiles. All you guys could be smoking puros Habaneros, not just me in Paris. He looks at me like I'm crazy, goes home and – get this, I hear through Cy Sulzberger that he's putting out word that the *Times* has a pinko publisher in Paris."

Gruson was enjoying himself, enjoying Swart's impatience. Let him wait, he thought. I'm paying. With guys like him no wonder Whitney went out of business in New York. Zero conversation: Doesn't know politics, doesn't know newspapers, doesn't know food, doesn't know women. Thinks Rockefeller will be the next president. How can you delude yourself like that? Why start with Swart? I don't get it. Probably doesn't know the pigeon he just ate from the ones shitting on Minerva's head in Herald Square. How does a guy like this get to be publisher of the *Paris Herald*? And they wonder what went wrong in New York. Episcopalians. Republicans. Cronies. Dad brings in his polo pals and the firm goes to hell. Swart would be lucky to be an ad salesman at the *Times*.

"So what's it like working for Kay Graham?"

Finally. Swart brought his gaze back from the Arab children whose uneaten plates of $50 food were being taken away. "Smart lady."

"Ambitious."

"Wants to prove a woman can do it."

"Word is that she's overreaching."

"Overreaching . . ?"

"The *Post*'s a family corporation, Ben. Not even B-stock. Pure family. Can't go around buying expensive toys like the *Paris Herald* on family money. Some old maid aunt will start screaming."

Swart was tired of sitting, eating, drinking, smoking, all things he more or less hated. He kept thinking of Martine. He wanted to be back by four o'clock and wasn't going to make it. "Maybe she knows that."

Gruson blew a smoke ring, leveling inquiring eyes across the table, contemplating what he'd just heard. Had Swart let something slip? "Meaning?"

Swart wondered if he should tell him, but figured he had to know. The *Post* was getting ready to go public – not with class B stock but a public offering to go toe-to-toe with the *Times* nationally and internationally. You can't keep something like that secret from the *Times* when you're raising the money in New York. Gruson knew everything else, why wouldn't he know that – though Swart had just learned of it himself from Walter Thayer.

"Nothing much. Maybe she would agree with you, that's all."

Gruson knew of the IPO, but no one at the *Times* thought it mattered. Even if they raised $50 million how could they expect to go head to head with the *Times* in Paris or anywhere else? With $50 million in assets against half a billion? With five foreign bureaus against thirty? Sure, the *Times* would have to come to terms with them in Paris, but the minnow doesn't swallow the whale. One way or another the *Times* was going to own the *Paris Herald*. It might take time, but the *Post* going public wouldn't change a thing.

"How much are you going to lose this year, Ben?"

"It's no secret. Maybe three."

"Not peanuts."

"Peanuts for Jock. Bennett lost money over here all his life."

"But he was making barrels in New York. What's Jock got left – his horses."

"You know what they say: the Whitneys and the Rockefellers."

"Here's how it is, Ben. Newspapers are our business, the business of the *New York Times*. No yachts, no horses, no investment houses, no trusts. We print the news – all the news that's fit to print. We're willing to come over here and start a newspaper that loses money because we think the *Times* should be in Europe. If showing the flag costs us a couple of cents off earnings for a few years, we can handle it."

"Maybe that's how Kay figures it as well."

"Except that nobody in Europe gives a shit about the *Washington Post* – that's the difference. That's what Jock and Walter have left out of their equation. The people who read newspapers over here want the *Times*, not the *Post*."

"So why's our circulation ahead of yours – not to mention ad sales?"

"You know why – habit, and habits quickly change. You don't even print the complete stock tables."

"So what do you want, Syd? What do you want me to report to Jock and Walter?"

"Punch is ready to talk if you are."

One more puff on the Partagas and Swart laid it down for good. Either the cigar or everything before it was making him nauseous. He watched Gruson who was watching him, each man stony-faced.

"All Punch has to do is pick up the phone and call around the corner."

"He figures that since it's a Paris deal, the talks should start in Paris."

He hurried back up the Champs Elysées under the mysterious flapping flags. He'd just finished lunch and it was already dark with streetlights on, approaching dinnertime. My God, he thought – WE'VE WON! He was almost trotting, trying to work poisonous food, alcohol and smoke out of his system and be back to call Walter at 4:30 – 10:30 New York time – as he'd promised. Walter would be ecstatic – well, maybe not ecstatic, Walter was never ecstatic, but he would be pleased. Punch is ready to talk could only mean one thing: They're ready to meet our terms.

The meeting of the comité de l'entreprise was, as always, set for 10 A.M. on the second Wednesday of the month. Eleven of them were at the table when he walked in the boardroom at precisely ten and went around shaking hands. If management is the brains of a French company, the comité de l'entreprise is its soul, bringing together representatives from every department.

The meetings were always in French, a custom dating to Bennett. Martine sat between Ben and Sonny so she could whisper or write out anything they didn't understand. The main tension, Swart discovered at his first meeting, was between the upstairs departments and the downstairs unions. There were more employees upstairs than downstairs, but they didn't have the muscle and weren't communists.

"You have said nothing to us, M. le président," began Tonton Pinard when his turn came, using Swart's formal title, "about your contingency planning to leave Paris." The beefy man with the

Gauloise cigarette paused to look around the table. "We know that M. le Tac has been seeing quite a lot of Europe lately."

"What can we say, M. Pinard," le Tac answered, "that is more eloquent than the figure of three million dollars, the amount the *Herald* will lose this year? Costs in Paris are high – especially union costs. Every company has the right to seek ways to reduce them."

Swart preferred to let le Tac deal with Pinard because it avoided translation. Hired by Eric Hawkins and working his way up, Theo le Tac had made himself indispensable to management. Along the way he'd learned excellent English to go with French and German and was fanatically loyal to the *Herald*. According to Martine, the conflict between le Tac and Pinard went back to the dawn of France. They represented the nation's irreconcilable divisions: land-labor, Christian-atheist, king-republic, capitalist-collectivist, union-management, Vichy-Gaullist.

"The company will lose three million this year," answered Pinard, "but the company has a new partner that is raising fifty million dollars – two hundred and fifty million francs – by going public. Surely that amount will help to offset any loses."

"We must examine every possibility," said le Tac.

"Are you serious about moving or is it a tactic?"

Swart understood and intervened. "We are not in business to lose money."

Martine translated, but everyone understood. No one believed that Tonton did not know English. The pretense gave him more time to consider his answer.

"Our contracts do not come up for renewal until March, 1968," he said. "I expect you to keep us informed and do nothing that might force us to take strike action or have recourse to the government."

Le Tac leveled his torturer's gaze on his antagonist. "The CGT would gain nothing by taking strike action – would in fact be displaying the very tactics that have led us to investigate other possibilities. As for asking the government to intervene in a matter of collective bargaining, I doubt you'd get very far."

"There are social laws in France, M. le Tac," said Pinard, his voice rising. "This is not America. You should try to remember that."

Swart understood and would have replied but by the time Martine finished translating Pinard was on to another point. "Would the president," he asked, "kindly inform the comité of the status of negotiations with the *New York Times?*"

So it has leaked, thought Swart, surely from Gruson. Nothing has leaked from our side because only Martine knows – not even le Tac, though oddly, his face registered no surprise at Tonton's question.

Gruson has done something to give us away. Why?

18

Standing in the driveway looking down the narrow street with its two-story stone houses and faux tile roofs, Frank Draper buttoned his coat against the March cold, took his dog's leash in hand, and began walking. One by one he passed the little gingerbread houses with their once-orange roofs turned to dirty polymer brown. Wealthier neighbors in Chatou and le Vesinet preferred terra-cotta or, better yet, authentic slate tile from Picardy or Lorraine, but working-class Maisons-Laffitte had no such pretensions, which is why the Drapers lived there. They, too, had no pretensions.

Draper didn't like Saturdays, never had. The *Herald* didn't publish a paper and he didn't go to work. He preferred the rigors of weekdays when you knew from the moment you rolled out of bed how you would spend your day. Early Saturday wasn't so bad for there was a routine to it, but later on he had trouble filling his day. It was not yet 7:30. No one else in the house was awake. They all slept better than he did. Lorca, his dog, was uncomfortable. Lorca didn't mind Saturdays as much as his master did and judged the early morning hours solely on the state of his bowels. Apparently he didn't feel anything yet, which made his eyes and tail droop. Man and dog needed exercise to get minds and bodies functioning properly.

This would be a seminal day in the Draper family. The merger negotiations that lasted all winter were over and Draper had accepted a $50,000 payment to retire at the end of the month. "You'd be crazy not to take it," Sonny said, "because I can't guarantee you anything."

At sixty-seven, Draper no longer was protected under French unemployment law, and the merger agreement with the *Times* meant layoffs. He didn't want to retire. But if he didn't he risked ending up adrift in France with neither money nor job.

"Good dog," he said and might have been referring to himself. Lorca was circling on the street between cars and clearly feeling it.

Dog done, they turned off the rue des Terrasses onto the rue de Bellevue. He bought a racing form and *le Figaro* at the kiosk outside the Café des Carrières and went in for a café-croissant and to get his Tiercé bets down. The horses were running at Maisons-Laffitte and if he didn't have more important things to do he'd be spending the afternoon at the track. The local meet was short, squeezed in among the richer Paris meets at Vincennes, Auteuil, and Longchamps. When they were running at Maisons-Laffitte it gave him something to do Saturdays.

With Lorca gently snoring under his feet, he ordered a second café-croissant, this time with a cognac. He had to prepare. By 8:30 most of the regulars had come in from the cold, loosening coats and warming themselves with cognac or calvados. They greeted Draper, recognized as an old and respectable member of the community and someone to take polite account of. They also kept their distance. He'd always been put off by the French reaction to his use of their language. He happened to be fluent in French. Maybe he didn't have an ear for languages and being a touch hard of hearing tended to speak up, but he spoke correctly. Words, after all, were his profession.

The matter coming to a head that Saturday had started a month earlier. Ben Swart came downstairs to announce conclusion of negotiations. The *Times* Paris Edition would close, staffs would merge, and anyone who left the *Herald* voluntarily would receive severance pay plus indemnity. Swart was named president of the new company, which included the *New York Times* as minority partner. All decisions would be taken jointly by the three owners. In case of disagreement, Jock Whitney and Katharine Graham, with controlling interest, would have the final decision, except in matters involving large-scale borrowing or capital expenditures, which required unanimity. Sydney Gruson returned to New York as vice president, assistant to Punch Sulzberger, replacing Sam Hecht.

At first, Draper had said nothing to his wife, Odile. He had to be sure there was no chance of keeping his job. Once that was clear, he told her of the offer and they began discussing what to do with $50,000 – 250,000 francs – his severance and indemnity in one lump sum. Odile's first thought was to move to Poissy to be near her family. Her mother still lived in the house where Odile was born. Draper did not want to move to Poissy. "We have the children to consider," he said, not entirely sure what he meant. Chantal, twenty, attended beautician's school in Paris and was surrounded by enough boys that he doubted he'd have to support her much longer. Jean, seventeen, in his final year at the local lycée, showed no interest in college. His goal in life was to work at the Chrysler-Simca plant in Poissy. Somehow, in one of the larger disappointments in a life full of them, both Draper's children had taken after Odile, a woman of limited imagination.

The question was what to do with 250,000 francs. The house was paid off and he had his small French pension and medical benefits. His children's educations, almost over, were free. Draper was out of a job but still vigorous. What was he supposed to do – spend the rest of his life walking to the Café des Carrières for coffee and croissants and greeting the regulars who didn't talk to him? Even if Odile would have agreed, which she wouldn't, he couldn't go back to the States, where he'd been blacklisted after the war for joining the Lincoln Brigade in Spain. What was he to do with the rest of his life?

It was the second Saturday after Swart's announcement that things changed so dramatically. He'd been at his usual spot at the counter, drinking coffee and reading *le Figaro*. He'd turned to the classifieds, just in case someone in Paris was looking for a sixty-seven-year-old unemployed editor. He skimmed quickly over the ads and just before closing the paper, just before rousting the dog and heading out again – that's how close it was – something in the real estate section caught his eye. It stood out from the rest because it was in bold type and standing off by itself. It was also in English:

VIVE L'ESPAGNE!
($50,000 net)

Unique offer. Beautiful avocado-producing property in hills above Mediterranean near Malaga offered at a fraction of its value.

Inherited property. OWNER MUST SELL Includes 30-acre, avocado-producing orchard. Annual crop value: $10,000. Get your money back in five years. Eight-room, ranch-style farmhouse with two bathrooms and separate servants' house. Once in a lifetime! Inquiries to Propriedades Saturnino Suarez, Paseo del Generalissimo 214. Malaga, Spain. 952 150333.

Lorca was up and ready to go but Draper continued staring at the ad, reading it over and over, his mind in full flight. He finished his coffee, gathered up newspaper and dog, and headed out, but not directly home. Instead, he turned down the rue de Champsfleur, walked through the park and over the bridge that crosses the canal alongside the Seine. The minute he'd seen the ad, he'd known. Only divine providence could have led him on that day to that page with that ad. The magic word played in his mind as he walked: Malaga, Malaga, Malaga.

Born with the century, Frank Draper had been thirty-six years old, working as an editor on the *New York Post*, single and solitary and worried about the fate of the world. One day he saw a story about the arrival of American volunteers in Spain to fight the fascists and six weeks later he was in Figueres enlisting in the Lincoln Brigade. A week later he was in a trench in the Jarama Valley defending the Madrid-Valencia line. "No pasarán," they shouted, and the fascists didn't pass. The Brigade held again in Malaga – for a while. Some of them made it to fishing boats to avoid the firing squads. Since that day, he'd never been back to Malaga.

Two days after seeing the ad he came to work early, sat by himself and looked out over the empty newsroom. He studied the dark, silent room. Lord, how he would miss it! In a few hours it would be bedlam – voices shouting, doors slamming, the rat-a-tat of teletypes and type-writers, clacking of downstairs linotype machines, rumble of the presses. What other business was like a newspaper – gathering information around the world, sifting it through the skilled minds and hands of people like Sonny Stein and Al Lodge and yes, Frank Draper, and offering it for sale the next day for fifteen cents? What other business did anything like that – not just make a loaf of bread or pair of shoes but a product on which the education of the world depended, on which governments were elected, democracies preserved, corruption exposed, wars declared.

He telephoned Malaga and learned there had been several inquiries but that the property was still on the market. Propriedades Saturnino Suarez would send photos, information and a contract by return mail. They recommended a personal visit. A down payment of $1,000, non-refundable, would give him first right of refusal, good for a week. The estate insisted on cash, paid in U.S. dollars.

He signed the contract as soon as it came, purchased a money order for $1,000, and mailed the package back to Malaga.

"Are you crazy?"

Odile's reaction did not surprise him. She was like that. "The children think you're crazy, too . . . just a crazy vieux."

Vieux. He hated the word, which she only used when she was very mad.

She called a family meeting for the following Saturday, one day

after his final day at the *Herald*; one day after he was paid an indem-
nity of $50,000 and wired $49,000 of it to Propriedades Saurez in
Malaga, located on the street with that detestable name: Paseo del
Generalissimo. Long after the other monsters of the time had met
their fates, Francisco Franco, the man responsible for the Spanish
Civil War, still ruled.

It was a week of silent tension in the Draper household, which
for two decades had drifted along on the principle that you could do
what you wanted as long as you stayed out of each other's hair. Frank,
a foreigner, was accepted in the family, as in the community, on the
basis of being odd but not troublesome. Odile, hardly more than a
girl, had married him after the war when Americans were still heroes.
It was a marriage of mutual convenience. A marriage is a contract,
not a communion, Odile liked to say, and Frank had always, at least
until now, respected the contract.

To his children, it was more complex. They knew Papa was an
immigrant, someone who talked and acted peculiarly, but he was loving in his way and inoffensive, meaning not an embarrassment, at
least when they were younger. As they grew older, he tried to influence
them in certain ways – his politics had always been on the left – but
he didn't press when they showed other inclinations. And they were
better off than some of their friends, whose fathers drank or were violent and couldn't hold jobs. But there was always an edginess when
Papa was around, especially at large family gatherings when no one
knew when he would start off in that loud voice and horrible accent
about the virtues of socialism and atheism and the evils of fascism
and the Catholic Church.

They gathered in the small living room in the only house the children had ever called home. Draper was the last to arrive. Chantal had
returned from Paris, and Jean finished his Saturday half day at the
lycée. With Lorca, Draper had been gone all morning, killing time
in the café, reading the newspaper and drinking two cognacs. Never

once had Malaga left his mind. He'd left the café and walked to the river as he'd done the day he saw the ad. The difference now was that the deal was done. He'd talked at length with Sr. Suarez about the circumstances of the sale, especially the OWNER MUST SELL phrase in the ad: Children moving from the land to the city, explained Sr. Suarez, *vida moderna, verdad?* Completely normal. They joked about it. He hadn't lost his Spanish.

Odile was on the brown velvet sofa, in the middle, which sagged more than the ends but which she preferred because no one would sit beside her. Chantal sat in the easy chair where Draper usually sat, and Jean was on the ottoman at her feet. The arrangement was such that Draper's only choice was the straight-back chaise Voltaire opposite the easy chair, which he entered like the accused entering the dock. Lorca made a quick inspection of the room and plopped at his feet. The dog felt the tension and wanted to show whose side he was on. Like his master, Lorca was ready for orchards in Spain.

"So Frank," began Odile, "it is the moment."

"I'm listening," he replied.

"No, Papa," said Chantal. "It is we who are listening to you."

She'd always been his favorite, mainly because she was feistier and cleverer than Jean. They'd had their best times when she turned ten, bored with her bourgeois mother and bursting with curiosity and prepubescent paternal love. Jean had always been more repressed, less physical than his sister. He had trouble getting his thoughts out in a normal flow. They came shooting out in venomous sprays that could land on anyone.

"My proposal," Frank began, helped by the cognac and careful to speak softly, "is to move to Spain. Obviously, you children would not come right away. You have your school here, your friends, your lives, soon careers. You would come when you could. You have seen the pictures. Imagine what it will be like in this big house on our own estate. Who knows how you will react when you see it – when you bring your friends to see it – you might even want to live there."

He smiled and saw a spark of curiosity in Chantal's eyes, but Odile intervened before either child could respond.

"And me?"

"All I ask is that you withhold judgment until you see it."

"Frank," she said, sharply, "come to your senses. There is nothing worse than a foolish vieux. You have led a full life. Don't make yourself ridiculous at your age."

"And what is your objection, Chantal?" he asked gently.

"We are not peasants, Papa. The life I see in these photos is not the life I want to lead. When I'm through beauty school I will work and live in Paris, become a Parisian. If you and Maman moved to Spain I would never see you."

"And you, Jean?"

"It is a question of personal dignity," said the boy. "Growing old with dignity, that is the responsibility of each one of us. How can you even think of doing such a thing, Papa? Do you realize how selfish it is? Do you realize you are trying to impose on us something none of us wants?"

"But I'm not seeking to impose this on anyone."

"That's why it is selfish," said the boy. "You choose this place over us."

"No, no, no! It is an opportunity for all of us." His voice rose for the first time.

"It is an opportunity for you," said Odile, "no one else."

"So you expect me to spend my life hanging around cafés and playing the Tiercé? Maybe a game of boules in the afternoon. Is that what you call personal dignity?"

"Hobbies, Papa," said Chantal. "Retirement gives you time for hobbies."

"I have no hobbies."

"Then get them," said Jean.

"Let me explain," he said, "what I am doing and why." He could have used another cognac, but it was probably good he'd stopped at two. Odile had a nose for alcohol on his breath. "I've had a different life from you three. Your lives have been similar to each other, but mine has no similarity to them. With age you will understand that you live more in the past than the present because there is so much more of it. And you will understand that the past is memory. My past – most of it – is in New York, where I grew up, went to school and worked. All your childhood memories are of France, and all mine are of America."

"Are you saying you want to return to America?" said Odile.

"No. I am not," he said, suppressing irritation at her obtuseness. "It is too far, and too foreign, not just for you but for me."

"So what does any of this have to do with growing avocados in Spain?"

"Some of my memories are of Spain. I risked my life to fight in Spain, for a cause that has never left me. In a way, you might say I have unfinished business in Spain. Franco is old and soon will die, and there is a chance that the cause I fought for will finally triumph. A quarter century later, I can be there on the day of victory."

He looked from one to the other. Chantal was the only one who seemed to understand what he was saying.

"Frank," said Odile, her lower lip turning down and quivering, "if you want to visit Madrid, the museums, the cathedrals, yes, especially now that we can go in style. But if you think I'm going to go about dressed in black gathering avocados, you are fooling yourself. French people go to Spain on vacation. It is the Spaniards who come to France to work."

His face was a blank. He listened but didn't hear, convinced it was the right step for all of them, opening interests and feelings they didn't know they had. They would come. Oh, they might not come at first; they would be hurt and angry and he would have to go alone and wait for them, but they would come. His children were young enough to be curious and adventuresome even if they didn't know it yet. Odile, too, would come. Her mother and sisters would say that Frank is crazy and she was right to let him go, but after awhile she would come.

He moved his hands along on the armrests of the chair and thought of Voltaire, twisted and shrunken, skullcap pulled over his ears, sinking back into such a chair until it consumed him. He let his fingers run along the brass-tipped upholstery pins the artisans had carefully and symmetrically driven into place a century before. He would install this chair in front of the picture window of his farm overlooking the Mediterranean and Malaga below. He would sit there with Lorca, named for the poet Franco had murdered, and wait for the old man to die.

He was seven years younger than Franco. He would be there at the end, victoriously toasting with vino tinto the tyrant's death.

19

There is simply no way we can stay in Paris," said Walter Thayer. "Nostalgia is a poor business counselor."

"We didn't buy into this operation to move to Zurich," said Sydney Gruson.

"We kept you advised at all times."

"It was contingency planning, Walter."

"And, sadly," said Thayer, "we have our contingency."

"The Middle East war," said Katharine Graham, still slightly out of breath from oversleeping and racing across town from the Ritz to be in time for the ten o'clock meeting. It was her idea to hold the first summer board meeting of the new *International Herald Tribune* in Paris, not New York. She could imagine what the men would be thinking if she'd been late.

"Our second quarter results, judging from April and May, will be good," said Ben Swart. "Because of rising costs related to the war, the third quarter does not look good."

"The Arabs say the oil embargo is aimed solely at the U.S. and Britain," said Thayer, "but oil is fungible – embargoes affect Europe as well."

"Thank heaven for the Shah," said Punch Sulzberger. "The Brits did something right when they put him on the throne."

"With help from the CIA," said Whitney.

"De Gaulle has suspended all arms shipments to Israel," said

Gruson. "Who in hell does he think started the war?"

"He thinks Israel started it," said Graham.

"So Israel is supposed to sit and wait while Egypt and Syria mass troops at the border and close the straits?"

"Our editorials on this have been very good," said Graham. "The blame lies squarely with the Arabs."

"We've written the same thing," said Sulzberger. "However that may be, I fear Israel will not gain from this conquest – either on the ground or with public opinion."

"Apropos," said Gruson to Swart, "I notice that you've been running *Post* editorials on the Middle East, not *Times*."

"Have you talked to Sonny?"

"I get the runaround from Sonny. I think he's overwhelmed."

They didn't ask for an explanation, and Gruson didn't offer one. They all knew he and his wife wanted to return to Paris. Ben's job was out for the moment, so why not take aim at Sonny, whom he had never liked.

"If you ask me," said Swart, "I think the *Herald* should have its own editorial writers. Both of you are writing for Americans at home. The *Herald*'s audience is fifty percent European."

"So what?" said Gruson. "The truth's the truth."

"Wait a minute, Syd," said Sulzberger, turning to Swart. "I want to hear Ben on this. Are you saying the *Herald* should tailor its opinions for a European audience?"

"Don't we all do that?" said Whitney. "Weren't your editorials different from ours in the *Herald Tribune*?"

"The Middle East is treacherous," said Graham. "I can see where an editorial written for New York or Washington might seem too pro-Israel over here. Our pro–Vietnam War editorials of a year ago wouldn't have made Sonny's job any easier."

"It was brave how you changed position on Vietnam, Kay," said Sulzberger. "Was it Lippmann?"

"Partly," she said, resenting the implication. "Though I went out there myself, you know. I wanted to see the war with my own eyes."

It was true. Of those present she was the only one who'd been to Vietnam. Since taking over at the *Post* she'd done everything possible to show she was a hands-on owner. She'd dealt with the unions, hit the campaign trail with the candidates, flown around Vietnam in a helicopter, even been given "the treatment" by President Johnson. Finally, she'd noticed, people had stopped referring to her as Mrs. Phil Graham.

Swart glanced across at Martine, who'd stopped writing and was staring at him. She gave him a little nod. The meeting was getting away from him.

"As for the Middle East," he said, looking for something they could agree on, "I'm sure de Gaulle will have something to say about that at his press conference tomorrow."

"De Gaulle has a lot to explain," said Gruson. "Expelling NATO, recognizing China, calling for an independent Quebec. Who does he think he is?"

Whitney let Gruson's comments sink in before speaking. "Do you know that de Gaulle wants the *Herald* to remain in Paris?"

"How do you know that?" said Gruson, surprised.

"Let's just say that the Elysée has sent us certain signals."

"When?"

"When was it, Ben?"

"A few months ago."

"You mean all the while we were negotiating the ownership agreement the Elysée was signaling you to stay in Paris?"

"I think that's a fair way of putting it."

Gruson was annoyed. The information had been kept from the *Times*. "We should have been kept informed."

He looked to Sulzberger, who remained silent.

"How is it that you're the ones arguing for moving and we're the ones who want to stay?"

Whitney's lips pursed. Gruson had struck a nerve. Thayer, Swart suddenly realized, making all the arguments for moving, was Whitney's stalking horse.

"Just what exactly were these signals?" asked Graham.

She didn't like how Whitney had dismissed Gruson. She had no affinity for Gruson, but wanted to be fair in her role as arbiter between New Yorkers. She liked Jock, whose wife, Betsey, was the sister of her closest New York friend, Babe Paley, but she wouldn't let friendships interfere with the Paris partnership. Moreover, in politics, she felt closer to Sulzberger, a Democrat. The important thing was that neither one take her for granted. Jock expected her blanket support, but it was more complicated than that. On moving the *Herald* she kept an open mind. Just like in Vietnam, she wanted the facts. And one fact was that she loved Paris.

"Nothing concrete," said Swart, "just that solutions can be found. The French way, they call it."

"But how can they help us with the unions?" asked Graham.

"Exactly," said Thayer. "De Gaulle has his own problems with the unions. I'd even say his biggest problem is the unions."

"There's really a very simple principle here," said Whitney. "Latin unions strike; German unions don't. Zurich is German-speaking. It would be a major accomplishment for this newspaper to work with union leaders we could trust."

"Will someone from the Elysée be at Charlie McCloud's dinner?" asked Sulzberger. "I'd like to talk about this."

"Charlie's dinner is for you all," said Swart. "He called me as soon as he heard you were coming. I wouldn't be surprised if someone from the Elysée was invited. On the other hand, with de Gaulle's press conference late in the afternoon – I don't know."

"Lots of reporters in town," said Whitney.

"Hundreds, Sonny tells me."

Thayer lagged behind as the others filed into the elevator after the meeting.

"I hear Rachel Stein has gone back to New York. How's Sonny taking it?"

They stood together in the hallway with Martine as the elevator went down. She pressed the button for its return. The question surprised Swart. "Sonny's fine."

The lawyer's luminescent eyes bored into him behind rimless glasses.

"It had been coming," Swart lied. "Maybe even before Paris."

Thayer's gaze narrowed on the man he'd not wanted for this job. Paris was a temptation, and he suspected that Ben Swart, like Jock Whitney himself, raised with money and privilege, might find temptation harder to resist than some others.

"So it has nothing to do with the young lady downstairs?"

Trapped, Swart adjusted. "*Now* it does, yes."

A soupçon of disapproval showed on his lips, somehow escaping through rigorous self-control. "I hope it doesn't affect his work."

The elevator returned. "The newspaper has never looked better."

Adjusting his homburg, Thayer turned to the elevator. Martine held the door. He turned back. "And how is Norma?"

Did he know? Why ask these questions in front of Martine?

"Norma has not returned to Paris. She wants the children to go to school in Newport. We are divorcing."

Both feet in the elevator, Thayer stood staring at Martine. "I'm sorry to hear that. So it's both Sonny and you. Strange, isn't it?"

Swart didn't answer.

"It must be Paris."

Lovely in a light blue silk suit and white shirt open at the collar, Martine closed the elevator doors. They watched the rickety old cage disappear down the shaft. He longed to kiss her and could not.

For the *International Herald Tribune*'s new board of directors, de Gaulle's timing was exquisite. Normally he gave only one press conference a year, an elaborate affair at the Elysée with the General seated on gilded chair behind gilded desk on scarlet stage, lacking only crown, scepter, and ermine robes. Journalists, diplomats, and cabinet ministers massed as subjects at his feet. But the 1967 press conference would be exceptional in every way. Some of the guests invited to dinner at the ambassador's residence barely made it on time. Two of them, British Ambassador Sir Christopher Lord and Elysée chief of staff Henri de Saint-Gaudens, fortunately had only to walk next door.

Swart stood watching from the foyer as Charlie McCloud went down the marble steps to greet his dejected British colleague, who'd just heard de Gaulle give the coup de grace to Britain's bid to join the Common Market, something Sir Christopher had worked on for four years. Right behind Sir Christopher came Henri de Saint-Gaudens, on foot from the Elysée. Swart watched fascinated as de Gaulle's right-hand man said something that made Sir Christopher put his arm around him. What could he have said to earn a hug so soon after de Gaulle planted the dagger? Next, Jean-Yves Cambronne and Charles de la Bellefontaine stepped from their limousines into the ambassador's courtyard.

Over whiskey and champagne guests milled about the salon of the eighteenth-century mansion elegantly restored by Ambassador McCloud's fortune. They had only one subject on their lips: Charles de Gaulle. The news had begun flashing at precisely 4:44 that afternoon. "For the British to join with the continent a profound transformation must first take place," de Gaulle informed her majesty's government.

He was the nineteenth-century man who had mastered twentieth-century technology. In every crisis, de Gaulle would take to television at 8:00 P.M. sharp, seated at his gilded desk and dressed either in a dark blue double-breasted suit or his khaki one-star brigadier general's uniform. From every living room, dining room and cafe, the nation watched, spellbound. Even in the tightest scrapes, as on the night the generals in Algeria revolted and prepared to drop paratroops on Paris, de Gaulle remained the stern and steady captain ready to guide the ship through the storm. "Well, well, my dear old friends," he began that night, "here we find ourselves together, alone once again."

Any one of a half dozen subjects could have led the news that day. Having opened with the British veto, he turned to America, condemning escalation of the war in Vietnam and accusing American corporations of using an over-valued dollar to buy up Europe on the cheap. He instructed Canada to change its constitution so Quebec could be "set free." He demanded a return to the gold standard. He was just warming up.

The last guests having arrived, Ambassador McCloud steered them to the salon to join the others. An American stepped forward.

"The president of the republic has slandered the Jewish people," announced Sydney Gruson.

McCloud started to say something and stopped. Henri de Saint-Gaudens was the only man in the room who could answer for the General.

Saint-Gaudens nodded to the ambassador and turned to Gruson. "You have misinterpreted the president's words, Sydney. Perhaps something was lost in translation."

"I wrote it down, Henri," said Gruson, producing a notebook: "'Les Juifs: peuple d'élite, sûr de lui même et dominateur.' I would translate that as the Jews, an elite people, sure of themselves and domineering. I don't think anything is lost in translation."

"And you find that slanderous?"

Gruson looked incredulous. "It's supposed to be complimentary?"

A waiter passed and Saint-Gaudens took a flute of champagne. "Let me ask you this, Sydney: If anyone else had uttered those words, would you call it slander?"

"I would."

"Not at all. The General chose to underline the character of this exceptional people, character by which they've been able to remain themselves after nineteen centuries spent in unheard-of conditions."

"Whatever he *meant*," said Gruson, "his words will be used by people who lack such subtlety of mind. The anti-Semites of the world today received from the president of France official authority to speak and act once again as they did during the Holocaust."

Standing together, Whitney, Thayer, and Swart had the same thought: Gruson doesn't know that this is the man whose help we need to stay in Paris. Should someone have told him?

"One week before war broke out," said Saint-Gaudens, "the Israeli foreign minister came to the Elysée. You know of that meeting, of course, Sydney. Whoever fires the first shot, the president told Abba Eban, will be blamed by France. 'Do not make war,' the president said. Israel, with armaments supplied by France over more than a decade, did not listen."

"Israel's survival was at stake."

"Israel's survival will be at stake if she does not find a way out of the situation she has created. You have seen Ben Gurion's statement: Israel must give back the land."

"Not all Israelis agree with Ben Gurion."

"Gentlemen," said McCloud, finally intervening. "I don't think we'll resolve this tonight and some of us must soon return to work. May I suggest we move to the next room for the excellent dinner the chef has prepared in honor of our visitors."

The ambassador gave his arm to Katharine Graham for the short walk to the dining room. Janet McCloud offered her arm to Henri de Saint-Gaudens. Franco-American relations were restored.

2 0

Dennis Klein had made himself a promise: He would not leave for Germany before breaking through the defenses of Gretchen Kilic. He knew it was just one more fatuous pretext to stay in a place he loved instead of going to one he didn't, but he couldn't help it. She obsessed him. He'd finished his research in Paris on the Nazi occupation. The rest was in Germany. He was ready to go and the only thing holding him back was his promise.

Obsession? He preferred to think of it as a challenge. She was the kind of girl who'd always attracted him, small, sharp, and feisty, just like he was. With Steve Fleming around he'd gotten nowhere, but Fleming was gone and he knew Gretchen had no permanent boyfriend. When she came to parties – at the Lodges, the Hallsbergs, Wayne and Jojo's, Dick and Suzy's – she always came alone. Sometimes he took her home by taxi but she never invited him up. Her resistance was as strong as his determination and he wasn't sure why. His obsession became his challenge, which became his promise, which became his frustration.

They'd never been on a date. She'd smile and say thanks anyway and after awhile he stopped asking. Occasionally they went places together. He'd have his taxi stop to pick her up on the way to parties or they'd ride out together with the Hallsbergs to l'Etang d'Hollande or with the Lodges to Archer's country house. He tried to put his arm around her but she wriggled away. He loved watching her in the library, scooting around in those miniskirts, doing little ballet stretches when she was stiff or tired, climbing the ladder to the high files. She knew he watched. Sometimes she'd smile down on him. She didn't care. She liked her body. So did he.

For his Nazi book, he had a contract, an advance, and a deadline. Promise or not, he had to get on with it and so he finally gave Sonny notice. A going-away party at the California was planned. Through the University of Munich he'd found lodgings near the English Gardens that were close enough to walk to the Bayerische Staatsbibliothek. He sent two months rent as down payment.

He decided to give Gretchen one last try and to his astonishment she accepted. He took her to the Tour d'Argent, across the bridge from his apartment on the Ile St.-Louis. They dined on the best ducks and wine. Afterward, he invited her back to his apartment and again she accepted. She'd been there once before, to a party he'd given.

"Who gets your place when you're gone, Dennis?"

So that was it! She was after his apartment. How could she possibly afford the Ile St.-Louis on a librarian's salary? They were on the couch sipping Courvoisier VSOP. She wore a little tiered red miniskirt, tight blouse and vest and ankle boots, which she'd unzipped to pull her bare legs up under her. How could she wear those things without stockings?

"It's yours."

She laughed. "Do you know how much I pay for my room? – two hundred francs."

"This costs a little more."

"I always liked it."

"So how come it took you so long to come back?"

"I'm here, aren't I?"

"So you *don't* want my apartment?"

"Are you crazy?"

"But why are you here just when I'm leaving?"

"Maybe it's *because* you're leaving."

He let it go. It could be taken either way. "So much wasted time."

She laughed again, a happy, girlish laugh. "Look, opposites attract. We're too much alike – short and dark."

He reached for her hand, warm and small, and she did not pull away. "I wouldn't describe you as short and dark. I'd describe you as" – they both giggled as he sought the right words – "as petite and deliciously seductive."

"That's because you're trying to seduce me."

Her snifter was empty. "Have some more cognac."

"See what I mean. You wouldn't happen to have a joint?"

He shook his head.

"You should try it sometime."

"Is that what you liked about Fleming – the joints?"

"Are you kidding? Gentlemen aren't the only ones who prefer blondes."

"So it was his blond hair."

"Among other things."

"Such as . . ."

Maidenly, her eyes fell to the ground. "Dennis, please."

"Can I tell you something: I thought you were anti-Semitic."

"Anti-Semitic! No way."

"Why not?"

"Because I *am* Semitic."

"No."

"Croatian Jews. My parents got out in time. I hate Germans as much as you do."

"So we really were wasting time."

"In a manner of speaking. So let's stop wasting it."

He reached for her but she pulled away, standing up quickly and taking off her vest. "I assume you have a bedroom in this house."

"Let me do that. I've dreamt of it long enough."

"I know."

"Then why . . ."

"Let's just say you deserve a reward for perseverance. A girl appreciates something like that."

In the bedroom, his fingers worked the buttons on her blouse while she removed his tie. She undid his belt buckle while he let her blouse drop and reached around to pop the snap of her bra. It was at that precise moment, somewhere between the drop of the pants and the drop of the bra, that the phone rang.

"You're not going to answer that?"

She was sitting on the bed, the breasts he'd dreamt of for years pointing accusingly at him in the dim light.

He hesitated. Nobody called at this hour on Saturday night. There was no Sunday newspaper. It had to be from the States, something wrong with his parents. "Just to get rid of it," he said, nervously, "keep them from calling back." Naked, cold, he returned to the living room and picked up the phone.

"Dennis," said the voice, "it's Helen. I need your help."

"Helen . . ."

"Would I call if it wasn't important?"

"But there's no newspaper tomorrow."

"It's not the newspaper."

She sounded tired, afraid, drunk . . . no, not drunk . . . desperate.

"Then . . ."

"Just come over . . . please. I'll explain when you're here."

"I can't possibly, Helen . . . not now . . . of all times . . . if you knew . . ."

He was begging.

"I called Archer. He's on his way from the country."

"Couldn't you just tell me . . . ?"

"Just come."

She hung up.

Back in the bedroom he saw Gretchen under the covers waiting, eyes closed, breathing softly, sheet peaked over breasts. He stared uncomprehending, unable to accept that this could be happening on this, of all nights. He picked up her trail of clothes and placed them gently, bra and panties on top, on a chair.

"It was Helen . . . some kind of emergency. Probably Al. Wait for me, Gretchen. Please. Wait for me . . . just like that, just as you are." He was pulling on his pants and pleading. "Whatever you do, don't move. Sleep. I'll be back. Soon. Please be here."

Archer drove like a madman, sure he could make the Arch of Triumph in forty-five minutes on a Saturday night when people were still trying to get out of the city. With the house in St.-Ouen and a second child on the way he'd traded in the Volkswagen for an Alfa-Romeo Giulia, maybe not the best thing for a family of four but with 1600 cc's it could run with anything the French had on the road. He'd planned to spend the night in the country with Sophie, Amy, and Vincent – the omnipresent Vincent who now lived there permanently as a caretaker though Archer had never seen him take care of anything. Mostly he painted ugly paintings and charged things at the shops in Berchères, a right to which Sophie said he was entitled as caretaker.

He took the back roads to Mantes and caught the freeway, keeping the Alfa at 180 kmh all the way to the city, zipping along the Bois to avenue Foch, broadest avenue in Paris and if it weren't for the mansions you'd think you were in Moscow or East Berlin or Bucharest where they'd cleared out the city to make room for armies to march. The French do that, too, or used to – twelve broad avenues run off the Etoile, nine of them named after famous battles – all victories. There is a Waterloo in London, not Paris.

Archer was closer to the Lodges than to anyone else at the newspaper. They'd helped him from the beginning. Al was an old-fashioned, green eyeshade, elastic-armband kind of guy who loved the tradition of newspapers and the legend of Bennett and the owls. It was Lodge to whom Eric Hawkins presented the bronze owl when he left, the owl that was the model for a fifty-foot owl to go atop Bennett's mausoleum in Washington Heights, to be designed by the architect Stanford White.

But White was murdered by Harry Thaw, and Bennett never returned. The model went to Paris.

They arrived simultaneously and walked up one floor to the apartment.

"Don't look too closely," Helen said, opening the door.

The apartment was stuffy and reeked of dissipation. Windows and curtains were closed, and the lack of street noise meant the outside metal shutters were shut as well. Except for the hum of the refrigerator, they heard nothing. Thick, total silence. No sign of Al. Helen padded to the bar and poured two whiskies, handing one to each. "Sit down."

She sat on the couch, crossed her legs, and lit a cigarette. The marble-glass ashtray on the coffee table was overflowing with butts. The mantel clock sounded midnight.

She wore a dark cashmere roll-neck sweater and navy slacks, both covered in fluff as if they'd been slept in. She was a mess – booze, tobacco, meds, newspapers, marriage, insomnia all taking their toll. The Jeanne Moreau look – high cheekbones, green eyes, full lips, luscious hair – had disappeared into lines, bags, and sags. The beautiful chestnut hair was unwashed and uncombed.

"Sorry, you guys," she said with her little lisp, "and thanks." She exhaled one more nicotine cloud to consume what oxygen still remained in the room. "Small crisis: It started last night. Up all night – booze, cigarettes, pills, no sleep. I've been working on him and I think I've talked him into going to the American Hospital. I *think* I have, but maybe not because he's not talking. At least when I mention it now his eyes seem to register what I'm saying. I don't know how he's going to react when he sees you."

She nodded toward the bedroom. "That's why I need you both."

She looked from Klein to Archer and back again. "Go in one at a time so you don't scare him, just sit on the bed and talk to him. He won't answer so just talk, softly, gently, get around to telling him that you came because he agreed to go to the hospital and you're here to help me get him there. Emphasize *me* because that gets his mind off *him*. It's hard. He's embarrassed and ashamed. Miserable. You go first, Rupert. Keep it soft and easy because behind that façade of silence he is scared shitless. I'll listen for a while and come in. I'd like to dress him myself but I may need help."

"What if he's changed his mind?" said Klein.

For the first time she showed just how close to collapse she was. Her face twitched as she lifted the cigarette to her mouth and her hand shook. "He's not violent. Al has never been violent. But one way or another we've got to get him out of here. I can't handle another day and night like the last one."

Archer entered a meticulous bedroom, bed made, dresser tops neatly arranged, clothes put away, everything in its place. It was dark, airless, and pungent with booze and sweat and cigarette smoke. One bedside lamp was lit and the curtains closed. In a rear corner crouched a man in the primeval position, the single light bulb illuminating him in the shadows. He was bare-chested and hairy, hunkered down in his skivvies, unshaven, unfocused, Piltdown man examining the enemy. Empty, slitty eyes saying nothing. If recognition existed it was not betrayed. Helen stood in the doorway a moment and backed out as Archer sat down on the bed and started talking about Charles de Gaulle.

Archer took the wheel of Helen's Peugeot with Klein beside him and the Lodges in back. He thought of the first time he'd gone to the American Hospital in Neuilly. Never a good thing when you're racing to the hospital after midnight with a sick man in the car. Eddie Jones didn't get out alive. They'd heard Al talking as Helen dressed him – had to shower, had to shave, had to get to work, Sonny off. Yes, of course, Helen said. You'll be fine.

Archer dropped them at the emergency entrance, parked and came back to give the keys to Helen, who was filling out forms.

"You going to be all right? You want us to stay?"

She smiled, maybe for the first time that day. "You two go back to bed."

They took a taxi back to the Lodges and switched to the Alfa, Archer juicing it down Malesherbes toward the Seine.

"They probably shot him up," said Klein.

"Sedated him until the Sunday doctors show up."

"What happened?"

"I don't know."

"Al's supposed to be working today. What do we do?"

"Helen's going to find Sonny. I think Eppinger's away."

At Concorde he turned onto the quai along the Right Bank. Klein quiet, no doubt wondering if the girl still would be there. What girl is going to leave a warm bed to go wandering before dawn on Sunday morning? Maybe Gretchen. Whoever it was, Klein would be leaving her behind. He would miss Klein, his best man, a good friend. He'd miss Al Lodge, too, his other friend. He didn't have that many. He still had Wayne, but he didn't see much of Wayne anymore. He didn't have any French friends. He had French neighbors, colleagues, sources, contacts, not friends. Philippe, maybe, his brother-in-law, was an exception. They got along, but were hardly friends, not in the sense of opening up like Helen had opened up or like he and Klein opened up. How could he open up to Philippe when Philippe was married to Sophie's sister?

Was friendship a matter of nationality? That would be too awful. A matter of language? The only way to bare your soul is with words. He thought of *Jules and Jim*, movie he'd just seen, Truffaut's portrait of friendship between a Frenchman and an Austrian, friendship that survives a war and loving the same woman. What greater tests? But Jules, the Austrian, spoke perfect French. How much of his problem with Sophie was caused by language? None, he'd thought, because his

French was serviceable and Sophie spoke English. Still, something was missing. With your own language you're able to dig deep, get to the bottom of things, form into precise words the intricacies of every thought. How can you do that in a language where you miss nuances and overtones and lack words; where you risk putting an imprecise word on a very precise thought? Is that what had thrown Sophie back onto Vincent, the fact that she could get to things with her cousin that she couldn't reach with her husband?

The dreadnought called Notre Dame loomed from the river mists as he sped by the Ile de la Cité. Jules and Jim, Jeanne Moreau at the center, Jeanne Moreau who reminded him of Helen. Or was it vice versa? Catherine was her name in the movie and if Catherine had lived another twenty years she would have looked like Helen, ravaged by time, worry, fear, not to mention the horrible physical things we do to our bodies, such perfect machines when we get them. Why was she called Catherine? Did it have something to do with the other Catherine, Brontë's Catherine, equally doomed? The names must have been picked for a reason. Why did the Austrian have a French name, the Frenchman an English name, and the Frenchwoman a universal name? The names seemed to mean something, but what?

At Pont Marie he crossed over to the Ile St.-Louis. Klein was silent.

"We're home, Dennis. You going to tell me who you have upstairs?"

"There is no chance she's still there. None."

"Of course she's there. I guarantee that whoever it is has waited."

"Why would she wait for me?'

"Because you are an estimable person."

"Thank you. Should I wake her?"

"I would say no, let her wake you."

"What if she doesn't?"

"She will. That's why she waited."

2 1

He'd never done anything like this before but Jojo had dared him and so here he was, sitting on a barstool in drag on opening night at Black Jack's on the rue Vavin. A guy had already bought him a drink so it must be working. Jojo said he looked stunning and the cabdriver hadn't said anything except "où allez-vous, madame?" Jojo helped dress him, turning around him like a couturier, smoothing this, adjusting that, helping with the blond wig. They'd wondered about the bra, should it be quite so stuffed, but Jojo insisted that a 175-pound man had to be a robust woman, not a gamine. His voice, never too deep, worked well enough with a slight falsetto.

Jojo's friend Jacques Taylor had the idea for the club, the first bunny club in Paris, though it had nothing to do with Playboy. It was not a gay club, though Jacques was gay, and when Wayne walked in he saw a good number of his friends scattered around at opening night tables. Jacques and Jojo were at a table with James Baldwin while two bunnies served hors d'oeuvres and champagne. Everyone was going back to Jojo's afterward for a post–opening night party. Jacques was taking a risk with the club, though he could afford it. He'd hired the chef away from La Coupole and for the music brought Dexter Gordon down from Copenhagen.

Opening night was packed. Wayne slipped onto a barstool, ordered champagne, and watched the pretty girls in long ears move among the tables. For some reason they didn't have bunny tails, just little satin bottoms. It was nearly eleven and le tout Paris had already arrived. Photographers flitted about the room. The bunnies, some of them very young, were a combination waitress and striptease, with two little rings of material passing for costumes.

He looked big but not at all bad. He had a round face, which helped when he dressed up, and was tan. He was nearly six feet and solid, maybe not as solid as he once was, but with makeup and Jojo's artistic touches he thought he made an attractive big woman. Looking in the mirror across the bar he was pleased. His friends could surely tell, but the guy who'd bought him champagne couldn't tell. At least he didn't think so.

Dexter was wailing "Willow Weep for Me" on his tenor sax, and Wayne thought back to the jazz club in Phoenix, Ernie's, on East Jefferson, the only place in town where blacks and whites could mix. Rupert Archer had introduced him to jazz. Archer had arrived from Honolulu, and Wayne was smitten from the first day. He never pushed it. He never pushed it with anyone. He could tell if someone felt it, and with Archer he'd sensed it was there if he'd just let himself go. They'd done a lot of things together, things that could be regarded as dates, at least for Wayne, but Archer never let himself go. Sometimes he didn't even know if Archer knew. You had to be careful in those days, especially when you worked on a right-wing newspaper in a place like Phoenix.

Eventually Archer had to know because he'd sent him four chapters of his manuscript in Barcelona and anyone could see the influence of Capote's "Other Voices, Other Rooms" except that it was about growing up in Gila Bend, not Monroeville. Archer said he loved the story and Wayne wrote him back just before taking off for Greece with Jojo. He wrote back because they were old friends despite everything and he figured Archer might need a job. So he wrote and dropped the letter in the box on the way to the airport and it changed Archer's life. Without that letter Archer would not be in Paris, would not have the best job on the newspaper, would not be married, would not have one child and another on the way.

And the thing was Archer didn't even seem to recognize it. Why hadn't he asked him to be his best man? They hardly seemed like friends anymore, at least not like in Phoenix. Not that Paris was anything like Phoenix. He'd needed Archer to survive in Phoenix but not in Paris. Nothing was a secret here, no one was in the closet. Imagine trying to open a club like Black Jack's in Phoenix – gays, blacks, transvestites, half-dressed bunnies – the whole police department would be out.

After awhile he saw Jojo, dressed entirely in white, get up to leave. People were invited for midnight and he had to get the apartment ready. He blew him a kiss. Someone slipped onto the empty barstool next to him. He saw his face in the mirror.

"Buy me a drink, sweetie?" Wayne asked.

Archer turned to the woman next to him and quickly away again. She had to be a hooker. His first reaction when Jacques Taylor called him was that a jazz dinner club in Paris would never make it. Jazz buffs aren't gourmets. A jazz dinner club with hookers would be a first in Paris. He called to the bartender to fill up the lady's champagne flute.

"Are you a reporter?"

"Maybe."

"A lot of press here tonight."

"Right."

"What do you think of Black Jack's?"

He'd bought the champagne to keep her quiet, not to talk. "How come you're not in bunny costume?"

She laughed a throaty laugh, drowned in champagne. "I'm the big bunny."

She was big all right, bulging in a red sleeveless crewneck sweater. He wondered if she worked for management or was a freelancer. The accent was definitely American, odd for a Paris hooker. Everything about her was odd.

"We're having a party at my place later. You want to come?"

"Thanks very much, darling, but I'm working."

"Dexter will be there."

He looked closer. Something wasn't jibing. "You're American?"

"James will be there."

"James?"

"James Baldwin, right over there at the table."

"Dexter will be there, you say?"

"Of course. You want to meet him?"

"I know him."

"Oh, then you should certainly come."

"And James Baldwin will be there?"

"I just said so, didn't I?"

"At *your* place?"

"You don't have to say it snooty like that."

The conversation was absurd. A blowsy blond hooker couldn't possibly be friends with Dexter Gordon and James Baldwin. He decided to move to a table. "Sorry, I didn't mean to be snooty. Enjoy your drink." He motioned to the bartender.

"You did so mean to be snooty! Oh, I know what you meant, all right. You don't think I'm their type. How do you even know what their type is?"

He stood up. She was about to make a scene. Why wouldn't the bartender come?

"Archer, you are such a fool."

The voice was lower. He stared at her, looking closely for the first time. She batted her long eyelashes.

"No!"

"Yes!"

"I don't believe it."

"You think everyone in here is straight?"

"I had no idea."

"You are such a pill."

"This is a transvestite jazz club?"

"No. It is not a transvestite jazz club. They just don't care how you dress. Look at those bunnies. Disgusting."

"How do you know they don't care how you dress here?"

"Because I know the owner. Do you want to meet her?"

"The owner is a man, Jacques Taylor."

"Sometimes."

"I'm over my head."

"Hang-ups."

"I'd like to meet Baldwin."

"Then come."

"What do you call yourself when you're in drag?"

"Je m'appele Winnie."

He looked closely at Winnie. No, he would not have known. Rouged, mascaraed, and lipsticked, it sort of worked. The face passed well enough for feminine and a long skirt covered his hairy male body. The boobs were as fake as the blond wig, but his blue eyes were limpid and appealing. He'd dropped the falsetto. The laugh was a little off.

"Winnie?"

"Comme Churchill."

They lived in a large fifth-floor apartment on the rue de la Bûcherie, around the corner from Shakespeare and Company. Jojo, a decorator, had torn down some walls and made a minimalist loft out of what had been a six-room bourgeois apartment. Everything was white – furniture, tiled floors, walls, ceilings. The effect of white paintings in white frames on white walls was hallucinatory. The last time Archer had been there, with Sophie before her country phase set in, decoration was not the only hallucinogen present.

For the party Jojo had decorated with every kind of white flower he could find – lilies, gardenias, roses, carnations, asters, anemones. Hors d'oeuvres were set out along with champagne, wine, and whiskey. Music played softly from white speakers. Shortly before one o'clock, Baldwin, dressed entirely in black, arrived and posed next to Jojo all in white as Wayne, changed back into himself, snapped pictures and everyone clapped.

"Decoration is contrasts," Jojo pronounced grandly, "and sometimes the best contrast is no contrast."

"Zen," said someone.

Two scotches later, Dexter still had not shown. Baldwin was surrounded by a coterie of cooing French admirers, and Archer, by himself on a white couch, was about to leave when he saw Baldwin start unsteadily toward him from across the room.

He blew out a rush of smoke. "Wayne says you want to talk." He nodded. "I saw your columns on Bud Powell."

He looked like he'd been drinking all day, wobbly but lucid, with a sad clown's face so expressive it was beautiful, a study in contrasts – broad-featured but delicate, lined and bagged with dissipation and suffering but alive with intelligence and curiosity. He had the head of a big man, but a delicate body, with a tiny waist and thin legs molded into tight pants, the contrasting large head and small body almost cartoonish. His chatty, friendly manner belied the aggression and anger of his writing. He was a civil rights fighter, spokesman for his people and his time and hated being known as a black writer, said somewhere that to be known as a black writer would be to be a failure.

"You caught why Bud came, why we all came. It's not just a bunch of black cats coming over to keep from being lynched. It goes way back. Mary Cassatt came because they wouldn't let women paint nude models in the States. Sylvia Beach published *Ulysses* because it was banned in the States. Edith Wharton came because of prejudice against female writers, Josephine Baker to dance the way she wanted. Richard Wright, my mentor, chased here by the FBI, probably murdered by them."

"Murdered by the FBI?"

"That's what his daughter says. Talk to Julia. She's here somewhere."

He was drinking whisky, not champagne. "He's buried here, you know, at Père Lachaise, number one literary graveyard in the world – Molière, Balzac, Proust, Wilde – great honor to make it into Père Lachaise, like winning a Nobel – posthumously, of course." His laugh was a sharp, cigarette rasp. "Now that Richard's integrated Père Lachaise I want to get in myself. If they can take a black commie writer they can take a black fag writer."

"And you? Why did you come to Paris?"

He smiled. "I'm like the others." He finished his whisky and took another as Jojo passed with a tray. "People come here to breathe, man. Say, speaking of France, what do you think of the piece in *Le Monde* about France being bored?"

"Good piece – Pierre Viansson-Ponté knows what he's talking about."

"Sounded like a provocation."

"How do you mean?"

"Saying de Gaulle has been so good for France that France is bored with him." He laughed. "An invitation to revolt."

"Springtime and Paris is restless."

A telephone sounded.

Wayne picked it up and shrieked. Jojo went quickly to him.

"You having a fit, man?" called Baldwin.

Wayne started to say something and stopped. People pulled in closer, forming a circle around him. He was crying. Someone handed him a handkerchief.

Jojo took his hand. "Wayne?"

He could barely get the words out. "They've just shot Dr. King."

Christopher Oliver Archer was born April 11, 1968, one week after Martin Luther King's murder, one month before France exploded in a frenzy of domestic anger and rebellion it hadn't seen in a century. Sophie returned from St.-Ouen and went into labor at four o'clock that morning. It was but a short drive from their apartment on the rue du Four, where they'd moved to be ready for the baby, to the Hôpital Enfants-Assistés in Montparnasse.

Three hours later, as Archer dozed in the waiting room, a nurse came out to tell him it would be a few more hours and he could go out for breakfast. When he returned shortly after eight, Vincent was there, black eyes squinting acknowledgment at Archer. How did he get here from St.-Ouen, Archer wondered? Does he expect to go in with me to see Sophie and the baby? He'd had only a few hours sleep and was angrier than he should have been. Into this clean, antiseptic place came this contaminating thing that never washed or shaved or smiled or changed its clothes. It clung to Sophie like a barnacle that needed to be scraped away except that Sophie liked having it stuck to her.

His hope was that the baby would bring her back to Paris and cut her off from her parasitic cousin. Only here he was in the waiting room. Why wasn't he taking care of St.-Ouen? Wasn't that what he paid him to do? He needed to have these things out with him once and for all, but obviously not in a hospital waiting room.

Staring at his nemesis, a thought darted across his mind, hovered a millisecond like a water bug on a millpond and flitted away. He'd hardly known it was there until it came back, up from the murk of his unconscious to settle in the clear waters of his consciousness. He closed his eyes. A chill ran along his spine. What if the baby had dark eyes? Both he and Sophie had blue eyes.

"I want to take the babies back to St.-Ouen," she said one morning over breakfast.

They were at the table in the sunny part of the living room that opened onto blue Paris skies looking south from the rue du Four. Archer thought of it as their solarium and they'd decorated it with ferns and palms and two deck chairs where they could sit with open windows in good weather and take their meals. It was Christopher's one-month anniversary and he was dozing in his wicker bassinet. Nearby, Amy played in her crib.

It had been a busy month. Paris was growing more agitated by the day, the Vietnam peace talks were about to start and Archer had moved his family – sans Vincent – back to Paris.

Her words surprised him. "I thought you liked being back in Paris."

"Pushing a pram along city streets is not good for them. They need country air."

"You'll be bored to death."

"I have a new project, didn't I tell you? It was Vincent's idea. I'm going to write the life of Diane de Poitiers. There's a marvelous library at the Chateau d'Anet, fifteen minutes from the house. The chateau was built for her by Henry II, you know."

She was still the very pretty girl he'd married, happy to be back in her body. With the arrival of spring and good weather she was dressing in little cotton skirts and blouses again. He wanted to keep her close. "Aren't married couples supposed to live together?"

She narrowed her pretty blue eyes on him and frowned. "You always knew, Rupert, don't say you didn't, that I intended to go back to work after the second baby."

"At *l'Express*."

"This is much better."

"It doesn't sound like a real job."

"Don't be a philistine."

"I repeat: Aren't married couples supposed to live together?"

"Of course they are. But modern couples also have two careers which means they cannot live together all the time. We are a modern couple, I like to think."

"I may not be as modern as you."

It was no secret that he didn't miss St.-Ouen or that St.-Ouen didn't miss him. Construction was advancing. There would be a nice profit when they sold. Except that no one but Archer wanted to sell.

"So either I drive out or we don't see each other?"

"That's what country homes are for."

"Why keep this big place then? A studio's enough for me."

"Don't be petulant, Rupert. We'll need this for when I come to the city."

"Which will be when?"

"From time to time," she said, happily. "But the children are better off in the country. Do you deny it?"

He stood and walked to the bassinet. His son stared up at him through beautiful dark blue eyes.

22

"Of course you're coming," said Suzy. "Why wouldn't you come?"

Three of them were sitting in her little apartment on the avenue Emile Deschanel and she wouldn't hear of leaving her friend alone on Saturday night while she and Dick trekked across town to Harry's. Penny had just arrived from Marseilles, having left a student group that cancelled its visit to Paris. The May riots were making things impossible on the Left Bank, but once across the Seine, Dick figured he could find a taxi, even on Saturday night. It was always easier with pretty women.

"I won't know a soul."

Suzy was wrapping his hand as they sat at the dining table in the front room. Penny sat across from them on the day bed.

"You'll meet new people," said Dick. "Paris is where you come to meet new people – to fall in love."

"Spare me," said Penny, sipping her glass of rouge.

Penny Schiller had been Suzy's roommate at Penn, a non-Quaker girl from Quaker country who'd come to Philadelphia to be educated as girls were educated in those parts – to be good wives and mothers. Though lacking Suzy's regal beauty, Penny was attractive in a tomboyish way that made her popular at Penn and landed her a husband as a graduation present. It hadn't worked out.

"Paris is not for the jaded," said Dick. "Paris is for the pure of heart."

"I am not jaded. As for being pure of heart . . ."

"That was always your problem," said Suzy.

"What was my problem?"

"Sex."

"If marriage taught me anything it's to have low expectations."

"You married too young, Pen," said Suzy. "I knew it, but what was I supposed to say, Oh, you can't marry Bobby Schiller because you two don't have anything in common but sex."

"You should have said it."

"Never confuse sex with love," said Dick.

"Profound, Dickie, profound," said Suzy.

"Those were still pre-pill days," said Penny. "That's why girls married."

"Some abstained," said Suzy.

"Oh, right. Did you know anyone at school who abstained – apart from the Quakers, that is?"

"I'm sure Suzanne Marie Vallette de Granville abstained," said Dick.

"No comment. By the way, how's the name search coming?"

"I believe I am of royal blood," said Suzy, holding out a hand to be kissed.

"Will there be any young people be at this party?" said Penny.

"The short answer is no. It's a party for a man in his eighties."

Eric Hawkins was abandoning the *Herald* office he never used. His unofficial retirement would become official. His real office was across the street at the California anyway. Just bad luck that he lost both offices at the same time: Lucien Montsouris decided to use the disappearance of tourism during the May riots as an occasion to remodel the bar.

Montsouris cornered Archer one afternoon in the Berri Bar, leading him across the street. "This barstool," he said as they picked their way through the construction rubble, "is the one on which M. Eric has planted his derrière for more years than I can count. If the *Herald* will host a farewell party, I'll present it to him. He can put it in his apartment and pretend he's here."

Archer took the offer to Sonny who shook his head. Connie Marshall, however, was nodding. "That," she said, "is an excellent idea. Sonny, get with it. A retirement party for Eric at the California. We owe him that."

"Except it can't be at the California because of renovations," said Archer.

"Then we'll have it at Harry's. I'll call and see when they can do it. What do you think – a surprise party?"

"Impossible," said Stein.

"Eric won't do it if he knows," said Archer.

"With all the people who will want to come – we're talking about half a century in Paris – he's bound to find out," said Connie.

"Maybe not with the California closed," said Sonny. "He won't be around."

"I wonder if anyone from the States would come," said Archer.

"Buchwald," said Connie. "Art Buchwald will come for Eric."

Sonny Stein stood smoking and looking out over the Marais, the marsh. Already dressed for the party, he waited for Connie. They lived just off Place St.-Paul in the heart of what everyone called the Pletzl, the little place, where Jews came to live when they were evicted from Paris in the days when the marsh was still outside city limits. Six centuries later the Nazis came and they had to move again – fast. Stein would never have picked the Pletzl. He was raised on Hester Street, New York City's version of the Pletzl, and was glad to get out. But the Pletzl is where Connie lived, and since leaving Rachel was where Sonny lived as well.

Connie loved her place, loved the neighborhood, loved being able to take the Metro straight up the rue de Rivoli and Champs Elysées or even to walk, as they'd been doing lately. With the strikes, everyone was walking, and empty taxis were as hard to find as a night without teargas. Sonny didn't complain, but found the apartment small and cramped. He'd cracked his head on one of the low ceiling beams a few days before and the headaches persisted. He began to wonder if it was a concussion, divine punishment, God taking Rachel's side. He didn't say anything because Connie would make him go to the American Hospital.

And what if it was a concussion? With Al Lodge out he couldn't take time off anyway. He'd never been busier and the *Herald*, despite the collapse of tourism, had never sold more newspapers. Helen said Al was ready to come back but Sonny said he shouldn't come too soon. Already he wished he hadn't said it. He began forgetting things, little things. It gets easier to excuse human weakness when you experience it yourself.

He'd started wondering about his own responsibility in pushing Lodge over the edge. It was an old problem, one he'd fought for years: he had to do everything himself. The riots and headaches were making it harder. In the composing room, Tonton Pinard was using an English-speaking union member to read Archer's riot stories on galley proofs before they were set into type. Twice Tonton asked him to make changes. Twice Sonny said he'd never give in to censorship and twice it resulted in a slowdown that cost thousands of copies. Suddenly the unions were talking about a press strike, something they hadn't done so far because they wanted full coverage of the revolt.

He watched Connie come out of the bedroom in navy patent leather high heels and a navy skirt and sweater set off with a gold Hermes silk scarf and gold brooch he'd given her, a picture of elegance and sophistication. Was this the same scraggily, baggy-breasted blonde who'd drifted into his office looking for a job not so long ago?

"Think we can find a taxi?" he asked.

"It's not that far. How about a martini before we go?"

Gin would be a problem but he didn't want Connie asking

questions. He went over and started mixing. "I didn't see the final guest list," he said. "Any surprises?"

"Just how many of Eric's friends are dead. It's great that Buchwald could come."

He stirred the martinis, poured one for Connie, and poured water into his glass, plopping in an olive and a little juice. She'd never know. He threw back two aspirins when she wasn't looking. "Ben coming?"

"He RSVP'd."

"For one or two?"

"Two."

"Martine?"

"I don't know. It may be over with Martine. Probably an age thing."

"How come they have it and we don't?"

"What?"

"The age thing."

"Maybe she has better sense."

"Hey, I don't like that. Suzy de Granville might have gone for me."

"Not unless you got an ascot and a particule."

He made sure he handed her the right glass. "What the hell is a particule?"

"The *de* in front of your name – like de Granville."

"De Stein – doesn't sound right. LePoint doesn't have a particule."

"You ever wonder why it's always older men and younger women?"

"Because it's Paris. Wouldn't be like that in New York."

"Shouldn't be like that," she said. "That's what women's lib is all about. Anything you can do we can do, better, honey."

Swart finished dressing and walked out to his car. It was a splendid evening, the beeches and chestnuts in the Villa Montmorency changing from bud to blossom. He stood a moment breathing the scented air of his little community. You'd never know a revolt was going on. The Left Bank was drenched in teargas, but in the Sixteenth Arrondissement the air was pure and the birds singing in high spring voice.

It was less than half a mile to Martine's, a distance he'd driven many times, though not lately. When he heard about Eric's party he wondered if she'd come with him. Their relationship had been cool for so long he'd almost given up hope. Coming to the office each morning he looked for little signs of sex that might give her away – beard burns, rosy cheeks, nipples too much *en fleche* under her flimsy bras. He used to think he could see the signs after they'd been together, but maybe not. Maybe he just thought he saw them because he knew what they'd been doing.

He didn't have to ask her, she asked him. She had great affection for the *Herald*, something that earned the respect of the unions even though she worked for management. The unions trusted her more than they would ever trust Theo le Tac, whom they regarded as a born traitor. Still, why would she want to go to a party for Eric Hawkins? Why would she even know Eric, who never set foot to the fifth floor?

For the first time in months, the first time since that horrid night at les Halles, he was heading for her place, tingling with excitement. He parked and crossed the lobby and thought of all the times he'd taken the elevator with only one thing in mind. Sometimes it was coming back from a date; sometimes it was going to pick her up. Sometimes they didn't make it to the date because he wanted her so much. That's how bad it was. And she never said no. Even when she was bathed and made-up and dressed to go, she never said no. Not until that horrible night.

Sometimes they would make love and then instead of going wherever they were going, just slip down to one of the cafés along the avenue Mozart for bistro food and cigarettes. Back in her place, they'd do it all over again. It was why he never feared Jean-Claude, never feared her French friends. She exulted in him and told him so. It amazed him that she would give him up, and he never believed it was for good.

Walking down the hallway he felt like he was on a first date. His last time here was the horrible night. He couldn't assume anything. That was the cause of the break, wasn't it – assuming too much? He wondered how she would be. Would she be tingling as well? Was it like a first date for her or just the convenience of being escorted to an office party by her boss? No one would think anything of them coming together. She wouldn't be expected to come alone, not in the madness of Paris. How would she even get to Harry's by herself, to the other side of the city? It was natural she would come with him.

The awful words at les Halles came flashing back, "you're my father's age," or something similar. And just after he told her he loved her. What a fool he'd been. He'd even said something about marriage that night. He pressed the buzzer. God, how humiliating! And here I am again, he thought, begging for more.

It was a short walk for Archer, two miles at most, not a walk he'd made before because they hadn't lived on the rue du Four that long and he didn't hang out at Harry's. When he'd come to Europe it was to escape America, and when he settled in Paris it was to learn about France, not to sit around in a New York bar schmoozing with Americans.

He headed down the rue Bonaparte, past the Ecole des Beaux-Arts with students bivouacked in the courtyard and spilling out onto the street. The Sorbonne was closed. The police had closed it, reopened it, and closed it again but hadn't touched Beaux-Arts on the theory that fine arts students were peaceful sorts. The anarchist flags draped from the windows and graffiti on the walls made him think there might be a story at Beaux-Arts. Some boys in black neckerchiefs eyed him and shouted something he didn't understand. He kept moving, crossed the quai and started across the Pont du Carrousel. His

Alfa was available, parked in an underground garage on the rue du Four, but he wasn't about to try it out on chaotic Left Bank streets.

Paris was bored and Paris had exploded. The spring fragrance of chestnut blossoms along the leafy boulevards gave way to the stench of tear gas. Barricades of paving stones lined the streets and iron grills ripped from beneath the chestnuts were shaped into iron pikes to defend against police charges. Stores were shuttered, cars torched, their cratered remains left on impassible streets. Across the country, students took over schools and fought with police. Soon the labor unions joined in, shutting down factories and joining students in marches and sit-ins in a massive strike effort to force de Gaulle to resign.

Trains and buses stopped at the borders. Ships stood idle in harbors. Airports were closed. Garbage rotted in the streets. As the Vietnam peace talks, which de Gaulle had worked so hard to bring to Paris, opened on the Right Bank, the Left Bank looked like bombed-out Hanoi. In the middle of it all, de Gaulle disappeared.

Archer paused in the middle of the river to look out over Paris. God, what a city! In four years he'd gone from replacing a linotypist on the copy desk to the writer *Herald* readers depended on to understand the madness of France, madness comparable to 1830, 1848, and 1870, when other legitimate governments, as de Gaulle well knew, were thrown out. His one regret, filling him with sadness as his eyes swept across the city, was that he was alone. Everything he did was alone. Paris is the city of youth and love, yet Baudelaire had it right: It is a terrible place to be alone, to tread the edge of the *gouffre*, the abyss; the Seine, so tempting, like the Lorelei, luring people to their doom.

They lived separate lives. Try as he might, he could not finesse that basic truth. He might blame her – when they married he had no idea she would make such a choice. But how could she know her true nature at twenty-one? How does a twenty-one-year-old girl living at home with her parents know what she'll want from life when she's a twenty-five-year-old mother of two? She might blame him – how could he possibly choose to live estranged from his wife and children? Separate interests had driven them apart, and natures as well. Their moment of experimental exoticism had passed and they had returned to their roots.

2 3

Eric was surprised when the car didn't turn at the rue Royale. Lucien had invited him to dinner at Maxim's but continued on St.-Honoré past Royale to the rue Castiglione, crossing Place Vendôme and parking on rue de la Paix. "A drink at Harry's," he said. They went back awhile, these two, had both survived Hitler and always been comfortable with each other. Some said Eric's French wasn't the best, but Lucien didn't agree. In a lifetime of dealing with people whose French wasn't the best, he thought Eric did fine, especially for an Englishman.

Andy looked up from behind the bar as they came through the swinging doors. It was a big, noisy Saturday night, business good because people were coming over to escape Left Bank chaos. When Andy pointed downstairs, Eric frowned. He'd never been downstairs except to pee, but Lucien had him by the arm and was guiding him toward the stairs. For the first time Eric grew suspicious. The noise, instead of fading, grew louder.

When Harry MacElhone died in 1958 son Andy took over. The New York Bar had been in operation on the same little street, rue Daunou near the opera, since 1911 and always been a hangout for the *Herald* crowd, whose first offices were close by on the avenue de l'Opéra and later on the rue du Louvre. In 1923, Harry, a Scot, bought out Tod Sloan, a top U.S. jockey who rode in England and France, and used his winnings to open the New York Bar. Harry added his name, nailed up some college pennants and hung autographed pictures of celebrities who stopped by because they liked how Harry mixed drinks, especially Bloody Marys, which some said – and Harry never denied – he'd invented and named after Mary, Queen of Scots.

The secret was out by the time they reached the bottom. Two banners were strung along the walls:

ERIC – MERCI POUR LES MEMOIRES

ERIC – THANKS FOR THE MEMORIES

To the banging of a piano, a chorus of "For He's a Jolly Good Fellow" filled the room. When the singing was over Art Buchwald bellied through the bustle to greet them. "Don't know why I should be here," he shouted to Eric over the din. "You didn't hire me – but then you didn't fire me either!"

"You didn't hire Buchwald," said Frank Draper in his loud voice, "but you sure as hell hired me." Suntanned under snow-white hair, Draper embraced Eric.

"You came all this way just to see me," said Eric, "all the way from . . . where the hell did you go . . . Malaga, right?"

The room barely contained the crowd. Eric, smallest man in the room, stayed close to the stairs, reluctant to wander too deeply into the crush. People came up whom he hadn't seen since before the war; some who'd worked with him on the rue de Louvre in the 1920s. From upstairs, Andy sent down heaping trays of the hot dogs and buns you couldn't find anywhere else in Paris.

Archer pushed around the room. Ben Swart, looking rosy, stood with his secretary. Sonny, looking ghostly, stood with his secretary. Archer supposed he would have brought his secretary, too, if he'd had one. He chatted awhile with Helen, getting the latest on Al's recovery. He met the muscled stud standing guard over Gretchen Kilic. He bumped into Dick LePoint and Suzy de Granville, who introduced him to a friend, Penny Schiller, a pretty girl with bangs from Philadelphia. A few bodies away he saw Theo le Tac and Tonton Pinard crushed together without hope of escaping each other.

He started to move on. Penny asked him something.

"Sorry, it's so noisy – what did you say?"

"I asked if it's safe for a girl to visit the Latin Quarter."

His first impression was of brown – short brown hair, brown sweater, brown skirt, brown foulard. The second impression was more striking: She had gray wolf's eyes, with what looked like tiny red dots in the center. "You mean alone?"

"Unless I can find some company."

The invitation was clear. "I have some mornings free."

"Oh, would you, Rupert?" said Suzy, regal as always in white.

"I live near the Latin Quarter," he said, almost shouting. "A few blocks away. The students haven't gotten to my street yet."

"Penny's staying with us," said Suzy. "Call her."

Ben Swart, with Buchwald, Eric, and Lucien in his wake, knifed his way through the masses toward the rear of the room, carefully tacking at the bar to avoid spilling anyone's champagne or getting mustard on their clothes. Swart mounted the piano stool and shouted something. Nobody could hear him. The bartender banged a knife on a bottle. Gradually the room quieted.

"A great occasion," Swart called out, "the celebration of Eric Hawkins's half century at the *Paris Herald*." There were cheers and toasts and when the room quieted Swart introduced Art Buchwald.

Swart stood down and Buchwald stood up as the crowd clapped for the little man with the big glasses and the lisp who'd been hired off the streets of Paris and gone on to become the most popular humorist in America. He told some stories to get the room laughing and when he was done introduced Lucien, standing beside a large object covered in printing paper. With a flourish, Lucien pulled off the paper to reveal the bar stool from the California. Attached to it was a lettered sign: ERIC'S STOOL.

More clapping. Just as Eric, teary-eyed from laughter and emotion, was throwing his arms around his old comrade to thank him, a woman's scream rang out. Heads turned toward Connie Marshall. Sonny Stein had collapsed in her arms.

He met Penny Schiller in a sunny café on the Place St.-Sulpice. The worst fighting yet, on the rue Gay Lussac by the Sorbonne, had broken out the night before. The students came armed with Molotov cocktails, hurling them at the police, who, furious, retaliated with tear gas and charges against the barricades. By morning the street was a graveyard of overturned, gutted, burned-out car carcasses. Archer got a taste of it. After checking his foreign press credentials, a policeman sent him sprawling into the street, shouting, "Bobby Kennedy! Bobby Kennedy!"

Kennedy had been murdered in Los Angeles two nights before.

She was taking coffee on the terrace of the Café de la Mairie, across from the fountain, across from the chestnut trees, next to the great old church with its famous organ. People wandered in and out of the church and religious shops. Pigeons clustered around the fountain in the quiet of the morning, just another peaceful spring day in Paris with no trace of the ruins or stench that marked the boulevards only blocks away.

Crossing the square he kept his eye on her, a pretty girl in sandals, short skirt, bare legs, pink blouse, reading her newspaper, taking the sun, alone in a café. Had he not known she was waiting for him, he still would have been tempted to stop. How long since he'd done such a thing? In love almost as long as he'd been in Paris, he'd never thought of trying to meet someone else. He felt good that this girl, this American girl reading her *Herald*, was waiting for him. The last American girl he'd dated was in Phoenix and that was in a different lifetime, before he'd given a thought to Europe, before he was a husband and father, back in the good old days, when the president and attorney general were both named Kennedy.

He ordered a café crème and croissant. She ordered another café express and lit a Marlboro. "How's your editor?"

"He'll be out for a while."

She nodded. "Sad."

"He needs the rest."

The orders came. She looked at him appraisingly. "You think the riots are over?"

"No. But students are like bats: only leave their caves at night." She seemed more attractive than at Harry's, the rare woman who looked better by daylight. "So tell me how you met Suzy."

"French majors at Penn. She came to Europe and I got married. Then I got divorced and went back for a teaching degree. This was our class trip to Europe. I left the group in Marseilles when they decided to skip Paris. I called Suzy and hitchhiked up here to see her and meet Dick. Too exciting to miss."

Afterward, they walked down the rue de Buci and across Place St.-Michel to the Latin Quarter. The boulevards were impassible. South of St.-Germain was filthy because street cleaners were on strike along with everyone else. The tiny streets of the Latin Quarter were bubbling with activity, students hanging around for a cheap lunch of croque monsieur or crêpes while awaiting the evening's activities. Across the bridge, Notre-Dame looked normal. The students didn't dare cross over for that would put them facing the préfecture de police, not a good place for a riot.

After lunch he put her in a cab back to Suzy's. Before parting they agreed to meet at St.-Sulpice the next day, same time, same table.

"You want to talk about your divorce?"

She was dressed in a yellow T-shirt and khaki shorts, legs stretched out in the sun. They ordered coffee and croissants and she lit a Marlboro. The previous night had been strangely quiet, as though Gay Lussac had worn out both sides and, like armies, they needed a day to assess and recuperate. It was already ten degrees warmer than the previous day.

"Bobby worked in Baltimore. We lived in a place called Ellicott City. He went off to work every morning and I tried to figure out how to spend the day. Marriages like that don't work anymore. Or maybe some do. It worked for the neighbors. I don't play tennis or bridge and don't like martinis. Didn't want to start breeding yet. Thank God for the pill. I knew about Suzy, how she'd come to Paris, was hired at the *Herald*, met Dick. I sat reading her letters and figured I had to do something. Poor Bobby. What did I do wrong, he kept asking. It was very sad."

He watched and listened and thought it was like the old paint coming off and getting down to the good wood again. She had a vulpine quality, like foxes that stand motionless, watching, waiting for you to make the first move; curious, cautious, nothing wasted, all energy potential.

"What about you?" she asked.

"My wife and I seem to be separated."

"That's an odd way to put it."

He sipped his coffee. "Actually it's the first time I've put it that way – the first time I've put it *any* way. I think I've been putting off thinking about it."

"I'm not prying."

"I need to talk about it . . . no, I need to figure it out and one way is to talk about it. Sophie is like your neighbors in Ellicott City . . . likes children, likes the country."

"How old was she when you married?"

"Twenty-one."

"That's how old I was. You just don't know. You hope you find out in time. Do you have children?"

"Two."

He noticed the little red dots again. Was that what led him to say what he said next? "I've been to Suzy and Dick's – never seemed big enough for house guests."

"There's a daybed in the living room. It gets a little crowded."

"I have a large empty apartment two blocks from here."

He found a taxi and they headed down rue Bonaparte. Past rue Jacob, Archer saw a crowd of students clustered outside Beaux-Arts, many more than had been there a few nights before on his way to Harry's. Traffic barely moved. The cabbie muttered he should have turned on rue Jacob, but it was too late. They inched into the mass, which slowly gave way. Suddenly someone shouted something. The taxi was engulfed.

"What are you doing?" shouted the driver. He was sweating profusely despite having all the windows open. "I'm a working man. I'm with you."

Black banners, symbols of the anarchists, were draped over the stone pillars in front, and from windows on buildings surrounding the inner courtyard a dozen banners and posters shouted their messages. Across the entrance to the courtyard, attached to the sculpted heads of Puget and Poussin atop the pillars, a banner proclaimed:

DIX ANS ÇA SUFFIT!

Two youths, unshaven, dressed in black, black scarves at their necks ready to be pulled up over their faces in case of tear gas, peered into Penny's window. "You are with us, grandfather, but what about these two?"

"Let us pass," cried the cabbie. "We've done nothing to you."

"You are French?" one of the youths asked Archer.

"We're American," said Archer. "I'm a journalist covering the events. I need to get to my newspaper."

"Ah," he cried, "American." He turned to the crowd. "Les Amerloques, les Amerloques!" They crushed up, trying to open the doors but were packed in too tight. "Tell me, Mr. American journalist," cried the boy, "why are you not in Vietnam? Do you work for the CIA? Was it the CIA that killed Dr. King and Bobby Kennedy?"

A boy in a red scarf said something, the door was pulled open on

Penny's side, and she was pulled out. "Hey," Archer shouted, trying to get out, but both doors were held tightly closed as the crowd gave way and the taxi bolted ahead.

He turned and saw Penny waving to him.

The cab raced ahead, pulling up as it reached the quai. Archer tossed him ten francs and raced back toward Beaux-Arts.

They'd turned the courtyard into a campsite, a bivouac, tents pitched on the stones, charred remains from campfires, debris, music playing, placards, sleeping bags, trash, a banner **POUVOIR AU PEUPLE** hung across a door, another **NOUS SOMMES TOUS DES JUIFS ALLE-MANDS** in honor of Dany Cohn-Bendit, the revolt leader who'd been shipped across the border to Germany.

"Who's in charge here?" he called out.

Stupid. Why would anarchists have anyone in charge? He ran into the building and up and down the corridors, looking into rooms, shouting her name.

"Get lost, bourgeois," a girl shouted. "Your nana has joined the revolution."

He ran back up the rue Bonaparte, toward the commissariat he remembered from the night with Errol Garner. A policeman listened, tapping his pencil on the desk. "Do you know how many young people are missing in Paris right now?"

"This girl is a foreigner, a tourist. She is not missing. She was kid-napped, pulled out of a taxi and taken away. This could be a capital offense."

"Did she resist being taken away?"

He thought back. The door opened, someone grabbed her and pulled her out. When she turned back to him, she waved.

"Of course she resisted. She was abducted."

"I'll send someone as soon as I have someone. It's not like we don't have anything else to do. Fill out this form. And don't worry. Beaux-Arts is not the Sorbonne."

The newspaper was chaotic. The unions were holding round-the-clock meetings in the ground floor front office. Even the distributors, who normally didn't arrive until 10 P.M., had come in, and trucks of various sizes lined street and sidewalk. Horns honked, traffic barely moved, crowds pushed in and out of the building, flowing onto sidewalks and street, into the Berri Bar, across the street to mingle with construction crews at the Hotel California. So far the *Herald* had had slowdowns and stoppages, but no strikes.

He hurried upstairs to the newsroom and told Al Lodge what had happened. Even with the riots, a kidnapped American girl was front-page news.

Archer still saw him crouched in the corner in his skivvies. Did he remember?

"*Was* she kidnapped?" he asked.

"That's what the cop asked."

"You better check. Go back to Beaux-Arts."

He went over to tell Suzy, repeating what the cop said: Penny was in no danger.

"She was so bored in Baltimore," Suzy said. "This will be good for her."

24

There's never been a better reason for leaving Paris," said Walter Thayer. "Riots every night. Government broken down. Anarchy reigns. We've been getting the paper out, but Ben tells me it's a daily battle with the unions and will only get worse."

They were meeting in the *Herald Tribune* building on West Forty-First Street just days after the Gay Lussac riots. It was to be a New York meeting of number twos, Thayer, Fritz Beebe and Sydney Gruson, but after the Gay Lussac explosion Jock Whitney said he was coming and so Kay Graham decided to fly up from Washington and that left Punch Sulzberger no choice but to walk over from Forty-Third Street. Thayer was working on Whitney to move the *Herald* out of Paris, and Sulzberger couldn't allow them to persuade Graham in his absence. The *Times* could block one of them, not both.

"Hold on, Walter," said Gruson, who'd never hidden his preference for Paris. "De Gaulle has called elections for the end of next month. Polls say he'll win handily."

"So . . . he'll still have the unions to deal with. How long can he stay in power?"

"The unions are as much for law and order as the Gaullists," said Gruson. "They want larger paychecks, not revolution. They're not crazy like New York unions."

"The question we must answer," said Graham, "is whether we'll be facing this over and over – even if de Gaulle wins. In other words, is the situation spinning out of control in a way that could permanently affect the *Herald*'s future?"

Finally she was getting comfortable with the boys. Thayer was a bit of a prig, but she found Whitney informal and pleasant. And *Times* or not, no one could hate Punch Sulzberger, a nice man, she decided. Any provincial complex she'd had toward New York was lessened by fact that the *Times* was their junior partner. The *Paris Herald* was the one thing the *Times* owned but did not control. They hated it and she loved it. She, not Punch, would decide whether to move from Paris. Jock favored moving; Punch did not, leaving the matter up to her.

"The anarchy in France today is not caused by the unions," pronounced Thayer. "The unions and the political left only joined in when they saw that the radical left – the Trotskyites, Maoists or whatever they call themselves – might bring down the government with them on the sidelines. Whether de Gaulle wins or looses, anarchy will continue – and not just in France. There's trouble in Italy and Germany, as well. The one place that's still quiet is Switzerland."

"Too much quiet is the Swiss problem," said Gruson.

No one laughed. They fell silent, each wondering if this was the moment they'd been putting off. The groundwork was laid. Tax breaks in Switzerland would allow them to pay off indemnities owed in France in ten years. For distribution, Zurich held the edge, but Geneva had the advantage of being French-speaking rather than German. On the other hand, the Elysée was promising help if they stayed in Paris.

It was a tough decision – tough for Whitney because he was Bennett's Paris custodian; tough for Sulzberger for if they moved he would have been outvoted, another *Times* humiliation; tough for Graham because she held the decisive vote.

She looked around the table, reading each face. "Change is always difficult," she said. "You all know how hard it was for me to change editorial policy on Vietnam. Some things just have to be done."

They watched her, wondering if she'd given something away. All her life she'd been in the shadow of powerful men – her father, her husband Phil, Fritz Beebe, all the confident and domineering men who ran the *Washington Post*. Five years ago in a meeting like this she wouldn't have uttered a word. She'd have patted her bouffant and smiled or nodded if someone happened to glance her way. She still liked listening more than talking, but no longer was shy about speaking up.

"Vietnam is at the core of the world's unrest," said Sulzberger. "On every continent. Vietnam fuels our race riots."

"What terrifies me," she said, "is that whether it's Humphrey or Nixon in November, Vietnam will go on, along with all the hate and violence. When Walter Lippmann came to us the first thing he said was that the line we'd been following on Vietnam – which went back to Phil and his ties to Jack Kennedy – had to change. He was right. How could I have a columnist of his stature arguing day after day that the war was a catastrophe and right next to him editorials saying stay the course?"

"In a way," said Sulzberger, "Scotty Reston played the same role for us. Jack Kennedy told Scotty after his humiliation by Khrushchev in Vienna that he had to show the Russians he was tough and the place to show it was Vietnam. Scotty never agreed with that and neither did our editorials."

Graham listened to the friendly, almost diffident man across from her and decided they could never be enemies. It wasn't in either of them. She remembered the story of the *Times*'s opposition to Punch after his father, Arthur Hays Sulzberger, retired, and his brother-in-law, Orvil Dryfoos, who replaced him, suddenly died. Some thought Punch too green and wanted a "regent" until the dauphin matured. It was the same thing she'd faced after Phil died. The men on the board didn't think she could do it, didn't think a woman could do it. She and Punch both proved them wrong.

"I guess what I'm saying," she said, looking at Whitney, "is I think

Sydney is right that the troubles in Paris are not endemic. But whether Paris is the best place for the *Herald* in coming years is another matter. I haven't made up my mind, but tend to think that Jock offers the best guidance. His love of Paris going back to Bennett is balanced by our need to make the right business decision."

"Thank you, Kay."

"Are we ready to vote?" asked Thayer.

Nobody answered. A long silence was broken by Whitney:

"We want this vote to be unanimous. I say we let the French have their elections first. It will clear the air for us."

"Absolutely," said Sulzberger, relieved.

"I agree," said Graham.

Thayer could hardly disagree. "Are we ready to adjourn?" he asked.

"While we're here," said Gruson, "there's one other thing: You all know about Sonny Stein. Hemorrhage stoke . . . out for weeks. Al Lodge before that. The strains are showing. Both these men, and Ben Swart as well, came from the *Herald Tribune*. With the new ownership it's time we talked about new management in Paris."

It was too abrupt. Had Gruson spoken to Sulzberger?

"You know, Sydney," said Fritz Beebe after a moment, "we could sit here all day trying to decide whether the publisher in Paris should be yours or ours, or the editor, or the managing editor, or the reporters for that matter. What we have now, it seems to me, is ideal. Stein and Lodge, with ties to neither of us, can be objective. As long as they're not incapacitated – and I've seen nothing to suggest that – I see no reason for change."

Gruson was shaking his head. "I'll say it again – and Punch will back me up: The *Times* bought into the *Paris Herald* as a means of keeping the *New York Times* in Europe. Yes, we have to share space with the *Post*, but what rankles is that those running the *Herald* are connected to neither of us. Ben Swart – to whom does he answer? I know Ben, knew him in Paris, but can't get him on the phone without practically calling a board meeting. What kind of deal is that?"

"That's the whole point, Sydney," said Whitney. "You *shouldn't* be able to order Ben around – or Sonny either for that matter. Decisions that affect us all should come from us all – that is, from the board."

"You can't," said Thayer, "expect Europeans to read a newspaper written for Americans."

St.-Ouen had no phone. For Archer to talk to his wife, she had to call him from the café in Berchères where she drove from time to time in the used Citroën Deux Chevaux they'd found in Dreux. She'd put Amy on the phone to chatter away in a French he barely understood. He was losing contact with his children. They agreed he would drive out on a mid-June Saturday, a week before the first round of elections. He would arrive in the morning before the cousins descended for the weekend's activities.

Amy darted across the courtyard when she saw the Alfa pull in. Sophie emerged from the kitchen carrying Christopher. The door to Mme. Mignon's house was open. Archer saw an easel. Vincent had moved in.

"How is it possible? The contract says these rooms belong to her."

"She's never come by."

"And if she does? Has Philippe agreed?"

"Well, not exactly."

Upstairs, workers had walled off the front and back halves, creating separate sleeping quarters for each family. Sophie's bedroom – Archer thought of it as hers though in fact it was theirs – was more or less finished, as was the children's bedroom next to it. A ceiling had been laid over the lower beams so the bedrooms were not directly under the rafters of the still un-repaired slate roof. The kitchen had a functioning stove and a table big enough for guests. For summer lunches, they set up outside. A new water heater provided hot water. The massive front room overlooking the valley of the Vesgre was used for storage. A smaller room across from the kitchen served as the family room. He wondered if the house would ever be finished – or if he would be there to see it.

Vincent had set up his studio in Mme. Mignon's front room. Through the doorway he saw piles of blank canvases. The easel facing the window was covered by a draped cloth. Vincent himself was nowhere to be seen.

"You can't imagine how well my work is going," Sophie bubbled as she set about preparing lunch. He still hadn't decided if he would stay the night. He wanted to sleep with his wife but to do that he'd have to endure ten hours of cousins and in-laws, paté and pastis. Outside, the children were playing, Christopher in his playpen and Amy along side, both growing up in the country to be good French peasants. Sophie nipped from red table wine in a plastic bottle.

"I go into Anet every day," she said. "Thank God for Vincent. I couldn't manage without him. By the way, I've raised his salary. I do all my work in Anet. I can't seem to work here. Everything is going so well. You should be pleased. I see now that after a year or two I'll have to move back to Paris. There's a lot about Diane de Poitiers in Anet but so much more in Paris."

It was as though they weren't married anymore. Her interest in him and his work, never great, had become nonexistent. Did she even know that Paris was in tumult, that de Gaulle had disappeared, that elections to decide the future of France were days away, that he'd been working twelve-hour days for weeks? He might tell her he had a different girl at the rue du Four every night and she'd just smile and go back to talking about Diane de Poitiers. He'd lost her, was probably losing his children as well, and what made it all possible was Vincent, whose last name he couldn't even remember.

Vincent had become more important in Sophie's life than her husband, whose only use was to pay the bills. However talented the two cousins were, neither of them earned a sou. Despite that, Sophie had clearly become Vincent's patron, which meant that he, Archer, was the real patron. He was supporting the man who had stolen his wife. Archer, the American, had become a disposable adjunct to this French family. He'd made some children, paid for an apartment in Paris, helped finance a country house, but sooner or later would be gone. Vincent, not Archer, belonged to the enduring family.

"I don't think you should stay out here for one or two more years."

Her face darkened. "One or two years at least – *at least*. Certainly I will return to Paris, I will have to, but I can't possibly come anytime soon. My work is here. This is where Diane lived, where her chateau was built by Henri II. If you could see it you would understand. It is the work I was born to do. I am in love with Diane. How could you even think of asking me to leave before I'm ready? How incredibly selfish you are."

"My God – you accuse me of being selfish. You leave our home, take the children, move to this place that was supposed to be a weekend country house, start a new life with your cousin and accuse me of being selfish when I ask you to come back."

"Oh, how you distort things! I never could talk to you seriously about my interests. You see everything your own way. All that matters to you is news, news, news – news and newspapers. As if any of that mattered. It's all gone the next day anyway. Only history matters. How boring you are."

She was agitated and got up to walk outside. He heard her calling to Vincent lurking in the bushes somewhere. If he made a scene it would just reinforce everyone's view that he was the vulgar, bad-tempered American. The moment had passed. Soon more cousins and in-laws would be arriving, the pastis would be opened, everyone would have a good time and he would be ignored. If he stayed he risked getting drunk on the licorice liquor he detested and making a scene that would embarrass everyone.

Better to return to Paris. Maybe he'd find some riots to cover. Or he could camp out at La Calavados with Joe Turner and drink

Canadian Club. Or he could go looking for Penny and she could come to live with him. She was on his mind lately. They'd run a little box on page two about her disappearance, the American student from Ellicott City, Md., still missing in the chaos that was Paris.

He took the country roads toward Mantes, past the farmhouse that belonged to Vadim-Fonda. He didn't blame Sophie. She was living the way the French of her class had always lived with their country houses and garden parties and servants. It just happened that Sophie's servant was her cousin. It was a fine way to live, elegant, chic, raffiné. He could see her wandering day after day hand-in-hand with Vincent through Diane's chateau.

It was he, Archer, who didn't fit. Had he been French he wouldn't be racing away, fleeing the family fun. Had he been French he would just now be arriving, arms full of packages with all the horrible things they love to consume: the unctuous pastis in every shade of green; liqueurs fermented from anything that grows; tins and jars of rillettes, andouillette, riz de veau, paté, tongue, boudin noir; lamb's testicles, the greatest delicacy of all, best swimming in blood with baguette and cornichons, washed down with a shot of plonk. Intestines, tripe. What better word for it all than tripe?

Were Archer French, Vincent wouldn't be around. Philippe would know how to deal with Vincent. He, Archer, couldn't deal with it because he was a foreigner and had no right to ask his wife to send away a cousin, someone she'd known long before him and the way things were going would know long after him. Vincent's omnipresence had something to do with him personally, with Archer, the American.

Were Archer French, Vincent would not be thinking that Sophie would be his again once they drove him back to America.

Were he French, he would be thrilled that his wife had embarked on a biography of Diane de Poitiers, mistress of the Henri II, great grandson of William the Conquerer, who had made England French – for a while, at least.

Were he French, he would find his wife's project charming, cultured, exciting – *ravissant, éblouissant, merveilleux*, something Proust himself might admire and praise.

But he was not French.

25

Penny Schiller sat drinking coffee on the eighth floor of a student residence at the Cité universitaire, a vast complex built between the wars as home for the thousands of foreign students who come to Paris each year seeking enlightenment. Located at the end of boulevard Raspail, on the edge of Parc Montsouris with its pretty little lake, the Cité is only a few Metro stops from all the Left Bank schools.

Guy, one of the two boys with her, was saying something she didn't want to hear. Julio, the other one, remained silent. She was being betrayed.

Guy had bruised her wrist extracting her from the taxi in front of Beaux Arts and never stopped apologizing. An hour later she could have walked away but decided the revolution was more exciting than another day at the Louvre. They'd taken her into a loft area on the fourth floor and put her in a chair across from Guy and Julio. It was good theatre. Behind them was a poster of Che Guevara in his scraggly beard and black beret.

She'd heard Archer calling. She could have called back. What stopped her was a gesture from Julio. He was a very handsome boy who with his scraggly beard and black beret – surely no accident – looked like the poster behind him. She'd thought his red scarf meant he was a communist while Guy's black scarf identified him as an anarchist, but Julio's scarf came from running with the bulls at Pamplona where the Basques wear red scarves, though dressed in white, not black. Julio was a Basque. They were all anarchists at Beaux-Arts. Communists were too bourgeois.

Hadn't she come to Paris for adventure? Isn't that why she'd left her student group in Marseilles? Isn't that why she'd asked Archer to show her the Left Bank? Archer said the students were like bats, and she was inside the bat cave. Maybe she'd write an article for the *Herald* on the revolution from the anarchist perspective.

They'd taken over the campus. They showed her workshops and studios. They went into a large amphitheater to hear Louis Althusser, a Marxist philosopher, though it was less a lecture than a shouting match between Althusser and the anarchists. In the evening they built fires in the courtyard and cooked sausages and argued and drank red wine. Julio sat beside her. Not once did she think about leaving. When they gave her pen and paper she started taking notes for the article she would write when she was free.

But she was free. Looking back on it, they probably expected her to leave after the wine and sausages but she didn't leave and so was given a sleeping bag and slept on the floor in one of the classrooms with the others. She didn't know whether Julio or Guy would share her sleeping bag, and was pleased it was Julio, one of the student leaders. She'd leave that part out of the story.

Guy was chubby and polite while Julio was dark and edgy with an ironic little smile that played on his lips. Both Guy and Julio were smart, talented, good-looking boys and she decided that if that was how anarchists were then anarchy wasn't so bad. Guy kept looking at her wrist and apologizing. One thing that annoyed her was that the girls threw out her T-shirt and bra, saying girls didn't wear bras anymore. The sweater they gave her was scratchy, definitely not cashmere.

They took her to the Cité universitaire, walking her around the complex, showing her the park and lake. She loved all of it, so unlike anything she'd known at Penn. She loved their good humor, their camaraderie, everyone tutoyering everyone else, calling each other comrade, kissing, embracing, students of all colors and shades, a little United Nations celebrating the student revolution. There was a flea market next to the campus where she bought jeans and T-shirts and underwear. She supposed somebody somewhere was worrying about her, but probably not too much.

With elections approaching, the violence had tapered off, though groups of students still headed for the Latin Quarter each night and sporadic clashes broke out. At Beaux-Arts they worried the police would find out where the antigovernment posters were made and lock it up like the Sorbonne. The Left Bank was occupied territory. Dark vans with caged windows parked along the boulevards with itchy police inside praying to get out and crack a few heads. She felt sorry for the flics, sweltering inside those stuffy vans like animals waiting for the trainers to come and open their cages.

"That's why they hate us so much," said Guy. "They are our prisoners."

Each night one of the leading lights of the revolution showed up at Beaux-Arts. After Althusser, Roger Garaudy, theoretician of the French Communist Party, came to debate Alain Krivine, the Trotskyite, and she filled half a notebook. "The left cannot take power in the street," Garaudy argued as the amphitheater filled with boos. "The street is the only path to power in a bourgeois nation like France," replied Krivine to cheers.

"You will provoke a backlash that sets us back a decade," Garaudy shouted over the tumult. "We must work within the system, win the confidence of the electorate and come to power legally." He was a nice, grandfatherly looking man in tweed jacket, blue shirt, and tortoise horn-rims. She felt sorry for him too.

Krivine, dark, angular, sinister in long hair and black glasses, ridiculed him. "The idea that the PCF could ever be elected in France is hallucinatory," he pronounced. "If Lenin had waited Russia would still be ruled by the czars."

"France is not Russia," shouted Garaudy to more booing.

In America, she thought, revolutionaries are arrested; in France, they become prophets and professors. They never knew who would show up. One night it was Jean-Paul Sartre and Louis Aragon. The next night Boris Fraenkel, the Trotskyite who translated Herbert Marcuse into French, came out to announce a special guest. From the wings stepped Dany Cohn-Bendit, and they were on their feet for the redheaded revolutionary who'd been exiled to Germany and sneaked back into France.

After a week she saw the paradox. Students were well into their twenties and still undergrads. Classes were free, housing was free, sex was free, food was almost free, and they received small allowances, subsidized by the regime they were trying to overthrow.

"You've got this great life and yet you're rioting in the streets to change the system," she said to Guy over lunch one day. "What is it – guilt?"

"Not guilt – justice."

"Justice means someone else is going to take your place."

"Good for society, not so good for me."

"So altruistic. I think I'd be on the other side."

"Who's going to do it if not us? Certainly not the unions who benefit from the class struggle. Most of us at Beaux-Arts are bourgeois. Julio's family owns half of San Sebastian. My father is a urologist in the Sixteenth, supporter of Giscard's right wing. Only ten percent of students come from workers' homes. We want to change things – end the baccalaureate system which rejects half the students who take it, stigmatizing them."

"You think the socialists or communists would be any better?"

"Of course not. They're part of the rotten system. Why do you think we're anarchists? We will create a new system, a non-system."

Julio was half French, half Spanish, swarthy, brilliant, and extremely sexy even in a dirty sweater. He kept an erection all night, periodically waking her. Studying to be an architect, he was formal and precise, strange qualities for an anarchist. Guy was a painter, slower, more serious, more cautious, not at all interested in sex. Guy was more concerned about her, always asking if she shouldn't let someone know where she was.

She'd begun writing the story she hoped to have published. Another week and she might be ready to leave. Or not. The problem was Julio. She liked Julio and thought he liked her. She wondered why there weren't other girls around him.

Drinking coffee with them on the eighth floor she was hearing something new. Guy was doing all the talking. Julio wouldn't even look at her.

"Your friends, your family, what must they be thinking?"

She looked out over the park. It was midweek between election rounds and the police had finally locked up Beaux-Arts. The entire Latin Quarter was patrolled, worse than under the Nazis, everyone said. The Cité was teeming with restless students with nothing to do. More riots would just mean more votes for the Gaullists.

"You're so sweet, so thoughtful," she said, voice heavy with sarcasm.

"They thought you'd show up the next day – or the next. But after a week, surely they expect the worst."

She riveted her eyes on Julio, still silent, still refusing to look at her.

"At least *call* them," said Guy. "Show them you're still alive."

"I told you I'm not ready to leave. I'll leave after the second round."

"We don't want you to leave either," said Guy. "It's just that – well, to be honest, the situation has changed."

"So the revolution is over?"

"No, the revolution is not over!" said Julio loudly, voice sharp, annoyed. Finally he looked at her. "We've been over it with you before. Mao teaches that the revolution is permanent, but until you have achieved the revolution you must play by their rules. That means elections; that means doing nothing to provoke a reaction on the eve of elections."

"Ha," she said, angry at his betrayal, "so you agree with Garaudy, not Krivine – Garaudy of the Communist Party you hate so much."

"What do you know about political tendencies, about tactics?" said Julio. "A little bourgeoise like you."

"That's not what you call me when we're in bed."

Guy laughed. Julio did not. "You can go back whenever you want," said Guy, "that's not the point."

"What's the point?"

"What Guy means is that you can go back – or not go back – whenever you want," said Julio. "Exactly right. You just can't stay with us."

"To be completely honest," said Guy, "others are coming."

"You're throwing me out?"

"Oh, come on," said Guy, "don't be dramatic. We're all friends. We'll always be friends. We'll come visit you in the States."

"I can turn you in, you know."

"For what?" said Julio, surprised.

"You raped me."

"You call what we did together rape?"

"You kidnapped me."

"Who kidnapped who? We can't get rid of you. Anyway, it's time for you to go out and spread the revolutionary message. You've been a good student. You're prepared. You must move on."

She took the train to Luxembourg Station and walked into the gardens. It was a late June morning and the gardens, protected by their gold-tipped iron fences, had been spared the destruction that surrounded them. Mothers pushed prams around the pond and old men sat reading newspapers in rented iron chairs. Children ran along the paths and pushed sailboats in the pond. Paris was beautiful. She'd thought she'd be depressed and was exhilarated. What she needed was a bath and clean clothes. She couldn't go to Suzy's. If she'd been kidnapped she wouldn't do that, she'd go to the police.

She came out of the gardens onto the rue Bonaparte and picked her way along to the rue St.-Sulpice, turning left and walking toward the church, still untouched by the riots. At a kiosk she bought a *Herald* and at the Café de la Mairie bought cigarettes, found a seat on the terrace, ordered an express, and opened the newspaper. The name Rupert Archer stared out at her under an election headline. She fished in her purse for his phone number, went inside and dialed the number.

The rue du Four was around the corner. He buzzed her in. No elevator. She climbed three flights. In pajamas, he was waiting at the door. "Give me a cup of coffee," she said, "and I'll tell you everything. Then a bath."

Over coffee in the kitchen, she told him the story – as much as she cared to tell.

"You want to go to the police?"

She lit a cigarette. "Did they know I was missing?"

"I reported it to the commissariat near Beaux-Arts. Five-minute walk from here."

"Do you think I could write about it for the *Herald*?"

She saw his surprise. "Talk to Helen. I have no idea what she'll say."

"What do you think?"

He sensed she'd come to stay awhile. He'd been planning to take advantage of the election break to drive to St.-Ouen, but no one would miss him.

"Innocent American captured by revolutionaries. *Were* you captured?"

"You saw me dragged off."

"But you waved to me."

She laughed. "I was being brave."

"Were you kidnapped or weren't you? It's the first thing Helen will ask."

"And the second thing?"

"Were you – well, you know – abused?"

She drew deeply on the cigarette. "They called me a bourgeoise, wanted to reeducate me to the anarchist point of view. I stayed because I found it interesting."

"So you were not abused?"

"I was not abused."

"The anarchist point of view – that's what they said? Not communist, not Maoist, not Trotskyite. Anarchist."

"They're all anarchists at Beaux-Arts."

He got up to put the cups in the sink.

"You'll put in a word for me with Helen?"

He turned back to her. The red points bore into him. She was wearing sandals, T-shirt, and old jeans. Her hair was longer. Her breasts bounced as she moved and he'd desired her from the moment she walked into the flat. Standing, he was aware that the flap of his pajamas posed a problem. She noticed.

He turned away. "Sure."

"Now that bath . . . and I don't suppose I could borrow some clothes. Like maybe a bra. Anarchist girls don't wear bras."

They walked to the rear of the apartment. The bed was still unmade. The fox eyes examined the prey, aware of its problem.

26

They worked together on her article. Archer had done interviews with Garaudy and Althusser, but Fraenkel was unapproachable and Sartre didn't give interviews. If any of them read the *Herald* they were going to get a surprise.

One day she told him about Julio with the permanent erection. "All Basques are like that," she said. "He said that's why Basques are in love with bulls, because, like us, they think the only thing more glorious than fucking is dying."

She didn't know politics but was interested in education. "The French education system is sclerotic. They're going to change it."

"I doubt it. *Le Monde* had it right. It's springtime and the French are bored."

They were at the kitchen table writing and editing. She was a decent writer, but had never written a newspaper article. "You're so jaded and so terribly American. The students are idealists. What's wrong with that?"

"Lenin was an idealist. Look what happened."

"These kids hate communism. There wasn't a communist among them."

They'd slept together on the first night. She'd bathed, slipped into some of Sophie's summer clothes, and they'd walked to the commissariat on the rue de l'Abbaye where the police dug out the missing person's report, checked it off and filed it away for eternity. At the *Herald*, Suzy and Dick hugged her, Helen encouraged her, and Archer wrote two paragraphs about the return of the missing girl from Philadelphia.

She was a good listener and easy to talk to. Growing up, Archer had a sister just enough older so that they'd never been confidantes. His mother, a frustrated socialite who detested his father for having no social skills, rarely had anything to say to her son. The girlfriends he'd had along the way weren't for conversation. Claire Lambert was the first woman he'd opened up to and he still had the scars. Sophie had become remote and self-centered and came with Cousin Vincent, her doppelganger, making intimacy impossible. Helen was a good friend. Then along came Penny.

She liked a cigarette after sex in the morning and they would lie under a single sheet in the hot weather and chatter away. Her body was smooth and soft and it was like running his fingers over the undulating glass of a finely blown bowl. They would lie back and talk about whatever occurred to them until the need for caffeine drove them into the kitchen for breakfast and to work on her article.

It was a very perfect summer affair, a seasonal thing, unique, impossible to extend, never to be repeated or duplicated, no complications. They had different lives. They knew it but never said it.

One morning she said: "A week ago I was a revolutionary member of the proletariat and now I'm a bourgeoise in a big apartment who lies in bed with sex and cigarettes until ten."

"So why did you leave?"

"They made me leave."

"Are you putting that in the article?"

"It has nothing to do with it."

"Why did they make you leave?"

"Their girlfriends were coming back."

"You didn't want to leave?"

"I needed a push."

"You know the whole student revolution thing isn't serious."

She came up on an elbow. "You don't think de Gaulle takes it seriously? So why are the police everywhere? Why are they having elections?"

"The carnival got out of hand. If the police hadn't shut down the Sorbonne none of this would have happened. The fatal mistake."

"The kids are determined. They're going to change the system."

"What system? France is a democracy."

"The education system. It's not de Gaulle they hate, it's the education system, totally run by the government. The order to send the police into the Sorbonne was given by the minister of education."

"Because French education is free. The taxpayers pay for everything, which means government control. No way to change that."

"Then they should expect the students to revolt."

"France is a rigid, authoritarian, hierarchical nation. Revolutions give the people the illusion of freedom. Each time, when the smoke clears, they go back to doing things the same old way."

"But isn't it great while it lasts? Everyone tutoyering everyone, garçons in the cafés smiling for once, people sitting on the grass right beside no-trespassing signs, nobody paying for rental chairs in the Luxembourg, people calling each other comrade."

"Innocent American girls being dragged from cars outside Beaux-Arts and disappearing for days of brainwashing."

"Re-education."

"Being awakened all night."

"Sometimes I woke him."

Helen was pleased and after some suggestions and rewriting Sonny decided it was good enough for the front page. "Captures the delirious illusions of the students," he said. He paid her seventy-five dollars.

Lying in bed one morning she said: "You know, I don't think I'm cut out to be a wife or mistress – though I prefer mistress."

"Maybe you prefer Paris to Ellicott City."

"And lovers to husbands – Odette lying in bed waiting for Swann."

"Odette didn't just wait for Swann."

"That was her charm."

"That was her business."

"Don't be crude."

"Is that why you got divorced . . . lack of variety?"

"With you I wouldn't need variety."

"For how long? Didn't you think that when you married Bobby?"

She reflected. "I suppose I did. Did you think that when you married Sophie?"

"No."

"You knew you wouldn't be faithful?"

"I knew that if I ever saw a girl like you I would want to make love to her. I might not do it, but I would want to. Do girls think like that?"

"Did I want to make love to you the first time I saw you? Yes. I did."

"Did you want to make love to Bobby the first time you saw him?"

"Yes. More than he did."

"Did you have boyfriends when you were married?"

"Did I cheat on him, you mean?"

"That's women's talk."

"Oh, because men don't call it cheating?"

"Correct."

"Now that's interesting. We call it cheating because it is cheating. Cheating on the marriage contract. We cheat, but we feel guilty about it. Just like any cheater."

"But you didn't do it."

"I didn't have the opportunity. Anyway, Bobby was the best-looking boy in Ellicott City. So if men don't call it cheating what do you call it? What are you doing with me if not cheating on Sophie? And in her bed."

"I'm making love to an irresistibly attractive woman after being abandoned by my wife. How can it be cheating if it is irresistible?"

"Oh, that is clever, Rupert," she said, staring at him with those foxy eyes. "I shall have to remember that one. But isn't temptation meant to be resisted?"

"Now you're getting into bourgeois morality. What would Guy and Julio say?"

"My bet is that Guy will end up in the Sixteenth with a wife who shops at Chanel and Cartier's, and Julio will die in front of a Spanish firing squad. What I'm saying is that in your place I would feel guilt. If I'd cheated on Bobby I would have felt guilt. I'm not saying I wouldn't have done it . . . just that I would have felt guilty about it. What you're saying is that men somehow rationalize so they don't have to feel guilty."

"In any case, if Sophie hadn't moved out of her bed you wouldn't be in it."

"And why did she move out?"

He had to think about that for a while. "I think that ultimately we were just exotic interludes in each other's life. We reverted to our natures."

"Yours being . . . ?"

"American."

It was a landslide. On June 30, 1968, Charles de Gaulle's supporters won the largest parliamentary majority of any single party in French history. The memories of the fragile coalitions that crippled France back to the beginning of the Third Republic, paralyzing the nation at key moments in 1936 and 1938, were swept away in a grand triumph of de Gaulle's Fifth Republic. The governing hopes of the opposition socialist and communist parties were wrecked. It would be more than a decade before the left recovered.

For a time it looked like things could go either way. During rioting on May 10, hundreds of cars across the Left Bank were set on fire; five hundred arrests were made and 367 people hospitalized. Three days later, eight hundred thousand protesters met on the Place Denfert-Rochereau to begin the long march across town to the Bastille. Dany the Red and fellow student leaders were in the front lines with politicians and union leaders right behind, ready to take over when de Gaulle resigned.

The nation was crippled. On May 29 de Gaulle went missing, rumors sweeping the capital that he'd resigned and returned to his home in Colombey-les-Deux-Eglises. He was located the next day in Baden-Baden, where he'd flown off to consult with General Jacques Massu, commander of French forces in Germany. De Gaulle wanted to be sure the army, with which he'd had tense relations since the night of the generals' coup in Algeria, was on his side in a showdown with the insurrectionists.

When it was over, the students were the biggest losers. University campuses across France were shut down for the year. L'école des Beaux-Arts was broken up, classes to be farmed out to suburban campuses when school reopened. For the labor unions it was a pyrrhic victory: 15 percent wage increases, reduced hours, and longer vacations led to inflation, a devalued franc, unemployment, and exchange controls. French GDP fell by more than 3 percent. The unions lost more than they gained.

Penny's stay grew to more than a month. When Sophie called from the country he pleaded the burdens of work. She made no complaints. He felt guiltier about not seeing his children than about having another woman living with him. Once Sophie asked if he would like her to bring the children into town to see him. After a hesitation he said of course he would.

She noticed the hesitation. "Well, it's certainly easier for you to come out here in the Alfa than for four of us to come into town in a Deux Chevaux."

"*Four* of you?"

"I'm not going to drive two babies into Paris alone in that thing," she said. "Vincent does the driving."

"Why don't you come in by train?"

"Why don't you come out by train?"

It was almost the perfect affair. They were totally open with each other because on August 20, 1968, the date stamped on her airline ticket, it would end. Penny's place was no more in Paris than his was in Philadelphia. Like Claire, she lived in one place and he in another. Separate lives had briefly intersected.

They saw a lot of Dick and Suzy during the final days, meeting for drinks in all the usual late-night spots. One night they went to le Grand Vefour in the Palais Royale, and Archer, whose salary had been steadily rising, splurged on a 1960 Chateau Certan Giraud Pomerol at 300 francs. Afterward, they walked across the Pont du Carousel and down the rue Bonaparte, stopping in front of the locked-up Beaux-Arts.

Penny pointed to the top floor. "That's where I was interrogated."

"By the boy with the permanent erection," said Suzy, tight from gin and wine. They all laughed.

He was taking it harder than she did. He thought of how it would be on the last day: watching her wake up for the last time, taking coffee, packing up, walk to the car, the drive to Orly, the final kiss and home again alone in an empty car to an empty apartment, an empty bed and an empty personal life. Thank God for the *Herald*, he thought, recalling Mauriac's words: "travail, opium unique."

But that's not how it was on the last day at all.

They were sleeping late that morning after being out most of the night. The bedroom had thick curtains and still was black when the street buzzer jolted him awake. The bedside clock said just after ten. He turned face down but the buzzing went on. He heard a groan. Wretched, dehydrated, needing to pee, he stumbled down the hallway to the intercom.

Pressing the intercom button he heard his daughter's tiny voice on the street three flights below.

Heart thumping . . . momentary panic . . . buzz open the street door . . . crack the apartment door . . . voices from far below . . . footsteps on creaking stairs . . . three flights to climb . . . little legs . . . still time . . . close the door gently . . . lock clicking . . . down the hallway Penny staring, understanding.

They doused their faces, threw on clothes, made the bed. No time to pee. Doorbell. Penny disappeared into the kitchen while Archer opened the door. Vincent carrying Christopher, Amy bubbling away that she'd made the climb without help. Spur-of-the-moment thing, Sophie said, kissing him on the cheek. Sitting at breakfast she'd said to Vincent why not take a day off and surprise poor Rupert so he could see his children and so here they were and they would walk over to Luxembourg together and let the children play. Vincent had errands to do.

They walked into the living room, the sunny room with potted palms and ferns they called the solarium. Noise from the kitchen and Penny appeared bearing coffee and biscuits, fortunately wearing her own clothes. Glances and silence. Children oogling. Vincent smirking.

"Penny Schiller was kidnapped by the revolutionaries," Archer offered, trying his best. "She did a story for us. She's flying back to the States today. I said I'd drive her to Orly."

Her face a mask, Sophie watched from the couch. "Of course."

Archer took the tray from Penny, offering a biscuit to Amy who took it and headed for her room. Christopher, in a diaper, crawled on the floor. Vincent kissed Sophie and left on his errands. Penny sat down on the couch facing Sophie. Archer poured coffee. The young women stared at each other.

"Kidnapped by the revolutionaries?"

Penny told the story well. Archer handed around the coffee. There would be no scene. After awhile, he got up and walked to the window overlooking the rue du Four and came back to pick up his son, who started crying. He put him back on the floor and went back to the window.

He would never forget. Two young women, one he slept with, one he used to sleep with, drinking coffee and talking about revolution. In crisis situation, the female of the species gathers herself. Hunkers down. What crisis? Life goes on. It is as if I am not even here, he thought. Drawing room comedy. Wilde, Feydeau, Molière. A man's desperate mind makes it impossible to sit balancing cups on laps, pinkies out, not even the soupçon of quiver entering the voice. Women act like old pals on the terrace at Deux Magots before heading out to the shops. If there is jealously it is undetectable, he thought. Perhaps there is none. Is it that they don't care enough?

"What an adventure," Sophie was saying. "Oh, I'm so glad to have met you." She turned to Archer. "Why don't we all walk to Luxembourg? Rupert. Where is Amy's old pram – in the cellar, isn't it? Can you get it out? I'll push Amy and you will carry Christopher – though it's funny, he doesn't seem to recognize you anymore. I'll probably have to change his diaper first." She turned back to Penny. "I always travel with a supply, you know."

Archer glanced at Penny, expecting her to thank Sophie but say she had to pack and a million things to do before it was time to leave and couldn't possibly accompany them to Luxembourg.

But Penny was smiling. "Oh, let me push the pram."

27

It didn't take long for Sydney Gruson to conclude that the *Herald*'s good fairy at the Elysée Palace was Henri de Saint-Gaudens. When Gruson heard that Jock Whitney would be at his estate in Surrey, England, after the U.S. elections and planned to cross to Paris for the monthly meeting of the comité de l'entreprise, he wrote Saint-Gaudens that the board was close to a decision on the *Herald* and that Whitney supported a move to Switzerland. He mentioned that Whitney would be in Paris in November and that he always stayed at the Hotel Bristol, directly across from the Elysée.

Whitney found a letter waiting for him at the Bristol. He called the Elysée to set up an appointment and then called Ben Swart.

"We're meeting tomorrow at 9:30. How did he even know I was in town?"

"No idea, except that he seems to know everything."

"Any idea what's on his mind?"

"A pretty good idea. He doesn't want us to leave town."

"Why don't you come to the Bristol for breakfast and we'll go over some things together first."

"You want me to guess how he found out you were in town?"

"You don't think . . ."

"Did Sydney know you were coming to Paris?"

"I believe he did."

The day was bright, the air sharp and clear as Swart drove to the

Herald, the kind of brisk November day when it's exciting to be in Paris with work to be done. Parking, he pulled his cashmere scarf tight and took off on long strides down Faubourg St.-Honoré. Glancing in the shops, his thoughts turned to Martine. Was there a crack in her shell? Was she a touch less cold, a touch less formal? Perhaps she was thinking how close they were to permanent separation. It's one thing to be in a pout with a lover when you see him day after day, something else when he's about to disappear forever. Whatever game it's been up to then must be resolved or it's over.

It was clear that Whitney agreed with Thayer. Paris, Jock told him over coffee and croissants, was too unpredictable; the communist unions were a constant threat to good business. De Gaulle had set a referendum on something called "regionalization" for April, and uncertainty about the outcome had destabilized the markets and accelerated the fall of the franc, neither of which had recovered from the spring riots.

"What's the point of the referendum?" Jock asked, sipping his café crème.

"The one thing it seems to mean is that if he loses, he goes. It's not a referendum on regionalization, it's a referendum on de Gaulle."

"Après moi, le déluge," said Whitney. "Political blackmail."

"The newspapers call it that."

"I don't see how we can tie the future of the *Herald* to the vicissitudes of French politics," Whitney said, stretching his long legs out from the gilded chair. "If he resigns anything can happen. The communists and socialists come in and the economy never recovers. For all we know the communists will close the free press. Or nationalize it. I don't remember seeing any opposition newspapers the last time I was in Moscow. "

"French communists aren't Stalinists," said Swart. "They were torn apart by the Soviet invasion of Prague in August."

"It must have been tough for de Gaulle as well, with his plans for detente. Poor man did not have a very good summer."

"Is Kay Graham on board for the move?"

"She'll follow my lead," he said confidently.

"Zurich or Geneva?"

"I suspect we'll make the decision at the January meeting."

"Gruson will be mad as hell."

"The *Times* is the junior partner – by the way, don't be surprised if Sydney demands his pound of flesh. He wants to bring his own people over. Kay might be tempted to pacify him, especially with Sonny still out."

"Sonny's back. As of last Monday, he's back."

"How is he?"

"A little slower. But a slow Sonny is still pretty fast. By the way, Al Lodge has done a hell of a job since he's been back. Strange. Two really good editors who can't seem to work together."

"Maybe it's time for a change."

"Maybe we won't have to. Maybe not everyone wants to go to Switzerland."

"How about you?"

"Is Gruson after my job, too?"

"I'll tell you this, Ben. Syd Gruson will replace you over Kay Graham's dead body – and mine, too."

After breakfast they crossed the street, checked in with the Gardes républicains, and were escorted across the courtyard and up the stairs to the anteroom.

"William the Conqueror," said Swart as Whitney stood looking at the tapestry.

"I'd love to have it for the Whitney. Have you seen our new museum on Madison Avenue? We could use a few tapestries."

Ever refined, composed, good humored, the pin-striped Henri de Saint-Gaudens advanced to greet them as they entered his office. Not a silver hair was out of place as he shook their hands and led them to the coffee service by the windows.

"So nice to see you again, Mr. Whitney. I think you've probably noticed a few changes in Paris since the last time you were here."

"I gather the revolution has ended."

"Oh, yes – over and done with." He smiled. "They come and go, you know."

"We've had some shows of our own in the meantime – like the Democrats' convention in Chicago."

"You know of course that President-elect Nixon is coming to Paris in March. I believe it will be his first trip abroad as president."

"Nixon has never hidden his admiration for the General."

Their host poured coffee, passed the madeleines, and sat back comfortably. A different world, thought Swart. As crazy as life at the White House must be at this moment, the Elysée Palace is as quiet as a country church. Crossing the courtyard, mounting the stairs, walking the halls, they'd seen no one. Here in this room, probably not ten yards from where de Gaulle was sitting, they heard not a sound.

"How is the General?" asked Whitney.

"Quite well. Quite pleased with how things turned out."

"A landslide," said Whitney, sipping his coffee. "And now on to the referendum."

"Ah, yes, the referendum."

"But why a referendum when you have this extraordinary majority in parliament? What if you lose?"

Eyes at half-mast, St.-Gaudens glanced from one to the other, nodded slightly, formulated his response. "You are not reporters," he said after a moment. "What I tell you is for you only, not to be repeated, certainly not to be published. It is for you to have a better understanding of why it is important that your newspaper remain in Paris."

He sipped the coffee, dabbed at his lips with a stiff linen napkin, and sat back, looking out at the gardens. "You are quite right, Mr. Whitney, that the General does not need this referendum, and it is possible we will lose. If we lose, the General will step down and go home. The succession is already assured. The political left has destroyed itself and its only hope would be to rally the nation against a declining de Gaulle. Against his successor, M. Pompidou, young and energetic, the left has no chance. Any concerns you may have that France will be engulfed in revolution without the General are unjustified. France, in all likelihood, will be reinvigorated."

They sat in stunned silence as the General's oldest and most trusted adviser explained that it would be better for all if the referendum was lost.

"The General understands. The man who liberated France, restored her honor, extracted her from the swamp of Algeria, gave her a new constitution, rebuilt her armed forces, restored political stability and economic prosperity, this man understands that his time has come. He knows he could have brought the army marching into Paris last spring – but you don't send soldiers against students. What you Americans have never understood – and it goes back to President Roosevelt – is that de Gaulle is, to his core, a democrat. Roosevelt's complaint that de Gaulle would be another Napoleon was absurd, if you'll allow me to be frank. De Gaulle does nothing without the support of the people. Churchill understood that de Gaulle represented the real France, the historic France, la France profonde, which is why Churchill was the first Gaullist. When the British rejected Churchill in forty-five and the French rejected de Gaulle in forty-six, they both went home – to return only when called back by the people, always the people. And they stayed – or will stay – only as long as the people want them."

He stopped, passed the plate of madeleines, and offered more coffee. A twinkle came into the limpid blue eyes and he looked almost embarrassed, a host who feared boring his guests.

"It has been a difficult summer for us, one shock after another. I'm not complaining. I know it's been just as bad in America. But I want to explain things so you have information for your own decision. I don't have to tell you that we were completely overtaken by events in May.

Yes, we knew Vietnam was empowering the left around the world, but we never saw it as a threat to the regime. We've been hurt: We lost three billion in production, and wage increases cost another one-point-five billion. We had to raise taxes. And then, on top of it all, the Russians invade Prague. The détente the General had worked so tirelessly for given the coup de grace by one more communist blunder."

He stopped, eyebrows arched over the aquiline nose. "But I suppose you think I should get to the point."

Before he could continue, the phone sounded and he got up to answer it. "Yes, of course," he said. "Gentlemen, I think we're going to have a visitor."

On cue, the gilded doors at the rear of the room opened and a tall figure with an ample stomach held in by the tight buttons of a double-breasted blue suit entered and strode across the Persian carpet in large steps. They stood while Saint-Gaudens made introductions and handshakes were exchanged.

"Messieurs," said the tall figure with the remarkable head, "I have visitors in my office, but I did not want you to leave without paying my respects. You have a fine newspaper." He spoke the clear, precise French in the slightly raspy voice that was familiar to the French for more than a quarter century. "The *Herald* belongs to Paris as much as any French newspaper. I trust you will see it remains so. Au revoir, messieurs."

They watched silently as he retired back into his chambers, and Saint-Gaudens came quickly to the point. He understood a decision was imminent and an appeal to history might not be enough to persuade the *Herald*'s directors to stay in Paris. He pointed out that if few newspapers were struck during the spring troubles it was because the unions understood the importance of a free press. "Even the communist unions understand this, and we were among those who made the point to them." He looked to each of them. "Paris is not New York. Surely you see that for the *Herald* to have survived, unscathed, during the troubles means you have nothing to fear in France."

Whitney started to reply, but Saint-Gaudens raised his hand. "Perhaps you will say that freedom from the threat of strikes is hardly enough to assure a prosperous newspaper, so allow me to say this: Social costs, of course, cannot be reduced for the *Herald* any more than for any company in France. But I have looked into a variety of tax, postage, and exchange control adjustments and have prepared a short report for you."

They followed him to his desk where he took a blue folder and handed it to Whitney. It was clearly marked: PARIS HERALD. He turned to Swart.

"In addition to the adjustments I have mentioned, which are itemized and detailed in this report, there is something else. As you know, Mr. Swart, the *Paris Herald* does not receive the same newsprint subsidies that the French press receives. Surely that is an anomaly that can be addressed."

Whitney had come to Paris for one reason: to explain the difficulty of the *Herald*'s situation to the comité de l'entreprise before returning to New York to inform Katharine Graham that he was ready to relocate to Switzerland. The arguments for moving from Paris had originated not with Thayer but with Whitney, who'd seen the *New York Herald Tribune* destroyed by suicidal unions and vowed it would never happen again.

Walking to the *Herald* along Faubourg St.-Honoré, the day after their meeting with de Gaulle, Whitney realized he'd become so persuaded they should move that he'd closed his mind to the advantages of staying, ones spelled out in Saint-Gaudens's report, which not only offered concessions but made the case that Paris was the best site for an international newspaper because Paris was the political heart of Europe. What's more, it referred to the day "not far away," when Britain would join the EEC, putting Paris at Europe's precise epicenter.

He mulled these things over as he walked and his mind went to another report, one done by Theo le Tac and somehow forgotten once attention turned to Switzerland. Le Tac's report made the case for relocating inside France, to Lyon, a move offering all the advantages of leaving Paris but none of the disadvantages of leaving France.

The thought of Lyon brought another idea to mind: if they could stay in France, why go as far as Lyon? What of the Paris suburbs? Other than the unions, the main problem with Paris was the plant on the rue de Berri, where the size of the building limited the press run and the narrow one-way street created a distribution nightmare. Sooner or later they had to move. But where?

Not since Bennett half a century earlier had an owner attended a comité meeting, and Whitney saw satisfaction on all the faces. Born at the start of the century when young men of his class were expected to know languages, Jock Whitney knew French. As the French members of the comité were introduced, he had a word for each of them.

Old business was dispensed with and Swart gave the floor to Whitney.

"Throughout the difficulties," he began, "we were able to keep printing, and I want to thank each of you for that. To publish every day in such circumstances is a testimony to your loyalty and esprit de corps. But as you know, the board is considering changes to guarantee the *Herald*'s prosperity far into the future. Technological innovation will be the salvation of our industry. Three years ago in New York we could not reach an agreement with the unions on the necessary changes with the result that three newspapers were closed – newspapers that together had served the city for more than two hundred years. Our hope in Paris is that we will have learned from that experience."

Swart recognized Tonton Pinard. "All these things, M. Whitney, must be addressed in negotiations. If they cost jobs, there will be problems."

Whitney nodded. "While we will do everything we can to save

jobs, there will be losses. As you know, we have outgrown the rue de Berri. Preparations are under way to move the newspaper, though no final site has been chosen. What the board ultimately decides will in large part depend on negotiations with the comité and the unions."

He looked around the table, seeking eye contact with everyone. "The choice in Paris is the same as it was in New York: Will you lose some jobs or lose them all?"

28

She moved from the Pletzl to the Place des Vosges while Sonny was still in the hospital. Maybe it was not the best time to move, but the doctor said another bang on the head could cause permanent damage. Checking the U.S. embassy list, she found the place on the Place des Vosges, a five-minute walk from the Pletzl, same Fourth Arrondissement, even the same Metro stop, St.-Paul. But it was like changing planets: The Pletzl was built by Jews expelled from Paris; the Place des Vosges was the old Place Royale, built not for Jews but for kings.

The timing was horrible, but when would such a place be available again? With the change of administrations in Washington, a new embassy staff would be arriving and would snap up anything decent on the rental list, certainly anything on the Place des Vosges. With four months down payment it was risky decision, but when the board voted to stay in the Paris region she was vindicated. When the new plant turned out to be in Neuilly, in the Western suburbs, it was even better. Neuilly was on their Metro line.

Sonny loved it. Each morning they took walks through the park, along its paths, around the fountain, under the linden trees bare in winter but arranged, like the paths, in geometrical perfection. They strolled under the arches that surround the *place*, which is a perfect square, examining each building, admiring the historical plaques: Mme. de Sévigné at No. 1; Sully, No. 3; Victor Hugo, No. 6; Cardinal Richelieu, No. 21; Georges Dufrénoy,

No. 23. Their building was No. 12, which had no plaque.

"I may be the first guy from Hester Street to live on the Place des Vosges," he said one day. They'd stopped to admire the architecture: two-story buildings of red brick and white mortar on all sides, topped by slate roofs so steep they could have been steeples. Dormers poked from the roofs, no doubt with exposed beams that had been knocking heads for centuries. Their apartment, too, had exposed beams, but was on the second floor, the beams too high for Sonny's head.

They agreed it was the most beautiful square in Paris, maybe the world. Connie missed the Pletzl more than Sonny did, missed Goldenberg's restaurant and the Jewish bakery with flat bread and kosher baguettes and missed the little bazaars. She even missed the synagogue, though Sonny had never set foot in it. She missed watching the little old men in black shuffling inside with their prayer books, mumbling to themselves, never looking up or around, lost in scripture, lost in rapture.

It was Saturday night and they planned to walk once around the square and have dinner at Coconnas, under the arches. Sonny mixed the martinis, lit a cigarette, and walked over to the window. Under doctor's orders he'd quit smoking for a while but had no intention of giving up something he liked so much. He cut down, enjoyed each cigarette more and had no idea how anyone could drink a martini without a cigarette.

"Dark now," he said, "but, ah, by summer we'll have light until nine or ten."

Connie sat on the sofa watching him, wondering if they'd still be there in summer. Everything at the newspaper was in flux and she wasn't sure she wanted to stay. Sonny worried her. Forgetfulness, little hesitations in his speech, short circuits in the brain. Everyone said he was the same but she knew he wasn't.

"You know, we've never really talked about things," she said, sipping her martini.

He was staring at the lampposts. The French word for lampposts, *réverbères*, popped into his head. The conk had done some funny things. He watched a couple stride briskly across the square, bundled up, illuminated by the *réverbères*.

"What things?"

"You didn't want to go to Switzerland, did you?"

He turned to face her. "What made you say that?"

"We've never talked about staying in Paris."

He frowned. "What's to talk about?"

"Why didn't you want to go to Switzerland?"

He saw where she was going. He sat down facing her across the coffee table. "I hate the Swiss."

"Seriously."

"Paris is far enough from New York. Switzerland is too far."

She'd let her blond hair grow out. She'd never liked makeup, but Paris had taught her some minimum requirements. "Everything is going to be new for you."

"So?"

For months they'd put off talking about it. It wasn't just the accident, but everything that had to be done when he returned to work: find a new site, negotiate with the unions, train employees on new equipment, complete the planning that would allow them to print the final edition on the rue de Berri one night and the first edition in the new plant on the next. They'd been so busy that never had they sat down together to discuss *whether* they wanted to make the move to Neuilly with the newspaper.

The *Herald* faced a big problem: its equipment was obsolete. Newspapers were on the threshold of a new era, one in which linotypes and hot lead would be replaced by photographs and cold type; one in which typewriters, pencils, paper and paste would be replaced by computers. Already they were buying facsimile machines to transmit pages electronically from Paris to London. It wasn't enough anymore for editors to be good with a pencil. They needed the new electronic skills.

Sonny dragged on his Marlboro. His mind was jumping. A few days earlier he'd popped up to Ben Swart's office to ask him to be his best man. They hadn't fixed the date yet but it would be a simple city hall wedding and then back to the Place des Vosges for the reception. He'd given no thought to anyone but Ben. They went back too far.

"I've asked Ben to be best man," he said.

"It's not best man for a civil ceremony, honey. He'll be your witness."

"If I tell him that he won't come."

"Ben will come. What about him and Martine?"

"Ah, he doesn't talk about her – at least not to me."

In terms of backgrounds, Ben Swart and Sonny Stein were from different planets. Swart was a descendent of William West, Revolutionary War major in Rhode Island. His grandfather was a Rhode Island plantation owner and his father a Newport investor who'd thrived during the Gilded Age and built one of the town's fabled mansions. He attended the Choate School and Princeton and served on a destroyer as a lieutenant in the war. He was a privileged scion of a distinguished New England family and grew up knowing he could do anything he wanted. He wanted to be a newspaper publisher.

Stein's grandparents came to America from Lublin during the great migration of 1890. His grandfather, Shlomo Rothenstein, shortened his name at Ellis Island. His father, Sam Stein, worked as a tailor to buy his own flat on Hester Street and raise four children. Finishing high school, Sonny, whose given name was Seymour (which he hated), started at the City College of New York, dropping out when he landed a job as copy boy on the *Herald Tribune*. He rose quickly through the ranks.

Social distinctions are meaningless on newspapers, and the two bonded the way many do in New York: You work in the same building, sit next to each other at the same deli, order the same pastrami sandwiches, and serve yourself from the same pickle jar. You exchange greetings. You chat. You get used to the other guy and worry about him if he's not there. That was it for fifteen years: deli acquaintances who sometimes took walks together after lunch in Bryant Park. Never did they consider socializing outside work or imagine they'd wind up working together – and divorcing together – one day in Paris.

"Enough about Ben and Martine," she said. "Maybe you'll tell me if you really want to make this move to Neuilly."

"You're going to tell me I'm a dinosaur. I should never have told you that."

"Oh, Sonny, honey, stop. Talk seriously."

"Ben wants me, you know."

"Of course Ben wants you. Why wouldn't Ben want you? You've been a team from the beginning. The question is – what do *you* want?"

"What are you getting at?"

"Let me tell you some of the things you've said over the past few months – starting with the dinosaur thing. You said you were a pencil and paste guy in a world of satellites. You said you were proud of the printers' ink that stains your fingers. You said you know how to use a linotype, know how to set type and move type. You said you know how to read metal type – little bitty upside-down letters swimming in oily ink and – and I quote – don't know shit about facsimiles and demodulators that transform light and dark areas into . . . into . . . into binary language for transmission . . ."

"God, what did you do – record it?"

" . . . to be decoded right? Decoded was the word you used."

He got up to go to the bar. "You want a refill?"

"Have I told you lately, honey, that you're looking better every day, finally starting to resemble your old self?" She knew she was lying.

"Thanks."

"I want to keep you that way."

"Paris is good for me."

"What about the mugging?"

"Oh, the mugging, right. So they stick something in my back

and tell me to please hand over my wallet. In New York I'd be at St. Vincent's with a broken skull. Here the only thing that hits your skull is the beams."

She laughed. "If we go back it doesn't have to be New York. The USIA job Burnett told you about is in Washington. I'd love to live in Washington."

He took her glass. "You don't think I can handle the new job, do you?"

"Oh, bullshit, Sonny, I know you can do it. You can do anything on a newspaper. I'm just not sure you want to do it."

He started over again, pouring the gin and vermouth into the shaker and adding ice. She'd never said anything like that before. It wasn't that he didn't *want* to do it but that he wasn't sure he *could* do it, wasn't sure anymore that he could do everything on a newspaper. The new stuff didn't interest him. He capped the shaker, shook hard, poured out the clear magic liquid, and dropped in the olive.

"I want to do it," he said.

He hadn't gone up to the fifth floor just to ask Ben to be his best man. He'd gone up to level with him. In New York, they'd never socialized, but in Paris, as the top two managers at the *Herald*, they couldn't have avoided it even if they'd wanted. And events had drawn them closer, starting with each one finding a girlfriend and losing a wife and ending with the new owners putting the squeeze on both of them.

Ben was relaxed that day, feet up on the desk, leaning back in the swivel chair brought over from the *Times*, glancing out at Martine. He watched Sonny closely and thought he looked fine, natty in pin-stripes, two-toned shirt with gold cuff links and a tie knotted just right, probably thanks to Connie. In New York Sonny hadn't worn cufflinks and his ties were always knotted halfway down his shirt. Still, there was something . . .

"I should have brought this up earlier," he was saying, running a hand over his bald pate, "but you know me, Ben, hate to get personal. Here's the thing: I've always been the best at what I do. Connie jokes that maybe some day I'll have my own plaque on the Place des Vosges. Ha-ha." He was leaning forward and Swart could see the veins throb on the side of his wounded head. "At the *Herald Tribune* nobody could lay out a better front page or put out the newspaper faster. Ah . . . why did they send us both over here, Ben? Because we're the best they had. Because they knew that two of us could run this newspaper and it would take four of anyone else."

He was rambling, his speech marked by strange pauses. The question was how much of what was bothering Sonny and bothering him about Sonny was bothering New York and Washington as well.

"What does it matter if you're the best if nobody wants what you do anymore?" He stopped, momentarily losing his thread. "But that's the thing, isn't it? If I get a plaque it will be because of what I was, not what I am. The fact is . . . ah, I don't like the new stuff, think the old way is better. I'm the Mills Brothers and people want the Beatles."

"It's new for all of us, Sonny," Swart said, "for everyone in this business. You think when I came over I knew any of this new stuff?"

"Sure, we all have to learn it, but the editor has to be the best, that's the difference. The only way you command respect in a newsroom is when everyone knows you're the best. You're making, ah . . . ten decisions a minute involving dozens of people and stories and you're always on one deadline or another and the only way it works is for, ah . . . everyone in that room to have total trust in you, total belief that however good they think they are, ah, they know you're better."

"You telling me you don't want to go to Neuilly?"

"That's what Connie wants me to tell you."

"And you?"

"You know, Ben, I trust you like a brother. I want to do it. I'm scared, that's all." His dark eyes were pleading. "But don't get me wrong, I want to do it. I know I can still be the best. I want you to tell them that when you're back to New York. They're going to raise questions. Gruson . . . now that we're staying in France, you don't think that, ah, Syd Gruson wants to come back to Paris? His wife would kill to come back here."

"Whatever gave you that idea? I've heard nothing about anything like that."

But Sonny had him thinking. If they took aim at Sonny, Ben's head would fall, too. They would replace both or neither. To get Sulzberger and Graham to agree – which they would have to do to override Whitney – it would have to be a package deal.

"Instinct, antenna, gut feeling."

"Look, Sonny, I wasn't born knowing this stuff. But I know this: once you've got it you wonder how you did without it. It's not just getting rid of hot lead and inky type but one of these days we'll have computers instead of typewriters. Imagine a day when instead of crossing things out with a pencil you just touch a key and presto, it's gone. Imagine a day when instead of a library full of yellow clippings and a morgue full of old photos it's all in a computer's memory. Think of it, Sonny. This is the biggest thing in printing since Gutenberg's movable type, bigger than linotypes."

"Maybe I'll get the hang of it. It's possible. It's just that there's so goddamn much to worry about. So goddamn much, ah . . ."

"Stress."

"I hate that word. Connie feels it more than I do."

"I don't want you to do anything you don't feel you can do."

"I know you don't."

Then he said it. Maybe he shouldn't have, but it seemed the right thing to say. "Sonny, I want you to come with me to Neuilly. You *have* to come with me. We came over together and we will go home together."

Stein felt his eyes well up. "That's good, Ben. We go back a ways, don't we?"

"I'll tell you this, straight from the top, straight from Jock. And I quote:

"'Syd Gruson will run this newspaper over Kay Graham's dead body – and mine, too.'"

Stein gave a wan little smile. "That's nice, but . . ."

"But . . . ?"

"There are so many others besides Gruson."

29

They were probably two dozen crushed together onto the balcony, waiting for the cortege to wind its way up from the Rond Point. Motorcycle police cruised the Champs-Elysées, eyes sweeping crowds, searching windows, looking up for the glint of blue metal that might be poking from a rooftop. From their place on the balcony, just below the rue de Berri, they heard the military band at the Arch of Triumph tuning up for "La Marseillaise." A huge French tricolor, probably thirty yards in height, flapped in the wind between the giant marble pillars of the Arch. The entire avenue was festooned with American flags, chains beating against lampposts in the icy wind.

"NIXON! DE GAULLE! NIXON! DE GAULLE!" came the cries from below.

"Nixon worships de Gaulle," said Don Cook of the *L.A. Times*, who'd opened his Paris office to members of the White House press corps and Paris colleagues whose offices weren't so well placed. Inside, champagne was being served and a buffet lunch had been set out for the guests.

"De Gaulle likes resilience," said Pierre Viansson-Ponté of *Le Monde*. "It's what he admired in Churchill and admires in Nixon."

Moving slowly, the cortege passed Rond Point and was a few hundred yards below them. The sidewalks were packed with people waving VIVE DE GAULLE! signs – a good omen for the coming referendum. Crowds pressed up against the lines of gray iron grills stretching along both sides of the avenue and guarded by police. The pungent scent of roasted chestnuts wafted up from below.

"They're here," called Cook when the cortege reached the rue de Berri, signaling to the people inside. From the Arch of Triumph they heard a slow drum roll begin.

The Citroën's rear window was open and they could see Nixon waving, occasionally sticking his hatless head out the window despite the cold. Elected narrowly because of Vietnam and disunity among Democrats, he was more popular in Europe than America. Out of office, he'd done due diligence with de Gaulle and was being rewarded for it. Archer could not see de Gaulle on the far side of the car and wondered if he'd broken down and spoken English. If not, it was a long ride up the hill.

Back at the newspaper, he headed for the newsroom. Mike Eppinger, who'd replaced Al Lodge as managing editor, was in the chair. "Sonny wants to see you."

Connie told him to sit down and wait. "He's with Ben . . . Ben's off for New York tomorrow. So how's Nixon?"

He took the same chair he'd taken five years before, waiting for Sonny Stein once again. His eyes fixed on the empty space where the owl had perched.

"Apparently worships de Gaulle."

Sonny came in and they walked back to his office.

Everyone noticed the changes in him – slower, kinder, gentler – and no one liked them. Sonny Stein had always been the fastest and the straightest, the kind of newspaper mind that could read a nine-hundred-word story in seconds and tell you what should go in and what should come out.

"Nixon–de Gaulle . . . good story . . . lot to it. How about a takeout, something beyond just reporting what they're talking about?"

Across the street, the Hotel California was lit up like an ocean liner as the gray winter sky turned to black. "What do you have in mind?"

"The parallel between the two men, both coming back from the dead. We'll run it on the front page for the weekend."

"Two days . . . no problem."

Sonny stared across at him, eyes strangely quiet, hands in lap, no cigarettes in view. "So why would de Gaulle have a different view of Nixon than we do?"

"Maybe because he's not a Democrat."

"I'm serious."

"Because Nixon worships him."

"Why?"

"Back to the war . . . Eisenhower's influence. Unlike Roosevelt, Ike had good relations with de Gaulle."

"If Nixon thinks he can run America like de Gaulle runs France, he's in for a surprise. You don't sit on golden chairs in Washington throwing thunderbolts. Get all that in." He smiled for the first time. "By the way, how are Sophie and the kids?"

Archer was standing. "They're mostly in the country now. Sophie's got this project . . . doing a biography of Diane de Poitiers."

"I'm supposed to know about Diane de Poitiers?"

"Don't feel bad. I don't know a thing."

Outside, Connie's phone rang and they heard her voice rising: "You've called an ambulance? We're coming . . . we're coming!"

She was in the doorway. "Eric just collapsed at the California."

Lucien held Eric's head as Marcel pressed his chest, down-up, down-up, fast, with force. A group of bar customers stood gaping. They heard a siren and two ambulance attendants rushed in with oxygen and a stretcher.

"He was at the bar," Marcel said, giving way to the professionals. "I saw him grab his chest. I caught him before he fell. Dropped my tray. He said something and closed his eyes. That's it."

Eric's half-finished sloe gin sat on the bar.

One week before, Eric had been toasting Al and Helen in that same room, standing on a box behind the bar. Everyone turned out for the Lodges that night.

The board's decision was unanimous. The Elysée's offer had changed Jock Whitney's mind and Kay Graham was happy to stay in Paris. The decision was kept secret until the unions agreed to sign a five-year, no-strike contract. Theo le Tac found an empty commercial building in Neuilly, a western suburb.

The attendant stood up. "I'm sorry," he said, shaking his head. "Anyone to notify?"

Stunned, the crowd stood silently. Lucien looked around. "We're all here."

Everyone had heard the ambulance. Word was spreading. M. Eric was down. A crowd spilled onto the street from the *Herald* and the Berri Bar, pushing through the open door of the California. Traffic was blocked, horns sounded.

"Is it true?" someone shouted from the door.

Lucien nodded. "It's over for him."

"Not a bad way to go," said Marcel. "He'd almost finished his drink."

The attendants covered him and placed him on a stretcher. They hoisted it and moved toward the door.

Sonny turned to Marcel: "You said he said something."

"He whispered to me."

"What did he say?" a voice called out.

It was Tonton Pinard, who'd crossed from the Berri Bar, glass in hand. He moved from the doorway to let the stretcher pass.

"He said – '*it's better than Neuilly.*'"

Tonton's heavy face lit up. As the stretcher passed into the street, he turned to the crowd. "Sacre Eric!" he cried out. "Did you hear that? Eric said it's better than Neuilly! Dying is better than Neuilly!"

The chant spread up and down the street:

"BETTER THAN NEUILLY! BETTER THAN NEUILLY!"

"Wait! Wait!" called Tonton, laying his hand on Eric before the attendants could slide the stretcher into the ambulance. Raising his glass, he faced the crowd that now filled the street, blocking cars back to the Champs Elysées.

"Here's to you, M. Eric," he cried out, raising his glass high. "You were the best of us all. Wherever you are – remember: IT'S BETTER THAN NEUILLY!" Glasses were hoisted and the chant picked up again:

"BETTER THAN NEUILLY! BETTER THAN NEUILLY!"

The air was alive. People leaned from windows of the hotel and the newspaper as the ambulance pulled away. Up and down the rue de Berri, strangers beside their cars honked their horns in rhythm and joined in the chant, having no clue of its meaning.

They buried him in Passy Cemetery, as close to Bennett as they could get, a few dozen people standing in the winter cold beside the coffin. Archer looked down the row of tombs to the owl on Bennett's mausoleum looming, like Poe's raven, from the gloom. Next to Eric's freshly dug grave stood the owl Archer had met on his first day in Paris, the owl that would perch for eternity atop Eric's stone – the model for the giant owl that would have sat on Bennett's tomb in Morningside Heights if things had turned out differently.

Connie Marshall, a lapsed Congregationalist, had asked the pastor at the American Cathedral to offer a prayer. An aging Episcopalian who had not known Eric, he hated the thought that anyone might slip beneath the sod without a benediction. Sonny would do the eulogy.

Erect, hatless, impeccably tailored in Brooks Brothers and London Fog, Sonny stood facing them, blinking as the winter sun made a stab at breaking through the branches into his face. Lucien, Eric's oldest friend, had been ready, but Connie wouldn't have it. Sonny was Eric's successor. Sonny would give the eulogy.

"It's like he planned it this way, isn't it?" Sonny began. "Eric would never have set foot in Neuilly. The move was breaking his heart."

Connie had written it out for him. He began reading:

"Eric Hawkins came to Paris in 1915, the day the *Lusitania* went down. He worked with James Gordon Bennett, Jr., until Bennett died in 1918. He was the last link to the man who started the *Paris Herald* in 1887, the man whose father, James Gordon Bennett, Sr., was born during the presidency of George Washington. That was his personal link, Eric always said, to the American Revolution."

A few handkerchiefs popped out.

"So here we are laying him to rest in the shadow of Bennett's tomb. He couldn't have asked for anything more: He lived the life he wanted, did the work he wanted in the city where he wanted to be, died among friends in the place he loved above all others but the newspaper itself, the bar of the Hotel California. We bury him next to the man he admired above all others: James Gordon Bennett, Jr., each of them in clear sight of each other, each man with his owl to watch over him. Neither has to go to Neuilly. We should all be so lucky."

30

Martine looked out over the countryside, which lay heavy under snow. They'd have to put on chains before long. It had been a harsh winter and even in March the snow cover grew thicker as they drove east. She had on her blue reindeer sweater, heavy socks, and snow boots. They didn't like too much car heat. She couldn't count the number of times she'd taken this route over the years, Paris-Strasbourg, but almost always by train. Papa or Maman would be there to meet her. The autoroute more or less followed the train tracks, crossing the Marne, the Aisne, the Muese, the Moselle, climbing up toward Nancy, over the Vosges Mountains, dropping down to Strasbourg on the Rhine. For Martine, Alsace-Lorraine was the most beautiful countryside in France. She knew it wasn't the most beautiful, but it was her countryside, her route home, and even more beautiful when covered in snow.

She hadn't had time to take him home. She should have done it but she hadn't. She should have told them but she hadn't. They knew about him, had known about him since she told them she was seeing her American boss. They didn't say anything, it wasn't their way, but it was easy to tell they were uneasy. Whatever happened to that nice boy at the bank, Maman asked? What was his name, the sweet boy you brought home on the way to skiing in Innsbruck? It was hard enough for them that she'd gone off to Paris. The thought of losing her to America was too awful. She knew how they thought. She was the first child, the loving child, the only child. There had been another baby, a boy born after the war, but he died. There would be no more babies.

The fields were plowed up in dirt rows hard as cement and stretched in their jagged snow blanket to the far tree line. She glanced at her hands, diamond ring jutting up like Mont St.-Michel from the sands of the bay – sharp, angled, glittering. She loved it. She hadn't liked diamonds, thought they belonged to the other part of Paris, but this one was different. You don't have to dress at Chanel or Dior to wear a diamond, don't have to have your hair done on the avenue Montaigne or your nails on Faubourg St.-Honoré. You can dress in snow boots and a reindeer sweater and still wear a diamond. The diamond wouldn't change her. She glanced up at Ben, blond and rosy behind the wheel. He felt her glance and reached for her hand, running his fingers over the diamond.

"You know, don't you," he said, "I'm a little nervous."

She smiled. *You're* nervous, she thought, what about me?

She would have told them but she was a coward. If she waited until they were all together it would be fait accompli. From the moment Maman saw the ring, which she would see before anything else, even Ben, she would know. If she'd told them on the phone, Maman would be wringing her hands and not sleeping until they arrived. Now it would all happen at once – see the ring, see that Ben was older, know she was engaged and Ben would be there and so it would be accepted, not only accepted, but embraced, had to be embraced on the spot because they were good people. If Maman had a problem – a really *big* problem – they would take a walk together in the woods and sort it out.

Whenever she made this trip east her mind went to poor Louis XVI and his flight from Paris. So close to escaping! A delay here, a wrong turn there, and instead of the carriage reaching the border, they were dragged back to Paris and the guillotine. The first time she heard the story as a girl, it terrified her. Something to do with mistakes at crucial times. Everything had gone so well: the disguises worked perfectly. But Louis got out to stretch his legs making them late to the rendezvous point by Varennes. The fatal mistake!

Ben brought her back. "I've never been out here before," he was saying. "The mountains, the forests, I imagine this is what Zurich must look like."

"Are you still thinking of Zurich?"

"Not really."

She patted his hand. "The borders don't make any geographical sense. That's why the Germans wanted Alsace. The Vosges are an extension of the Black Forest. So is Zurich. Same land, different tribes."

The stillness of the winter countryside was a drug. She listened to the hum of the engine and closed her eyes, letting her mind run back over events. She'd gone back to Ben. That much was clear. Less clear was why. For months she'd resisted. The affair was over and they'd become comfortable as colleagues again. Almost comfortable. His eyes stopped devouring her each morning when she came in. Almost stopped. She'd gone back to her banking friends, back to Jean-Claude. She was happy. Almost happy. But they were all kids and she wasn't. Not after New York. How could she be?

What changed her was fear: fear that he was leaving, fear that the *Herald* was leaving, fear of the mistake at the crucial time. Why did she care? Older married man leaves mistress and moves on. Hardly news. But she *did* care. And he did, too, which was why he'd risked so much. She was used to him, used to the *Herald*, used to newspapers, used to Americans. Wasn't that love? Isn't love refusing to let something go? He was a clever, handsome, decent man desperately in love with her – why wouldn't she want to stay with him? What would she do without him, without the *Herald*? Women had no future in French banks. And why would a mistress leave her lover just as his wife was divorcing him?

And she, Martine Treuherz, she of the true heart, had caused the divorce. She had seduced him. How could she leave him now?

Over the mountains, still west of Strasbourg, they turned, heading south down two-lane roads shielded from the low sunlight by tall evergreens, running along the mountains they'd just crossed, toward Mutzig where they turned up toward Mollkirch. Outside, everything was white or green in the fading light. There was no noise or traffic. Hermetically sealed and cozy in the car. At Mutzig they stopped for gasoline and Ben put on chains for the ascent up the mountains. It was bitterly cold, close to freezing. Ben turned up the car heater.

He'd just turned fifty-two. They'd gone to Robert Vattier's in les Halles to celebrate his birthday, the first time they'd been back since that horrible night. He'd insisted. She didn't want to think of that night but it was his birthday and so they went. "You have to live down some things," he said, "get past them. I won't be poisoned for the rest of my life against les Halles. I like choucroute too much and so do you." They both laughed. It felt good to laugh about something like that.

He told her about growing up in Newport, about the life he'd led and everything he wanted to show her. She didn't want to go to Newport but she had to see his children, who would be her step-children, step-daughter, step-son, one of each. How ugly the words were in English, she thought – step, meaning removed, apart, different from natural children. How much more beautiful it was in French, beaux-enfants, beautiful children. At some point they would have to go back but they were too busy to take vacations. When they returned from Alsace, Ben would leave for New York and the March board meeting. Just over and back. She wouldn't be going this time, would not be spending another weekend with him at the Barclay.

She hadn't told him that Papa also would soon turn fifty-two; that Papa was six months younger. She tried to put it out of her mind. Ben and Papa were the same chronological age but had nothing else in common: Ben looked ten years younger, Papa ten years older; Ben, son of wealth and privilege, vigorous and in perfect health; Papa with his sad wasted life; Ben a dashing naval officer in the war – she'd seen pictures of him in his whites – Papa a shell-shocked infantryman wasting in a Nazi Lager, unable even to send word home that he was alive; Ben with a new life ahead of him; Papa hanging on as a part-time forester, trying to stay in touch with life, even on its fringes.

Slowly, they'd put things back together. He'd taken her to lunch and then dinner and then to her place and finally to the big empty house in the Villa Montmorency that needed a woman's touch. They might have gone on like that except one day he brought home the diamond and she saw it was the only way, that despite different countries, languages, religions, backgrounds, families, and ages, they were in love. And she saw that although she could never leave her parents she was ready to marry an American who one day would want to leave. She would deal with that when it happened, and maybe it wouldn't. For now the decision was to stay by Paris. The *Herald* was not leaving. The new location in Neuilly was closer to the Villa Montmorency than was the rue de Berri.

"You didn't tell me it would be this cold."

"I told you it would be cold – though this is bad for March."

They'd turned off the autroroute onto regional roads and off regional roads onto country roads and then onto narrow cuts through the woods. As they climbed, they passed mountain houses on both sides, handsome chalets with broad eaves and sloping roofs, not too steep because you have to get up there to shovel the snow off.

"I think I need a drink."

"Oh, Papa will have the Schnapps out. He knows something about cold weather."

She was thinking about her Papa who never was the same after the war. For Papa, like for France, the war was over almost before it started. They'd married in the spring of 1940 and by summer the French army was defeated. For nearly five years, Maman never heard a word, and then one day he knocked on the door and met his four-year-old daughter.

"I have to say, it's all very strange," Ben said. "Why am I more nervous than the first time I met Norma's parents."

"How old were you then – eighteen?"

"That's exactly how old I was. Drove up to their place on Narragansett Avenue in my old Ford and knocked on the door just as jaunty as Fred Astaire."

"Around two more bends and we're there."

"I don't feel very jaunty right now."

"When they see the ring everything will be all right."

And then they were there, headlights shining through the snow tracks onto the mountain chalet where she'd lived until being sent to the lycée in Strasbourg. Curtains pulled back, Maman's face at the window, curtains quickly closed; the front door opening, Papa standing in the doorway, Putzi, the old dachshund, at his feet. All her life she'd dreamt of this moment: Bringing her fiancé home to meet her joyful parents. She never imagined she would be so nervous.

De Gaulle repeated the ritual in each Breton town: stand at city hall, wait for the band to finish La Marseillaise, clasp hands high over the remarkable head, and through myopic eyes implore the crowd to vote "oui! oui!" in the vote no one understood. It was hardly the reception he'd received in 1944, but these were less thrilling times. At Quimper, the second stop, Archer stood beside Viansson-Ponté in the town square. "They keep waiting for him to cry 'Vive la Bretagne libre!'" the Frenchman said. "He never will."

They came back through Rennes, Laval, and Le Mans, crowds polite and well behaved except in Rennes where Breton separatists came out to protest. Nowhere was there was much enthusiasm. It was as though the French didn't care about the vote but wanted to see the great man one more time, suspecting it might be the last. Most in the crowd were over forty or under fifteen – those who remembered what he'd done and those just learning about it. Missing were the young people of May, '68, those who'd decided that whatever he'd done, it wasn't enough anymore.

The campaign tour ended late Friday night, and the press plane took off from Mans at 5:30 Saturday morning, landing forty minutes later at Orly, where Archer had left the Alpha. He'd had little sleep and so instead of driving to Paris decided to drive through the countryside directly to St.-Ouen. He wasn't expected until noon but might arrive early enough to go back to bed. The map showed the main routes from Orly leading north and south, but he'd be heading west on rural roads, through the Rambouillet Forest, near the Etang d'Hollande, where Sophie had paraded her girlish body before the lecherous ogles of Hallsberg and Klein before they'd returned to Paris to make love for the first time.

At Massy he caught the autoroute, zipping along at 180 kmh, few cars out so early, no gendarmes, no bouncing Citroëns in his rearview mirror thinking they were fast enough to pass him. He hated those cars, great dreadnoughts that with a head of steam could cruise with anyone but took all day to get up the steam. At Lemours he switched to two-lane roads, heading due west. At 6:30 A.M. there wasn't much country traffic, just an occasional tractor heading into the fields. It was the start of a crisp, cloudless day, crops and insects just coming alive in the early spring. He'd had coffee in Mans and was hungry but could wait. He could surprise them by fixing breakfast, but was more tired than hungry. He would slip into bed with Sophie and surprise her that way. He wondered what little nightie she was wearing.

In Quimper he'd found a costumed Breton doll for Amy and a miniature Celtic bagpipe for Christopher. He didn't have to bring presents, they'd be excited to see him anyway, but he enjoyed playing papa. For Sophie, he'd found a flowing Breton dress and bonnet perfect for St.-Ouen. Expecting him at noon, she'd asked him to bring a bottle of Pernod, which meant there would be cousins coming. In Rambouillet, he looked for a shop, but it was still too early. He passed the castle where Louis XVI used to ride over from Versailles for the hunts before his luck turned bad. Leaving Rambouillet he turned northwest through the forest toward St.-Léger.

He remembered the surprise on de Gaulle's face in Rennes when the chants, "Liberate Brittany," began. For the president's first visit to Brittany in eight years police had rounded up members of the Brittany Liberation Front but apparently missed a few. De Gaulle pointed a finger at them, a small faction in a crowd that must have numbered ten thousand, and called out in his raspy voice: "These people forget that we liberated Brittany twenty-five years ago." The crowd roared its approval and that was the end of the chanting. He reminded them of his family's Breton ancestry and spoke briefly in Breton as the bagpipes squealed in the background.

The Rambouillet Forest was lovely, dark and deep, no sun admitted by the high trees. Archer slowed down along the narrow road, aware that animals might be out for breakfast. He liked the looks of St.-Léger, pretty little rural village, not a bad place for a writer if he could earn a living. Find a little slate-roofed cottage, walk to the boulangerie in the morning, the charcuterie in the afternoon, the patisserie in the evening. On Saturday nights drive into Paris to hear Slim at Trois Mailletz and then up to Calavados for Joe Turner and spend the night at the George V across the street.

He saw a sign for l'Etangs d'Hollande and thought of turning but the beach didn't open until summer and maybe he was getting too heavy into nostalgia. Those were good days, no question, his first year in Paris when he was reinventing himself and every day was filled with something new. Some people, some Americans, come to Paris and live exactly as they do at home. There were people at the *Herald* – McGillicuddy, for example, or Eppinger – who spoke French like tourists, put their kids in the American school, and socialized strictly with Americans. For Archer, coming to France had been to discover a new world, not live like he always had. Somewhere along the line he had reverted.

At St.-Léger he turned west again. He got the Alfa up to 120, hoping no cows decided to cross the street. It was after seven when he ran through Bourdonné and heading northwest saw the dungeon of Houdan in the distance, Houdan where he would catch the familiar road to St.-Ouen. He was thinking about Sophie now. Sophie was a sleeper, could easily sleep until eight or nine. The children were sleepers too. As babies, she'd gotten up to feed them on occasion, but they'd learned to sleep as late as she did. He would make love to his wife and sleep into the afternoon. Skip the pastis.

For months they'd lived parallel lives, drawn apart not by necessity but by choice. Sophie could have come to Paris. It was just as easy to live in Paris and drive to St.-Ouen as vice versa. In Paris there were crèches for the children and they would hire a full-time nanny and install her in one of the maid's rooms upstairs on the rue du Four. But she preferred to make her life in the country with Cousin Vincent in ineradicable residence.

What if he decided to return to the States? What if the *Post* or *Times* decided to replace him with one of their own? With Lodge gone, Hawkins dead, Stein slipping, and the *Herald* heading for Neuilly, soon nothing would be left of the newspaper that had saved him – as it had saved so many – from foundering. Even Ben Swart – how long could he hold out against the new owners, the new powers? How long could Jock Whitney keep them at bay? At some point Archer would have to go back. No cozy maisonette in St.-Léger. From time to time he hinted to Sophie about returning. She smiled and changed the subject.

Beyond Bourdonné he left the forests and entered pure farm country. The cornrows were sprouting and soon the corn would be edible. Later in the spring, he'd go into the fields behind the house and cut a dozen baby ears and it would be the sweetest corn you ever tasted, so tender you could eat the cob. Maybe he would do it today, take Amy to check out the cornrows and walk down to the stream and into Berchères for the Pernod. It was a nice walk. He would have sex with his wife, sleep until noon, and take his daughter walking when the cousins started arriving. Of course Amy was little and he'd have to carry her on his shoulders part way, but she liked that too. He liked Houdan, stately medieval town switching between English and French hands until Joan of Arc gave France the upper hand at the cost of her life. Like de Gaulle, the Maid was alone at the end, abandoned by those she'd saved. Remarkable: starting with nothing, they'd both saved France and been tossed aside – de Gaulle not yet, but it was coming. "Alone and deprived of everything, like a man on the shore of an ocean he had to swim," was how de Gaulle described his arrival in London in June, 1940 – the only Frenchman, in Churchill's famous words, "who still believed in England's victory."

At Houdan he caught the road to Anet and past Berchères turned onto a side road toward St.-Ouen and their house, stopping outside the walls instead of driving noisily into the courtyard. The sun that had followed him west from Orly was finally high enough to do some good. It would not get very high and the day would not get very hot, but as he climbed stiff and tired from the car and lack of sleep its warmth felt good. He unloaded his bag and packages and stood there, leaning against the car and listening. Country sounds are always there, though you have to listen. There was a dog and then a cock and another cock answering. They liked the morning sunlight too.

He slipped through the gate in the wall and glanced around. Cobblestones, a few of which he'd pounded into place himself, stretched to the kitchen. The roof was almost finished. He saw the curtains drawn in Mme. Mignon's rooms where Vincent was living. He pushed opened the kitchen door. Nobody locked up in the country. Any thief breaking into this house would be disappointed. Sophie had scribbled messages to herself on the kitchen blackboard:

Diner Samedi: 12 personnes. poulet, macedoine de legumes, pommes de terre franconia, baguette. Gaston passe 10 hr. Rupert rentre midi. Pernod!

Big party. Archer smiled, noting he'd made the blackboard right behind Gaston, the roofer from Houdan. He put down his packages. Not a sound. He took off his shoes. It was still dark in the hallway but there was light from an upstairs window. On the stairs he stayed to the side to keep the boards from creaking, though they were new boards. At the top he stopped. From the children's room, on the far side of Sophie's room, he heard nothing. Sophie's room, straight ahead, was just as still.

He eased quietly into the room, curtains drawn, dark, spying her unmoving under the crumple of quilt. He took off his trousers and stood listening to her soft breathing. Soft? No, not as soft as usual. Close to waking. He was just in time. He dropped his socks and shirt on a chair and advanced toward the bed, conscious that he had an erection. It had been too long. He stood over the bed a moment looking down on her dark head.

No, he was looking down on two dark heads. They lay in each other's arms, snuggled under the quilt, faces inches away from each other, cousins, breathing gently, rhythmically together, as one.

POSTSCRIPT

Fifty-three percent of French voters opposed the referendum on regionalization held April 27, 1969, a totally unnecessary vote on a technical matter that could easily have been passed by the Gaullist parliamentary majority that had won such a crushing victory ten months earlier. De Gaulle knew all that of course, but after the challenge to his government and his vision of France the previous May, he wanted the French to declare, once again, their love for him.

They wouldn't do it. They thought about it and decided it was time for a change. De Gaulle had been there for the great events of the forties and fifties, returning France, as he explained, "to her nobility and her rank." They'd had enough of him. He hadn't said he would resign if he lost, but no one had any doubt. It was a suicide pact.

There was no press conference, no television, no tears, no recrimination. He drove home to Colombey les-Deux-Eglises to vote that weekend and when the results were known Sunday night, simply stayed home. Shortly before midnight he called Paris and his resignation was announced by the Elysée Palace. After a short campaign, Georges Pompidou, his longtime prime minister, was elected to succeed him. The transition could not have been smoother.

He never spoke again in public. A few months later he told André Malraux, his longtime comrade in arms, that "yes, age had something to do with it, but I had a contract with France. The contract was broken." Malraux wrote an elegant little book about his last meeting with de Gaulle, lunching at his home with the family shortly before Christmas, 1969. "My only international rival," de Gaulle told him, "is Tintin. We are the little guys who don't let themselves be pushed around by the big ones. People don't realize it because of my size."

He died at home eleven months later, age seventy-nine, after working all morning in his study on his memoirs and meeting with a neighbor to discuss his use of a tract of land adjacent to the de Gaulle home. As deaths go it was a good death, a pain in his chest as he played his afternoon game of solitaire. A doctor and priest arrived but it was all over. An envelope held in safekeeping at the Elysée was opened and the instructions carefully followed. A private funeral in Colombey was arranged by his children. Meanwhile, one hundred miles away in Paris, the greats of the world came for a memorial mass at Notre Dame. At 3 P.M. on that rainy November 12, 1970, as the two ceremonies began, the church bells in every parish in France started to toll. Three hours later, one more great march down the Champs Elysées began, the Gaullist faithful undeterred by the weather. They would not let him go easily. A giant Cross of Lorraine was erected on the hill overlooking his home at Colombey, visible for miles.

Thanks to Henri de Saint-Gaudens, the *International Herald Tribune*, née the *Paris Herald*, stayed in France. The Neuilly plant became a base for using satellite technology to beam facsimiles to printing presses around the globe. For a while, Jock Whitney tried to resist his two powerful co-owners, but it was little more than a holding action. Whitney Communications was in decline while the *Post* and *Times* were in ascendancy. When Whitney died in 1982, the *Post* and *Times* split his shares. But the *Times* had never hidden its desire for total control and eventually got it. The *Times* lost the battle of 1966 but as Sydney Gruson always said, it was just a matter of time.

Sonny Stein did not make the move to Neuilly. The board wanted an editor more in tune with the new technologies and he was let go with a nice indemnity. With Connie, he returned to the States and worked awhile for the United States Information Agency. Ben Swart had no time to shed tears for his old friend for neither did he move over the hill to Neuilly. As a Whitney man, he too was rewarded with a handshake and an indemnity. Returning to the States, he worked awhile on Wall Street and bought a house in Westport.

None of the top three at the *Herald* when Rupert Archer arrived in 1965 would live to a ripe old age. Leaving Paris can do that. Though it can be a lonely place, lonelier still are the memories that linger when you are gone. It would be impossible to say that Ben Swart, Sonny Stein, or Al Lodge died of chagrin, for in each case medical causes existed – cancer, stroke, and heart attack in that order. But those who knew them after they returned saw the decline. Hemingway called Paris a "moveable feast" – the idea, from Christianity, that some things are not fixed in time or space but travel with you, live on inside you. In that sense it's fair to say that chagrin played some part in their early deaths. Leaving Paris was leaving the best part of their lives behind, and they knew it.

The wives did better. Helen Lodge worked on various New England newspapers as an editor until her retirement on Cape Cod. Connie Marshall Stein returned to Vermont to shed the inlay of Parisian style and chic that never really was her. Martine Treuherz Swart returned from the States with her young daughter to marry Jean-Claude Fauvet, by then a branch manager at Barclay's Paris. Papa had died, but Maman, content at last, came to the wedding at Paris's Sainte Madeleine.

Some others also did well. Wayne Murray and Jojo moved to Corfu, where they bought an old wine and olive estate near Ipsos and became known for their international parties. Dennis Klein spent many years in Germany and Austria, marrying an Austrian pastry and becoming an authoritative writer on the Hitler era. Steve Fleming and Byron Hallsberg spent decades as reporters and writers on the *Los Angeles Times*. Frank Draper made a success of his avocado farm near Malaga. Odile adapted well enough to her role as dueña. Their children, along with grandchildren, visit on holidays.

Suzy de Granville, with the aid of Dick LePoint and the archives at Bayeux, was able to trace her name back to the Norman nobles who accompanied William the Conqueror to England in 1066. Suzy returned to Philadelphia and made a good marriage. With his indemnity, Dick moved to the Côte d'Azur. Gretchen Kilic married a Serbian businessman in Paris who later was killed in a shootout with French mobsters. She returned to Chicago with her baby.

About half the French employees made the move to Neuilly, including most of the leaders of the comité de l'entreprise. Tonton Pinard, representing the printers' and typesetters' unions, did not make the move for the newspaper no longer needed printers and typesetters. The union was paid off and a handful of men taken to Neuilly to be trained in the new art of computerized photo-typesetting and transmission of pages to rented electronic presses belonging to other newspapers.

Theo le Tac not only made the move but was promoted to general manager by the new president of the company, the man who replaced Ben Swart, a man from Buffalo who spoke no French and knew nothing about France or printing presses or Bennett or owls but was a technological whiz. Le Tac became even more important than he'd been with Swart. Vichy triumphed at last.

Rupert Archer did not make the move. He thought about it for he had a good job and it would have made his personal life easier. But to take the *Herald* from Paris was to take Paris from the *Herald*, and that he couldn't do. He had several good offers in the States and after a stint in New York returned to journalism in California. While in New York he visited Penny Schiller in Philadelphia where she taught high school French. They had dinner but she didn't ask him to stay over. New friends, she said. She was as cute and feisty as ever, but Paris is not a moveable feast for everyone. He invited her to New York, but she never came.

Sophie never remarried. When St.-Ouen was sold at a nice profit, she moved to Paris with the children to finish her book on Diane de Poitiers. St.-Ouen was purchased by the French actress Dominique Sanda, who turned the house into an elegant country estate (by that time Mme. Mignon had died) eventually featured in a photo spread in *Elle* magazine. When the children were older they came to the United States for school before returning to Europe to live. Vincent left Paris for Avranches, where he lived off family largesse and the sale of an occasional painting until dying of cirrhosis at age forty.

The people came and went, but the institutions they created endured. Unlike the first four French Republics, de Gaulle's Fifth Republic proved a model of political stability, even after Socialist François Mitterrand was elected president in alliance with the communists. De Gaulle created a solid presidential system that can be slowed down by parliament, but unlike in America, cannot be paralyzed by it.

As for the *Paris Herald*, today the *International New York Times*, it became a sober and serious newspaper owned completely by the *Times* and modeled after it. No more Paris jazz columnists and ambulatory paperboys. No longer does Bennett's owl look down on ex-linotypists, unemployed authors, and refugees from European civil wars hired off the street for 500 francs a week. Salaries at the Neuilly newspaper run into in six figures, paid not in francs or dollars but in euros, which are worth more.